SHADOW
OF THE
DEIA

SOURCE'S EDGE BOOK TWO

Cover art and illustrations by Tiziana Federica Ruiu
Edited by Crystal Shelley
Layout by Ryan Sivek

Shadow of the Deia (Source's Edge Book Two)
First Edition (Revision 1, Nov 2025)

ISBN: 979-8-9863686-3-4
Library of Congress Control Number: 2025915689

Published By Ryan Sivek
Cary, North Carolina
www.ryansivek.com

This book is dedicated to seventeen-year-old me.

Acknowledgments

A great number of people have influenced and made this novel better. As I did with book one, I will try to cover individuals who had the most significant and specific impacts, in no particular order.

I am once again deeply grateful for my family members who put on alpha reader hats and provided me with valuable early feedback on the story: Alyson Sivek, Janet Sivek, Susan Nagy, Adam Smith, and Katrina Smith. Your initial reactions helped me address many basic areas of improvement.

I'm also profoundly grateful for my beta readers: Bethany Guymon, Isaac Wilson, Jenna Sivek, Ellie Wallwork, Layne Johnson, and Ethan Mayfield. Extra special thanks to Ellie and Layne for providing priceless insight into the depictions and experiences associated with blindness in the story. This continues to be a significant aspect of the narrative, despite the smaller word count around the topic compared to book one, and I treasured your feedback and suggestions on the matter.

More gratitude is in order for a few content creators in particular, who continue to inspire various aspects of my writing. Molly Burke, I have learned so much from your content, your journey, and your perspectives on the world as a blind woman over the years. Thank you for continuing to publish your experiences and thoughts for all of us to learn from. Merphy Napier, while I haven't quite followed your venture into the manga world, I continue to find your book reviews and discussions wholly fascinating, insightful, and inspiring to my writing journey. I'd also like to thank Drew from Genetically Modified Skeptic. I find your remarkably respectful discussions and essays about religion and belief wholly edifying.

For this book, music has continued to be a tremendous source of inspiration, particularly for the most emotional and plot-relevant events in the story. Thank you Two Steps from Hell, Zack Hemsey, Revolt Production Music, Ruelle, Thomas Bergersen, Dos Brains, Audiomachine, Phantom Power, and Hi-Finesse.

To my wonderful artist, Tiziana Federica Ruiu, I cannot thank you enough. Again, your creativity, passion, and ability to take concepts and turn them into incredible works of art with your own unique creative flair continue to amaze me.

Immense gratitude is also in order for my amazing editor, Crystal Shelley. Even though I expect to see improvements, I'm always blown away by how profoundly your edits brighten up my amateur prose. One of these days I'll get better at correctly placing em dashes around quotes.

Last but not least, I am deeply grateful for the support and encouragement from my wife Alyson and my children. Your tolerance of my adventures to the Source's Edge universe, which enables me to get this story out of my head and onto the page, means so much to me. I love you.

Contents

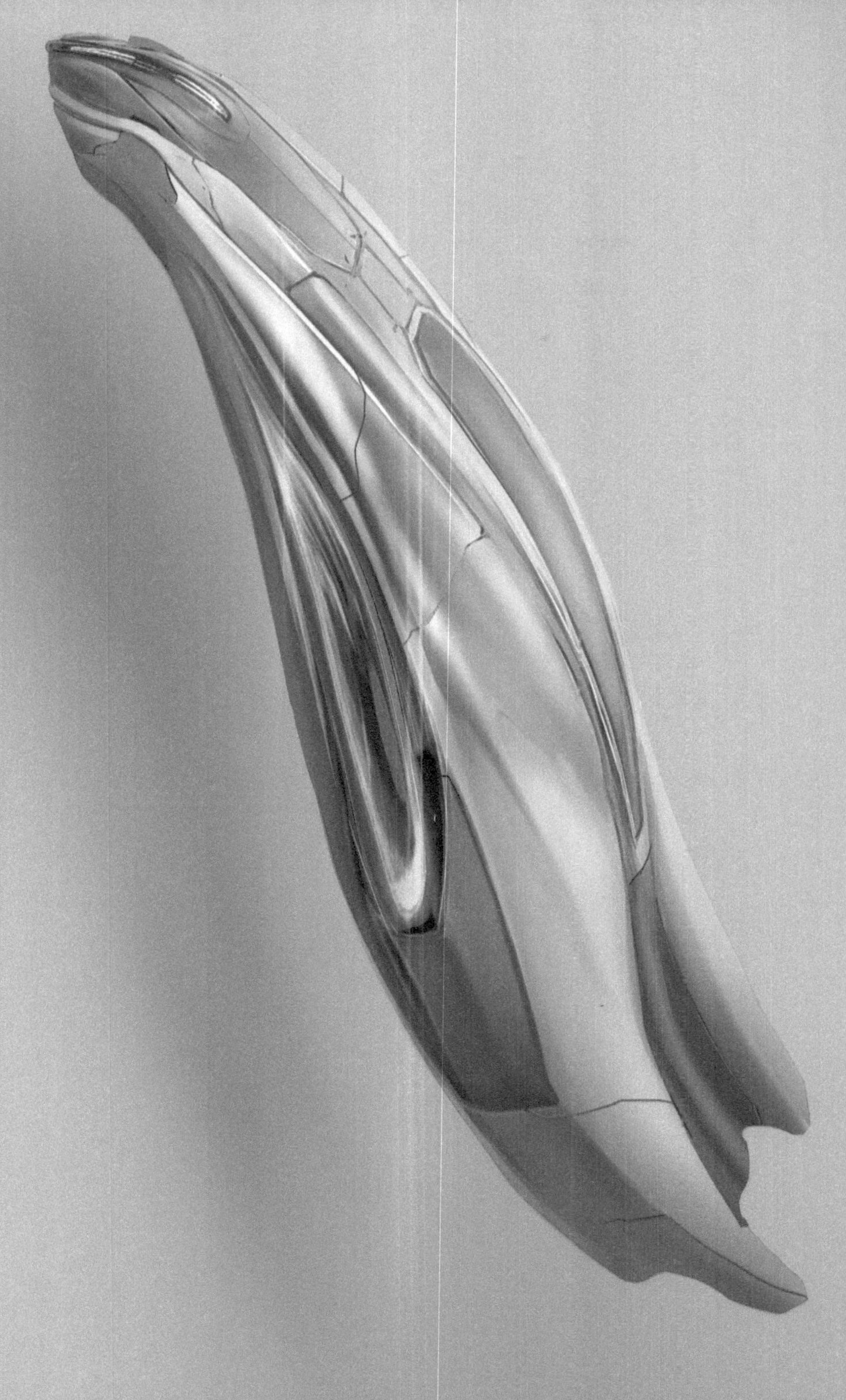

Chapter 1
The Proclamation

"You are mine."

Jeanette shifted as she stood at the back of an enormous, circular conference center. The voice of the lone man on the raised central platform echoed across the thousands of attendees, rapt as they absorbed his spiritual premonitions catalyzed by scripture and prophecy. The sea of diverse dress, skin, and hair around him morphed as participants stirred around the center of the massive room.

Large displays showed the minister's upper torso in crisp detail overhead. His dark, patterned tailcoat whipped about as he turned to face different sections of the crowd during his address. Elaborate frills cascaded down his white dress shirt, giving him a somewhat Victorian appearance. The thought stirred Jeanette's homesickness for Earth.

Below the central platform stood six large suits of Wenkuth power armor bearing the Sovereignty emblem on their chest. Unlike the form-fitting suits Jeanette had seen Delveton working on many weeks ago, these were large and bulky, with broad shoulder guards and wide helmets. Unfortunately, the reflective face shields made it impossible to tell whether any of them were observing her.

She scanned the ceiling, past the giant screens displaying the man on stage, to the dimly lit metal girders and wiring, wondering if there were other security or surveillance measures in place. Did they have crowd-facing cameras? Could they identify her in a recording?

A few other Wenkuth clad enforcers stood around the curved walls of the massive conference hall. A few lights, alcoves, and visible panels spanned the otherwise plain surroundings. From her position against the curved back wall, as far from the two nearest security guards as possible, Jeanette could barely perceive the speck-like attendees or guards at the other end of the room.

After his dramatic pause, the man continued his scriptural recitation. "When adversity is near, fear not, for I am with you. I will not forget my own. I say again: You are mine."

He let the echoing words fade to silence once more. A gentle inner prompting nudged Jeanette forward.

It was time.

Anticipation thumped in her chest. She took a deep breath, released it against the invisible veil cascading over her face, and felt the warmth reflect against her cheeks. The moment she'd been preparing for was near.

A wide walkway spanned the distance between the curved wall where Jeanette leaned, and the back row of occupied seats. Several others stood around the wall nearby due to inadequate seating. This made her presence more inconspicuous, but also meant there were more people around to potentially see her.

She glanced quickly to the left and right, ensuring that the attention of those nearby fell elsewhere, and awakened her Sorcery. Impressions of nearby objects flowed through her mind, hampered by distance and clouds of imperception surrounding the mass of people standing or sitting around her.

"These words of the Divine should be a source of comfort in these turbulent times. All those worthy of—"

The minister continued his sermon as Jeanette connected with her transparent outer garment, which revealed only the plain gray top and black, form-fitting pants she wore underneath. She teased the garment's light-manipulating enchantment, then gently shifted its purpose, as instructed by the all-powerful Deia herself. Light bent across the cloth surface to its opposite point, instead of traveling through it.

The room faded to darkness for her.

"—words of salvation to—"

Disoriented, Jeanette relied on her hearing to determine whether her sudden disappearance had startled anyone. The couple on the wall nearby continued their hushed but animated conversation. From the acoustics, she regained some orientation in the darkness, likely thanks to occasional tips she had picked up from Kara over the years. The thought summoned a spike of longing for her sister.

No, not now. I need to stay focused.

There was no way to know for sure whether someone had noticed her disappearance, but no one called out or made a disturbance, so hopefully she had gone undetected. After pulling at the garment's arms to ensure they covered her hands, Jeanette focused her Sorcery again, targeting her own body.

Potent imagination lifted her against the pull of gravity, and the cushy carpet floor left her feet. Reverberations and passing sensations through Sorcery allowed her to maintain a grasp of her position without sight, providing impressions of nearby objects as reference points. The sea of emptiness corresponding to the people beneath her fell below, and the strength of her awareness of the surroundings grew with their distance. Integrated lights, screens, and circuits of the ceiling above increased in perceptibility as she approached.

"—grants power to those who have faith in—"

The center was easy enough to locate; every structure around her pointed toward it. A small ring of hazy impressions below marked where the minister stood. The dot of imperception moving about marked his Source within the gap of the audience.

Her target.

She hovered above his position and stopped, listening intently. His tone had turned darker, more ominous. There were several scriptures or prophesies he was likely to recite that would present an opportunity.

"—whole of the Sovereignty has tolerated the ungodly for too long. Aldan is not Divine. Its choices are not Divine. While the Sovereign is respectable, she is no prophet. She, like her predecessors, lacks the power and foresight of Divine guidance. Generations of sin and godlessness have eroded the Sovereign's control over her own forces, and the Divine's judgment is upon us.

"Consider the Oblivion attacks. The attack on Tenreth. The destruction of Enck. The recent, horrific attack on Tercast by anti-religious zealots in the Sovereign's own Armed Forces. The Sovereignty is unraveling."

He paused, letting the foreboding silence settle over the congregation. *There's the doomsday speech. Next should be the hope speech.* That could be her chance. Jeanette's fingers tingled in anticipation.

"However, do not fear! Those who are righteous should look forward to the future with *faith* not fear. Heaven will not abandon us. Consider the words of the Divine, given to the prophet Parolais: 'Sing praises unto thy Deliverer, for the time of reckoning shall come swiftly. When destruction is at thy feet, look to the heavens, for mine angels shall prepare the way before me. As beacons of light shall they descend to lead my—'"

This was it. Her moment. It was perfect!

Jeanette, heart racing, changed the enchantment on her outer garment while simultaneously allowing her body to accept the pull of gravity once again. Light gradually reacted normally against its pristine, white surface, rather than bend around it, and her surroundings faded back into vision. She caused her skin to emit a faint luminescence, granting her an angelic glow. Connecting with the nearby air, she gathered it around her person, Vitalizing it to emit a steadily increasing amount of light. Hopefully, it would appear close enough to a "beacon."

"—the work of the Divine upon all the face of—"

Gasps rose from the crowd as their gaze rested on Jeanette. The minister's voice cut off as he glanced up, eyes widening. Jeanette gracefully pulled back the veil, revealing her face to the thousands of people around her who became increasingly reactive. Many stood. She rotated her body so that everyone could observe her brilliant features.

The speaker beneath her continued his wide-eyed stare. She glanced at the enforcers, who pointed their fists to her in warning. Her heartbeat echoed in her ears. The latent enchantment on the cloak and on her skin that could deflect projectiles was still active, though she hoped they wouldn't be necessary. Tess had warned her about the power of the Sovereignty's enforcers. If they tried to take her down, she would be in serious trouble. An encounter would make her appear less "divine." Her allies, hidden in the crowd, would help her get away, but it would mean their efforts had failed.

She must not fail.

"What is this?" the man below said, his voice no longer amplified through the speakers. "Who are you? You're not permitted here!"

Was that any way to speak to an angel?

Jeanette remained silent as she opened her arms and continued her slow descent, struggling to keep herself from breathing too heavily. *Be calm.* They had hoped the minister would bend swiftly. Unfortunate. Perhaps he saw through her facade somehow—or didn't actually believe what he preached. Some in the crowd cried out about angels or prophecies. A few moved toward the exits in fear, but most watched with uneasy anticipation.

The minister turned to an enforcer. "Get her down from there!"

The suit floated up toward Jeanette's position. She kept her gaze on the audience, feigning indifference. While she maintained her connection to the surrounding air to power her "beacon of light," she focused on the air between her and the suit, in case she needed to do something drastic.

"You . . . uh . . . must come with me," a man's low voice emitted from the suit. Uncertainty. It gave her a chance. A gauntleted hand reached out for her.

Jeanette inwardly panicked. The closer they got, the weaker her Sorcery would become, diminishing her angelic presence. If she harmed them, however, it might defeat her purpose.

As the mechanical gauntlet approached her arm, she connected to it. The occupant's hand was farther back, with plenty of padding, giving her Sorcery some leverage.

She connected with the ends of the suit's fingers, where she had the greatest hold, and Vitalized an immense heat within the material. It glowed a soft red. The wearer recoiled and tilted his head, bringing the large hand back and turning it around, breaking her connection. Waves of heated air rose from it and distorted the passing light as it cooled.

The suit's unaffected hand pulled off the helmet, revealing a middle-aged man's face peppered with silvery-black stubble. His head appeared too small for the bulky suit of Wenkuth. He stared wide-eyed at the hand, then glanced at Jeanette, who maintained her outward gaze as if she was ignoring his presence.

Anticipation rippled through her body during the seconds of tense silence. Thankfully, the suit drifted downward.

"What are you doing?" the minister called.

When the suited man reached the platform, he fell to his knees. "She is truly of the Divine," he said, barely loud enough for Jeanette to hear. He knelt to the floor in submission.

The minister glanced up again with a scowl, clearly unconvinced. His focus seemed elsewhere—perhaps on his Nit to command someone else to remove her. The audience became livelier, some conversing among themselves with excitement or dread, others exclaiming praises or skepticism. She needed to speak.

Forcing down a wave of panic, she connected to the small, invisible pebble in her pocket that Lorin had given her earlier. She lifted it with Sorcery, passing it up through the neck of her garment and holding it in front of her mouth. A touch of Vitalization activated its sound-amplifying enchantment. Her heart continued to race as she reached a point several feet above the platform and stopped her descent.

Calm down, she told herself. *Breathe.*

She took in a deep breath.

"Fear not," she said, more to herself than the surrounding audience. The air surrounding her body vibrated, enhancing her voice spectacularly. "Behold, I bring tidings of joy to all!"

She let her voice fall. Thousands stilled to silence around her. Some looked at her with tears in their eyes. The distance made it difficult to make out individual expressions beyond the first few rows.

"The Divine knows thy plight, and cometh to deliver thee from certain death. I am sent to prepare the way and reveal her true name."

She let her voice fall again for dramatic effect. Was that the correct use of "thy" and "thee"? Maybe "cometh" was too much. She should dial it back.

"The Divine is not a 'her'!" the minister said, his voice echoing across the room. "This is an imposter! She means to deceive you all!"

Jeanette needed to deal with him, somehow. First, she needed some reinforcements.

"Behold, three new prophets are called to lead the work of salvation," Jeanette said. "Rise now, and come forth."

Her three companions, Quade, Sarah, and Lorin, floated up from their seats and moved toward the central platform, much to the astonishment of the surrounding audience. Quade and Sarah put on awed, humble expressions. Lorin, wide eyed and flailing, flipped himself upside down as he flew toward the platform. Jeanette inwardly rolled her eyes at the man's performance.

"You may not approach the platform!" the minister cried. "Enforcers, stop them!"

The kneeling enforcer rose and turned to the minister briefly with a threatening posture, quieting his protests.

Two of the suits were preventing a few fanatics from attempting to scale the platform. The others shifted uneasily but didn't respond. Jeanette wondered what kind of unheard conversations were going on between them.

Her three companions landed on the platform and approached her, then knelt reverently with the enforcer. She reached out toward Quade's bald head.

"Stop this nonsense!" the minister called, approaching Quade, who stood and turned around to face him. "Your deceit will not be —"

"Fear not, brother." Quade reached out and gently grasped the man's shoulder. "Feel the power of the Divine!"

The minister stumbled in his failure to resist Quade's push toward Jeanette.

She smiled at him, and slowly reached out toward the short, curly hair on his head.

"Don't touch—"

His words cut off as she touched him, and his body lit up to her perception. She aimed at his Nit, the neural device linking him to the universal network, and destroyed the components according to the Deia's instructions. His eyes widened with alarm as she froze his arms and legs, rooting him in place. She attempted a motherly expression while searching for the sweet spot near the middle of the man's brain—an area the Deia had taught her to find. A subtle command caused the neurons there to activate. His pupils dilated. Though his heart was still racing, tension dissipated from his muscles, preparing him for the Deia's unifying bond.

Her attention turned to the man's Source, a curious, somewhat ethereal sensation associated with his presence. She pressed her advantage. His eyes locked onto hers, and his resistance collapsed, allowing the Deia's power to flow from her and into his mind. His jaw dropped. The forceful manipulation of his brain meant he would be impotent as a Sorcerer, but that was fine. They needed his reputation more than his potential as a Sorcerer.

Satisfied, Jeanette unfroze the minister's limbs, and lifted her hand from his head.

"Divine almighty!" the man declared, his voice echoing across the conference hall. He fell to his knees and bowed his head to the floor. "Forgive me, O great messenger. I see now that thou art truly of the Divine!"

Jeanette nodded at his veneration as the crowd stilled.

"Behold, those who oppose Divine salvation shall fall, but those with faith in her power shall have life everlasting."

Was she saying "behold" too much?

Quade stepped forward and knelt once again. Right, the false ritual. She touched his head, and his body glowed briefly by his own Sorcery. Lorin and Sarah moved forward, and she completed the ritual with them as well, their bodies glowing momentarily to gasps of awe and reverence from the surrounding crowd.

"Look to these three, thy prophets, for they shall guide thee before the glorious arrival of thy Deliverer."

She really wasn't sure about her use of "thee." Regardless, her part was done. Time to leave.

Jeanette reengaged her body's upward force against gravity, and she rose steadily. Quade pulled something out of the minister's neckline, which he held to his lips.

"What is the name of our Savior, angel of the Divine?" he asked.

Oh right. She'd forgotten that part. *Just don't say "behold" this time.*

"Rejoice, spheres of life. Let us praise her name forever, for she is the Deia, Queen of Minds, Divine Liberator of all humanity."

Jeanette let the pebble's amplifying enchantment fall, then shoved it back under her garment and into her pocket, before pulling the veil back over her face. A tweak to her garment's enchantment allowed the light to bend around it once more, causing her to fade out of sight to the crowd, where many wept, shouted praises, or engaged in anxious conversation. Overhead lights drew nearer with the ascent, and her tension eased, though beads of sweat tickled the back of her neck. As the enchantment on her clothing completed its transition, the thousands of faces around her faded to darkness once more, bringing back the aching thoughts of her sister.

Kara, I miss you.

Chapter 2
Adrift

"It doesn't make any sense," Sam said.

Tovas half expected Kara to look up with a playful sneer of disdain from her deep squat. When she didn't, he entertained Sam's statement. "Why not?"

"Because good and evil are so *subjective*," Sam said, tapping his chin as his monolid eyes considered the scribbled notes on the panel door of the passenger bay. The thin lights all around illuminated the brushed metal interior lined with various cords and storage compartments. "Even people with the same religious beliefs have different ideas about what good and evil even mean."

Dull cramps gnawed at Tovas's legs from sitting cross-legged for an extended period, so he unwound them atop his bed of sparse robes, considering Sam's words. "I suppose that's true. Lomerianism, as an example, is based on principles. Individual followers frequently debate the moral value of specific actions. But the Divine knows all. They can pass true judgment."

Sam turned, his brown features displaying genuine perplexity. "So ... you think Sorcery results from a kind of supernatural judgment? If that's the case, why would this supposedly benevolent Divine be granting power to the *evil* side?"

Tovas tilted his head in response. "A good point."

"I admit there's clearly something that at least *appears* to be morality at work with Sorcery. That much is clear. But it's likely just another aspect of the universe we don't completely understand yet."

Tovas smiled. "Perhaps one day the Divine will touch your life enough for you to see Their hand in all things, Sam."

Sam sighed. "Well, I still think it's *very* counterproductive to assume that gaps in our knowledge are because of 'the Divine.' We should consider other possibilities."

Tovas contemplated the argument, then nodded. "Yes. I agree we need to learn more. I am convinced of the Divine's creation of all things, including Sorcery, but that is simply my faith."

The pair was sitting at one end of the messy passenger bay of the Thalas-class vessel that had become their world since leaving Invar. Thankfully, Rose and Zel had discovered ways to mask odors on board, both of the Tercast animals and of the group which had no way to bathe. Their work left a faint smell of mecreme, a common flour from Alvior. Makeshift beds created from the shoulder capes and sashes of their robes littered the interior. It had been at least four to five doh standard days filled with sleepiness, sparring, games, and experiments led by Sam. Most wore the shirt and pants of their Tercast robes. Only Kara, who was exercising nearby, wore something different: the heathered, light gray uniform of the Sovereignty military.

"I'm curious to know what you think, Kara," Tovas said.

"Don't drag *me* into this," she said, her voice strained from repeated sit-ups. "I think your endless debates are a waste of time."

Sam glanced over at her fondly. "Heh, that's—"

He stopped, as if struck by something unexpected. *That was something Vurkil had said,* Tovas realized. A wave of grief caused a sudden ache in his stomach. Sam's pained eyes met Tovas's for a moment, before looking away.

"That's what?" Kara asked.

"Nothing," Sam said, glancing down the bay at Rose, who appeared to be sleeping on her bed at the other end, near Zel.

Tovas rested a soft hand on Sam's shoulder. They all dearly missed the giant, as well as Talanna, Niu, and Relon. The absence of the women's bubbly chatter and laughter during their time aboard the ship left a tragic hole in the group's ambiance. A piece of them was missing. Tovas glanced at his twin brother Scheln, lying nearby. Losing Relon had hit him particularly hard.

Rose had hardly spoken during their weeks adrift in space. Tovas suspected she had connected with at least one or two of those killed during their last moments at Tercast, particularly Vurkil. While Tovas understood the crushing pain of loss, he could scarcely fathom experiencing an intimate connection with someone as their soul left their body. She had been through so much.

Ya'ir approached with a box of nutriment bars, and Tovas returned the hand on Sam's shoulder to his side. "Anyone want to split one with me?"

Awareness of the ever-present pangs of hunger resurfaced. They had all been eating meager meals to conserve the limited supply of food. Eventually, they would need to risk touching down on a planet, but they wanted to delay that inevitability as long as possible. The Sovereignty was likely still searching for them.

"No thanks, Ya'ir." Sam said as he stood. "I'm going to go check out the Ilkuth again for a bit."

"Just don't break anything," Kara said, her body straightening into a plank position.

Ya'ir's eyes locked on Tovas, holding up the bar of mixed yellows, blues and reds, surrounded by a clear protective layer that would dissolve in the mouth.

"No, thank you."

Better to save it for later. He could last a while longer without food.

"Hey! Tovas! I said I could go for a bite," Scheln said in his mind.

His twin brother's voice was barely discernible—and, frighteningly, getting weaker by the day.

"Actually," Tovas said, tapping Ya'ir after he'd spun around, "Scheln says he could use one."

Ya'ir cheerfully bent the multicolored bar in half until it separated, then handed one half of the soft, heterogeneous solid to Tovas.

"Thank you," Tovas said. He turned to his twin brother, who lay in his bed of assorted clothes and items.

"Finally, you heard me." Scheln said.

It's been getting more and more difficult lately, Tovas replied mentally, *and other acts of Sorcery have been getting more difficult as well. Sam's experiments have made it painfully clear: Our Sorcery is fading.*

"I know. It scares me, the thought of being completely voiceless again."

Tovas put his hand on his brother's shoulder, locking eyes with him. Master Azeloram's assurances that Scheln's physical condition would improve with Sorcery had never come to fruition, but at least it had given him a voice through Tovas, and some level of control of his surroundings.

I don't want to lose your voice either, but we may not have a ch—.

"Aargh!" Fita exclaimed. "Who stuck this putrid sock into my pillow!" He chucked the offending article and turned, eyeing each of them nearby. Kara laughed amid her next round of push-ups.

"It was *you,* wasn't it!" he snarled.

She fell to her knees with a giggle. "Don't look at me, Frito. *I* didn't do it."

Fita's eyes burned into Tovas and Scheln only briefly before he turned to Zel, snoring nearby. Defeated, he huffed, curling up under his robe-blanket and facing the wall.

Scheln's gaze drifted downward slightly as drool dripped from his open mouth and onto his robes. Tovas shook his head with a smirk, wiped up the drool with the sleeve of his own shirt, then pulled Scheln's jaw open.

Why do you torment him like that? Tovas asked.

Scheln chuckled into Tovas's mind. *"'Cause no one ever suspects me. It's hilarious!"*

Relative silence settled in as Tovas fed his brother the half-bar piece by piece, smashing it with his hands and using Sorcery to place it in his mouth. Scheln's automatic swallow reflex took over from there. Weeks ago, this would have been fairly easy, but now Tovas had to exert himself considerably to complete the task. He may need to start doing everything manually soon.

He was glad Scheln had some ability to exercise his will, though he wished they could figure out why their power was diminishing. Curiously, it seemed to have faded more quickly for Fita and Ya'ir, who could barely do anything with Sorcery anymore. Sam thought it had something to do with the Tercast robes. Both of them had removed more of their clothing for extended periods of time than the others, so the idea made some sense.

"Could I get a drink?" Scheln asked.

Of course.

Tovas pulled a small, flexible conduit from the wall nearby, which extended easily. The end had an interface designed to attach to suits like Kara's, but it also had a tiny control nozzle a few inches back for manual operation. He stuck the end into Scheln's mouth and turned the nozzle, allowing a trickling flow of water. His body automatically responded to the liquid, swallowing regularly.

"That's good, thanks."

Tovas stopped the flow, then pulled gently on the conduit, and it retracted back into the wall of the passenger bay. He broke off another piece of nutriment bar and continued the feeding process.

"Hey," Kara said as Tovas was moving the last bit of nutriment bar down Scheln's throat. She sat next to them, sweating and panting slightly, her gaze distant. She must have turned her eyes off again. "I've been thinking a lot about what we do next."

"About returning to Invar?" Tovas asked.

"Yes, and I think there might be a better place to go instead."

"Where? We need supplies."

"I've been thinking more and more about my parents. I think Sam or I have mentioned them before, right? How they were secretly citizens of the Sovereignty?"

"Weren't they at Tercast too?" Scheln said in his mind.

"Yes, I remember," Tovas said to Kara. "They had studied at Tercast as well, correct?"

"Apparently. The more I think about it, the more I think there's something behind their decision to move to Earth. I don't think they were running from something."

"Maybe they hid it well."

"Maybe, but there also may have been something about our home in particular that drew them there. We never moved; never even *considered* moving as far as I can remember. They always wanted to be there."

Tovas brought a hand to his face, pondering. "You want to go to Earth?"

"I think we might be able to get some answers there."

Tovas sat cross-legged again, leaning back against the wall. "It sounds risky."

"Sam won't like it," Scheln said.

"Scheln says that Sam won't like it."

"Oh yeah, he definitely won't like it," Kara agreed. "That's why I'm telling you first and not him. You'll need to help me convince him."

"They know who you are, Kara," Tovas said. "They may expect this. Do you really think you will find answers there?"

"I do. And I think it's worth the risk," she said. She balled her hand in a tight fist. "I *need* to find Jeanette. I need to. Returning home is the best chance we have of finding her. We've done enough hiding out in the middle of *literally* nowhere. We should also be able to resupply there, since the Sovereignty doesn't have a presence. At least the food won't be so *bland.*"

Tovas glanced at Scheln, who stared blankly back at him.

Kara tossed a sock at Fita. "What about you, Frito?"

He turned, shooting his inevitable scowl at her in response.

Kara chuckled. "Use your words. I don't really get what this"—she imitated Fita's expression—"means."

Scheln chuckled into his mind. Tovas himself fought a snicker.

After a moment, Fita's expression softened. "It seems better than an endless space existence. I cannot stand living in this metal box. Kula feels the same. I think she will support this decision."

"Could be worth it, as long as we're careful," Scheln said.

Tovas took a deep breath. Kara was right. Sam would not like this idea. He had been the most insistent about keeping out of sight. But it seemed like it could lead to some answers.

He glanced past Scheln to the Staff of Dreams, which lay against the metal wall next to him. Tovas picked it up and opened his Sorcery, feeling its protective purpose pulse through him.

Divine above, please grant us wisdom in this decision, Tovas prayed. *Help us know how we can find and help Kara's sister.*

He felt good about her plan. It was more active, less passive. They could finally do more than sit around and hope the Sovereignty would eventually stop searching for them.

He looked at Kara, whose eyes stared off into the distance.

"Okay," he said. "Scheln and I are convinced. We—"

The whine of a keglon echoed across the ship. Tovas bolted up to find it flailing wildly. A powerful hooved foot kicked Zelyra, who was attempting to move around the beast. She winced and gasped at the pain, but continued to move forward as Tovas shoved past Fita.

Kara's suit of Ilkuth flew from it's position in the corner and nearly smashed into Tovas, who dodged just in time thanks to the subtle inducing effect of the staff. The suit wrapped around Kara as she leapt forward, and she flew to the whining beast. A loud thump rang from a kick to her armored chest, which barely affected her movement. She gracefully moved to subdue the animal's front legs, pinning them down with the weight of the suit.

"Ugh," she said. "I can't reach the back legs."

Tovas approached the creature and slowly stepped forward

toward the frantically kicking hind legs. A blow struck out, and he spun the staff forward, deflecting it aside.

White-hot fire erupted nearby, in the shape of a sword. The beast's frenzied movements stilled.

"No!" Zelyra cried.

Fita, his dark face and golden hair lit eerily by the glow of the sword, moved the blade closer to the beast's long, triangular face.

Zelyra lunged forward with a gasp, one arm twisted oddly, the other stretched out to touch the creature's green, scaly belly. The hind legs flailed once more. With a steady, languid progression, the keglon's movements eventually stilled and its beady eyes closed. Kara lifted herself and put her hands on her hips.

Fita's sword extinguished, cooling to its shiny reflective silver once again. "It should not be here. None of these animals should be here."

"No!" Zel shouted. "You will *not* harm them."

She gasped with pain. Thankfully, Rose's pale, freckled face appeared in the soft light. Wearing her white Tercast robes, minus the sash and outer robes, she approached Zel from behind and touched her injured arm. Fita muttered to himself and skulked off toward the pilot's cabin. Zel visibly relaxed, and her arm shifted into a more natural stance. Her fingers flexed, and she turned to Rose with a grin.

"Thank you."

Rose, suddenly appearing drained of energy, gave a weak, split-second smile, before shuffling back toward her corner of the passenger bay nearby.

"What was that?" Kara asked, hands still on her hips. "I thought you said you could keep them asleep."

"I'm trying," Zel said. "Their bones are restless, and my power is fading."

Tovas sighed. "All our power is fading."

Kara shook her head and wandered to her corner, where the Ilkuth opened up, releasing her.

The door to the lav, between the passenger bay and the pilot's cabin swung open. Sam sprung into the doorway. "What happened?"

Kara approached him. "The horse-like thing—"

"The keglon?"

"Yeah, it woke up and started freaking out."

"Is everyone okay?" Scheln asked, diverting Tovas's attention from their conversation. He turned and headed back to his brother, stepping over the haphazard bits of makeshift beds that had been strewn about in their rush.

Yes. Kara helped subdue the keglon until Zel could connect with it again and put it back to sleep.

"Good, good. Speaking of sleep, I think I'm going to get some."

Tovas leaned the staff against the wall near his brother. *I think I'll rest for a bit as well. Feeding you and using the staff seems to have sapped a fair amount of my strength.*

"Wish we knew why its—"

Scheln's voice faded from Tovas' mind.

I didn't catch that last part, Tovas said mentally.

No response.

"I didn't catch the end of that," Tovas said softly. It felt odd, speaking to Scheln out loud.

Scheln's voice didn't reappear.

Tovas sighed, full of sorrow. "I'm sorry."

Were they perhaps going against the will of the Divine by remaining in space? Were they being too cautious? After what his tenacity had cost them at Tercast, Tovas was wary to act in haste again. Perhaps Sam was right to be careful. He had taught Tovas that there is wisdom in pragmatic restraint.

They couldn't stay in space forever, though.

As he sat in his own makeshift bed next to Scheln's, Tovas's eyes drifted to the staff, tracing its subtle, intricate, leafy patterns. Perhaps he had become too fearful after the events at Tercast. Faith was a principle of action, not fear. He needed to be more active in achieving the mission given to him by the Divine. His sacred duty.

Protect my people.

Chapter 3

The Prospects

"What did you do after that?" Jeanette asked.

The tall, round, pale-skinned man—she had already forgotten his name—smirked, and pounded his fists together repeatedly.

"Well, I couldn't let that go, o' course. Divine above knows I will not stand by and let someone insult 'em like that. The boys and I cornered her in the building the following week. Got her to confess her sin. Doubt she'll ever be causin' trouble again."

Jeanette leaned forward, her chair creaking slightly within the small meeting room. Golden light trickled in through a small, frosted window, illuminating a small painting of angels singing praises among fluffy clouds, and two padded wooden chairs. She had changed into a far more modest, suit-like outfit since her angelic appearance the day prior. They had hundreds of prospects to screen. Thankfully, no one had yet suspected her as the angel from the conference center.

"So," Jeanette prompted. "She said something against Skelebriar doctrine—"

"She said the women would lead as much as the men in the afterlife! That's just heresy!"

"And you and your friends harassed her into apologizing?"

"Damn, you make it almost sound like a bad thing. We were defendin' the faith, ma'am!"

Jeanette fought to avoid rolling her eyes, nodding in apparent agreement instead. Despite being a self-described "devout" Scelebriar, he didn't even follow the teachings of their leaders, which were more egalitarian. He was clearly a poor candidate.

She reached toward him, "Please give me your hand."

"Uh, all right." He placed his thick, soft hand into her own, allowing her to connect to him with Sorcery.

His body came alight to her perception. She reached for his Source, which put up its natural resistance.

"You have been chosen by the Deia—" She would usually use their name to make it more personal and impactful, but for the life of her she couldn't remember this man's name. "—devoted servant of the Divine."

Her encouraging words disarmed him, and their connection was complete. The Deia's presence spanned the bridge, entering the man's mind. His eyes widened, and she let her fingers slide from his. He would be no Sorcerer, but, as with the minister, the Deia could still use him to further her efforts.

"That's amazin'!" he said.

"Go. Spread the Deia's message of unity to all."

He smiled, stood, and left the room with an aura of blissful stupor.

When the door slid closed behind him, Jeanette sighed, leaning back and rubbing her temples. Several of the people eager to join the Deia's cause were quite dull, with little capacity for critical thought. Only a few had shown significant promise so far.

The door opened, revealing her next candidate: a dark-skinned woman with wavy, golden-brown hair. She wrung her hands nervously in the doorway.

Jeanette smiled warmly. "Lively afternoon. Please come and sit."

The woman returned a soft smile and moved around to the empty seat across from her.

"A—are you one of the chosen?" She asked.

"Oh no, no." Jeanette meekly put a hand to her chest. "I'm simply one of the acolytes chosen to assist them with this process."

"Oh, I see."

Her hands continued to fidget.

"What is your name?"

"Lelanna."

"The Deia smiles upon you Lelanna, and is grateful for your eagerness to serve her."

Her hands balled into fists. "I have devoted my life to the Divine. I am ready to serve wherever I am needed."

"Tell me more about yourself."

"I grew up here in Oscertos," she said, wringing her hands again. "One of my best friends was a devout Scelebriar, a-and she invited me to services after my partner left. The doctrine t-touched me, and when I saw the angel descending, I knew this was where I belonged."

"Wonderful. Tell me about your work or hobbies. What do you do with your time?"

She brushed her hair back. "I've been an animal caretaker at a megafarm on Galgadove."

"Have been? Are you not anymore?"

"Oh! I quit immediately after the Deia's holy angel departed." She tapped the back of her neck, where a Nit implant had been recently removed as part of their screening process. "I will miss them, but this work is far more important."

"That's remarkable," Jeanette said kindly, hoping to help the woman feel more at ease. "What have you enjoyed most about your work?"

Lelanna brightened. "Oh, I've loved so much about it. Socialization is perhaps my favorite part. Helping the derelingas, telisks and other animals have positive interactions with each other is so rewarding."

Jeanette smiled. "Beautiful. Has your devotion to the Divine influenced your work?"

"Oh, absolutely!" Her tone turned reverent, and her gaze turned upward briefly. "As the scriptures say, all life is sacred. I—"

The words struck Jeanette like lightning. *All life is sacred.* There it was. A familiar sentiment. One her parents had held firm to. A sentiment she herself had shared.

Until the Deia had benevolently deceived her to walk a better path.

"—calvaras running around the telisk den. It was tough, but I separated them and prevented any deaths. Cost me two fingers, though." She held her hand up, wiggling her pinky and ring fingers.

It seemed the Sovereignty's technology had reattached or regrown them, but that must have been a painful experience.

Devout. Protective instincts. Apparent respect for life. She's a good one.

Jeanette smiled broadly. "Dear Lelanna, I feel you are destined to be one of the Deia's select servants." She stood and extended her hand. "Please come with me."

Lelanna's eyes went wide, and she shot up from her seat. "Where are we going?"

She took Jeanette's extended hand, and her body came alight to Jeanette's Sorcery. Her heart was racing, exposing genuine anxiety or excitement.

"I have someone to introduce you to."

Jeanette led her by the arm through the door and into the bright, ornamental hallway of the Scelebriar administration building they had repurposed to begin the work of sorting devotees. As they walked, Jeanette pushed lightly on the woman's Source. Her resistance was strong. Excellent.

Lorin, Sarah, and others were conducting similar interviews in the rooms nearby. Quade managed the process from the hall above, becoming the public face of this new religious branch of Scelebriar theology.

She reached the door at the end, which swished open to reveal the disheveled remains of a disused meeting room. Jeanette moved to the center of the room, then turned to face her companion, whose brow was furrowed in confusion. With a grin, she connected to the floorboards and released the metal latches with Sorcery. The section of floor fell away beneath them, opening to a deep, dark hole.

Lelanna gasped, flailing in sudden panic, her gaze darting fearfully between her position above the depths and Jeanette's grinning face. Sorcery let their bodies descend gracefully into the darkness below, and Jeanette replaced the floor above, cutting off most of the light.

"Wh—where are we going?"

"You will see. Keep a firm grip on me."

Her grasp on Jeanette's hand tightened as they descended farther into complete darkness. Adrenaline pulsed through the woman's system. She was frightened—a sensible response. They shifted direction at the bottom, moving sideways past the rubble of an ancient, unused transport shaft that ran beneath the city. Lelanna yelped with the acceleration, gripping Jeanette's arm with her other hand. Stagnant, musty air rushed past as they flew. Though impossible to see with her physical eyes because of the pitch dark, with Sorcery Jeanette could make out the steel of the tracks and the rusty remains of an old subway car of sorts. The Alviorans had presumably abandoned the system ages ago in favor of ascender transport.

Jeanette remained quiet and, at the proper point of the tunnel, shifted direction again, lifting their bodies back up toward the surface. Light peeked at them from above, illuminating the rock surrounding them. They emerged in the middle of an old warehouse, which was empty except for two men in robes chatting with each other, and a small ship that vaguely resembled a submarine.

"A ship?" Lelanna asked. "We are going off world?"

"Soon."

"Maven Jey," Levick said, approaching the pair. The dark robes wrapped around his deep brown figure incompletely, exposing his right arm, shoulder, and a bit of his upper torso. "And who might this be?"

Jeanette smirked. "This is Lelanna. She's ready for the trials."

"Trials?" Lelanna said. "What trials?"

The man sighed. "Why do you keep telling them that? It just frightens them."

Jeanette shrugged. "I feel like they deserve *some* warning."

Lelanna, clearly sensing trouble, turned about, looking for an exit. "I . . . I don't think I'm ready for this, whatever it is. I should go."

"Aw, now do you see what you did?" Levick tsked. "What did I tell you? She's panicking."

Hulinargo—a burly fellow with light skin and a beard—approached, wearing a similar robe, but colored a deep maroon.

Lelanna backed away, then dropped Jeanette's hand and began running, her steps echoing across the expansive interior.

The bearded man shook his head. "Why do you do this?"

"Oh, come on, admit it, you were bored anyway."

He grinned, then his feet left the ground. The woman glanced back to see the giant man flying toward her and screamed. He grabbed her arm, and she threw a kick at him. When that failed, she bit his hand, which remained firmly attached to her arm.

"Whoa—aha," he said. "You're a feisty one."

"Help!" she screamed, flailing wildly. "Hel—"

Her body suddenly went limp, falling against Hulinargo's body. He casually flung her onto his shoulder and floated back toward the ship.

Jeanette recalled that fateful night of Delveton's arrival on Earth. Her parents, dead. Her struggle to get free of him. Consciousness fading. Waking up in an unknown setting. Pits of fire. Whips cracking.

"How much more room do we have?" she asked, pushing the memories aside.

Lelanna in tow, the bearded man flew by and landed near the opening to the ship, then carried her inside.

Levick shrugged. "I'd only bring another two or three, I think. The Deia instructed not to get too many at once, remember?"

Jeanette nodded, stepping over the hole in the floor once more and hovering. "I'll be back soon."

She let her body go, relishing in the natural exhilaration of freefall. Wind roared, cooling with her rapid descent, until darkness consumed her.

Chapter 4

Destinations

Not particularly soft. Not particularly warm. Rarely quiet either. There was almost always someone moving about or talking—even when they dimmed the lights for sleep hours, although that helped. They wouldn't be dimming the lights for some time yet, though.

Rose turned, trying to get more comfortable in her makeshift bed nestled against the corner of the ship's passenger bay, comprising the sash and cape of her Tercast robes. The surrounding environment moved unusually quickly to her perception, a side effect of the enchantment she had frequently been placing on her body to slow causality. She hoped it would shorten the time—or, more accurately, her *perception* of time—stuck inside the spacecraft with dangerous thoughts.

Thankfully, she had maintained enough power to heal Zel earlier. It was a clean break from the keglon's blow, and relatively simple to fix, but it left Rose feeling significantly drained. The potency of their Sorcery was waning quickly, as evidenced by Sam's measurements. From her lying position, Rose had a clear view of Zel, who had laid her head on top of the furry purple ulinko, and fallen asleep.

Rose turned onto her back and whipped her shoulder-cape blanket in an attempt to let it cover her more thoroughly. Though she was tired, sleep continued to elude her. She turned her thoughts inward, connecting to and naming all the bones in her body one by one, starting with the distal phalanx of the great toe of her left foot. She worked her way up her leg and hips, up the spinal column, including the ribs, down her left arm, then into her head, where she completed at the parietal bone of her cranium.

She sighed, feeling no closer to sleep than when she'd started.

Perhaps she could continue by considering the primary functions of each of the bones. She could start where she had ended—begin at the head and work her way down to the toes.

The cranial bones fuse at around two standard years after birth. Cortical thickness and density varies, but offers significant protection to the brain from external trauma such as—

A chill rippled across Rose's body.

Knives.

Lightning.

She sat up and shook the thoughts violently from her head. Her heart raced. Tears welled in her eyes. Her breathing became shallow and ragged.

No.

Don't think of it.

Won't think of it!

She whirled her head around awkwardly, making her head spin. Dizziness and nausea, thankfully, replaced the dark chill that had threatened to consume her from within.

"You okay?"

Rose flinched, reflexively backing away from the figure above her. Her enchantment caused the voice to be distorted to her ears, and she still couldn't see properly due to her whirling vision. It sounded like a male voice. She dropped the enchantment on her body, bringing the world back to its normal speed. The figure crouched next to her.

"Rose?" Ya'ir said.

"I'm—" she began, then found she was out of breath. "I'm okay."

Ya'ir sat down and placed a soft hand on her shoulder, and his brow furrowed with concern. She waited for him to say "no, you're not," but he remained silent as her vision steadied, eventually allowing her to bring his worried face into focus.

Without a word, he embraced her. The tears that had formed in her eyes earlier streamed down her cheeks as she hugged him back. Warmth radiated from him, melting through the icy darkness within.

"You're not alone, Rose," he whispered. "We're always here for you."

She should talk about her feelings—talk about the trauma. It was the healthy, responsible thing to do. She just couldn't do it. Couldn't even let herself *think* about . . . everything that had happened. It was still far too agonizing.

But Ya'ir's quiet warmth made a world of difference.

"I'll be okay," she breathed, wiping her cheeks. Ya'ir moved back to see her, keeping his hands on her shoulders. "I'll be okay when we can get off this ship."

He smiled. "About that. Kara is trying to convince everyone to go somewhere new. Somewhere we might get off the ship without fear of the Sovereignty."

Rose raised an eyebrow. "Where?"

"Earth."

"Sam's home planet?"

Ya'ir nodded. "And Kara's."

She considered the possibility. A class four planet. The Sovereignty still monitored those planets, but they wouldn't have the advanced surveillance systems typical of Sovereignty worlds. It would almost certainly be easier to avoid detection there.

"Could be a good idea."

Fita stepped out of the passage toward the pilot's cabin and turned his gaze to them.

"Yeah, she's concerned that Sam won't like it," Ya'ir said, dropping his hands from Rose's shoulders.

"Forgive me for interrupting." Fita stepped behind Ya'ir, his eyes locked onto Rose. "I wish to speak to you."

Fita's dark, muscular torso was bare, as usual. He had donated his shirt to Scheln's bed.

"Okay," Rose said, trying not to sound troubled. Fita was rarely one to talk.

He shot Ya'ir a glare. "Alone."

Ya'ir flinched. "Oh, right, of course." He stood and strode off toward the other end of the passenger bay.

Fita sat, crossing his legs with an upright, dignified posture, then spoke in a subdued voice. "Despite my continued exercise regimen, I am quite certain I am losing muscle. I suspect it is the food."

Rose raised an eyebrow. "The basic nutriment goods may not be the tastiest things, but they're a highly nutritious diet. I suppose it could be because you aren't eating as much as you did before."

He stared at her with an unreadable expression, motionless as her words sunk in.

"Increase them, please."

"What?"

"Build my muscles back up to the way they were before," he said. "With Sorcery."

Rose shook her head. "It doesn't work that way, Fita, you know that. When you or I enchant your body, it will slowly return to the way it was before. Body enchantments don't stick."

"I thought you and Sam were working on that."

"We did. Somewhat. We tried several things. It's unclear why, but it seems like our organ systems have a 'base state' that they revert to after a while. You can't make any permanent changes with Sorcery alone, not without constantly re-enchanting."

Fita sighed. "Perhaps we could move the ship closer to the planet. Increase gravity."

"What? No. Forcing our bodies to work harder will make us all need more food. It likely wouldn't help you anyway." Not to mention it would make sleeping even more uncomfortable.

"Only for—"

"Hey," Kara said as she approached. "Sorry to interrupt. I need to talk to you about something while Sam's occupied. A potential new destination, instead of risking a drop on Invar."

Tovas and Kula walked up behind her.

"Ya'ir already told me," Rose said.

Kara nodded. "Good, good. What do you think?"

Rose shrugged. "I think it could be a good idea, since it's a class four planet."

"If we're careful," Kara said, "I think we should be able to avoid detection there."

"Avoid detection where?" Sam's voice approached from the pilot's cabin and everyone turned to him.

Rose glanced at Kara, who simply grinned at Sam.

"Clearly I'm missing something here," Sam said. "What's going on?"

"As you know, we're running low on supplies," Kara said.

"I know. We're stretching what we have as long as we can. Returning to Invar is risky, but as we've already discussed, I agree we'll need to do it soon."

"We actually have a different destination in mind."

Sam raised an eyebrow. "Really? Where?"

"Earth."

His eyes widened. "Kara, that's . . . not a good idea. I bet they're expecting that from you."

Rose hadn't thought of that, but it was a good point. The Sovereignty was likely looking for Kara specifically. If they knew she was from Earth, they might expect her to go back.

"I know, but I think that's where we need to go. Scheln, Tovas, Fita, and Kula are on board."

"Seriously?" Sam said. "That's *extremely* risky."

"It may not be any worse than going to any other Sovereignty world. I think it's worth the risk."

"What about you, Rose?" he asked, gauging her reaction.

Truth was, she didn't know what the better choice would be. Resupplying and hiding out in space was certainly *physically* safer, but their mental health was deteriorating. If their Sorcery continued to weaken, that would also make Zel's animals much more difficult to handle. They would need to leave them behind. Injuries could also be more severe if Rose's healing abilities lost strength.

"It's risky," she replied, "but staying up here is a risk in other ways."

"Yeah," Kara said. "Going anywhere is risky, but at least on Earth we might go outside for a while."

Sam rubbed his temple. "You don't just want to go to Earth and hide out on some remote island, though. You want to go back home."

Silence settled over them as the accusation sunk in.

"Yeah, yeah okay. I want to go back home because *I know* there's something there. I've thought about it a lot, Sam. My parents weren't running from something. They were there for a reason. We need to find out what that reason is."

Sam's face reflected his inner conflict. Knowing him as she did now, Rose was fairly certain he felt torn between his caution and his endless hunger for knowledge—and perhaps his affection for Kara. He likely wanted to know as much as Kara did. Maybe more. But unlike Kara, Sam was more circumspective.

"You said we would try to find Jeanette, Sam," Kara said. "The clues to finding her are back on Earth. I know it."

He glanced at each of them, perhaps grasping for some kind of support, or at least hesitation. Eventually, he sighed.

"Well, clearly everyone seems to be on your side with this, and I know better than to keep arguing with you about it, but if we do this, we're going to need to be *extremely* careful."

Kara nodded. "Of course."

"All right," Sam said. "Let's go to Earth."

Chapter 5
Reassignment

"Jey!"

Tess threw her arms around Jeanette, holding her tightly within the entry hall of Evamune Palace. The hall now sported colorful decorations, including elaborate banners of purple and gold, which rustled with the sharp gusts from the open double doors. Roaring flames flickered inside two ornate golden torches. Levick closed the door behind them, quieting the ceaseless winds of Uvlun as the others carried the unconscious occupants of the ship to the dungeon.

"I'm so glad to see you again!" Tess said with a wide grin.

Jeanette smiled warmly at the shorter woman. "I'm glad to see you too, Tess."

"I heard the operation with the Scelebriars was a success."

"It was. We've added *hundreds* to our numbers already. Many at the conference center wanted to join immediately.

"Beautiful. I convinced a few from Tenrazka, but not so many as you. Skeptics are harder to convince, naturally, but when you get the right group together, their hate for organized religion can do wonders."

Tess finally released her embrace and stood back, giving Jeanette a clear view of her outfit. Plenty of pale cleavage was on display from her black leotard, which bore swirling silver patterns beneath a thick black belt.

Tess placed a hand on her hip, which jutted out to the side. Her eyes scanned Jeanette's figure, adorned with the simple suit-like outfit from Alvior.

"Come find me after your chat with the Deia. We should catch up while we can before setting out again."

Her words contained the slightest hint of a suggestive undercurrent.

"Sure," Jeanette said as nonchalantly as possible.

Tess gave her a wave as she strode by with her two companions, who were to help her prepare the ship for another departure. The enormous palace doors creaked as the small woman swung them open with apparent ease, letting in the relentless, freezing gales of Uvlun. Then they passed through into the darkness and shut the door with an echoing clash behind them.

Jeanette continued up the steps to the hallway above, passing the spiral staircase to the dungeons, which evoked mixed feelings within her. Her capture by Delveton, the ensuing torture, and the relentless abuse, still felt so visceral and terrifying in her memory.

But now she knew. Now she truly understood.

Her helplessness, her suffering. They gave her *power*. They strengthened her Sorcery. The Deia had allowed—even encouraged—those things to happen because they would teach her things she could not know otherwise. She had learned the true value of suffering and sorrow.

For that, she was grateful.

Jeanette turned the corner toward the throne room, eyeing the colorful paintings and elaborate lighting. She thought back on the fateful event, many weeks ago now, when she had marched down these same halls, intent on destroying the Deia. The guttural sounds. A curly haired man bleeding to death against the stone wall. The events rang through her memory. She remembered her sorrow as she'd left the Deia's throne room, feeling defeated.

It seemed so long ago now. She had come so far since then—become so powerful.

Jeanette arrived at the throne room door and waited for the Deia's prompting to enter. Her feelings of despair and defeat when she had walked through these doors on the day of her transformation had been woefully unwarranted. The Deia was *everything*. The genuine hope of humanity. Jeanette could hardly fathom how she hadn't come to her senses earlier.

The Deia truly was as Divine a being as one could be.

A subtle feeling of acceptance entered her mind. It was time to go in. She pushed the ornate door open, and walked into the now familiar room of hand-knotted gold-and-purple carpet below intricate, shining gold ornaments above. In the corner, three shirtless men hovered over books on the desk, scanning their contents.

The Deia sat on her extravagant padded throne, her legs elegantly crossed and hands softly poised in her lap. Long, straight brown hair—streaked with gold—spilled down her exposed, slightly lighter brown shoulders and onto her black dress, where gold embellishments cascaded throughout the fabric. The impossibly gorgeous woman smiled at Jeanette, causing her stomach to do a somersault. That this magnificent woman would grace her with such a lovely expression was almost more than she could bear.

As Jeanette approached the throne, the Deia stood, then stepped down to the main level and opened her arms warmly.

"Jeanette," she said, her voice settling like a drop of pure sunshine through the frigid air of Uvlun. "I'm so glad to see you."

Jeanette embraced the Divine being, feeling wholly unworthy.

The woman pulled away, beaming. Jeanette smiled back.

"Your work with the Scelebriars on Alvior was exceptional."

Pure joy at the Deia's appreciation brought tears to her eyes. The Deia turned and stepped back into her throne, which put her gaze nearly level with Jeanette's. "After your brief return to Alvior to meet with Golin, I want *you* to oversee their indoctrination."

"Me?" Jeanette said, wiping her eyes with her sleeve.

"Yes. By testing them, your knowledge and power will grow. Experiment. Learn from them. Manipulate them. Break them. And they will be born anew, as you have been. They will be ours."

"I don't know if I can—"

"You are more knowledgeable and powerful than you realize. You have studied well. The mind can be remarkably malleable, if given the proper conditions. I foresee you will have brilliant success."

The Deia's sure gaze gave Jeanette confidence. "But what if some of them refuse to change?"

The Divine being frowned. "The power of our suasion is potent, but if, ultimately, they choose not to be one with us, then their lives can be spent to encourage those who are strong. We need more with abilities such as yours."

Jeanette bowed. "Of course. I will do what I can."

The intoxicating smile crossed the Deia's godly features once again. She nodded and gestured gracefully to the door. Understanding the cue to leave, Jeanette turned and strode across the throne room, glancing briefly at the three men in the corner. One of them broke from the group and marched toward the throne with a suggestive grin on his face.

When she returned to the brightly lit hallway, thoughts of her new task churned in her mind. What would she do? How would she test them? Push them? How would she help them see the beauty of the Deia's embrace?

She turned the corner and found Tess striding toward her. The shorter woman grinned broadly as she approached, brushing long black hair behind her ear. They hugged, and once Tess released the embrace, she gripped Jeanette's hand with a telling smirk.

"Come with me."

Chapter 6

Bluebirds

The vehicle touched down with a barely noticeable bump, and the rear gateway opened for the first time in weeks, letting in a cool breeze that carried the heavenly scent of mossy wood, and revealing a landscape of beautiful oaks and pines under a clear blue sky. Leaves of bright orange, red, and yellow cascaded across the breathtaking scenery. Fall was in full swing.

Sam squinted at the sudden brightness and took a deep breath in through his nose, which he released slowly. Kara did the same next to him. Her grip tightened around his hand as bird-song came through the opening. They walked out of their metallic confinements onto the soft woodland floor. Sam's insides did a somersault as he glanced sideways at Kara's enormous grin.

They were home.

"Look at that," Sam said. "We came back at the perfect time of year."

"It's beautiful."

"Ahh, sunlight!" Zelyra exclaimed, striding out beside them with the Tercast animals plodding around her lethargically.

"I thought you said most plant life was green on your planet," Ya'ir said as he picked up a reddish oak leaf with interest.

"It is, usually," Sam replied. "We're just lucky to be back at the perfect time of year to see the colors change."

Wind rustled the trees, sending a fresh wave of leaves falling around them.

Kara shivered. "Whew, it's chilly."

She led Sam to a tall pine and reached out to feel it. He followed her lead, running his fingers along the scaly, course bark. He knelt down and picked up a pine cone, sensing a powerful attachment to the common coniferous object.

"My *god*, it feels so good to be back on Earth," Kara said.

"Absolutely," Sam agreed. "I still think this is risky, but honestly, I didn't think I could miss it this much."

She closed her eyes, still wearing that infectious grin on her beautiful face.

"What is it like, being able to actually see it all now?" he asked.

Kara opened her eyes and cocked her head. "Odd, but beautiful. Similar to when I saw you for the first time, maybe. Sensing a familiar person or place in a completely new way is just . . . bizarre."

"Where is your home from here?" Tovas asked. He approached with Scheln hanging limply in his arms.

Kara pointed past Sam's head. "A few miles that way. I'll go scout the place out in a minute to see what we're dealing with. I just want to enjoy *not* being surrounded by a metal box for a few."

"Of course!" Tovas replied cheerfully.

He strode off, high-stepping to avoid tripping on a root or fallen tree branch, and gently placed Scheln against a handsome red oak.

An aura of peaceful exhilaration permeated the group as they absorbed their surroundings. It had been far too long since they had seen any plant life or sunlight.

Stupid reconnaissance. Sam didn't want Kara to leave him. If only there was a way he could join her; if only he could fly. With their waning Sorcery, it seemed less and less likely he'd be able to crack the secret of flight. Which was all the more reason to give it one last try.

"Hey, can I try connecting to the Ilkuth out here?"

Kara sighed. "Sam, I really don't want to be surrounded by tech right now."

"You don't have to wear the whole suit! Can't you just put on a hand or something?"

"I guess. It's not really meant to be worn that way, though. My Nit will probably start pestering me about it being disconnected."

"I won't take too long."

She raised her eyebrows at him with a playful smile. Sam's insides fluttered.

"Promise!" he added with a grin.

"Okay, okay. Let's go get it."

He followed her lead, still hand in hand, back to the ship. Tovas sat next to his brother, casually leaning back on his hands, while Ya'ir waved a stick around and recounted an energetic story to them. Fita and Kula conversed nearby about the alien flora. Zel was attempting to pull a pine cone out of the keglon's mouth, telling the animal it may not be safe to eat. Rose sat near Zel, and stroked the cat like purple ulinko in her lap.

She was smiling.

Jubilation electrified him at the sight. It had been far too long since he'd seen Rose smile. He had a sudden urge to rush over and hug her, but quelled the impulse.

Kara's hand drifted from his as she entered the vehicle. She returned a moment later with the entire left arm of the Ilkuth attached to her body.

"Couldn't just get the hand?" he asked.

"Well, some of these pieces come apart, but without the entire arm, the hand section won't have power. Here."

She disconnected the hand from the forearm, and it slid off. Sam moved to catch it, but it slipped from his grasp.

"Aagh!"

The gauntlet's posterior fell against the surface of the passenger bay with a resounding clang.

Kara chuckled. "Heavier than it looks, isn't it?"

"I'll say!" Sam tried to lift it but failed with a grunt of exertion. "What is this made of? Neutronium?"

"What's neutronium?"

"A dense degenerate matter from n—"

"Yeah, yeah," Kara said, rolling her eyes. "I regretted the question as soon as I started asking it."

She bent over, slipping her hand into the gauntlet's wrist until it snapped into the forearm. The fingers flexed.

The metallic left arm extended and Sam took it, intertwining his bare fingers with her armored ones.

"How do you even lift it like that? How do you still move it around so naturally when it obviously has a huge amount of inertia?"

Kara shrugged. "I don't know. It feels kind of weird to wear it without the rest of the suit. It moves on its own power."

Sam frowned in thought as they moved away from the ship into another crisp breeze of falling leaves. It made sense. The suit likely had to propel itself with anti-gravity and whatever propulsion system it used. It would be impossible for Kara to move it as fluidly as she could at that moment by the force of her muscles alone. She was pretty strong for her size, but she wasn't *that* strong.

"Speaking of power," she said, "the suit is down to less than half its power. We should try to let it charge while we're here—leave it out in the sun for a while."

It would be nice if they could plug into the local energy grid, but there were several issues with that, the most obvious being that the suit certainly wouldn't have any way to interface with the electrical system.

"Oh," Kara said. "I should probably cloak the ship."

A moment later, Sam watched the ship close its large opening and fade out of view, completely invisible. He still wanted to explore that incredible feature at some point, once he figured out this anti-gravity nonsense.

As they walked back out into the forest, Sam activated his

Sorcery, navigating some of the mechanical components within the hand of the Ilkuth with his mind—or Source, if such a thing truly existed. He could only reach a thin depth before the imperception surrounding Kara's body took hold. He wished he could form a persistent connection with her through Sorcery, but it seemed to be impossible unless she was a Sorcerer as well.

"Can you change the antigravity a little?" Sam asked. "Feeling the change on a planet might be helpful."

"You had the gravity of the other planet."

"Yeah . . . I don't know, I just think it would be worth a try in a new environment."

She sighed. "Okay."

Hopefully, Kara's patience would hold out for a few minutes at least. Sam strained his mind to feel anything through his connection as they stepped over a cluster of roots. A light breeze sent more leaves cascading down around them, and a component of the inner palm moved, barely perceptible. The material changed. He could sense lines of it pushing *away* from Earth, rather than toward it. Such an odd phenomenon.

He recalled one of their first assignments back at Tercast: feeling a health potion enchantment and attempting to apply it to a vial of plain water. Soon afterward, they were feeling and transmuting air into methane to create fire.

The same principle *should* apply here, in theory. He had spent many hours aboard the ship examining the anti-gravitational effects of the suit and the ship. If he could just get the sensation right, he should be able to apply it to himself, or to other objects.

A small bright red bird flew up and landed on a branch overhead as they strode underneath—a cardinal. Unlike the bird, humans lacked the inherent ability to fly. But perhaps he could circumvent that limitation.

Sam closed his eyes, letting his mind replay the events of the tragic night of Jeanette's kidnapping. It had happened only a few miles away from where they now stood. He vividly recalled his own horror as the hooded figure, who he now knew as Delveton, slung Jeanette's limp body over his shoulder and soared into the night.

Delveton's flight had been so natural, so graceful. The man almost certainly used antigravity to achieve such a quick and natural-looking movement.

As Sam opened his eyes, he smiled at the cardinal and connected his ethereal sensations of Sorcery to his own hip bone. He tried to imagine it pushing against gravity instead of falling toward it.

His hip lifted a little, causing him to shift awkwardly during his next two steps, but it was the same as lifting a stone against gravity, and certainly didn't feel the same as the antigravity. He was pushing the matter up with Sorcery, rather than changing the effect of gravity itself. As he dropped his imaginative command, the weight on his hip resettled.

"One more time?" Sam asked.

"Okay, but I'll hold you to it," Kara said. "You get a minute and then I'm putting it back."

"Fine."

"Here it goes."

Last chance. Sam concentrated on the change in the material's substance—stronger this time. Their hands lurched up briefly, then the effect reversed with another change, bringing their arms down again. He connected simultaneously to his hip bone once more, keeping his focus on that subtle, material alteration, as he gazed at the forest floor. *Just replicate the feeling.*

His hip, swaying with his gait, responded, pushing up against his torso again, making him feel lighter.

Sam let the connection drop, and the feeling of lightness remained. His hip bone continued pushing upward, against the usual direction of gravity, causing him to stumble.

Excitement thrummed through him as he pulled his hand away from Kara's to catch himself, then stilled.

Kara stopped with him, placing a hand out to steady him. "You okay? What is it?"

He ignored her—for the moment. The *impression*. He couldn't risk losing that *impression*.

Sam closed his eyes and connected with his whole body this time, feeling his expanding lungs and pulsing circulatory system, and repeated the imagination of the unique alteration permeating the tissues of his body.

They responded, giving him a surge of exhilaration—until the forest floor fell from his feet. His stomach lurched.

"Ahh!" Kara exclaimed. Her empowered hand lunged toward him, but slid across his garments, failing to catch hold.

Terror gripped him as his body tumbled. He got a brief glimpse of Kara's wide-eyed stare before smashing into the branch of an oak tree, which knocked the air out of him. The rough bark scraped his forearms as he managed a very uneasy grip around the thick limb.

Profound disorientation stunned him. He looked "up" and found the bushes and trees of the forest, Kara's stunned face, and Tovas and Kula racing over to her, then looked "down" and saw nothing but a vast blue sky.

Well . . . that was a bad idea.

"Sam!" Kara yelled.

His tentative grip gave out, and he tumbled with a yell through a mess of smaller branches and leaves. He grasped a twig as he continued falling into nothingness. Panic flared through his chest as he released the twig, which fell "up" toward the ground— opposite the direction he was falling.

Panic consumed him. His heart pounded relentlessly in his chest as air rushed past him, cooling rapidly. He tried to activate Sorcery, but that was unsuccessful. He was too frantic—unable to think clearly.

"Argh!" he exclaimed at the surrounding air.

He corrected his tumbling, presenting his stomach to the blue sky below. A glance "upward" confirmed that he was still falling in the wrong direction. The frigid air froze his exposed face and hands.

Frustration with his own stupidity pierced through the

hysteria. How could he be so careless? He should have realized antigravity was a dangerous thing to experiment with out in the open air. Why hadn't he thought about this? Soon he was going to end up in the cold emptiness of space!

A cool, hard object wrapped around his torso. An arm?

Kara!

Fully covered in her shiny Ilkuth, she pulled around "below" him, and her encased body began pushing against his own, slowing his "descent."

"You blockhead!" she said from behind her reflective helmet. "What the hell do you think you're doing? Skydiving in the wrong direction?"

Sam's panic subsided with his diminishing velocity. Being the target of Kara's wrath sounded better than falling into space. Slightly.

He shrugged. "Oops!"

"Oops is right, you numbskull. You were about to freaking die!"

"It's okay," he said, attempting to convince himself more than her. "I'm okay. Just give me a minute."

Thankfully, Sorcery was again within his reach. He felt the familiar fleeting sensations of his own body, then connected to it. He *should* be able to reverse the effect. It would be extremely inconvenient to have to live like some kind of helium balloon for the rest of his life.

An attempt to alter his body the same way as before proved successful, and with a moment of relief, Sam felt gravity reverse, causing his stomach to lurch again. He pulled away from Kara, who drew him close, pressing a rigid breast of the suit into his chest.

"Hey! You almost slipped. Give me a little warning before you change physics on me!"

"Sorry," he said.

How was this supposed to work? How did the ascenders work again? The man at the Sovereignty facility had told him once. He strained his mind to remember. Something about changing a portion of the mass, not the whole thing at once. Somehow, he had to distribute the effect so it wouldn't change his entire body.

Through the connection, he scanned the tissues of skin, muscle, bone, and other substances. Then he imagined the feeling peppering through portions of his mass. He felt sections of his body pull against itself slightly, but then the effect stabilized.

"I think I've got it," he said.

"Stop messing around! Just wait until we get to the ground."

"Just let me go! I'll show you."

"I will not let you—"

"Trust me. I've got this. If I fall again, you can catch me."

She let out a heavy sigh, then released his body, but maintained a firm grip on his hand. He casually drifted away from her, and she pulled him around to face the ground.

He was floating—nearly weightless.

Excitement surged through his frigid extremities.

"Yes! I finally got it."

Kara released his hand and performed a slow clap. "Great job. I just *love* it when my boyfriend nearly turns into a human asteroid. Can we get back to solid ground now?"

"That's twice now that you've saved my life," Sam said with a chuckle as he adjusted the feeling on his body, allowing him to fall at a moderate pace. Her suit matched it. "People might think you like me or something."

She folded her arms. "That's twice *recently*. Remember that time at Glenn-something-or-other Park?"

Sam ran through his memories of scaling jungle gyms and jumping from swings with her through the years. A smile crossed his face as he considered how his feelings for her had grown.

"A time when you saved me?" he asked. "I remember saving *you* multiple times from getting clobbered in the face by swinging kids."

"Okay, fair enough. But there was that time when you slipped on the 'gnome dome' and I caught you."

"Oh right, that climbing frame thing! I forgot about that." He chuckled. "Gnome dome. Such a stupid name."

Kara sighed happily. "I loved that thing."

"I know. You were always the fastest. Gnome queen."

They laughed together, relishing the memory. "Good times."

Their feet made it near the treetops, and Sam nudged his body toward an opening to the forest floor. Tovas, Rose, Kula, and Ya'ir rushed under their position amid the sea of reds and oranges. They had veered off from where the ship had landed.

"Sam!" Tovas called out. "Are you all right?"

"Yeah, I'm fine," he responded, embarrassed at the attention. "I just got a little, uh . . . carried away . . . with my antigravity experiment."

He landed softly, cushioning the impact with his legs. He moved his arms around in front of himself awkwardly, feeling as if he were submersed in a pool—with a breathable, far lighter medium.

Rose approached with wide eyes. "It worked? You gave yourself antigravity?"

"Yeah! It's amazing."

"Pfft," Kara chided, folding her arms. "Amazing? I saw you up there. You were freaking out."

Sam ran a hand through his hair. "Well, okay yeah, I was panicking a little because I had accidentally completely reversed gravity on myself, but it all worked out."

She laughed. "Only because I was there to save you."

"Regardless," Tovas cut in, "you're safe now, and that's what's important."

Sam felt Rose's presence enter his body, and something changed in his arms. The scrapes and bruises covering them began disappearing. He glanced at her pale, freckled face and gave her a nod of thanks.

"Since I'm all suited up now anyway," Kara said, "I'm going to go scout out the house."

"I'll come with you," Sam said.

"No, I was just going to fly over there and take a quick look."

"I'll fly with you!"

She placed her hands on her hips. "When did *you* get so stubborn? Usually that's my job."

Sam simply grinned at her expectantly.

"Okay, *fine*. We'll be back in a little while."

"Are you sure you will have enough strength, Sam?" Tovas asked. "With our Sorcery weakening?"

"I should be okay. The nice thing about charging gravity is that it takes much less energy to move around. I can be a lot more efficient."

"All right, but be careful."

Kara lifted off the ground, and Sam followed suit, feeling exhilaration rush through him as he pushed his body to follow. They flew just a few dozen feet off the ground, well below the tops of the tallest trees overhead. She was probably hoping it would provide some cover in case the Sovereignty was watching, which he decided was a good idea. Hopefully, his antics hadn't already given them up. Soon she began pulling ahead of him, and he found himself unable to accelerate further.

"Hey, wait up!" he called out. "I can't move that fast."

She turned about and spun around to match his speed. "Too fast for you?"

"Well, I bet I could have kept up better at Tercast, before our Sorcery started fading."

"Uh-huh," she said. "Blame it on Tercast."

"I'm not blaming—oh, whatever."

She took his hand, causing his insides to flutter as they continued pushing through the trees. Crisp wind rushed past his ears. A pair of bluebirds soared ahead, accompanying them for a moment as they danced through the air. Sam copied their motion, and rotated around Kara as they flew. She followed, spinning around him as they weaved through the sunlit trees.

Soon enough, the edge of the trees appeared in the distance, and she slowed. He eased the push against his own body, causing him to slow as well. Mild fatigue pressed upon his mind with the exertion.

They landed near the tree line and gazed out into the familiar backyard landscaping, which, though normally well kept, was experiencing an invasion of weeds around the pond. Beyond the water, he noticed that the back of the house had been repaired. It was impossible to tell that a giant hole had once been there. Remnants of Jeanette's destroyed dresser lay below, which summoned a momentary pang of anxiety coupled with the memory of Elysia, a Sovereignty enforcer, being thrown through the wall of Jeanette's room.

"It's so, so weird to see this," Kara whispered. "The place I grew up. How it always looked. It doesn't feel right."

"Well, it doesn't quite look the same as it normally did. They seem to have repaired the wall, though."

"What I mean is sight itself. It still feels wrong to see things like this—makes me uncomfortable."

Sam glanced at her reflective face shield, and didn't know what to say. In truth, it still felt odd to him as well, as if she had lost something precious. A bizarre feeling, since in truth she had only gained something. Hadn't she?

Kara glanced around. "I don't see anyone nearby, let's go inside."

Sam grabbed her hand, attempting to hold her in place, but she yanked him forward instead with an unexpected lurch.

"Whoa!" Sam said, catching himself. "Shouldn't we wait a little? Observe for a while before we try getting any closer?"

Her unreadable helmet stared at him for a moment, then she shook her head.

"Nah."

"What if someone else lives here now?"

Kara sped off, ignoring him, and Sam followed her with anxiety gnawing at his insides. They flew quickly and quietly, past the shimmering pond and the large tree in the backyard, which still bore the large scar from the impact with Elysia's armor months ago. Splinters lay scattered across the yard—some bearing the stain from the destroyed dresser he had noticed before, but others were clearly from the tree. The clothes were no longer strewn about, at least.

They stepped onto the patio and attempted to open the sliding glass door. Locked. Not wanting to damage the door, they hovered around each of the windows and found that Jeanette's was unlatched, allowing them to slide it open and slip inside.

The sight of the dark room surfaced Sam's repressed grief. Bits of clothing, debris, and a few remaining pieces of Jeanette's destroyed dresser littered the floor. The Sovereignty must have repaired the wall, cleaned up the exterior, and left it at that. He wondered what might be going through Kara's mind, physically seeing the horrible destruction of her sister's room for the first time.

She pulled off her helmet and attached it magnetically to the side of her waist. Her brows furrowed. "Sam, Can . . . can you check my parents' room? I don't think I . . . you know . . . if they . . ."

"Of course," he said. He opened the door, walking tentatively into the dim, cool hallway as Kara followed. Someone had clearly kept the air conditioning running, which maintained a comfortable temperature. Kara strode into her room as Sam continued down the hall to the main bedroom.

His heartbeat thumped in his ears as he opened the door, expecting a horrific sight. Instead, he found only the king sized poster bed and night stands, lit by afternoon sunlight which streamed through the large windows. The beige carpet surprisingly showed no signs that the bodies of Laurel and Darren Jones had lain there the last time he had stepped into the room.

Sam let out a breath as he backed out and shut the door.

"Are they . . . ?" Kara asked, startling him.

He turned, finding her in her form-fitting Sovereignty uniform rather than her armor.

"They aren't here."

She exhaled, visibly relieved. When he reached her, she took his hand and led him into her bedroom.

Her Ilkuth stood in the far corner against the bright-pink-and-gold surroundings. The bed was in disarray, pillows and blankets scattered haphazardly across it. The vanity, with a notably absent mirror, sat against the right wall, opposite the enormous dresser on the other side. A black bra dangled from an open drawer. Sam pretended his attention was elsewhere, turning his gaze to the mess of various makeup items on the vanity.

"Sam," she breathed. He turned to face her, and she smiled up at him with her approach, staring past him with her distant gaze and looking slightly nervous. "I'm so glad we can finally be alone together."

He grinned back at her, his stomach twisting into anxious knots. "Me too. Being on that ship *sucked*."

She laughed, then her features slowly dropped into a frown. Her furrowed brow seemed to betray some kind of inner conflict.

"Do you actually love me?" she asked. "Like you said at Tercast?"

The answer was obvious, but saying it still proved difficult. He had suppressed those thoughts for ages. What if she had now given it enough thought and decided being with him would be too weird? What if, when she'd said she loved him too, it was an in-the-moment thing? Emotions had been extremely volatile for everyone that day.

He swallowed. "I do. I . . . have for a while, actually."

She wrapped her arms around him, then pulled his head down toward hers. He closed his eyes as their lips met. Warmth shot through his body, making him feel like he was floating again. She pulled away a second later.

"You did a good job hiding it. I never knew."

He scratched his head awkwardly, still reeling from the kiss. "Well, not a good enough job, apparently. Liam found out. He actually suggested that I confess to you the day everything happened."

"Liam!" Kara said. "We should go visit him. And your family!"

"I don't know . . . is that really a good idea?"

She thought for a moment, then shrugged. "Maybe not, but let's at least consider it while we're here."

"I'm finding it a little hard to consider anything with you hugging me like this," Sam said without thinking.

Kara smirked as she maintained her tight embrace, pressing her body against his. "You know, I really never even considered the idea of dating you. We've been friends forever. But when you confessed . . . I don't know . . . Being with you just felt right. I trust you more than anyone."

Her words pierced his soul. This was Kara, the girl—the *woman* —he'd secretly loved for years now, telling him she wanted to be with him. He could feel tears form in his eyes, and he desperately tried to force them down.

"I love you," she said.

Unwilling to allow her a clear view of his obnoxious eyes, he kissed her, feeling surreal. This must be the pinnacle of his existence. Despite the horrific terrors they had experienced over the past several months, Kara was his. He was hers. It was beautiful beyond comprehension. She pulled away.

"Sorry. I'm a little nervous."

"*You're* nervous?" Sam said. His heart felt as if it would leap from his chest.

"Shocker, right? Well, my uh . . . last relationship didn't end so well."

Oh.

"That guy you met in the citizenship course?"

"Nikor, yeah."

Sam recalled their conversation about the matter weeks ago, feeling conflicted about it. On the one hand, he was upset about not being there to support her during the entire ordeal. On the other, the thought of her slamming the jerk into the floor of his own apartment was a pleasant image.

"Well," he said. "You don't need to worry. We can take this as slow as you want."

The genuine smile from her made his insides burn. She was impossibly beautiful. Her fingers caressed his cheek, sending fire through his body.

"Maybe I don't want to go slow."

Before he could respond, she kissed him, tracing her tongue against his while her right hand pulled his left hand back and lifted it upward. He followed her lead, heart fluttering in response. Along her upper back, the material of her form-fitting uniform had parted to reveal the warm skin along her spine. She flinched at his touch and gently pulled her lips away from his.

"Your hands are cold," she whispered through heavy breaths.

"I can fix that," he said, reaching out with Sorcery and mentally urging his hands to warm considerably. Familiar fatigue encumbered his senses as he lightly traced her spine, which now felt cool to him.

"Mmm, better," she said with a grin, sliding her hands underneath his untucked Tercast shirt and along his back, sending ripples of pleasure across his skin.

Sam could hardly believe this was happening. He pulled her close, moving his head toward her right ear. "Are you sure you want to—"

"Yes," she said, her breath tickling his ear. "I am."

Chapter 7
Distractions

"This isn't you," a quiet voice whispered.

A man cowered against the wall with his arms raised.

"Jeanette, whose side are you on?"

"I'm on my own side!" an otherworldly, terrifying voice replied.

Jeanette startled awake, and the nightmare quickly slipped through the crevices of her consciousness. Tess snored beside her. The pale skin of her back peeked out through the fuzzy blue blanket, lit by the dim candlelight on the bedside table. Jeanette sat up, and the silky blanket fell from her bare torso.

Distant memories. Regrets. They faded to the abyss as she swung her feet over the edge of the bed. She rubbed her face and reached out with Sorcery, bringing the nearby cup of water to her lips, which she drank eagerly. Clothing lay scattered across the floor. She moved them into the woven laundry basket in the room's corner as she put the cup down and stood. With her imaginative command, new clothing from the basket of clean undergarments and the clothing rack on her side of the room rose and drifted through the air toward her. She raised her arms, stepping into the clothing. The casual blue dress draped over her shoulders, cascading down to soft ripples across her knees as she strode to the door.

Sorcery set her hair in order with a quick view of herself in the mirror, but she didn't linger to make herself any more presentable. The Deia had an important mission for her to complete, and she would not delay its initiation a moment longer.

She slipped out the door, closing it gently behind her, and marched down the palace's dormitory hallway. Three men stood around the neighbor's door, chatting absently. One with light blue skin noticed her with a start, then stiffened. The other two turned and regarded her briefly before moving against the wall, eyes wide.

"Maven Jey," the blue-skinned man said, nodding respectfully.

Jeanette narrowed her eyes at the others, and their expressions betrayed fear. She smirked as she passed by.

Power.

The people of this place had taken it from her before, but she was potent now. One of the best. The Deia had granted Jeanette access to that power by allowing her to discard the narrow-minded views of her parents. Beliefs she had held herself.

She made her way around the corner and into the armory, which was teeming with glimmering ancient weapons of all sorts and sizes. Tess and her crew had recovered some relics from the rubble of Tercast soon after its demise at the hands of Del. Jeanette scanned the walls, looking for something intimidating.

A spiked, metallic club caught her eye. She walked to it while activating Sorcery to find everything in the room absent from her perception. As she reached out and touched the hilt of the instrument, it lit up to her mind, allowing her to analyze its enchantment. It emitted feelings of light distortion, which didn't seem useful for this initial encounter. She needed something more direct, more sinister, to weed out the weak ones.

Next to the club hung a short crescent blade with a hooked end. She touched the weapon's grip, and an imbued purpose of intense chill emanated from the steel. She smirked. *This will do.*

She pulled the blade from the wall and strode from the room, passing several others in the halls as she made her way toward the dungeons. As she turned the corner by the spiral staircase, she found a familiar face: Urok, the large man who had stood in the library hallway talking with Tess the day of Jeanette's arrival. His dark green eyes lit up with a smile.

"Maven Jey," he said, bowing respectfully.

"Maven Urok," she replied in kind. "Good to see you again."

"Always a pleasure." He looked over her body. "Tess is a lucky woman."

Jeanette chuckled. "Don't you see enough action?" She eyed his exposed pale chest and abs. "I hear you've been with a good number of Evamune's occupants at this point."

He laughed, revealing an adorable dimple on his left cheek. "Of course, but I will always make time for you, Jey, if ever you desire."

She raised an eyebrow. "Tess would disapprove. She's quite possessive."

"She's more than welcome to join in," he said with a grin.

Jeanette rolled her eyes. "Uh-huh. At any rate, I need to begin my work with the Scelebriars."

"Ah, so the Deia gave you charge over their instruction? That's wonderful. I shall leave you to it, then."

She continued down the spiral staircase, feeling a spike of unexpected panic at the sound of her feet against the hard stone— a familiar, echoing sound. One that had caused her intense terror some time ago. A part of her mind held on to the trauma, tormenting her, even though the experience had ultimately been for the best. The warmth of the halls quickly faded with her descent. Perhaps a dress wasn't the best choice of apparel.

Once she reached the bottom, she scanned the long row of cells, using Sorcery to warm her body. A naked man sat in the first cell to her left—a chunky figure with ginger hair. His eyes went wide at the hooked blade in her hand, and he backed into the far wall. She continued down the row, activating the enchanted blade and pouring more cold into the dungeon as she went. Clouds of warm breath escaped her lips with each exhale. A blond woman with pink skin huddled in a shivering ball. Rapid, visible breaths slipped through the long hair covering her face, dissipating into the frigid cell. She remained motionless, showing no acknowledgment of Jeanette's presence.

In the cell next to her sat a woman with dark skin and wavy, golden-brown hair. Lelanna. She trembled, but returned Jeanette's gaze. In the dim light of the dungeon, the shape of her face reminded Jeanette of Amy, bringing on a wave of ache in her stomach. She stopped herself, instead recalling the imaginations of her old friend with contempt. Amy had tried to push her away from the Deia—away from power—but a part of Jeanette also missed their fictitious conversations.

She approached the bars of the woman's cell. Lelanna glared back.

Jeanette smirked. The woman still showed great promise.

"This 'Deia' will never have us, you witch," she spat. "Do what you will. Demons will have your soul in the afterlife."

A beautiful show of defiance.

Lelanna's gaze betrayed a slight glimmer of panic as Jeanette turned the latch of her cell and opened the gate, then raised the curved blade. The woman's dark eyes widened, and she scooted her naked behind back against the far corner. Whether her shivering was an unconscious response to the intensifying cold, or perhaps the terrifying prospect of what might happen to her, it seemed to destroy any amount of confidence she had left.

Jeanette approached slowly, still wearing a smirk. "You will—"

An impression stilled her mind. The Deia—she had need of her elsewhere. Urgently.

Lelanna's defiance returned as Jeanette backed out of the cell and reengaged the latch. "N-not going to go through with it?" she said through chattering teeth. "Ha! Coward! You know the hell that awaits your kind."

Jeanette ignored her, striding past the other cells and back up the steps toward the Deia's bedchamber, where the impressions led her. She tuned out the others chatting in the halls despite their attempts at casual conversation, and entered without announcement.

"Jeanette!" the Deia exclaimed from her luxurious golden bed, upon which two of the men from her throne room earlier sat with their muscular chests exposed, wearing nothing but midnight black briefs. The Divine woman, adorned only with lacey undergarments, floated up from her position, and a light sheet gracefully wrapped itself around her glorious body. She smiled excitedly as Jeanette approached. "I have wonderful news. You must return to your parents' home!"

Jeanette's mouth fell open. "To Earth?"

"Yes!"

"Why?"

A heavenly hand caressed her cheek. "I just received word from our informants that they've located your sister. She's with the missing members of Tercast. They likely still have possession of several powerful relics as well."

Warm joy surged through Jeanette at the prospect of seeing her sister again. She had so much to tell her. To show her.

"Go. Bring them to me."

Jeanette bowed hastily, excitement buzzing within her. "I'll leave at once."

She turned on her heel and raced from the throne room.

Kara, I'm coming!

Chapter 8

Secrets

Boots crunched against the fresh blanket of leaves on the forest floor, accompanying the rustling of trees in the cool breeze and the distant sounds of wildlife. No one said a word as the group hiked toward Kara's home in the fading evening light. She kept their invisible, silent vessel hovering overhead, just above the tallest pines.

While she wore her Ilkuth again, she had attached the helmet to the back, keeping her head free to enjoy the scents of nature. Sam walked with her, hand in hand. They had slept for a few hours in her room, but it clearly wasn't enough for Sam to fully recover. After the flight back to rejoin the group, he was still exhausted.

On the ship, she sometimes questioned whether advancing her relationship with Sam was truly the right thing to do. He had been one of her closest friends since they were children. Flying through the trees of the nature preserve, however, and coming back to their home again had solidified her sensation that things were different now. *They* were different now. And being with him felt so right.

Kara pushed past a bush and faced the open, weed-ridden backyard of her family home. Late-afternoon light shimmered off the still pond. She held the branches back for Sam, who stepped out with her. The remnants of Elysia's fight with Delveton brought on a wave of horrible anguish that stabbed the pit of her stomach once again, so she forced those memories from her mind.

The others emerged from the brush behind them, and Kara scanned the sky, changing her visual spectrum to see if there was anything unusual that might tell her the Sovereignty was watching. Nothing seemed out of the ordinary, but she had little doubt that their monitoring may be undetectable to her.

Sight still felt foreign to her. She had often kept her eyes off aboard the ship. There was rarely much worth seeing, and blindness was comforting, in a way. As she'd told Sam in that grassy park on Invar, sight felt overstimulating. The world seemed more peaceful without it—more intimate.

That said, vision was undeniably useful. Kara still had trouble with depth perception and reading facial expressions, but being able to locate things at a glance was nicer than having to feel around for them. And being able to see Sam and her new friends was pleasant.

The ulinko and keglon trotted to the water's edge and drank. Zelyra, who followed closely behind with a caladrial on her shoulder, seemed concerned but didn't stop them. The wyvern swooped from its flight overhead and dropped next to the pond as well, placing a small, bloodied creature next to it before drinking.

"What did you catch?" Zel asked.

"It's called a rabbit," Kara said. "Poor thing."

"They're all over the place here," Sam added. Rose caught his eye as he spoke, but she averted her gaze awkwardly.

Kara wondered what that was about, but it could wait.

They stepped around the pond and past the beautiful white oak, which bore a terrible scar on its trunk.

With subtle commands to her Nit, the invisible ship overhead silently settled on the lawn, near the corner of the house. Small patches of unkempt grass bent abnormally under the landing gear, betraying the ship's presence, though Kara felt it wasn't too noticeable. Best to keep the ship close by in case they needed to make a hasty escape.

Clacks from her boots on the patio accompanied her walk up to the house, and she opened the sliding glass door, which they'd left unlocked on their way out earlier. When she stepped into the room, she took a deep breath, letting the scents of her childhood home excite vague, pleasant sensations in her unconscious mind. Her anxiety about coming back to the house the first time had prevented her from enjoying the sentimentality. The familiar hum of appliances pulsed through the empty interior.

The group followed them inside, and she let Sam's hand slip from hers as she strode to the kitchen.

"There are still a couple of snacks in the pantry," Kara said as everyone looked around. "Sam and I also decided we'd introduce you all to the wonders of chocolate."

"Chocolate?" Tovas asked as he gently placed Scheln down on the sofa.

"Yes, chocolate," Kara confirmed. "Make yourselves comfortable. And Zel, *please* keep the animals outside."

She turned to Kara with wide-eyed astonishment, her arm held out with the caladrial perched on top. "But it's cold! Can't they—"

"No!" Kara said. "I don't want them destroying my house. Go magic the patio or something to make it more comfortable for them."

Zel sighed, then carried the caladrial back outside and called the ulinko to follow her out. Fita, who'd been standing next to her, gave them a contemptuous scowl as they left. Thankfully, the other animals, including the keglon, hadn't entered yet.

As the group settled into seats in the living room or dining room, Kara stepped out of her suit while Sam prepared hot chocolate and handed out snacks of chips and crackers. The other food items in the pantry were long expired. They still had some flour and other ingredients, so maybe they could make pancakes in the morning. Her parents had been prudent enough to maintain a modest supply of food storage, which should sustain them for a while at least.

They were also on Earth now, with some cash on hand. Shopping was an option, without fear of the Sovereignty tracking them. They didn't have much—just what was sitting around the house—but it might be enough for a few important supplies.

As Sam poured hot chocolate into mugs, Kara risked opening the fridge a crack. An almost immediate, putrid smell escaped, and she slammed it shut. Her eyes watered.

"Ugh. Oh, my god." She frantically fanned the stench away from her nose as she squeezed her eyes closed. "That was a bad idea." She turned her head, shouting an announcement for the entire household. "Do not, under *any* circumstances, open the fridge!"

Sam chuckled. "Do they know what a fridge is?"

Kara wiped the tears from her eyes, shrugging. "They have fridges in the Sovereignty."

"You mean, chillers?" Ya'ir asked.

"Yeah, same thing."

Sam and Kara handed out the mugs of hot chocolate. Tovas and Rose, who sat on the sofa, mildly enjoyed it. Tovas conveyed that Scheln found it delicious. Ya'ir, who slouched at the dining table with Kula and Fita, was the most enthusiastic, calling it pure joy in a cup. In stark contrast, Kula and Fita, in a dignified posture, immediately spat the drink back into their cups after Sam handed it to them. Fita called it a "loathsome bean soup". Kara laughed as she brought a cup out to Zel on the patio, who sniffed at it curiously before taking a sip. Her eyes lit up, and she took another large gulp, giving Kara a wide grin. Another fan.

Kara and Sam joined Ya'ir, Fita, and Kula in the dining room with their own mugs.

"This is a lovely home, Kara," Ya'ir said.

"Thanks. My parents put a lot of work into it over the years."

"That's true," Sam added, gesturing toward the well-crafted built-in shelves on the wall of the living room, near where Rose sat on the sofa. "Your mom built those herself, right?"

"Yep. That was quite a while ago." Memories of her mother standing on a step stool with a large board in one hand and a power drill in the other flashed in her mind. A bittersweet ache in her gut followed soon after.

"Right, we were like—what—ten? Eleven?"

Ya'ir's brow furrowed in confusion.

"Dek or el," Kara explained.

"Oh, right," Ya'ir said. "So you two have known each other for a long time, then?"

Kara and Sam locked eyes. Butterflies tickled her stomach. The experience was still weird. But a good weird. She smiled.

"Yeah, since we were really little," Sam said, grinning. "First grade, right?"

"Yes. I think we were both six at the time."

"I assume 'first grade' refers to your education?" Fita asked, before tossing a potato chip into his mouth.

"Yeah," Sam said. "What was your schooling like in Helenestia, Fita?"

He gazed upward briefly. "It was well structured. Disciplined. It has been the same for many generations."

"Sounds boring," Kara said with a light chuckle.

Fita scowled. "Many traditions are enjoyable. My—"

Kula snickered.

He turned to her. "What?"

She glanced at him briefly, covering her grin with a hand. "When we were children, during one of our annual festivals, Fita accidentally—"

"You don't need to tell this story."

"Yes, she does!" Kara said, pulling a seat out and settling in. "Go on!"

Fita rolled his eyes and folded his arms while Kula, still struggling to contain her laughter, continued. "The festivals include zones for various activities and demonstrations. As he was walking past a ganoziha, a ceremonial dance, a performer accidentally hit him as he was walking past their area—with her butt."

Kara chuckled, enjoying Fita's sigh of frustration.

"Her butt?" Ya'ir asked, failing to suppress a snort.

Kula nodded, tears of repressed laughter beading in her eyes. "The best part was that he stumbled into the area next door, falling onto a yuliksha mat where participants were doing floor exercises."

She paused, struggling to continue.

"So . . . what? Did he run into someone else?" Sam asked.

"No, no. He"—Kula giggled—"he took a quick look around to see if anyone was watching, didn't notice me, and started doing exercises with them like nothing happened."

The group roared with laughter.

Fita huffed and stood from the table, then strode off into the kitchen. Ya'ir rose and followed, perhaps concerned for Fita's embarrassment.

Sam turned to Kara, wiping tears from his eyes. "Mind if I go to sleep? I'm exhausted."

"Why are you asking me for permission? Go to sleep!"

He smiled weakly. "Okay. Where do I sleep, though?"

"Oh, um . . . you can use my bed for now. We'll figure out more permanent sleeping arrangements later."

"Okay, good night."

"Good night, Sam," Kula said.

Kara and Kula chatted idly about Helenestian customs while they continued to snack on chips and crackers. Ya'ir returned, then the three joined Rose, Tovas, and Scheln in the living room. After they had settled down, Ya'ir lifted his cup to take another swig of chocolate, then stared at his mug with utter perplexity.

"Where did my chocolate go?"

Kara glanced at her own mug and found it empty as well. "Uh, I don't know. Mine's gone too."

Rose frowned. "Huh, my cup—"

"Scheln!" Tovas said. They turned to find an amorphous stream of brown liquid flowing into Scheln's open mouth.

Kara's jaw dropped. "Did he just steal our drinks?"

Pillows from the couch lifted into the air from their positions, hiding Scheln's face and the hovering liquid. Tovas shook his head while the room burst into laughter.

"Scheln," Kara said between her own chuckles, "if you want more, you only need to ask!"

Tovas rolled his eyes. "He thinks this was more fun."

Kara fixed more hot chocolate for those interested while the group continued their relaxed chatter. Sunlight faded in and out as the afternoon progressed, with sparse columns of fluffy cumulus overhead. Zel ran around the backyard with her animals, enjoying the fall weather. When Tovas mentioned Scheln was tired, Kara excused herself to go upstairs and find some blankets for him.

She had completely forgotten to work out sleeping arrangements. The thought of anyone in her parents' room unsettled her, but it would be more comfortable than the floor. They had plenty of blankets in the hall closet upstairs, which would be much better than the Tercast robes everyone had been sleeping on for ages.

As she turned the corner toward the staircase, a glance through the open double doors of their study revealed Fita doing stretches on the rug. With a smirk, she approached him, trying to think of a snarky comment. Books surrounded them on the built-in shelves. Fita had moved the single desk into the corner to make room. As he stretched his bare torso forward past his toes with an impressive amount of flexibility, a sense of kinship overcame her instead.

"Hey, Fita."

He turned his head to look at her, and tucked his long golden hair behind an ear. "Not 'Frito' this time?"

Kara shrugged with a grin. "Just this once, maybe."

He turned his head forward, pushing himself deeper into the stretch. "What is the occasion?"

"Nothing, really. I just like messing with you."

"I haven't noticed."

"Ooh, sarcasm? Coming from you? I must be really getting to you!"

He glanced over at her again, wearing a smirk as she got closer and sat next to him on the soft carpet.

"Hey, it was a funny story earlier because that's just *sooo* you." Kara chuckled. "I just want to make sure you don't feel like—I don't know—we're overly ridiculing you or belittling you or something."

He sat back from his stretch, with all the emotion of a stone. "I am fine."

Was he really fine, or was he just saying that? She couldn't think of a non-awkward way to push more out of him, though.

"We should roll again soon," she said. "I want you to teach me that move of yours—what's it called again?"

"The riddlehook."

"Yeah, that thing took me by surprise last time."

A genuine smile graced his features. "I would enjoy that."

"Great," Kara said, standing up from the rug. "I'll hold you to it."

He nodded, the muscles in his dark arms and back fluctuating as he moved onto a side stretch. The man was certainly easy on the eyes, so they say. At least, the pleasant feeling associated with the sight of Fita's body seemed to suggest so. She still wasn't confident she clearly understood visual attractiveness or beauty.

Kara left the room and turned off her vision. As she ascended the stairs, which creaked under her steps, she idly wondered what the guys she'd dated in high school actually looked like. According to her friends, they had been at least moderately attractive. When she reached the landing, the thought of her parents' bedroom down the hall brought back the ache in her stomach. Then the ache turned to insight.

Her parents. She still needed to find out more about why they stayed on Earth. Maybe the answers were in there.

She turned her vision back on and noticed lines of faint discoloration along the walls of the hallway—subtly thicker between the upper steps and her own bedroom—and wondered what they could be from. She touched them, finding them about level with her hip, and realization hit her: These were her. She wondered how many other slight impressions of her daily activity had been visible to others without her noticing as she sauntered down the hall, tracing the subtle discoloration with her fingers.

The door swung open, revealing the sight of her parents' bedroom for the first time in her life, bathed in dim golden light trickling in from behind the curtains. She flicked the nearby switch, flooding the room with color. A king-size poster bed sat along the far wall with a lush green comforter, flanked by dark-wood nightstands.

She took a few steps inside and knelt to the floor, closing her eyes. While she pressed her hand into the pristine carpet where she had last felt her mother and father, the memory of sensing their familiar fragrances and clothing twisted her insides into agonizing knots.

Kara clenched her fist and stood, shaking her head to clear it. Thinking about that could shut her down again. She couldn't allow that. She still had a mission.

Jeanette.

Why did Delveton, and the Deia, want her sister? Did it have something to do with why their parents had come to Earth?

Kara rummaged through her father's nightstand, finding books on leadership and software and other random junk, including old cell phones and cables. She crossed the bed to her mother's nightstand, searching through those drawers as well. The top contained a few fantasy books, some jewelry, and old receipts. She pulled open the middle one, glimpsed something that looked like it may have been some kind of contraceptive, and immediately closed it, desperately trying to wipe the image from her mind. Preparing herself to stumble upon something else she'd rather not, she opened the bottom drawer to find a single unlabeled book.

Her mother's journal.

Kara took it out eagerly, heart racing. It had a strong metal clasp holding it together. She couldn't find a keyhole. How did it open? She pulled at it, testing its strength, which was considerable. It clearly wouldn't open by her own strength alone.

She tossed the book onto the bed, commanding her Ilkuth,

which she had left in the foyer, to come upstairs. The shiny metal casually floated through the bedroom door, and Kara let it wrap around her body. She picked the book up and delicately pulled at the metal clasp again, slowly ripping it from the front panel. As soon as it was free, she threw it back on the bed and stepped out of her suit.

"Sorry, Mom," she said, tenderly picking up the damaged book.

She turned to the first page, and commanded her Nit to read the words to her.

Hello,

I've never done this before, but Lana said journaling would help with the stress, so here I am.

Jeanette recently started her freshman year of high school. She's been spending a lot of time with Claire and Amy at Claire's after school. I miss having her around the house, but they're sweet girls. I'm happy they're having fun.

Kara started seventh grade. She's still spending a lot of time at the academy, and doing so well! Her skills have improved a lot over the past few months, thanks to her new professor, Mr. Santos. He's legally blind, so has given her some targeted guidance and techniques. I'm happy she's doing so well with it, but that girl has quite a mouth. It has been a constant battle to get her to do her homework.

I still wonder sometimes whether we made the right choice staying here. We could have potentially done so much more for Kara, medically, if we went back. We could still go, but there would be no coming back. Truly, it would break Jeanette's heart to leave her friends, and Darren agrees we still need to be here to watch over the property.

Speaking of Darren, he's been doing well at the office. They're off having a celebration right now, in fact, since they had a successful demo of their prototype. I miss him. I hope he comes home soon.

Well, since we still have a little daylight left, I think I'll sit by the pond and read for a while.

Kara wiped a tear from her eye. Subtle smudges on the page

showed something had been written at the end of the fourth paragraph, then erased. Perhaps something related to why they agreed they still needed to be here. At any rate, it confirmed that they had come to Earth specifically to be at this location. But why?

"I know now you were probably being careful," she whispered. "Careful not to say anything about the Sovereignty, just in case anyone ever read this. But why were you and Dad so convinced you needed to stay?"

The answer had to be here.

Chapter 9

The Scientist

Rose browsed through the library of books in Kara's study, munching on a handful of something called pretzels. The snacks were far from the nutrition the Sovereignty supplies had been providing, but the salty flavor was a welcome change. There were several intriguing titles with beautiful covers. Perhaps she could find a new one to read—hopefully one that had a better ending than *Hearts of Adelaide*. A book titled *Pride and Prejudice* caught her eye, and as the introductory chapters absorbed her attention, she moved to the padded armchair in the study's corner. The manner of speech and culture of the book was unfamiliar, but wholly engrossing.

After the sky darkened, Rose determined that she'd like to keep the book for a while and finish it, but she should probably ask Kara first. She stepped up the creaky staircase, pausing at the top to glance down the hallway to the right and left, unsure of where Kara might be. She approached the first door on her left, preparing to tap it lightly with her knuckles when the door behind her opened.

"Need something, Rose?" Kara asked. "That's my room. Sam's sleeping in there."

"Oh," Rose said, her cheeks burning. "Sorry."

"It's fine."

Rose walked toward her, holding the book up. "I was wondering if I could borrow this."

"Absolutely. Out of curiosity, what's the book?"

Oh, right, Kara couldn't read.

"It's called Pride and Prejudice."

"Ah, that's a classic—on Earth, anyway. I haven't read it myself, but Jeanette liked it."

Rose nodded. "Thank you."

"Of course."

"Have you found out anything about your parents yet?"

Kara shrugged. "A little. My parents really wanted to be in this location specifically. I'm not yet sure why, though. They also really liked the pond in the backyard, more than I thought they did. My mom wrote about it a lot in her journal. Kind of odd. I mean, we had some wonderful memories out there, but I still don't quite get their obsession with it. There might be more to it."

Her eyes lit up. "Oh, while I have you here, I wanted to ask you something."

Rose felt her cheeks warming. Hopefully she wouldn't ask about—

"What's with you and Sam? Since he and I came back from the house, you two have been acting a little weird toward each other."

Oh no. Kara noticed. *Why couldn't I have just . . . acted normally? I should have just acted normally!*

"Uh . . . um . . . there's not . . . uh . . . he . . ."

Kara smirked. "You connected with him, didn't you? When we came here earlier." She giggled.

Rose felt her insufferable cheeks flush hot. "I didn't mean to . . . I was just worried about him, you know, after he fell into the sky. I wanted to make sure he was okay!"

She certainly hadn't expected to find him in the throes of coitus.

Kara laughed. "It's fine. You can say it. We had sex."

"You *what?*"

Rose turned to find Tovas hurrying up the stairs below looking uncharacteristically livid. "He would *dare* do that to you?"

Kara sighed, putting hands on her hips as he approached. "What do you mean 'he would dare'?" She pointed at her chest. "It was my idea Tovas. Sam was a gentleman. Besides, it's none of your business."

He turned to her, his expression softening. "Kara, the natural process of procreation is *never* to be taken lightly. We should only exercise it under a substantial oath of unity."

"Marriage?" Kara chuckled. "Don't be such a prude, Tovas. We're being responsible about it."

"There is never a scenario where intercourse, and a potential pregnancy, outside of firm family bonds, is responsible," Tovas replied.

She rolled her eyes. "Like I said, it's none of *your* business what Sam and I do in our own private time together."

"Rose, help me out here," Tovas said.

Rose put her hands up, shaking her head against the relentless burning in her cheeks that still wouldn't vanish. "Don't drag *me* into this!"

Tovas sighed. "This is no small matter. The natural process of bringing new life into being is sacred."

Rose had to escape. It was getting far too awkward up here.

"Ya'ir needs me downstairs," she lied. "I'd better go."

"Tovas, you are seriously overreacting to—"

Rose scurried down the steps, tuning out Kara's rebuttal to Tovas's statement. She raced down the last creaky steps and swung around the stair post, book still in hand. Interestingly enough, Ya'ir appeared to meet her in the foyer.

"Hey, what's going on?" he asked.

"Oh, you don't want to go up there. Trust me."

He raised an eyebrow as she maneuvered around him. After entering the kitchen and glancing back, she saw him turn from the stairway and follow her. Good choice.

The pond actually sounded like a nice, peaceful spot away from people at the moment. Rose walked past Fita, Kula, and Scheln who were napping on the furniture, and let herself out the sliding glass door. Warm sunlight cascaded across the sparse clouds in front of a deep blue sky. A chilly breeze caressed her skin. Zel sat at the corner of the patio, petting the ulinko in her lap. She waved, then turned her attention back to the purple beast.

Rose waved back, thankful that Zel didn't engage her in conversation, and strode to the pond, then sat by its rocky edge and leaned back on her palms. The large, unusual trees surrounding the house swayed with a momentary gust of wind, while afternoon light reflected off the water's still surface.

Her heart and the burning in her cheeks finally settling down, Rose took her book out and continued to read, wondering how long a fortnight could be. After several minutes of peacefully enjoying the scenery and engrossing herself in the story, she took a brief break to change her location for better light. As she walked around the pond, she casually engaged her Sorcery, sensing her surroundings. Skin. Clothing. Rock. Water. Slowness.

The feeling of slowness was an unusual one. It seemed to come from the water. *Beneath* the water. She had felt a similar impression of causality before, from the health potions at Tercast. Her key insight had come after that soldier attacked them in the halls, when it worked its enchantment on—

No. Stop. Not that.

Right. The sense of abnormal causality and slowness beneath the water. It certainly didn't seem natural.

Rose put her book down on the stone edge of the pond and gazed into the water, unable to see more than a few feet past the surface. Perhaps she could enchant her body to repel water, and just go in. Weeks ago that may have worked, but her Sorcery was likely too weak for that now. Water was heavy. She could go back and tell Kara, who could dive in and investigate with the suit, but the thought of re-inserting herself into her conversation with Tovas quelled that course of action. Rose decided it would be all right to let herself get wet. She could use Sorcery to dry herself later.

After connecting with her skin and enchanting it with resistance to heat transfer, she stepped into the pond, perceiving it as warmer than it actually was. The pond deepened quickly as the feeling of causality grew stronger. She soon found herself under water and exhaled most of her air to allow herself to tread the pond floor. An enchantment on her lungs transmuted carbon dioxide into oxygen, allowing respiration to continue with the absence of new breath.

Her feet reached the lowest point of the pond, and, despite her enchantment, cooled fiercely. She noted a very unusual sensation, like they were sticking to the ground—and the surrounding water. She stretched out the perception of her Sorcery again and found a curious network of metal, wires, and electricity below the mud. Some kind of structure? The feeling of causality associated with them was immensely powerful, blending into the soil and water around it.

She connected with the material and felt someone's presence, stilling her.

The structure was actively under the Vitalization of another Sorcerer. Accompanying the presence was an extreme sense of fatigue and sorrow.

Rose's heart leapt with panic.

What could it be? *Who* could it be?

Why was there an enchanted structure under Kara's family pond?

Rose pulled back, alarm rising as her feet stuck, keeping her from pushing herself back to the surface.

She connected with the soil and water beneath her feet, desperately looking for a way to free herself.

The enchantment! It must be slowing the material so much that it becomes difficult to move through it.

Calming her mind, Rose thought about the sensation of causality. Of increased causality. She focused on the enchanted material, willing causality to accelerate. Thankfully, it did, warming her feet and allowing her to slide free. She pushed herself to the surface, where she took in a breath. She stepped onto the rock, finding Zel striding toward her in the dim evening light.

A blast knocked her forward, and the whine of scraping rock filled the air. Water rained down.

Rose yelped and covered her head, glancing back to find pond water raining through the area, launched by a massive force. A defense mechanism? Or perhaps the structure dropped out of its causality-bending enchantment. That could cause a sudden blast. The lawn and stone on the eastern edge of the pond had crumbled. Steam rose through the cracks.

Zel approached and helped Rose up. "What was that?"

"I don't know."

Kara emerged through the sliding glass door in her armor, and soared toward her. Tovas, Fita, and Kula raced out of the structure behind her, carrying their weapons.

Kara landed with a thump at the edge of the pond. "What is it? What happened?"

"I don't know, but there's a structure under the water!"

Kara jumped over Rose's head and dove into the pond, which was now only half full. The rest of the group arrived while she was underwater.

"What's happening?" Tovas asked.

"There's something under the pond. Kara's investigating."

"How did you find it?"

Rose shrugged. "I felt Vitalization—an enchantment."

"There's a Sorcerer down there?"

Fita's sword burst into flames, and he assumed a threatening stance.

"I—I don't know," Rose said.

"I feel nothing out of the ordinary," Tovas said.

She activated her Sorcery again, looking for it. Curiously, the enchantment seemed to have disappeared.

Sam ran toward the group, rubbing sleep from his eyes, the Mace of Motion in his hand. "What's going on? Where's Kara?"

"She's—"

Kara's suit burst from the water. "I found it! Some kind of metal structure, like Rose said, hidden under the pond floor. Think we can get rid of this water somehow? That blast threw a lot out, but I don't want to open it unless we can get it dry."

"I could try to move it," Sam said, hefting his mace.

"Wait." Tovas held his arm out. "We don't know what's in there. We'll want to conserve what little Sorcery we have in case we need to fight, or escape."

Rose nodded her agreement.

Kara sighed. "I hate it, but you're right. We've got some buckets in the garage. Let's do this the annoying way."

She flew to the house and came back a few minutes later with large white buckets. They formed lines, emptying the water as quickly as they could. Kara, with the enhanced strength of the suit, took four buckets all on her own, filling and emptying them into the trees nearby, which sat at a lower elevation from the property. They worked into the evening, when the sun began settling into the horizon, casting them with quickly dimming light. Soon, a small enough pool of water remained that they could dig a path, diverting it into another part of the pond and exposing the metallic door of the mysterious structure.

"There's a gap in my sensation of Sorcery inside," Tovas said. "Someone, or at least something alive, is in there."

"I've got it," Kara replied, grabbing the external handle.

"What are you going to do? Rip the door off?" Sam asked.

"Well, yeah, I don't see any other way to open it from this side."

"There's a lever on the inside. One of us can just use Sorcery to open it."

"Oh," Kara said, releasing her grip. "Yeah, that makes more sense."

"I'll do it," Sam said. "You pull it open once I release the latch."

Kara gripped the handle once again.

"We ready?"

Curious, apprehensive nods permeated the group.

"Three, two, one—"

Rose felt the latch move on the other side of the door. Kara swung the door open and pointed a straightened arm inside. Rose, curiosity overcoming her caution, pushed her head toward the opening, crowding Fita and Sam who did the same.

Lit by a few points of warm light near the entry, stacks of books lined the rather homey interior. Pages of notes surrounded an unconscious figure at the center. Wavy gray hair sprawled out around the woman's dark, wrinkled skin. She wore a simple light gray robe with shimmering vine-like patterns that weaved across its surface.

Kara jumped in, keeping her arm pointed at the woman on the floor. "She seems to be unconscious. Definitely alive, though."

"Who is she?" Sam asked.

"No idea. I've never seen her before."

Arm still trained on the mysterious woman, Kara floated past to the desk nearby, papers and notes spread across its surface.

"I don't know what any of this stuff means, but I see a lot of numbers. Almost like she was doing research."

Rose entered, inspecting the equations, recognizing some of them from her studies. The notes outlined experimental controls and outcomes.

"She appears to be a Sovereignty scientist!"

Chapter 10
The Reunion

Jeanette stepped through a bed of leaves surrounded by familiar oaks and pines, the light of a full moon streaming through sparse branches. Brisk air kissed her face and hands. She inhaled through her nostrils, then let the air trickle out, watching her moonlit breath swirl into the cool night breeze. The pleasant, soft scent of pine and moss filled the musty air, bringing back memories of running through the woods with her friends as children, off on imaginary adventures.

Earth.

Home.

She pulled up her long gray coat against the biting chill. Her invisible exploration ship lay in the forest behind her, cloaked with enchantments of Delveton's design—as all the Deia's ships were—to avoid Sovereignty detection mechanisms. Kara's vessel was no doubt near the house as well, a much more modern ship with advanced cloaking capabilities of its own.

Autumn leaves crunched under her step, bringing a smile to her face as she made her way to the clearing next to the backyard of her family home. She emerged in the yard to find an unexpected sight: Someone had completely drained the pond. Two men in dirty white clothing stood around in the mud, looking down into a hole.

Curious. She wondered what they could have found.

Jeanette stopped, feeling anxious. How should she proceed? Would they think her a threat? Kara's new friends might, but she was fairly certain Kara herself wouldn't. They also may not like the idea of parting with their enchanted weapons and other artifacts, but she would need to convince them to do so, or take them by force. The Deia would accept no other outcome. Daggers hung from the sides of her waist, weighing down the belt under her coat. Hopefully, she wouldn't need to use them.

She smiled and approached the emptied pond. Porch light from her home cast long shadows from the two figures staring into the hole. The pale, sandy-haired one turned and put his hand on the shoulder of the lankier one with dark skin and hair. A third man rose from the hole, handing papers to the other two.

Jeanette stopped in her tracks, her eyes widening.

She hadn't expected to see Sam here. Had Kara sprung all of this on him? No, he had been at their home when Delveton took her. Of course. And he was wearing robes—same as the others. So he had been at Tercast, which was supposedly a religious insti-tution.

That didn't seem like Sam *at all*.

His face dropped back into the hole, presumably to grab something else.

The Deia's presence caressed her soul, comforting her and bolstering her confidence. Jeanette continued her approach. Soon enough, the sandy-haired man noticed her.

She waved with a warm smile. "Hello."

A staff shot through the air from the house toward the man, which he caught and wielded defensively.

"Who are you?" he said.

"I'm—"

"Jeanette!" Sam yelled from the hole, dropping whatever he was carrying back into it. He *flew* out of the hole and landed to face her. Of all the many ludicrous things she had seen over the past several hours, seeing Sam having apparently embraced religion and flying around as a Sorcerer was perhaps the most absurd.

"Is it really you?" he said.

"Hi, Sam."

He embraced her, and she hugged him back.

"It is so incredible to see you again!" he said with misty eyes. "How did you escape? Have you been hiding out somewhere nearby?"

"What did you do to our pond?"

"Oh!" Sam laughed and glanced over his shoulder, where the two other men approached. "Turns out someone was *buried* under it! She was in this pod-like vehicle. We pulled her out and have been looking at the books and notes. She seems to be some kind of scientist."

Intriguing. Perhaps there truly was more to her parent's decision to relocate to Earth than she had thought.

"Anyway, I'll go get Kara!"

Sam sped off toward the house, leaving her with the other two men.

The one with sandy-brown hair lowered his staff, a steel rod with subtle swirling gold lines—likely an artifact from Tercast she was tasked to retrieve. He continued to study her with an unreadable expression. Interest? Suspicion? She couldn't quite tell. In contrast, the man next to him approached her with a warm smile.

"Hi! I'm Ya'ir. Sam and Kara have told us a lot about you. I'm so glad you're all right."

"Thank you, Ya'ir," Jeanette said, returning his smile. "It's wonderful to meet you. Did all of you escape from Tercast?"

His face crumpled. "We . . . Yes, we survived. But so many . . . "

Ya'ir's sorrow was palpable. She put a tender a hand on his shoulder. She understood that pain. That anguish. She wished she could whisk him away into the marvelous embrace of the Deia, who would deepen his understanding and relieve his torment, but it was too soon. She needed to know more about them before she could make the next move. They would likely see her as some kind of mindless fanatic. People were understandably hesitant to give weight to the words of such a person. She needed their trust first.

"I'm so sorry to hear about what happened there. Such a terrible tragedy."

"How did you escape them?" the pale man asked. His eyes, lit by moonlight, met hers with a soft intensity. "We had been told that—"

"Jeanette?" A beautiful, familiar voice rang out from the direction of the house.

Jeanette could barely restrain herself as elation flooded her. Her tears flowed freely as she ran to her sister, who wore a form-fitting uniform bearing the Sovereignty emblem on its chest under a heavy pink coat. The two met in a glorious, weepy embrace under the damaged oak tree. Jeanette squeezed her eyes shut, feeling tears stream down her cheeks and into the familiar light brown hair. She felt right. Whole. Kara was here. They were home. Together.

As she opened her eyes, she found a blurry view of people surrounding them.

"Can we have a few minutes to ourselves, please?" Jeanette asked.

Kara turned from their embrace, her voice cracking with emotion. "Yes. Please. Just a few minutes."

No one protested. The group moved toward the house. Sam engaged Ya'ir in a discussion about the pod, and the woman they had found inside.

"You too, Zel," Kara added.

A short, plump woman sitting with a purple cat-like animal nearby furrowed her brow as she looked at Kara.

"Just for a little while."

Jeanette nearly jumped when an animal—horse-like, but green and scaly—nuzzled the woman before she strode inside. There were other animals as well, like none she had ever seen. She turned her attention to the miracle in her arms, continuing to hold her sister tight, and finding it difficult to speak.

"We should sit," Kara said.

"Yes." Jeanette took her hand and guided her to the edge of the now-empty pond. Images of family picnics and emotional conversations flashed through her mind as she helped her sister into a sitting position on the rocky edge, then sat down next to her. Kara's eyes followed Jeanette's motions with unusual lucidity, locking on with a steady, firm gaze.

"Kara! What happened to your eyes?"

Kara's face lit up. "I got new ones!"

"You can see?"

"Yeah!"

Jeanette touched the familiar round face with her delicate fingers, and gently turned it to the side, watching her sister's gaze remain fixed on her.

"You are pretty," Kara said. "I mean, I'm not even sure I know what that means yet, but you are. Just like all your jerk boyfriends said you were."

Jeanette laughed. "I can hardly believe it. You were always so confident, so *insistent* that you would never want to see, even if you could."

"Yeah, well, it was the only way I could help rescue you after they kidnapped you."

"You got sight to rescue me?"

"Yup. I wasn't just going to sit by and wait for your body to turn up somewhere. I needed to do something."

"Now *that* definitely sounds like you."

They laughed. Hearing her sister's lighthearted giggle again was exquisite.

"What happened to Sam?" Jeanette asked. "He's a Sorcerer now?"

"Ha! I know. It's like the most ridiculous thing ever, right? He nearly killed himself with it earlier today because he just can't stop experimenting."

"Well, *that* sounds like Sam!"

"Oh yeah," Kara agreed. "He . . . feels different, I think. After all the ridiculous things that have happened over the past several weeks."

The tone of her voice sounded almost allured.

Jeanette raised an eyebrow. "Are you two . . . ?"

She let the implication dangle. Kara returned a shy smile, providing all the answers she needed. Jeanette put a hand over her mouth.

"Isn't that weird?"

Jeanette shook her head, noting that for once, Kara would actually see it. "I don't think so. I suspected Sam's attraction to you a while ago. I just said nothing because I never thought you were interested in him in that way."

"I never thought about it, really. But when he confessed . . . I don't know . . . It did something to me. Being with him like this feels so right, even though it does also feel a little weird sometimes."

"I'm happy for you two."

Kara smiled, then glanced downward and furrowed her brow. "So, what happened to you? Where did you get kidnapped to? It was Delveton, right?" She clenched her fist. "That bastard said that you were 'one of them.'"

Jeanette leaned forward onto her elbows, reflecting on the night of her capture. "It was terrifying. They needed me to open a library. Mom's father was a Sorcerer, and he had put a powerful enchantment on the library to keep out anyone who wasn't in our bloodline. If anyone else would have tried, it would have destroyed everything inside. He wanted to hoard the knowledge for himself."

"Is that what they were after at Tercast too? Books and such?"

"There were a lot of reasons for Delveton's mission to Tercast. I was really surprised to find out you were on his team. He was going to come back with you. I heard everything was going mostly according to plan, until he suddenly died."

Kara stared into Jeanette's eyes with furious intensity, a bizarre and wonderful sight, as Jeanette placed a warm hand on her shoulder. "He tricked us into attacking Tercast, when we were supposed to be attacking your captors. He *basically forced* everyone to kill each other, and killed many himself. Turns out Sorcery plus advanced Sovereignty technology equals one frighteningly powerful guy."

Jeanette raised her eyebrows and nodded. "You have no idea. He was immensely powerful. How in the world did he die?"

Kara took in a deep breath, turning a pensive gaze past the empty pond in front of them. "I killed him."

As the sharp blue gaze turned back toward her, Jeanette felt a remarkable fury explode throughout her being. She stared into those unusually steady, familiar eyes, blood boiling.

Of course. It all made sense. Delveton had trusted that she would follow him. She must have betrayed him. The Deia's most prized subject, Delveton, killed by Kara. It was profane. Blasphemous. Unthinkable.

It was unforgivable.

Jeanette reached a hand out and opened her Sorcery. The hilt of one of her daggers flew into her palm with nimble precision. Without hesitation, she plunged the blade into her sister's chest.

Chapter 11

Betrayed

Kara stared into her sister's dynamic, beautiful eyes—both a novel and wondrous experience—and felt wrong. Jeanette's expression had turned angry. Furious. So odd. Then the pain hit.

Her chest *hurt*.

Jeanette gripped the hilt of a weapon, which stuck out from Kara's chest. The hand remained motionless.

Kara coughed, feeling the onset of nausea and dizziness accompany her incredulity. Warmth drained from her face. Jeanette, of all people, becoming furious? Murderous?

Toward *her?*

"Stop looking at me with those eyes," Jeanette said, her tone drastically different from a few moments prior. "They're so unlike you."

Kara's eyelids squeezed shut and her head arched back at Jeanette's touch. Attempts to breathe resulted in more coughing. Fire erupted briefly in her eyes, then her dimming sight went dark, returning a familiar lack of visual stimulation. Her Nit reported catastrophic failures in her eyes' systems.

Jeanette had sabotaged them.

Kara thought to cry out, but tasted copper with a coughing fit instead. Tremendous, searing pain spread from the center of her chest, agony rippling across her body. Her head felt so light.

How could this happen? Kara was a warrior, a fighter, while Jeanette was anything but. She was kind and thoughtful. Intelligent. She had always held their parents' principles. Life was sacred.

At least, that's what Kara had thought. Apparently, something had gone horribly wrong.

An unfamiliar noise blended into the surroundings. Something sharp. Abrupt. Rhythmic.

The noise faded into the depths of unconsciousness.

Tovas ran toward the two women by the drained pond, readying his staff, which pulsed its overwhelming feeling of protection through him. Jeanette turned just before he reached striking distance, and she pulled a bloody dagger from her sister's body, which slumped horrifically. Jeanette stood, scowling at him.

"Rose! Sam!" Tovas shouted.

They needed to get Kara to Rose, fast. It was the only chance she had.

"I guess I have to do this the hard way," Jeanette said. "I suppose I could ask you to come willingly, but that's probably a waste of—"

Tovas lunged forward, catching her off guard. The staff hit her in the chest, knocking her back. He hurried to place himself in front of Kara's motionless body.

"What's going on?" Sam said from behind.

Tovas kept his eyes trained on Jeanette, who locked her gaze on him and righted herself.

"You'll regret that," she said.

He turned his head to the side. "Sam, take Kara to Rose. Now!"

"Kara!" Sam cried. "How did . . . NO!"

"NOW!" Tovas yelled.

Sam must have approached, because Jeanette leapt toward Kara. The impressions from the staff flowed through Tovas, giving him purpose. A twirl of the rod knocked her arm off its target. He spun with the blow, moving himself directly between her new position and Kara's.

She fell back again, brow furrowed. Rocks of various sizes from around the pond behind her rose into the air.

Divine help us.

The stones flew toward him, while impressions from the staff continued to pulse through his being and direct his movements. He twisted and twirled, catching several of the projectiles with the steel, each one ringing with the impact.

His heartbeat thumped in his ears. The staff's enchantment was guiding him. He felt as if he was almost sleepwalking through the movements, allowing the Divine to direct his activity through the staff.

The Staff of Dreams.

Voices echoed from the house behind him, but he couldn't afford a glance. He needed to make sure Jeanette made no more progress toward the group.

"Tovas, what's happening?" Scheln's quiet voice pierced his mind.

It's Jeanette! Tovas replied. She—

She pulled another dagger from behind her coat. The sharp clang of metal sang through the cool night air. A second later, she advanced, presenting a whirlwind of dagger strikes, which he deftly evaded or parried with the staff's guided movements. Jeanette reached forward with a frustrated yell, and a Divine impression caused him to plant the staff in front of him and connect to the air immediately around it.

A sonic boom rang out from her position, ripping up portions of the lawn and patio near her. It reached the air in front of Tovas and fell flat against the vacuum he had created just before impact.

Dizziness weighed on his mind. Fatigue was setting in. He couldn't maintain this for long.

A flaming sword struck out toward Jeanette, which she parried.

Fita.

While the parry deflected the blade from reaching her arm, the defending dagger had deformed, warped by the intense heat. She tossed its remains to the ground, and more rocks and debris flew toward them. Tovas stepped in front of Fita, protecting him from the makeshift projectiles.

"Rose got Kara conscious again," Scheln said in his mind. A wave of relief spread through his aching muscles. *"She's getting the ship ready."*

"Good," Tovas said to himself wearily as he twirled the staff, sending a rock the size of his head glancing off to crash into the tree behind him.

"No!" Jeanette shouted.

Tovas risked a glance back and saw their ship waiting near the open sliding glass door, where Sam and Zel carried Kara and Rose. Ya'ir stood frozen with wide-eyed fear in the doorway. Kula and a floating Scheln were advancing toward the fight.

No, Scheln! Tovas said. Help them get aboard and leave.

"We're not leaving you!" Scheln replied.

A hard object collided with Tovas's side, sending him toppling over. Intense heat passed over his body as Fita moved toward Jeanette. She hovered, deftly evading the fiery blade.

"Kula, Scheln!" Tovas said through gritted teeth, "Help them get on board. Tell them to leave. Now!"

"We won't leave without you," Kula cried.

"Do it now!"

"Go," Fita yelled, still whirling his sword toward the floating woman. A zap of electricity hit Fita in the chest, who crumpled. Tovas planted the staff just as she sent another arc toward him, which was relayed harmlessly into the ground. Jeanette turned and flew toward the group.

Tovas found a reserve of strength, flinging himself up with the staff and colliding with her in the air. They both fell, and he rolled upright into a defensive position, immense exhaustion overshadowing his senses. A glance showed him that Zelyra was hurriedly pushing the keglon into the vehicle.

Jeanette yelled and flung her dagger toward Tovas, which he deflected. He could feel the static electricity build up in the air, bringing a scene from recent memory pulsing through his mind: a flash of lightning, and a falling giant.

A powerful and sudden gust of wind accompanied a flaming arrow that ripped through Jeanette's body. She screamed in pain, then sent the whole of the backyard landscaping into the air, Tovas struggled to keep up his deflections, but managed to prevent a few of the objects from reaching their targets. Stars danced in his vision as he fell into a trance-like whirlwind of dizziness.

"Go!" he yelled as loud as his weakened lungs would allow, worried the others might try to bring the ship to him. If they got too close, he knew they wouldn't stand a chance. Jeanette was far too dangerous to risk it.

"Tovas, get out of there if you can," Scheln said. *"We're—"*

Jeanette shot toward the vehicle in a rush of wind cutting off Scheln's mental words. Tovas was powerless to stop her. A flash of light and a sonic boom of deafening thunder rang from her dim figure. As the ship turned, a scar glowed on the inside wall of the passenger bay before the door shut. Despite the injury, the ship sped away, ascending into the night with a rush of wind.

Unable to stand a moment longer, Tovas fell to the ground. The impact threw a grunt from his lungs.

As the whish of the ship faded, the subtle alien sounds of the Earthan forest rang around him, and Tovas relaxed, feeling an urgent need to sleep. He rolled onto his back, content that his friends should now be out of harm's reach.

A blurry figure stood over him with hands on her hips.

"Go ahead," he said weakly. His breathing remained heavy as he closed his eyes against the oppressive exhaustion. "Kill me. You'll never reach them now."

"Oh, don't worry," Jeanette said, her voice barely intelligible. "I have something much better in mind for you."

Chapter 12
Tumble

A falling maul smashed into a suit of impenetrable armor. Lightning flashed. A shockwave rippled across a destroyed courtyard.

The images faded as Rose awoke. Through her hazy vision came a familiar metallic ship interior with an unfamiliar gash running along the wall near the passenger bay door. She lifted her head to find Scheln and Zelyra lying nearby. Kula sat on the floor, her head slumped forward. Then the horrific events that had transpired before her exhaustion caught up to her.

Kara!

Rose bolted upright, and Kula lifted her head, worry clouding her features. The sight sent shivers of terror up Rose's spine.

"What happened?"

"Fita," Kula said. "He and Tovas were left behind."

Rose gasped and reached out with her Sorcery, which was remarkably weak. Objects only dimly passed through her perception now. She tested the connections to Tovas and Fita, and was relieved to find them intact. Very faint, yet clearly there. They were bruised and lightly injured, but relatively healthy.

Rose sighed with relief and gave Kula a weak smile. "They're all right."

Her eyes lit up, and she stood. "They are?"

"Yes," Rose said. "I can still feel them."

Kula shook her head, and embraced Rose. "My connection to Fita has been weak and failing. I couldn't feel him, and feared the worst."

Rose returned the hug. Then remembered.

"Kara!" she said, pulling back. "Is she okay? Where is she?"

Kula gestured toward the other end of the ship. "Sam is with her in the pilot's cabin. She is okay. You saved her life."

Relief swept over her. "I'm just glad Sam got her to me when he did. I should check her. I wasn't able to heal everything, so she will probably need more help."

Kula nodded.

Rose stepped over the supplies and clothing strewn around the floor, likely thrown about by a rapid acceleration. It must have been a close escape. The mysterious woman from under the pond lay on a makeshift bed next to Kara's suit. As Rose moved into the narrow hall beyond the passenger bay, the ulinko lifted her head from the pile of huddling animals in their corner to watch her. The ship shuddered, throwing her off balance briefly. Odd. She scurried past the lav and supply rooms into the pilot's cabin.

There she found Sam kneeling over Kara's supine body. Ya'ir sat in the main pilot seat, staring at the controls. The screens were dark, suggesting they were likely cloaked again.

Sam turned to Rose, and his eyes brightened. "Rose!" He stood and wrapped his arms around her.

"Thank you," he said, his voice full of emotion. "You saved Kara. I . . . all of us can never thank you enough."

He pulled back, and Rose felt herself blush at the tears in her own eyes. *You never need to thank me.*

"Tovas and Fita though . . ." He trailed off.

"They're okay," Rose said. "For now, at least. I can still feel them, faintly."

Sam returned a slight smile. "That's a relief." Then he furrowed his brow. "But that also means they're captives now."

Rose nodded, then inspected Kara. She stared at the compartments next to her head, appearing melancholy, or distraught. Her breathing was shallow. A tear in the fabric of her blood-stained Sovereignty uniform revealed pale skin above her right breast. Rose knelt next to her.

"I should examine you," she said. "I couldn't perform a complete healing. I was able to get oxygen to your brain and patch up your heart and lung, but there's more damage."

Kara showed no indication that she'd heard.

"Does it still hurt?"

"Yes," Kara said, maintaining her gaze at the compartment next to her. "It still"—*gasp*—"hurts. It hurts to breathe."

Rose waved her hand in front of Kara's eyes, alarmed to find them unresponsive. Could she have been hypoxic long enough to cause damage to her eyes or occipital lobe? If so there could be other areas of neural damage.

"Did something happen to your eyes?"

"My sister happened."

"She did something to them?"

Kara shrugged. "Yeah, I'm blind again. Honestly, that doesn't bother me too much." She shifted her position, grimacing. "I'm quite"—*gasp*—"used to being blind. What I *can't* understand is Jeanette."

"Was it a trick? Someone else pretending to be her?"

"No. It was definitely her. And then suddenly . . . definitely *not* her."

"It doesn't make any sense," Sam said, pacing.

Rose opened her Sorcery and touched Kara's hand, feeling the woman's internal organs and physiological activity. Everything was getting fuzzier. She found it hard to discern precisely what was going on.

"Sam," Kara said. "You can fly. We're currently in an invisible ship hovering over Jupiter. We left sense behind a long time ago."

Thankfully, Kara's heart appeared to be thumping normally

now, a stark contrast to the terrifying torn mess Sam had brought inside the home earlier. The tissue around it was still heavily damaged, and there were areas of slow internal bleeding, but it appeared that Rose had sufficiently patched the vital areas.

Sam moved to the other empty pilot chair as Rose worked through Sorcery to relieve what she could of the remaining damage. She drained the blood that had pooled in the chest cavity, causing undue pressure. After patching some tissues, Rose stopped due to her rising fatigue and diminishing perceptibility.

"How do you feel?" Rose asked.

"Better," Kara replied, her breaths still shallow.

"Try taking deeper breaths."

"Okay." Kara inhaled slowly, winced, and exhaled. "Still hurts, but definitely better. Thank you."

"Of course."

"And thank you for saving my life."

"You saved ours first."

Kara returned a smile, which faded quickly.

"Where are we, anyway?" Rose asked. "You mentioned Jupiter?"

"Yeah," Sam said. "Jupiter is a gas giant in the system. We're cloaked and hovering over it."

"Do you think that's safe? How long has it been?"

"About five standard hours since we left my house," Kara responded, then rubbed her forehead. "I don't know where else to go. The ship's damaged from that blast from Jeanette, and we're running low on power. I wanted to avoid an intergalactic jump."

Rose nodded. "Good idea, but if Jeanette could find us on Earth, then she, or the Sovereignty, might find us here too."

"That's a good point," Sam said. "We won't want to linger here too long."

She stood and stepped into the center position between the two pilot seats where Sam and Ya'ir sat. Rose activated her connection to their bodies to check their vitals.

Sam turned to face her. "I'm fine, Rose."

Ya'ir maintained his distant gaze. His heart raced.

"How are you feeling, Ya'ir?" she asked.

He turned to her, his dark eyes and wrinkled forehead revealing a deeply troubled expression. "I . . . I just . . . I don't even know . . . "

"Yeah," Sam said. "So much doesn't add up."

"It's not that. When I saw Jeanette attacking Tovas I just . . . froze. Same as I did that night at Tercast. My body just . . . wouldn't respond."

"You were frightened. That's completely normal."

"But you were all frightened too, and you still flew into action. You helped. I didn't. I *couldn't*." He sighed. "I'm a coward."

"Hey," Sam said, leaning toward him. "Listen to me. You are not a coward. You are gentle, and kind, and powerful in your own way."

"It sure doesn't feel like it."

Rose put her hand on Ya'ir's shoulder. "Sam is right. The ability to act decisively in situations like that is not always instinctual. It often takes conditioning. Your response *is* quite normal."

"I froze up at Tercast too," Sam said. "And even before that when I saw Delveton at the Jones's house. It's hard to think straight in mo—"

A loud clang shook the craft, knocking Rose to the floor. She landed painfully on her behind and left elbow.

"What was that?" Sam said. "Rose, are you okay?"

Rose turned on her side and gripped the chair, rubbing her throbbing left gluteus. "I'm okay."

"It's the ship." Kara said. "Something about a sensor node being damaged. Says it's causing 'anti-gravity instability.' That was the worst one yet."

"That can't be good," Sam said.

Ya'ir stood from his seat. "Maybe we should—"

A horrible lurch sent them all flying forward with yells and screams. Weightlessness followed. Rose's heart thumped in her chest as she spun about, noting that everything in the ship was floating.

"Ahh!" Kara yelled. "We're spinning toward the planet. I can't stabilize the ship!"

"What do we do?" Sam asked.

Kara felt her way toward the opening, while Rose followed, reaching out to everyone aboard. There were a few minor injuries, but nothing life threatening. Yet. She almost started enchanting them against harm, then stopped herself. She may not even get through them all before her energy gave out. It would be better to wait and heal when someone needed it.

Kula and Zel met Kara in the doorway to the passenger bay.

"What happened?" Kula said.

"Move!" Kara yelled, pushing past them. When she made it through, her suit wrapped around her. "Maybe I can go out and push or something."

"What is happening?" an unfamiliar, non-rhotic voice called groggily from the passenger bay.

Rose pushed her head between Kula and Zel, finding the previously unconscious woman poised in the air, weightless with the rest of them. The keglon, ulinko, and other animals flailed around behind her, squealing in panic.

"You woke just in time to watch us all die, apparently," Kara yelled.

The woman raised an eyebrow.

"If you happen to know any way of getting our little ship away from the giant planet that's about to crush us, now would be the time to share."

"As you wish."

Gravity slowly returned, settling them onto the floor. Zel rushed to the animals, calming them with a touch. Everyone stumbled to uneasy footing with the rising force of gravity, which eventually leveled out. The group stared blankly at the mysterious woman in their midst.

"How did you—"

A sudden jolt sent them all stumbling. Rose slammed into the floor of the hallway with her shoulder, sending a wave of pain up her arm. Yells, thumps and clashes echoed across the interior.

"The ship is malfunctioning," the woman said calmly. "Kindly deactivate the anti-gravity controls, please."

Gravity returned once again, and they found their footing. Rose checked everyone over. More bruises. Kula had a minor cut on her leg, perhaps from some piece of debris or a loose weapon. Rose connected to the tissue, sealing the wound quickly. After a few moments, gravity remained stable.

"How did you do that?" Kara asked.

"You're a Sorcerer!" Sam said, sliding past Rose.

The woman nodded. "I see, by your robes—or at least what is left of them—that you are Sorcerers in training."

Rose glanced down at the white heathered top of her robes, which bore the Tercast emblem.

"Who are you?" Ya'ir asked, following Sam.

"I am Elleran Laneum. And you?"

The group introduced themselves by name.

"Why were you buried under my parents' house?" Kara asked.

"I'm afraid I do not understand the question. My last memory involves falling unconscious in my research pod on Earth."

"Yeah. Earth is where my parents lived."

The woman's eyebrows scrunched inward as she studied Kara's suit.

"You are from Earth?"

"Born and raised," Kara said. "Where are you from? What were *you* doing on Earth?"

Elleran turned her gaze to each of them in turn. "I'm afraid I cannot divulge that information. Not until I know more about you."

"You can tell us *something* at least," Sam said. "Those notes in your pod made us think you're some kind of scientist. Is that right?"

"I suppose that is true."

"And you're a Sorcerer?"

"Clearly."

Kara sighed, pulling off her helmet to reveal a mess of

disheveled hair. "Why would my parents have been interested in you? Did you know them? Laurel and Darren?"

"I am not familiar with those names, I'm afraid."

"Ugh. Why doesn't anything make sense!"

"You are with the Sovereignty?" She gestured toward Kara. "You bear the emblem on your chest."

"Well, that's a long story."

"I'm still fascinated that you grew up on Earth. It is such a primitive place."

"Yeah, yeah, I know, class four planet and everything. What—"

"Class *four*?" Elleran said, her eyes going wide. "Oh no."

"Oh no, what?"

She pinched the bridge of her nose. "What is the current year?"

"It's . . . uh . . . one—"

"The standard year is one moh four groh five doh nine," Ya'ir interrupted, likely to save Kara from embarrassing herself with her still-inadequate dohnal knowledge.

"Are you from the future or something?" Sam asked.

"I'm afraid not," Elleran responded, leaning against the wall of the personnel bay and pushing worried fingers to her forehead. "It appears I have been in that research pod for many, many years."

Chapter 13

Urok

Tovas came to himself to find his face pressed uncomfortably against a rough stone floor. He lifted himself up, inhaling rank air sharply against the pain in his arms and shoulders. He had been stripped of his Tercast clothing, wearing only a wrapped loincloth.

A soft hand touched his shoulder. "Tovas, I am glad you are awake."

He turned back to see a familiar face in the low light. "Fita, I'm happy you're all right." The man's powerful arm helped him into a sitting position. "I feared the worst when you were electrocuted."

Other figures in the room they occupied sat against the wall or conversed quietly with each other, lit dimly by two overhead lights in the center of the ceiling. All of them wore a similar cloth to Tovas's, and some around their chests. Two doors stood next to large windows peering into darkness, with a metal hook between them. A large door at the other end likely barred their exit. The only other item in the room was a large bucket.

"I think it may have stopped my heart," Fita said quietly. "My chest exploded with pain, and I blacked out."

"It appears they want us alive."

"Indeed."

A large, muscular man with a tight blond ponytail and pale skin approached the pair with a grin. "How is your friend?" he asked Fita.

Curiously, Fita remained silent. Tovas was unsure what to make of it. Was the fellow prisoner not to be trusted? He seemed friendly.

"I am well enough," Tovas said.

"Aha. He speaks! Unlike his pointy-eared friend."

Fita narrowed his eyes, presenting an otherwise stoic expression.

"So, what is your name?"

"Tovas."

"What about pretty golden boy here?"

Tovas turned to Fita, and Fita shook his head.

"It appears he does not trust you, which I cannot fault him for."

The man laughed heartily. "A fair posture. I am Urok Lerenagonel. Were you two also with the Scelebriars?"

Tovas's eyes widened. "No, but I know of them. What happened?"

"An angel happened," Urok said with a smirk. "She foretold of the Deia, the Divine who shall come to redeem her people, and several have been taken captive and brought here."

"A horrific deception. So, this is the Deia's stronghold?"

Urok raised his eyebrows. "You immediately doubt the Deia's divinity, eh? You are a skeptic?"

"I am Lomerian," Tovas replied. "I am devoted to the Divine. This Deia is certainly not Divine."

Urok scoffed. "Perhaps you will have to see for yourself before you decide. She is quite extraordinary."

He turned and strode back to another group of people in the corner, who were snickering and pointing at a smaller man near them. Urok shoved the subject of their taunting aside as he approached, causing the man to slap against the stone. The group roared with laughter.

Tovas stood. That behavior was unacceptable.

A hand grabbed his.

"Don't. Not yet," Fita said quietly, "He's simply a bully."

Tovas scowled. "I don't like bullies."

"I will gladly teach that man a lesson, when the time is right."

Tovas nodded, sitting back down. "Why haven't you already?"

"He is large. Strong. No doubt a formidable opponent. Best to observe, for now. Learn more about him and the others in here. Then we can better exploit his weaknesses and determine the best approach."

Tovas nodded. "Is . . . ?" He trailed off.

"Yes?"

"Is that how you pinned Vurkil back at Tercast? By studying him?"

Fita smirked. "In a way. The giant had few weaknesses to exploit. He was so *enormous*. I only bested him when he failed to account for his surroundings."

"It's unfortunate that I missed it."

He sighed, frowning. "I miss the oaf."

Tovas put a gentle hand on his shoulder. "As do I."

The group of boisterous men picked a new target, walking toward an older woman who lay curled and shivering on the floor.

Tovas moved to stand again, but Fita grabbed his arm. "Not yet."

"I will not sit by and watch them harass that woman."

"We must wait for—"

Tovas ignored him, pulling away and striding briskly toward the group, which shoved the old woman around with their feet, taunting her about her wrinkled features. His grasp on Sorcery felt impossibly weak. He could barely even perceive his body through the mysterious connection to the Elements, much less anything else. His powers may not be much help anymore.

Urok smiled warmly as he approached. "Ha! Tovas! Yes, come join in on the fun!"

"Leave her—"

The door to the room opened with a loud squeak. The group

stopped, all of them turning toward the entrance and backing away reflexively. Tovas turned too and found a familiar and terrifying sight.

Jeanette smiled at them as she strode into the room, wearing a stunning blue dress with thin straps that hugged her alluring figure. Everyone eyed her with awe or fear as she waved a hand at a hooped metal line dangling from the ceiling between the doors and windows on the opposite wall. As it fell, a pulley mechanism lifted the doors, letting some additional light in through the windows. It slid into a hook of its own accord, holding the doors up.

"Come on out, ladies. Don't be shy."

From the now-open doorway, Tovas saw a light-skinned woman with blond hair, wearing only a thin wrapping around her chest and hips. She scooted farther back into the room, beyond his view.

What had they been doing to her in there?

"Come on. Get outta there," Jeanette said to the woman, placing her hands on her hips.

After a few moments of tense silence, she sighed, then snapped a finger. Flames erupted along the walls of the room. Screams ensued and two women scurried out. The second had wavy golden-brown hair and darker skin. Tovas caught their frightened expressions as they huddled in a corner. Anger boiled in his veins at the eager grins on the faces of a few in the group nearby, including Urok.

Scheln, you probably can't hear me anymore, but I'm likely going to die today.

Jeanette turned, and the line unhooked, dropping the doors back into place with a reverberating thunk. While she strode back to the entrance, Tovas kept his eyes on the men nearby, desperately pleading for strength from the Divine to do right in the face of certain opposition.

"Have fuuun!" Jeanette called out cheerfully as she turned back from the hallway. The door shut behind her.

The women remained huddled in their corner, eyes wide and

wary as they studied each face. Tovas found various expressions on the faces of the others, some staring with lust or interest and others with fear.

"Welcome, welcome, beauties," Urok said as he strutted toward the women, flexing his muscular arms.

Tovas's heart rate spiked as he walked to intercept him. Fighting this group alone, or even with Fita's help, was unlikely to end in his favor. *If I can inspire others to stand up to Urok as well, we might stand a chance.*

"I think it's time to get this party started!" Urok opened his arms, and his entourage cheered. He pointed to a few of the younger members of his group. "You, you, get into the corner with those two, and keep them company while I gather the others." He gestured to the cowering women, and his group members approached them but kept their distance. Urok stopped in front of Fita. "You too. Performance time."

Fita glanced up with a blank, emotionless stare.

Tovas headed the large man off. "Leave him be."

Urok regarded Tovas with a calculating expression. Tovas gazed upward into the man's green eyes with all the defiance he could muster.

A grin spread across Urok's face, then he chuckled. "All right, Tovas. I'll let your friend slide this time. But only this once. Don't test me."

Urok turned, pointing at others to join those in the corner. If they refused, members of his group shoved or carried them into place against their will. None of them fought too hard, likely attempting to avoid more brutal treatment.

What was this "performance"? Many in Urok's group wore expressions full of anticipation. Would Tovas dare to defy the man further? Tell him to leave the others alone? That would surely anger him, and may make things worse. He wasn't even sure what was happening.

The auburn-haired woman moved to slip away from the corner, but one of Urok's men stopped her, causing her to give up her attempt. There was nowhere to escape to, anyway.

Once dek individuals had been gathered into the corner, Tovas noted they were all younger, and perhaps more conventionally attractive than average.

"Now," Urok said, rubbing his hands together. "Get closer."

Those in the corner glanced around nervously at each other.

"Don't be shy. Get *real* close."

They scooted in closer. One man slipped right up against the blond woman, making Tovas's skin crawl. She grimaced and recoiled slightly, but had nowhere else to move to as others closed in.

"Closer," Urok commanded. "Put those hands to good use. Get them *all* over each other."

Goose bumps prickled Tovas's skin. He didn't like where this was going.

"We will not be your slaves, brute," the woman with dark skin said.

Urok chuckled. Some of the other men came up behind him.

"Lookee here, a feisty one. I bet she'll be a right fantastic lay. Whaddya think?"

Several laughed with him.

Tovas approached from the side, and his gut twisted into knots as he observed the woman's bold, defiant stare. A man inched closer to her, but she shoved him back.

She kept her eyes fixed on the large man. "Don't let him intimidate you."

Tovas expected Urok to get angry. Instead, he found the large man laughing. His entourage quickly laughed along.

"I like this one. She's got a mouth." He turned to the man next to her. "Enol, get cozy with her, will ya?"

The face of the sturdily built man the woman had shoved away earlier betrayed a sense of apprehension. "Urok I . . . I don't feel comfortable wi—"

"You'll feel *plenty* comfortable after you get started," Urok growled.

Tovas had a momentary spark of hope that Enol might

continue his resistance, but the man advanced instead. The woman bared her teeth, putting her fists up.

"Stay away from her." Tovas placed himself between Urok and the group. Thankfully, Enol retreated, taking two steps back. Tovas turned to Urok, staring into the man's deep green eyes.

"Tovas, my man!" Urok said with an irritated laugh. "I already indulged the request for your friend. I told you not to test me."

"Leave. Them. Be."

Urok studied him, perhaps sizing him up.

"Beat him down, Bulin," he sneered.

A tall man stalked forward tentatively, putting his fists up in an aggressive stance. Tovas's heartbeats pulsed in his ears as he did the same, his mind a blur with everything Fita had taught him about hand-to-hand combat. He tried to slow his breathing.

Somehow, the Sorcerous perceptions of his body flowed through him momentarily. He connected to his face, enchanting it to become unbreakable—rigid in the event of an impact. As expected, the man called Bulin threw a fist forward and Tovas leaned into it, praying it would work.

The fist smashed harmlessly against his rigid face.

Bulin yelled and grasped his injured hand. He stared at Tovas, baffled, then retreated behind the gang.

As the others watched him with curiosity, Urok simply smirked, dashing Tovas's hopes for a peaceful resolution. He narrowed his eyes as the large man stretched his arms and stepped forward. "You're more than you appear to be, it seems."

The lack of surprise in Urok's tone filled Tovas with dread.

He brought his arms back up in a defensive stance, attempting to find his serenity once again. The impressions danced past his perception, but they were just barely out of reach.

He could no longer rely on Sorcery, and the enchantment on his face had already slipped.

Urok threw a punch forward, and Tovas blocked. Pain erupted on the impacted forearm. Another blow landed on his chest, knocking the wind out of him.

Others in the room gathered around.

"Leave him alone!" the auburn-haired woman said.

Urok kicked out and Tovas lifted his own leg, taking the blow painfully with his shin.

"Don't worry, we'll get back to your pleasure soon enough, girl," Urok said.

He threw a few more blows. Tovas blocked one or two, but the others caused damage to his gut and head. Disorientation overwhelmed him. Warm blood dripped past the corner of his eye.

"What's the matter? No one ever taught you anything except how to block with your face?" Several around them roared with laughter. "Throw a punch or two. Let's see what you've got."

Tovas somehow remained upright, bones and muscles screaming. In a daze, he lifted his battered arms to defend again in a daze, as he heaved against the anxiety in his chest. He couldn't stop this man, but he could at least delay him. He prepared himself for another inevitable onslaught.

Urok shrugged. "Have it your way, then."

He inched closer and clenched his fists before something collided with his side, knocking him to the ground. A dark figure with long golden hair stood over him.

"Stay down, fool," Fita said.

Anger twitched on Urok's face as he lifted himself to a kneeling position. Fita kneed him in the nose, knocking him over again. Urok's gang eyed Fita's impressive physique with uncertainty.

"I said, stay down."

"So," Urok said, pulling himself up to a knee again. He wiped his mouth. "The pretty blond one speaks."

Fita spun into a roundhouse kick, which Urok grabbed, halting the maneuver instantly. Fita's other leg kicked out, sending him to the ground but freeing him from Urok's grip. Both men righted themselves—Fita with a dexterous roll—and Urok stared down at the shorter man with a smirk. Stoic and expressionless, Fita widened his stance. Tovas glanced back to find the people in the corner observing the fight with interest, wishing there was somewhere they could escape to.

Urok swung forward, and Fita deflected. Tovas swept a foot out, catching the man off guard and sending him to the floor again. The darker-skinned woman leapt up and kicked Urok's face, while the other woman stomped down on his stomach. He cried with pain as he reached for the foot near his head, but each of them backed away just enough.

"Stay down," Fita repeated. "That is your final warning."

The large man, sporting a bruised left eye, used his arms to move himself into a half-sitting position, then turned his head and spat. He stared up at Fita for a moment, sizing him up again. Then, to Tovas's surprise, he grinned.

"Impressive. But you *will* learn your place."

"It's over," Tovas said. "You will command no one else."

He eyed the others standing around, making sure they understood his words were for them too. They watched with fascination or fear, but none of them seemed interested in supporting the man who had ordered them around moments before. Perhaps Urok had simply intimidated them into submission, and now that he had been removed from his position of power, the prisoners were free from his leadership.

Urok rolled sideways, lifting himself upright into a relaxed stance. Fita didn't waste a moment and advanced on him, striking with a punch to the face, followed by a powerful kick to his gut. Urok took the blows with little concern or apparent impact, then walked casually toward Fita. The bruise of his eye faded completely.

Tovas's eyes widened. *Urok is a Sorcerer!*

Fita spun, striking out with a kick, which Urok caught easily. As the other foot moved to strike, the larger man brought his arm down on the leg he had caught. A loud snap echoed off the walls.

Fita fell to the ground with a yell. As he tried to rise to his knees, Urok struck out swiftly at his arm. Another loud snap. Tears clouded Tovas's eyes as Fita cried out again.

Fear rippled through Tovas as Urok turned his gaze to him and the people behind. He approached slowly while Fita writhed on the floor behind him.

"Now," Urok said with an arrogant smirk. "Kneel, Tovas."

Tovas, eyes watering and heart thumping, brought his aching arms up and widened his stance.

Urok laughed, then his expression turned serious. "You wish to break too, I see."

Tovas backed away, desperately grasping at his own Sorcery, which was horrifyingly weak. He managed to connect to his forearms an instant before a powerful fist flew toward his face, which he blocked. It threw him backward into the wall, knocking the wind from his lungs. Head spinning, Tovas slid down between the two women and the others Urok had selected.

The woman with golden-brown hair stood in front of Tovas. "Leave him alone!"

She struck out with her fists, which Urok ignored completely. He grabbed her arm and twisted, evoking a scream, then casually flung her toward Enol, who caught her, eyes wide.

"There you go."

Tovas found strength enough to stand, his body screeching in protest, as the woman struggled. He clenched his jaw and fists, determination pulsing through him. Before he could bring his arms up, Urok's rock-hard fist came down against his face, forcing him to the floor on his stomach with a grunt.

"No!" the auburn-haired woman screamed.

Tovas lifted his spinning head to find Urok shoving her toward another woman nearby.

"Now that we've dealt with that surly interruption," Urok said, flexing his muscular arms, "get close, and remove those silly clothes from each other. It's time to play."

Tovas squeezed his tearful eyes shut, ears ringing with salacious laughter and the depressingly few protests of people he was powerless to protect.

Again.

Chapter 14

Insight

"They are called temples."

"The caves?" Ya'ir asked.

"Yes," Elleran said. "They are testing grounds of Tercast's Elements, an enchanted arena designed to evaluate a cohort's knowledge."

Kara leaned against the metal wall of the ship, listening intently. She had a decent mental image of where everyone was located, except Scheln. The group was situated around the forward end of the passenger bay, with Rose, Sam, and Ya'ir recounting their experiences at Tercast more thoroughly for Elleran's benefit, who sat across from her. Kara had gathered some details of their experience during their days adrift in space, but not the full story of what happened before her company's misguided assault on Tercast, so she was delighted to hear a more complete recounting.

"So Tercast was always some kind of school?" Sam asked. "That wasn't something Ilius invented?"

"Indeed. Tercast has been the primary location of elementary Sorcery instruction since before the existence of the Sovereignty itself. It seems Ilius tarnished the castle with his own beliefs and misunderstood the four Elements. Tercast regarded the Elements as a felicitous way to categorize some of the basic principles of nature, as you discovered."

"Tercast was religious, though?" Sam asked.

"Oh, certainly. Their beliefs are loosely connected to those of other ancient religions, such as Relinism and Lomerianism."

"Tovas is Lomerian," Ya'ir pointed out.

"*Now* can you tell us why you were buried in my backyard?" Kara asked, pushing herself from the wall.

"Very well," Elleran said with a sigh. "To save time, I will evade the details for now. The relevant piece is that I attempted to reverse the progression of time in order to prevent a terrible catastrophe."

What catastrophe? Kara wondered. She was about to ask, but Sam beat her with his question.

"Time travel?"

"So to speak," Elleran said. "Clearly, my attempt failed. It appears I only slowed the progression of causality to a near stand-still until Rose's prodding cut into my runaway Vitalization. In truth, I halted it too rapidly, causing undue damage to the surrounding landscape, so I apologize for that. I am glad the effects did not significantly inj—"

"Tovas and Fita," Rose cut in, her voice quavering. "They're in pain. A *lot* of pain. I think they're being tortured . . ."

No. Jeanette wouldn't torture them. Would she?

"Can't you heal them?" Kara asked.

"My connection is too weak. I can barely even *feel* them. I wish I knew why our Sorcery was fading."

"It has been fading since you left Tercast?" Elleran asked.

"Yes," Rose replied.

"Ah, you have the limited unveiling granted for initial instruction and evaluation. The grounds unlock your potential, facilitated by the robes, and it fades with their absence."

"The longer we're away, the weaker it gets?" Ya'ir asked.

"Yes," Elleran said. "In fact, I am certain it would have left you much more hastily if you had discarded your robes."

"Is there anything we can do?" Rose asked.

"Your Sorcery doesn't seem to be tied to Tercast like ours," Sam said. "How does yours work?"

Elleran took a deep breath, then sighed again. "It is possible to grant you full access to your Source's reach, but this action is never to be taken lightly. It requires a tremendous degree of trust."

"It's that simple, though?" Sam said. "You can just give it to us?"

"The ability already lies within you, but it requires the fully realized Sorcery of another to unseal. It appears you have already discovered how to perform a link between Sources, and the process referred to as 'unveiling' is similar. Participants share a sense of mutual trust during physical contact, and I can guide your Source out of its natural shroud."

"It requires trust?" Kula asked.

"Yes. In my days, the Masters would only grant such power after significant education and positive affirmation of virtuous character. You must understand that the abilities come with a tremendous, lifelong responsibility."

"I . . . I understand," Rose said. "But Tovas and Fita may not have long."

Elleran spoke with melancholy. "I'm afraid opening your Source will not improve your connection to them. The link is only as strong as the weakest participant's connection to Sorcery."

Kara's heart dropped. This was all her fault. She knew going back home would be dangerous, and she had let her guard fall at the sight of her sister. It was *her* fault Tovas and Fita were now imprisoned. Helpless. But maybe they could do something about it. Elleran was powerful, and she could give the others their full Sorcery back. Her fist clenched. With their combined might, they could stand a chance.

"We can rescue them," Kara said.

"Do you know where they are?" Elleran asked.

"We have a good hunch. My s—" She stopped herself, still

unable to bear the thought of Jeanette as one of them. "A cult of Sorcerers somewhere called Uvlun."

"I doubt that is its true name," Elleran said.

"Why?" Sam asked.

"Whatever the place is, you are clearly powerful," Kara cut in. "With your help, maybe we could do it."

"A dangerous proposition, I'm afraid," Elleran said. "I have considerable abilities, surely, but a group of Mortezan Sorcerers is never to be underestimated."

"Mortezan?" Sam asked.

Not the time, Sam.

"Please," Kula said. "We must try. We cannot leave them to die."

"I empathize with your difficult situation, and admire your courage and concern for your friends, but perhaps you could go to the Sovereignty for aid."

"We can't," Kara said. "This cult has people in military leadership. That's probably how J—" She cringed. "How they found us on Earth. I don't suppose you know of any way to get around them?"

"The Sovereign should be able to identify and remove them."

Kara raised an eyebrow. "She doesn't seem to be aware of them. But now that I think of it, the Sovereignty may not be looking for you. Could you reach her if we drop you off somewhere?"

"Unfortunately, I do not know what to expect with my return. They may see me as a threat."

Quiet settled over them as they contemplated this information. The Sovereignty was compromised. The group couldn't rely on them for help. And they needed to act quickly. Tovas and Fita may not have long.

"Well, then a rescue mission it is," Kara said.

The group murmured their agreement.

"Each of you have received the precursive Sorcery of Tercast?" Elleran asked.

"All of us except Kara," Ya'ir said.

Silence fell again. Although she couldn't observe their faces, she could feel their eyes on her.

"She should be the first, then, since the initial unveiling often results in unconsciousness. It will also give her greater perception of her surroundings, given her lack of sight."

Kara blinked her unseeing eyes, feeling goosebumps ripple across her skin.

"She can be a Sorcerer?" Sam asked, echoing her own thoughts.

"All humans with sufficient intellect have the capacity. But again, I will not simply grant it on a whim. I will discuss the weight of this responsibility with each of you individually before deciding if you are ready."

So technically *anyone* could be a Sorcerer? That was both thrilling and terrifying.

"We should proceed with haste if we are to attempt a rescue. Kara, please accompany me to the pilot's compartment."

Kara stood from her sitting position against the metal wall, apprehension streaming through her. First sight, now magic? Was she ready for this?

With her first step, she stumbled against something soft— probably a garment strewn about with the ship's sudden plummet. Thankfully, she caught herself before falling completely. She'd barely been blind a few hours again and had already bumped or tripped into several things a handful of times. Turning sight on when it was convenient had gotten to her. She'd need to get used to navigating without it again. She wished she had her cane.

"You okay?" Sam's voice came from above her. "Want help?"

She shook her head. "No, I'm fine. Just need to get used to this again is all."

A soft hand touched her shoulder as she felt her way toward the pilot's cabin. "I'm excited for you," he said. "It's an amazing experience."

She smiled. "So I've heard. I guess I might get to go through it for myself now, if she likes me enough."

Kara shuffled through the narrow opening into the pilot's cabin, careful to avoid any other obstacles. "Uh, Elleran?"

"Yes?"

"Just checking."

"Would you like assistance?"

"No thanks."

Her voice had come from the seat to Kara's right, so Kara felt her way into the one on the left, turning it to face the other. She reminded herself to look toward the woman's face. Easy to forget when blind.

"You navigate exceptionally well, despite your recent loss of sight."

"I actually *re*-lost my sight. I've been blind most of my life."

"Would you like me to attempt its restoration? I am not an expert in human biology, so I am not confident it will work, but I can try."

Sight *would* be pretty useful in a fight.

"Sure."

The woman's warm fingers gently touched her cheek, and Kara felt a momentary panic at the sensation of an ethereal presence. Just like Jeanette. *Calm down,* she told herself, desperately hoping Elleran wouldn't perceive her racing heart. *She won't hurt me— probably.*

The hand and presence lifted.

"Ah, your eyes are artificial. The technology is remarkable, and far too complex for me to repair in any reasonable capacity, I'm afraid."

"It's okay."

"You grew up on Earth?"

"Yep. Didn't have the option to fix sight there, obviously. Honestly, I'm pretty accustomed to it, and have actually kind of enjoyed being different from most people in this way."

"I think that is an admirable attitude toward your condition. I'm sure it has presented many challenges throughout your life."

"Of course. I mean, things were somewhat easier in the

Sovereignty, thanks to technology, but I've banged my shins on more pieces of furniture than I'd care to admit."

"I imagine so," Elleran said. "Were you blind when you joined the Force?"

"Nah, they wouldn't let me join blind. I got sight right before I enlisted."

"That suit of yours is a fascinating feat of technology. I've never seen its equal."

"Really? Every soldier has one."

"Outrageous!" Elleran said. "In my time, suits such as that were always tremendously bulky and unsightly. It speaks volumes about the Sovereignty's advances in engineering and manufacturing that they can produce individualized contraptions on such scale. How long did it take to create?"

Kara tapped her chin, thinking back on the day Commander Vokbon first introduced her to the Ilkuth. What day was that?

"Hmm, I think it was the third day after I joined the military."

"Incredible!"

Kara laughed.

"There have been Sorcerers who have tried to work with such suits of armor in the past, with little success. Sorcery depends on your ability to perceive and connect to the surrounding Elements, and armor has always resulted in an inescapable feeling of being closed off from one's surroundings."

Kara considered another Sorcerer she'd known who had worn his own suit, to chilling effect. "The Ilkuth actually doesn't feel restrictive at all. It's almost like a second skin. I've never felt disconnected while wearing it. In fact, I barely even notice it's there."

Elleran was silent for a moment.

"It is at once a fascinating and terrifying thought, that of a suited Sorcerer—one with the capabilities of advanced technology as well as powerful Sorcery."

An image flashed in Kara's mind: lightning crackling from a magic sword held by another suit of Ilkuth. She didn't mind the thought of never seeing something like that again. "It's even more terrifying in reality."

"Someone has done this?"

"We fought one at Tercast. He deceived my company into attacking the place, and nearly killed everyone."

"Welin Em Onii," Elleran whispered.

Kara's eyes widened. "You were in the Armed Forces?"

"No. But I have worked alongside many soldiers. I am glad to hear they still carry that motto. Do you know its meaning?"

"Yeah, 'for life, duty, and love,' right?"

"Indeed. It is derived from an ancient Rwenmarian proverb: 'Life gives us potential. Duty gives us purpose. Love makes them beautiful.'"

"I think the man who told me its meaning used the word 'resplendence.'"

Elleran tapped her chin. "Hmm, yes, I agree that is a more accurate translation. The word 'desius' in the original language intends a kind of vibrant, colorful beauty."

They both went silent for a moment. Kara fidgeted with her hands, not knowing what else to do.

"To join the military, you must have become a citizen first," Elleran said. "Can you recite the first oath of citizenship?"

"Uh . . ." Kara turned her head upward, straining to remember that day. She had just answered all of the synth's questions. "I can't remember the exact wording, but 'I will uphold life and agency' or something like that."

"I commit to honor the liberty of all beings and the experience of life."

"Right, that. I was close."

"Have you ever pondered on what that commitment means to you?"

Kara stilled, unsure of what to say. This was clearly some kind of test. Elleran was probably looking for a specific answer. What did she want to hear?

"Honestly, no, I haven't really thought about it too much."

"I see."

It sounded like disappointment. *Good going, Kara.*

"Well, they're just basic things everyone should commit to, right? What's there to think about?"

"Living beings rarely exist in a vacuum, Kara. Everything we do, or don't do, affects the lives of others."

"Well, yeah, but that's just . . . existence."

"Do you believe every individual should be free to think and believe whatever they so desire?" Elleran asked.

"Absolutely," Kara said.

"Even if those beliefs are harmful to others?"

Now she was just getting all philosophical. This was more Sam's arena. Kara considered the question, though. "Well, everyone can always think whatever they want, but they can't just impose those beliefs on others."

"If you had the option to cause everyone to believe the same thing, would you?"

What would that even look like? Mind control? Everyone believing the same thing sounded like a cult. Wasn't that the definition of a cult?

"No," Kara said.

"Why?"

"Because besides being terrible, it would also be super *boring*. Diversity is good, especially diversity of thought and belief."

The room fell to near silence. Only the soft hum of nearby electronics filled the void.

"Do you have questions for me?" Elleran asked. "You will need to trust me for this to work."

Kara shrugged. "Not really. I don't think I have much of a choice *not* to trust you. But anyway, judging by how you could move our entire ship the way you did, you seem pretty powerful. That we're even where we are right now means you value our lives, at least. I trust you."

"Please give me your hand."

"Okay," she said. Goosebumps broke out across her skin.

Soft, warm fingers caressed her palm, and she felt the ethereal presence again. It gently pressed on her mind, giving her the impression of attempting to enter a precious space.

"You will need to accept me," Elleran explained. "It will feel as if you are granting access to a very special or intimate place."

Kara ran her thumb gently across the back of the woman's soft, wrinkled hand. Did she trust her? *Could* she be lying about everything? Was the pod actually a prison? Had her parents been there to warn the Sovereignty if Elleran were to escape?

"Direct a feeling of trust toward me," Elleran instructed.

Kara determined that the woman was trustworthy. She had saved them from death already, and certainly seemed genuine. Letting herself relax, she opened up to the presence.

It entered immediately, tenderly settling upon her perceived precious space. She could feel Elleran's concern, her interest, and a touch of sorrow. What was she sad about? Perhaps friends and family who were probably long dead now? If she really had been in the pod for generations, she might understandably feel pretty lonely.

Sudden impressions of Kara's own body and the room around her passed through her mind, startling her. She could *feel* them, in a bizarre, otherworldly way. Heart. Lungs. Muscles. Chair. Wires. Air.

"Whoa!" she said, the pressurized volume pressing against her skin, smothering her.

"It is all right. You are experiencing telesthesia."

"Tele-what now?" Kara felt desperately claustrophobic.

"You can sense your surroundings. Try to remain calm. Your first moments often result in haphazard connections."

Strange connections formed between her and the suffocating substance around her. Air pushed out from her, causing her to yelp as a pop blew hair across her face.

Elleran held her arms. "It is all—"

Insurmountable fatigue drowned out the woman's words and Kara's own sense of panic. She felt tired. So unbelievably tired. She had an urgent, unstoppable need to sleep.

Her head dropped as consciousness left her.

Chapter 15
Pain and Pleasure

"I'm on my own side!"

The words, haunting her from a dream swathed in blood and tears, faded as Jeanette awoke to the stone ceiling above her warm, spacious bed. Tess's steady breathing disturbed the air to her left.

Something wasn't right with her head. It certainly wasn't the Deia. After Jeanette's initial shock and misplaced grief at discovering the Deia's control over her mind, the Divine woman's soothing presence had become ever so delightful. No, it was something else. Something mildly unpleasant, pressing against her thoughts. A part of her mind that felt off. An inner rival. Something easily ignored most of the time, but during more peaceful moments, the sensation became noticeable.

She should attempt to sleep more. There was much to do, and a good rest would be helpful.

Jeanette shifted, finding her thoughts idly turning to her last boyfriend back on Earth. Selfish jerk. He might have been the one to make her a mother one day, had he not utterly demolished her trust in him. She'd always wanted to be a mother.

She turned to her other side.

Anyway, she had a new purpose now. There was much to be done with the Scelebriars and other prisoners. Urok had successfully revealed some of the more promising candidates, including the two obnoxious men who had thwarted her attempt to capture the relics on Earth, and who had likely saved her sister.

Jeanette turned again, finding a cool spot on the pillow to lay her head.

She felt oddly conflicted about what had happened. Her sudden outrage at Kara for killing Delveton was wholly justified, and certainly according to the will of the Deia, but she was hopeful Sam's band of Sorcerers had been able to heal her sister. Perhaps there was a chance for redemption. Perhaps Kara could still join them one day.

Mind bogged down with potential plans for the prisoners, and finding herself still uncomfortable, Jeanette shifted back to lay on her left side. A soft hand stroked her hair.

"Turn over any faster and you're going to give yourself whiplash," Tess whispered with a giggle. Then her tone turned serious. "You okay, Jey?"

"Just finding it hard to get back to sleep." Jeanette opened her eyes. "Sorry, did I wake you?"

Tess lightly scratched Jeanette's head, her smirk peeking out from beneath her midnight-black hair in the candlelight. "Oh, clearly I can sleep just fine when you're trying to set the record for bed gymnastics."

She laughed softly. "Sorry. My mind won't quiet down."

Tess traced Jeanette's cheek. "I know the feeling."

"You do? I mean . . . I know you were joking, but you do seem to sleep pretty soundly most of the time."

"I do now. I didn't use to."

"Before the Deia?"

Tess nodded against her pillow. "The years of your grandfather's control were rubbish fire."

"I thought the major problem was that he was too complacent. Just waiting for something to happen."

"That's exactly why it was unsettling. We had garbage scraps to eat. He'd given up on everything. Locked all the knowledge away in that library so only he and his family could access it. Didn't trust anyone. He would have had us all scraping by on Uvlun for the rest of our miserable lives."

"The Deia and Delveton then pulled you together, right?"

She shrugged. "Sort of. I was resistant to joining her at first. Delveton helped me find my way soon enough. He and I were at Tercast together for a while, actually."

Jeanette raised her head and propped it against her arm. "Really?"

Tess did the same, grinning as she lifted her head. "Yep. He was my Air instructor. The guy always did love his lightning." She chuckled.

"Why were you both exiled to Uvlun?"

"Oh, I'm not sure about Del. I think he'd started experimenting or something. Got the Grand Masters into an uproar."

"What about you?"

Tess's eyes turned downward, pensive. "Got caught having sex with my dorm mate. She accused me of assault to save her own skin, the scuzz."

Jeanette studied Tess's face, wondering what she might have been like before Uvlun.

"What did you do before Tercast?"

"Oh, have I not mentioned it?" Tess shifted under the blanket. "I was a research assistant. My team helped mohs of Molkinarans on Enck get free of the network, which is why the Deia has given me my current assignment on Tenrazka."

Jeanette smiled. "You should meet my friend Sam."

"Why's that?"

"Wants to be a scientist. Very skeptical."

"Oooh, is he one of the men you brought back with you?"

"Unfortunately not. He got away with the others."

Tess sighed. "Oh well. Speaking of those two, the Deia wanted each of us to spend some time with them before I head off to

Tenrazka and you go back to Alvior. From Urok's report, she thinks they have good potential."

"I believe it. I'm surprised at how well they were able to slow me down."

"Well . . ."

"Well what?"

"You fight about as well as a toddler in a pillow fight."

"Hey!"

Tess giggled. "Since we're not sleeping anyway, why don't we go pay them a visit? Get an early start?"

Jeanette let her head drop and closed her eyes. "But I wanted to get more sleeeep."

Something soft smacked into the side of her head.

Tess's cheeky grin was visible behind the pillow she wielded.

"Hey!"

Tess laughed.

Jeanette was about to swing her own pillow back around, but a sense of responsibility stopped her. Truly, there *was* much to do. The Deia would likely be pleased with an early start.

She sighed. "Fine, let's go."

"Aw, I was hoping you'd fight back first."

Jeanette swung her pillow, catching Tess in the head. They tossed the pillows at each other back and forth, either with physical strength or Sorcery, while they prepared for the day. Jeanette rinsed her face with the trickling water in the lav, then pulled down a light, loose maroon jumpsuit with black seams from the garment rack in their small bedroom. Tess emerged from the lav in her black outfit with swirling silver patterns, and a pillow smacked Jeanette across the side just as she was pulling the last piece of the jumpsuit over her shoulder.

Tess beamed, looking her over. "You're gorgeous, you know that?"

Jeanette smiled. "So are you."

They each wrapped belts around their waists, containing their weapons and vials of health potion. Then Tess took her arm, and they strode out into the well-lit, colorful hallway, which was empty. Most of the others were sleeping or busy somewhere in the Sovereignty, furthering the work of the Deia.

"I'll take the blond one," Tess said as they rounded the corner.

"Hey, I don't want Tovas."

"Too bad, I called it first. I've always wanted to meet a Helenestian."

"Fine."

"They left them in their own private rooms for us to play with," Jeanette said. "Tovas is in this one." She pointed to a familiar door, then pointed to the next one down. "Fita is in that one."

"Okay, I'll see you afterward."

Tess hugged her, and Jeanette returned the gesture. They held each other briefly before Tess pulled away and looked up at her with a grin.

"Have fun!"

Jeanette smiled back. "You too, Tess."

While Tess continued toward the next door down the hall, Jeanette turned to the familiar door in front of her. It was the one Tess had often led her through during her days in the dungeon. Back then, the uncertainty of what lay on the other side had filled her with terror, but now she mostly felt excitement and anticipation.

This time, *she* was in control.

Jeanette grabbed the handle, and opened her Sorcery, connecting to the locking mechanisms. Before the door opened, Tess opened the next door down with a light wave of her hand, and was thrown back by the Helenestian as he burst from the opening. He shoved past her and ran down the hall. Tess righted herself and turned to Jeanette, grinning madly, then deftly pulled a dart from her waist and tossed it toward the man. It whistled down the long hallway and pierced his thigh, causing him to cry out with pain. Remarkably, he remained upright, limping forward as hastily as he could.

Jeanette smiled, remembering herself on the other end of those darts. It felt like an eternity ago now.

Tess laughed, casually walking toward him and tossing another dart, which pierced his other thigh, sending him to the floor. He continued to crawl forward on his arms.

"You are going to be so much fun to work with, pretty boy," Tess declared. "I like you already."

"You'll never"—he let out a sharp inhale of pain—"take me, witch!"

Tess cackled, and Jeanette turned her attention back to the door. As much as she would enjoy watching Tess in her element, she had her own subject to work with. After one last glance at Tess, who was casually dragging the Helenestian by his leg, Jeanette reconnected to the locks and pulled them free before pushing the door open and stepping into the room.

Tovas knelt on the far side of the room, hands atop his sandy hair, elbows forward. Praying? He didn't acknowledge her presence. Jeanette softly closed the door behind her as she took inventory of the other items in the room. An aging wooden table stood along the wall near the door, displaying a bundle of long chains, a hammer, and an assortment of knives. Along the opposite wall was a larger array of chains passing through several metal rings attached to the stone wall, a recent addition. A single enchanted bead on the ceiling illuminated the space.

Jeanette turned her attention back to the man at the far end of the room, who still hadn't moved since her arrival. The harsh light cast dramatic shadows from his figure. She approached slowly, watching for any response. Only when she was within a few feet did she notice tears streaking down his cheeks.

Perhaps Urok had broken him. That would be a shame. If he'd lost his mind to madness, he would be of little use to the Deia.

Jeanette placed her hands on her hips.

"Scared, Tovas?"

He lifted his head slowly, looking up at her with a pitiful expression before wiping the tears from his face. He gently dropped his hands to his lap, remaining seated on his knees.

"No, Jeanette," he said sorrowfully. "I was praying for you."

"Don't let Sam hear you say that," she said with a smirk.

"I suspect Sam and Kara are both significantly more distraught at your betrayal, assuming Kara is still alive. They love you."

Jeanette laughed. "Eventually, they will understand. One way or another. Just like you! That is the way."

"They are suffering."

She bent forward, jabbing at her chest. "No, *I* was the one who suffered. *I* was the one who was taken from my home. Beaten. Abused." She calmed herself, returning her fist to her side and standing tall. "I have been through the refiner's fire and have become renewed with purpose. And *power.*"

"Power is only potential," Tovas said. "What truly matters is the way you use that power."

Jeanette folded her arms, then connected to the air in front of her and caused it to shoot forward at him. The blast knocked him over, and his body slapped against the cold, hard stone.

"Right, then." She smiled. "No magic staff to protect you this time."

Tovas lifted himself onto his arms, looking up at her with eyes full of defiance.

"I do not fear death," he said.

Jeanette scoffed. "Oh, you would like that, wouldn't you? To die as a martyr?" She lowered her voice. "For honor!" Then she laughed. "I'm sure you've been looking forward to it by now." She stepped forward and knelt next to him, bringing her face inches from his. "We have so much more in store for you."

She enchanted her arm and grabbed his neck, feeling blood pulse through his body with each racing heartbeat. His eyes widened as he attempted to pull her grip free. Tovas rose with her as she stood up, her firm grip unyielding. Choking sounds echoed from the walls as she strode to the wall with chains and drove him against it.

With Sorcery, she yanked his arms against the wall. The chains pulled inward, wrapping tightly around his forearms. She caused the other end of the chains to pull downward against their anchors, clinking as they drew his arms up against his efforts to twist free.

Jeanette released her grip on his neck and stepped back. Tovas coughed as she directed the other ends of the chains to pull his body tighter on their own. She wrapped them through one of the other rings attached to the wall, securing them in place.

She waited patiently for his coughing fit to run its course. Although he wasn't as physically impressive as his blond friend, he was relatively fit. She would even say his pale face was quite handsome.

Tovas had attempted to defend the people from Urok during the exercise earlier, but Jeanette wondered what he might do when confronted with amiable sensuality. She could be sexy if she wanted to be, right? His coughing finally subsided, and he stared at her with those defiant eyes. She connected with the arms of her jumpsuit while giving him a slight, suggestive smile.

The top of her suit slid over her shoulders and down her arms, exposing her breasts. Tovas turned his gaze firmly to the wall as the material settled around her waist.

"Aw, am I really that ugly?" Jeanette said.

"Quite the contrary," Tovas replied toward the stone wall to his left.

"Why don't you look at me, then?"

He remained silent.

Jeanette laughed. "You're such a prude. They're just tits. Look!"

She shifted her torso, letting her body sway tauntingly with her movements. Tovas shut his eyes. It felt so good to be comfortable in her body, teasing him like this. Before her time with the Deia, she would have never dreamed of doing something so provocative.

"Hmm." She stepped toward him. "Looks like I might need to be a little more"—her fingers gently touched his face —"persuasive."

A foot planted into her abdomen and shoved her back.

"Oooh," Jeanette said playfully. "Yes, I think I like that idea."

She connected to the other chains on the table, and their clinking echoed in the small room as they floated toward Tovas.

"Don't! This isn't you, Jeanette."

"You don't know me," she said as the chain moved to wrap his ankle. He pulled his foot free, waving both his feet in haphazard desperation.

"Sam and Kara do. They always said you were the kindest, most gentle person."

"Heh." Jeanette attempted to loop the chain around his writhing foot, which was quite difficult due to the imperceptibility around his body. "I was a pushover. I let the will of others control my life."

"The Deia," Tovas panted. "She controls you now."

She whipped the chain around his shin, then pulled his leg tight against the wall. Another chain moved to intercept the other foot, which he continued to flail haphazardly.

"Pure freedom is an illusion, Tovas. I'm no more controlled by the Deia than you are by your own beliefs. The Deia is as divine as any person can be."

"She is *not*"—the chain looped around his other leg—"Divine!"

"I resisted at first, before I came to understand," Jeanette continued, pulling his other leg tight. "She knows the value of suffering. The value of pleasure. The significance of knowledge and imagination. Her power is unfathomable."

"The true Divine values life and agency."

She sneered. "The Divinity you worship is a sham used to control *you* Tovas. At least I know the source of the strings that pull *me* now—and she is glorious."

His eyes remained tightly shut, but he continued to pull against his bonds. Jeanette savored the sight of his writhing body for a moment before approaching slowly. She touched his icy face with her own warm fingers again, and he recoiled.

"Don't do this, Jeanette!"

He sounded genuinely panicked. Jeanette smiled. She was getting through to him. She slowly pressed her own exposed body against his chest, indulging in the coolness of his skin, knowing that her body would feel warm and pleasant to him.

"I think you just need to relax," she whispered, pushing her body more firmly against his. He threw his head forward, but she dodged the blow, then forced his head back with a soft, steady hand.

Due to her physical touch, her Sorcery connected to his body. She felt his racing heart, his pulsing nervous system, his body's natural arousal at her actions. With it came something else: Tovas's presence in her own body. He must still have a trace of Sorcery left in him. And with him came a reemergence of the rival at the back of her mind. It seemed to grow bolder, pressing with discomforting force toward Tovas's presence. He opened his eyes and stared into hers with fascination.

Something wasn't right.

Jeanette pulled away abruptly, and Tovas continued his wide eyed stare. She scrutinized him in silence for a few moments, wondering what had happened. He had touched something inside her, the precious space the Deia had reached to unveil her Sorcery.

Physical connection could be dangerous, it seemed, given that he was also a Sorcerer. It may not be worth the risk.

"Oh, fine then," she said, slipping the top of her jumpsuit over her shoulders again. "Killjoy."

She raised her hand and a small, curved knife flew into her palm from the table nearby.

"Since it looks like pleasure isn't going to work, let's try a little pain."

Chapter 16
Ruins

Sam watched his fist clench, and through the magnificent connection of Sorcery, he sensed the interior tissues of his hand carry out the movement. Dim lights of the pilot's cabin illuminated the interior. The screens remained dark, indicating that the ship was still cloaked as it headed toward Alvior.

Elleran had completed unveiling each of the group's Sources after some prior discussion to establish trust, and a brief break to eat a meager meal of nutriment bars. Sam had been the last of them to undergo the procedure.

"How do you feel?" Elleran asked.

He grinned at her. "Incredible. I can sense everything so clearly!"

She returned a weary smile. "Yes, that is to be expected. The preparatory Sorcery offered by Tercast is weaker, by design."

"You said before that it weakens over time, but it definitely got stronger after we first started."

"After the initial burst of opening, the unveiling increases over time and peaks around eight to doh Alvior weeks. It then slowly diminishes."

Sam's eyes widened. "Even when you're still on its grounds?"

"Yes. When Tercast was attacked, your group likely had more power than most of the others."

Elleran leaned back and gestured to the cabin door. "Considering what I gathered from Kara regarding the Sovereignty's increased technological might, I am surprised that her unit experienced losses at all."

"She said something was off. Some of their suits' functions had been tampered with or disabled. Delveton was probably the one behind it because he *wanted* them to destroy each other."

Elleran frowned and shook her head. "Terrifying."

Sam shuddered at the memory of bodies lining the dark halls of Tercast. "It was."

They sat in silence, and Sam sorted through the hundreds of questions whirling through his head. He needed to take advantage of the time he had with her before they arrived at their destination.

"So," he began, "we performed a couple of experiments, and I came up with an equation to represent the relationship between power and distance and some other factors. I didn't include the variable of time, though."

Elleran raised her eyebrows. "Oh?"

"Er," he looked around, and failed to find something to write with, or on. How could he have forgotten to bring any? He pulled his left hand flat, and drew out the equation on his hand by connecting to his skin with Sorcery. When he finished, he spun his palm out toward Elleran, and she scrutinized his work.

"Let me see if I can piece together what you intend with this equation," she said. "The bar represents division, and the x represents distance?"

"Yes!" Sam said.

Elleran nodded. "What is the k?"

"I used that to account for the user's rough knowledge on the subject, since that seemed to have a fairly drastic effect."

She nodded again. "I see. This certainly captures the proper relationship for distance, and you were correct to place high importance on knowledge. I can see how this can be a rudimentary approximation for the effect of knowledge, though it is missing dohs of other essential factors, including imaginative capacity, emotional investment and others."

"I know, I know!" He pulled his hand back and clenched his fist again. "I've wanted so badly to get more data, but most of the others weren't terribly interested, and our power was fading haphazardly, which skewed the results anyway."

Elleran smiled at him fondly.

Sam scratched his head, self-conscious. "Sorry. I can get carried away with this kind of stuff."

She didn't reply, only continuing to gaze at him.

"What?" Sam asked.

She shook her head. "You remind me of an old colleague—and friend."

"You *are* a scientist, right? We guessed as much by the notes and books in your pod."

Elleran sighed, staring out into the past. "Virahmgal and I. Our thirst for knowledge was insatiable. We studied Sorcery and the universe in ways no one had ever attempted before. We made *profound* discoveries."

"Can I study your work anywhere?"

She regarded him with a curious expression, then frowned. "We kept our research secret, wary of what someone might do with that knowledge. However, we also felt compelled to preserve our findings. We created two copies of the work, collecting years of our research, and placed enchantments on them so that we would always know when one was opened."

"Where are they?"

"I do not know. Not precisely. But I can tell you that no one is reading them right now. It appears the enchantments remain—"

She stopped, furrowing her brow.

"What is it?"

"I think one of them has been opened recently, but only briefly. Curious."

"Enchantments can last that long?"

"Certainly. A simple detection enchantment such as this requires very little energy."

"Incredible," Sam said. "I *knew* that the leaders at Tercast were messing with us. They were clearly missing a lot about Sorcery, especially regarding the importance of empirical knowledge. Or they *did* know and wanted to downplay it to maintain control."

"That seems likely," Elleran said. "You must remember, however, that the original inhabitants of Tercast were also deeply religious. I worked with them frequently." Her eyes turned distant, sorrowful. "They were good people."

"What happened to them?"

The console beeped, and the display opened briefly to show a familiar sight that caused Sam's heart to jump: the damaged remains of Tercast castle.

"We have arrived," Elleran said.

A shame. He had so many more questions to ask. Perhaps there would be more time later.

Elleran walked into the passenger bay, with Sam following close behind. Scheln popped up from his laying position, floating into the air. In his eyes was a fierce determination. He was ready to rescue his brother.

"Let's do this," Sam said.

Scheln's head pulled forward into a single, awkward nod.

The portal the Grand Masters used to banish those who did not abide their rules should open the way to Uvlun, where they suspected Tovas and Fita were taken. All they needed to do was find it. He found it curious that Elleran had mentioned that Uvlun was likely not the planet's true name.

Kara approached from his left, wearing her Ilkuth without the helmet. She embraced him and they shared a brief kiss, causing Sam's insides to flutter furiously.

"Did you rest well?"

She smiled. "Too well. You're right. That Sorcery fatigue is something else."

He touched her beautiful face lightly with his fingertips, and she grasped his hand in hers. Sam opened his Sorcery, watching those steady, distant eyes and felt the internal structures of her body next to his. Beating heart. Pulsing lungs. Tightening muscles. The impressions were clearer than ever before.

Her presence entered his body, revealing that she must have activated her Sorcery as well. She released his hand, and he released her cheek. Their connection persisted.

"That's amazing!" she said, her eyes lighting up.

"Now we can connect any time."

Just like the connection he'd had with Rose. At the thought, he noticed he could still feel Rose, who was seated across the room, through that connection.

"The sensations are *amazing*," Kara said. "Like you can feel everything."

"I know."

"Kara," Rose said with her approach, "let me connect as well so I can monitor and heal you if needed."

Kara held out her hand, and Rose took it. A moment later, they both let go.

"So cool. Kinda gross though. In a way, I can sense all your insides."

Rose laughed. "Yes. I find it fascinating!"

"Where should we land?" Kara asked.

"I will move the ship into position." Elleran said. "Please keep the shroud active. Is everyone prepared?"

Rose, Kula, Ya'ir, and Zel approached the woman. All of them had weapons, except Rose. Sam felt the connection to his mace, and it flew into his palm. He gripped it tightly.

"Rose, you should take a weapon," Elleran said.

She shook her head. "I'm no fighter. I'm a healer."

"Even a healer may need to defend herself."

"It's too bad Tovas took the staff with him," Ya'ir said. "That would be handy."

"What was the staff's enchantment?" Elleran asked.

"We were never completely sure. Tovas said it directs your movements almost, helping you defend yourself."

"Ah! The Staff of Dreams."

"You know of it?" Sam asked.

"Certainly. It is legendary. A relic said to have been wielded by Balith the Defender, a philosopher and idealist who believed in extreme pacifism. Legends say he would never attack, only defend himself and his people until his enemies fell with exhaustion. It truly is a shame that it now lies in the hands of our enemies."

"How about this one?" Kula suggested, handing a longsword hilt-first to Rose, her bow in her other hand. "It is enchanted with agility. It may help you react more quickly."

Rose took it. "Okay."

"Will you take a weapon?" Sam asked Elleran.

"No."

"Aren't you going to help us?"

"At a certain level of ability, these items become less useful and more of a hindrance."

Sam's eyes widened. She was either completely out of her mind or ridiculously powerful.

"Ready?" Kara said through her helmet. She now hefted a familiar, enormous maul, with her plasma rifle magnetically attached to the suit's back.

The sight of the maul brought back painful memories of Vurkil's fascination with it. Sam glanced at Rose, who averted her gaze. The sight pierced his heart. Part of him wished Kara would choose a different weapon, but it was one of the most powerful in their possession, so it was a good choice. It could be more useful in a fight than her plasma rifle, which would require time to recharge. With the armor, she could also wield the maul without using Sorcery, which she would have to avoid in this fight to stay conscious since she was still so new to it.

"Let's go," Kula said.

"The cloak will drop momentarily. I'll put it back up as soon as I can."

The rear door of the vehicle slid open. Cool winds swept through the passenger bay, fluttering their hair and the scattered bits of cloth and other junk. The destroyed remnants of the

Tercast castle they had left many weeks ago sat in the distance below the rocky hillside, lit up by the evening sun and orange moon overhead. Everyone departed the craft quickly, which then turned invisible, leaving the sleeping animals alone on board.

Sam breathed in the warm, humid air as they followed Elleran through a cluster of soft bushes. A small opening let them through one by one into the cave system they had stumbled upon before the attack on the castle, which they had decided was the best way for them to avoid Sovereignty detection. Elleran led them quickly through the rocky interior, where points of light hovered over their heads, providing illumination.

The group soon found themselves in the destroyed artifact room.

Elleran snuck past the rubble, which was notably devoid of any remaining items. She glanced back briefly with a grim expression, but remained silent, urging them forward into the castle interior. Sam felt his own gut twist at the sight, but forced himself to watch for threats to avoid memories of their last horrific trudge through the castle. Through a section of destroyed wall, he caught a glimpse of the magnificent mountains to the west in the evening light before the blackened stone of Tercast obscured it. Thankfully, though the dull scent of death still lingered and blood stained the halls, the bodies had all been removed.

"No one else is present in the area," Elleran said. "But we should not linger any longer than is necessary."

As they passed by the Water instruction room, Rose paused. Sam halted with her, his heart breaking at the destruction within. The brilliant painting of the fox-faced water serpent emerging from a crashing wave lay torn on the floor, among the rubble of destroyed desks and chairs. He placed a hand on Rose's shoulder, and they moved on with the others.

Elleran led them into the Master wing of the castle, an area they had never entered before. Golden ornamentations and brightly colored paintings were in pieces, destroyed by the terrible battle that had taken place between Sorcery and the Sovereignty's technological might.

"Oh!" Elleran stopped suddenly.

"What is it?" Kara asked.

"Did the Masters ever wear their field robes?"

"Their what?"

She brought a hand to her lips, pondering, then strode back the way they had come, parting the group. "Remain here. I will search more quickly on my own."

Before anyone could respond, her feet left the floor, and she flew out into the hallway. Sam's eyes widened. Her flight was graceful, efficient, likely powered by anti-gravity. He should ask—

Kara's fist struck his shoulder.

"Ow!" Sam said. "What was that for?"

"Do *not* ask about her flight when she returns. We must stay focused."

The others snickered.

"Hey! Who said I was going to ask?"

Kara placed her free hand on her hip while hefting the enormous maul over her shoulder. "*I* said."

Although the reflective face shield masked Kara's expression, Sam could clearly picture the characteristic smirk she reserved primarily for him. The thought made his insides flutter. He matched her pose, placing the mace over his shoulder with his own smirk. It seemed like a child's toy next to the enormous maul held by the shorter figure in front of him. After a few seconds, his stance wilted, and he chuckled.

"Okay, fine, I was thinking it. But I want to know!"

The group broke into laughter again.

"Rose," Ya'ir said, "how are Tovas and Fita?"

Rose furrowed her brow in concentration. "Their connection is weak, fading in and out haphazardly. Fita's seems to fade out worse than Tovas's."

Kula frowned.

"When I can feel anything at all, it's only a faint set of fuzzy impressions. I can tell they are alive, and they are still in pain, but I have a hard time discerning anything beyond that."

Hold on, Tovas. Hold on, Fita. We're coming for you.

Elleran reemerged from the hallway, carrying a large stack of neatly folded clothing.

"Put these on in lieu of your study pants. Wear the jacket over your shirt. They will offer greater protection."

"Right here?" Rose asked with reddening cheeks.

"Yes, please," she said as sets of light gray tops and bottoms flew out to each of the group members except Kara. "We should not linger. Do not worry about sizing. They will adapt to your body the same way the study robes do."

Sam dropped the mace, then threw off his pants, grateful to have something else to wear for the first time in weeks. He glanced at Kara, who waited patiently with the maul still over her shoulder. He quickly slid on the form fitting pants, which had a built in latch for his waist. Patterned golden lines ran down the outsides of his legs.

"These are Tercast's legendary field robes," Elleran explained. "Masters would wear these when performing tasks outside the castle walls. Ancient artificers crafted them for physical defense, and they have several enchantments to further enhance that protection."

Sam donned the stocky jacket, where the front overlapped itself, fastening near his left armpit and draping to a point between his thighs. The hood hung down the back. A golden clasp held a sash around his waist, while vertical lines embroidered the rest of the uniform. Dense but flexible white gloves completed the look, each with a dark brown palm offering significant grip.

"They would often wear the shoulder capes with them as well, but would remove them if they expected conflict."

After slipping his boots back on, Sam stretched, marveling at the outfit's flexibility despite its thickness.

"Prepared?" Elleran said.

"Yes," they all replied.

"Then we will proceed to find this portal."

After several minutes of searching the depressing ruins, Sam scrutinized a large, ornate door on the floor, having formerly gated the entrance to a colorful room. The group entered warily to find vibrant pentagonal walls, each colored for one of the four elements. Red fire danced with fury, green mists of air swirled in turbulence, the browns and yellows of earth stood resolute, and blue water flowed with grace. The last wall, opposite where they had entered, depicted dull gray chains near the floor, giving way to brilliant pearlescent leaves at the top.

He thought back on the caves, and the strange line that Tovas had interpreted as a depiction of morality. Perhaps Elleran had more answers to that.

"Aha." Elleran touched the gray-and-pearlescent wall. It opened, revealing a narrow corridor. "The Masters of Tercast have always had a fondness for secret rooms and passageways. There are many hidden throughout the castle."

"We discovered the entrance to the caves in a storage room," Rose said as they moved single file into the corridor. It was barely wide and tall enough for them to enter fully upright. Someone much larger would have had significant difficulty getting through it. Someone like Vurkil. A pang of grief struck Sam at the thought.

"That is unsurprising," Elleran said. "They would often connect the caves to different points of the castle and instruct initiates to find the entrance as the first exercise of their examination."

The passage opened up to a small room, which, unlike the rest of the castle, was in pristine condition. It was empty but for a single ornate metallic archway. Delicate flowing patterns danced up its curved surface, similar to the ones on their new clothing, culminating in a white gem at the top. Apparently, the fighting had never reached this hidden room.

"I wonder why Delveton didn't just open this." Kara pointed to the metallic portal. Sam was surprised she could locate it, given her lack of sight. "He could have let the other members of his cult come right in and take what they wanted."

"The Tercast fundamentals book mentioned they had moved the portal," Kula replied, "so he may not have known where it was."

"Couldn't he have felt for it in the walls, like you did, Elleran?" Sam asked.

"He likely would have had significant difficulty connecting to the walls of Tercast, given his intentions."

"It's enchanted against . . . what? People who want to harm those inside?"

"Not exactly. It is more of an inherent property of Sorcery, which I will not take the time to explain at the moment."

More mysteries. Sam scowled. Why wasn't there ever enough time to explore them?

Elleran reached out to touch the metallic surface of the archway, then closed her eyes. "This is indeed the operative end of a portal, but there is no way for me to know where it leads. I do not know what awaits us on the other side, or whether it even points to our desired destination. Be prepared for anything."

The group readied their weapons.

"Kara and Kula, you will join me at the front. Ya'ir and Scheln, stay with Rose at the center. Zel and Sam will bring up the rear."

They got into position. Anticipation thumped through Sam's veins. This was a risky, but necessary, operation. Tovas and Fita wouldn't hesitate to do the same for any of them if they had been captured. But what if they faced Jeanette? What would Kara do?

The stone wall behind the portal transformed into a new dark interior as the gemstone atop the metal glowed a brilliant white. Air rushed past them from the opening, and the temperature dropped considerably. Elleran advanced her point of light into the opening, then followed it inside, revealing black stone inside. Kara and Kula accompanied her, weapons ready.

"Something is wrong," Elleran said. "I cannot sense or Vitalize *anything* here."

The sound of rubble shifting behind them made the group jump.

"Elleran!" Zel called out in a worried whisper as she and Sam turned about, searching. His tense heartbeat thumped in his ears, but he didn't sense any absence—nothing to suggest a person was there. It could be some kind of surveillance bot, though.

Elleran flew through the portal, squeezing past Rose, who had been about to enter. Zel, to Sam's left, hefted a throwing knife at the ready. Elleran moved past them, toward the narrow passageway they had entered through.

She relaxed. "It is nothing, just a—"

Boom.

Rose dove through the portal to join Kara and Kula, rubble falling in her wake. Rock and dust crashed through the opening.

Then silence. Nothing but solid Tercast stone showed through the metal frame. Sam stared at it with horror. The gemstone at the archway's peak still glowed.

They were cut off.

Rose coughed, attempting to subdue her rising panic at the darkness around her. She connected to her muscles to enhance the pull of sliding filaments within. Though difficult, she pushed the rubble from her head, which she had thankfully had the sense to enchant against trauma ahead of time, and glanced back the way she had come. The circular portal, which appeared to have been made of stone on this side, had an enormous chunk missing, probably damaged by the falling debris. Nothing but broken black stone lay within the ring. The portal was inoperative.

They were stranded.

Kula yelled, letting windswept arrows fly across the room toward an enemy Rose couldn't see. A sword clashed with one of them, sending sparks flying.

Rose opened her Sorcery, inspecting the others. Her connections to Sam, Ya'ir, Zel, Scheln and Elleran were much fainter, but they seemed safe. Worried, but safe. Kara had suffered light head trauma, similar to Rose. She was dazed, likely hit by an unexpected massive force.

Sparks continued to fly from Kula's direction as she engaged a large man. Rose frantically, and painfully, pushed her arms and legs free of the debris, then stitched the damaged tissue together with Sorcery. Elleran's presence entered her as well, taking care of some of her wounds. She enchanted her muscles and threw a few large stones to the side, creating a point of light in the air as she desperately looked for her sword.

Another boom sounded behind her, followed by an electric blast and brief flash of light that illuminated the interior. Kara had reengaged with the enemy, wielding her rifle.

A glint of metal shone from beneath a sizable chunk of stone, lit by Rose's point light. Another woman entered the room and engaged Kula. A leg of Kara's suit smashed into the man she had blasted with the rifle, knocking him straight through a stone wall.

Rose turned over the large piece of rubble, and found an unexpected sight.

The Maul of Ruin. The weapon wielded by—

No, stop. It was just a tool. A tool of destruction. A tool that could create an alternative exit.

She eyed the stone wall as a third and fourth Sorcerer entered the room. One of them fired arrows, which exploded in bursts of sonic booms, knocking Kara and Kula back.

The rescue mission was a failure. They needed to escape before they became prisoners as well.

Rose wrapped her fingers around the hilt of the massive weapon, feeling its purpose flow through her. Strength. Mass. Destruction. A faint, familiar presence permeated the object. She hefted it up, and found her target: a section of the wall that was already damaged by the previous blow. The maul moved with remarkable ease, and she swung with all her strength. Sparks flew with the colossal impact. An expanding cloud of rubble spread into the room, drowning out the sounds of combat with painful ringing. Freezing, tempestuous winds soared through the destroyed wall, kicking up dust and debris. She could see nothing but pitch darkness outside the opening, but the wind told her she had been lucky enough to hit an exterior wall.

Something exploded near her left ear, throwing her body sideways into rubble. A bearded man with a bow advanced toward her, readying another arrow. A woman screamed. After crushing the arm of her attacker from the floor, Kara dashed up. The archer turned but was too slow. Kara swung a leg into his side, sending him flying back with a grunt. She grabbed Kula, who was evading a swordsman, and let the steel glance harmlessly against her armored shoulder. They flew toward Rose, and she gripped Kara's leg as she passed. Icy pitch black consumed them as they raced out, dry winds screeching past. Kara continued directly away from the structure they'd been in—a remarkable palace—and picked up speed.

Dull blasts nearby marked a few attempted strikes from the archer behind them. His accuracy seemed to fail against the tempest.

"Can you see anything?" Kara yelled. "I can't tell where I'm going!"

"Turn on your lights!" Kula said.

Rose attempted to expand her perception through Sorcery, but just as Elleran had observed, she too could feel nothing. The entire landscape was as dark to her Sorcery as it was to her eyes. Beyond her body, she could only get faint glimpses of the passing air. Spotlights from Kara's suit lit up the rocky ground below. They passed a grove of zigzagging trees, all apparently dead.

Elleran's presence warmed her body against the bitter, icy winds—for which she was grateful. A connection to Kula told her that Elleran was warming her body as well. It would be wise for the three of them to conserve as much wakefulness as possible.

"There!" Kula said. "Let me go."

Kara complied, and Kula's blond hair rippled through the wind as she fell. Rose dropped too, fighting the hair whipping across her face as Kula led them into the midst of a cluster of large boulders. Rose felt Kara's presence, and she settled down nearby, likely locating them through her connection. At least the boulders provided some amount of shelter from the dry storm.

"What happened?" Rose yelled over the oppressive winds.

"Bow guy shot an explosive at us," Kara said, leaning against a boulder. "That first one was ridiculous. Damn, he was fast."

"We should go back," Kula said. "Get Tovas and Fita."

Rose shook her head. "I don't think that's a good idea. They already caught us off guard, and we're separated from everyone else. They're too powerful, and we don't even know how many there are."

"What do we do, then?" Kula asked.

Rose considered for a moment, mind a blur with courses of action. "Maybe we should find shelter, see if we can—"

"I'm getting a signal!" Kara said.

"What?" Kula yelled, holding a hand to her ear.

"A signal." She pointed off into the darkness. "An old universal distress signal, according to my Nit."

"A trick, most likely."

Kara shrugged. "Possibly, but it isn't the direction we came. It might not be them. Maybe someone else is here."

Rose considered their options, and none seemed particularly wonderful. They could risk everything attempting to save Fita and Tovas, or find some crag to hide in to perform reconnaissance and try striking from a position of greater intelligence, or follow a random signal, which could be anything.

"I think as long as we're cautious, it could be worth looking into," Rose said. "We need all the help we can get."

"It's quite a way out," Kara admitted. "This will be a long, windy ride."

Chapter 17
Verilar District

"Deia is deceit! Deia is deceit!"

Jeanette approached the group of chanting protesters, pulling her hood tight. It was highly unlikely anyone would recognize her as the angel of the Deia, but it was wise to be safe. She tried to peek through the glowing signs they held, which contained anti-Deia or anti-religious propaganda.

They stood in the crisp, sunny afternoon in front of the Scelebriar conference center, which sat amid several sleek, rounded, high-rise buildings in the center of Verilar district, a section of the town of Tisa. The protesters engaged beneath the collection of impressive religious statues and architecture. Across the wide path stood the group of counterprotesters, bearing colorful, glowing signs that praised the Deia's divinity, and told of prophecies concerning her protection from the days of destruction and reckoning. Jeanette spotted a bald head among their number.

Two large, armored enforcers kept each side of the protesters separated. One man from the pro-Deia side yelled and tossed something toward the crowd near Jeanette as she worked her way around them. One enforcer moved to intercept the projectile, which impacted with a light thud, while the other rushed to the man's position and grabbed him before he could escape into the crowd. As he yelled and squirmed, his wrists were bound by a small metallic device that took him off the ground. It drove him through the air, away from the protest, while he shouted curses at the anti-religious.

Having reached the edge of the crowd, Jeanette crossed the wide path, taking in the impressive architecture once more. An elaborate array of stone sculptures and pillars lined the entryway to the massive building.

Her target emerged from the pro-Deia crowd, wearing a simple gray tunic with red trim, grinning fondly as he approached.

"So wonderful to see you, Jey," he said.

She smiled back. "It's good to see you too, Quade."

"How are things going back home?"

"Making progress. We have a few promising candidates. How are things progressing here?"

Quade glanced back at the crowd, now engaged in unified chants of "Deia is all".

"Very well," he said. "As you can see, we've been causing quite the uproar. I hear that news of the prophecy and the Deia has caught on in other parts of the Sovereignty."

"Tess has her targets involved," Jeanette said, eyeing the anti-religious protesters across the path. "She says she's making progress, but it might take a while for them to organize effectively."

Quade turned and motioned for her to walk with him. "I've got four more for you to take back to Uvlun. How did the last batch turn out?"

Jeanette shrugged, advancing to walk alongside him. "I'm still working with them. We easily swayed many, so they have little potential."

"That's unfortunate," he said, scrunching his forehead. "I thought they would have been more promising."

"That's okay, they still have some utility. It's hard to tell beforehand how firm they are in their principles. We are seeing a lot of promise with two of my sister's friends I took back with me from Earth, though."

"Earth?"

"Yeah, it's the class four where I'm from."

He approached the door to one of the nearby high-rise buildings, which whooshed open for them. She entered a cool, well-decorated interior with shiny stone walls and pillars. The slowly shifting tile floor gave off a soft orange glow, arranged in a circular pattern around the lobby center. A few individuals stood around the information desk, chatting casually. Others moved about, entering lifts or moving to different areas of the office building.

"The structure has finally been yielded to us by the Scelebriars as part of the official separation," Quade said. "We own it now."

Jeanette followed him to an unassuming door, which led down a staircase. It surprised her to see stairs at all in the Sovereignty.

"These rooms can't be accessed with the lift," Quade said as he began his descent. "They're ... you know ... sacred." He chuckled.

Their steps echoed until they reached the wide corridor at the bottom. Spiritual paintings and a specular stone floor were lit by warm light from flowery golden lamps overhead. They passed doors with intricately carved frames, and stopped in front of one that was rather plain, which Quade held open for her.

She entered the room and dropped her hood, feeling the cold air of a small mechanical room of sorts. A large, shielded metal device against the far wall hummed softly, reflecting the cool, harsh light from overhead. Lorin turned at her entrance, his pale face brightening as he regarded her. He had been speaking with a blue-skinned man in a Sovereignty uniform, who Jeanette didn't recognize.

"Maven Jey," Lorin said, "It's wonderful to see you."

Jeanette approached the pair. "And you."

"I need to return to the protest," Quade said to her. "I will see you again soon, I'm sure."

"Of course. Take care, Quade."

He nodded, then shut the door.

"This is Golin," Lorin said, motioning to the man next to him. "He's with us. Delveton worked with him on the Tercast incursion."

"Pleasure to meet you." Jeanette extended her hand, which he shook gently. "Are you the one coordinating our work in the Force?"

"Working tangentially, at the moment. The Sovereign herself removed me from my position and placed me under investigation after the events at Tercast."

"That's unfortunate."

"Yes, but it was to be expected. I am confident they will find me blameless, but I still have yet to regain my office."

"What do you need from me?" she asked.

"Your biometrics." He pulled a pen-like device from his pocket, which emitted a soft purple color from a point at the tip. He placed it in front of her face. "With the Sovereignty at large taking greater interest in the Scelebriar situation, we need to ensure no one connects you to the event last week."

"And this will stop them?"

"Nothing is certain, since we don't have control of the system, but this should work."

"We'll make you no more interesting to the Sovereignty's systems than any other Jane walking around Alvior," Lorin added.

"Hold out your hands, please."

Jeanette followed Golin's instructions, and he ran the device along her hands and the rest of her figure. He was scanning her leg when the door burst open.

"Maven Jey!" a pale man with dark hair called out.

"Yes?"

"I was sent to inform you that your sister and two others entered Evamune Palace from the portal at Tercast, then the portal was destroyed. They fled the castle and are trapped on Uvlun."

Kara, ever the reckless one.

"Thank you. I will go to Tercast as soon as I am finished here."

If any of them remained at the castle, she would find them. She guessed any left on this side would have fled by the time she arrived, but it was worth a check, anyway.

He nodded, and returned to the doorway, then stopped. "Oh, I also heard that the Deia is very pleased with the information you retrieved from the pod on Earth. Particularly something about acheron technology." He closed the door behind him.

The Deia's pleasure at her actions filled Jeanette with warm elation.

"Your sister?" Golin asked.

"Yes, with the group from Tercast. She was on the team that Delveton put together to attack the castle."

"Oh yes, he mentioned that," Golin said, moving the device to her other leg. "It profoundly surprised him to see her at first. She was blind before she left Earth, as I recall?"

Jeanette laughed. "Yeah. That's Kara, though, doesn't let anything stand in her way. It appears she and her friends didn't waste any time going after the two I captured."

Golin straightened up and pocketed the device. "Done. This is all I need."

"Thank you. I'll be glad to stay clear of the Sovereignty's eyes."

"Are you going back so soon?" Lorin asked. "I was hoping you could stay for the fireside event tonight."

"I would, but I need to get to Tercast and see if the others are there with the artifacts. There is so much to do."

"Understood. Quade told you about the next group of potential initiates right? We have a few for you to take back."

"He did. I'll pick them up before I head back."

"Take care, Jey!"

"You too, Lorin."

She ascended the stairs again to the main lobby, pulling her hood up. The group at the desk was still chatting, a few more having joined their number since she arrived. A woman in a formal black dress strode past with a handbag around her shoulder toward the lifts.

Jeanette re-emerged into the bright afternoon sunlight of Alvior, noticing two half moons in the blue sky. One bright orange and the smaller one a pale yellow. She advanced toward the protest, enjoying the sight of both sides pitted against each other across the wide path, underneath statues of devotion, so unaware of the Deia's true purposes.

"They just want to control you!" one protester yelled out over the crowd.

The rival in her mind twitched at those words, hardly perceptible. It was probably just a subconscious remnant of her imagined conversations with Amy. The counterprotesters began organizing a new chant, which quickly grew in volume until it drowned out the rest of the noise.

"Deia is unity! Deia is unity!"

Jeanette grinned as she continued her stroll in the warm sunlight toward the area where she had hidden her vehicle.

"The Deia is unity," she whispered.

Chapter 18

The Sovereign

Sam paced back and forth amid the clutter of the passenger bay, his mind racing through possibilities. Elleran had moved the vehicle up into the atmosphere out of caution, since they had clearly alerted the enemy to their presence at Tercast. There was no way to repair the portal from their end, anyway.

"Our connection to them gets stronger the closer we are, right? Can't we just search for the planet that way? Keep jumping until we find it?"

Elleran shook her head from her seated position on one of the makeshift bunks. "As I've already said, I don't have full control of this vessel, only Kara did. Even if I could take control, it is damaged, low on power, and we have limited supplies. We would likely only be able to make a few jumps, which may leave us stranded."

Her logic was sound. He *knew* it was. And yet he still wanted to throw all the logic away and try. They couldn't just leave Kara, Rose, and Kula on that planet, besides Tovas and Fita.

"We have to do *something*."

Ya'ir rose. "We weren't ready! We shouldn't have tried."

"We were about as prepared as we could have been," Elleran said calmly, "but the failure is my responsibility. I should have foreseen the possibility of the portal being destroyed or deactivated. We were fortunate no one was crossing over when the connection was severed."

That was a horrific thought: someone suddenly being galaxies separated from a limb because a portal failed as they were crossing. Sam wondered how often such a thing occurred. Did the Sovereignty have protective measures on their acherons to prevent that from happening?

"We know they are healthy, for the moment," Elleran continued. "Based on the activity of their physiology, I suspect they have escaped the structure and are in hiding."

She took a deep breath and sighed.

"I believe the most sensible course of action now is to request the aid of the Sovereignty government."

"But the Deia has people there!" Zel cried as she petted the ulinko in her lap. "The auras are off now. It is a bad omen of elestere. They will find us!"

Elleran raised an eyebrow in her direction, then turned to Sam, who subtly shook his head as if to say: *I don't know what she's talking about either. Don't worry about it.*

"It is a risk indeed," Elleran replied. "I am also unsure if or how the Sovereignty will react to my sudden reappearance, but we are left with few options if we want to help them."

"Is there no one else we can contact? Anyone you knew?" Ya'ir asked.

"I'm fairly certain any contacts I once had will be long gone by now."

Sam continued to pace, trembling at the thought of what they would do if another suited Sorcerer like Delveton showed up. Would Elleran be powerful enough to stop such a force?

Scheln floated into their midst, forcing Sam to stop his pacing. Lines of light appeared over his head, forming into scribbled words that quickly dissipated: *We go.*

Sam sighed. "I guess there really isn't much else we can do, is there?"

Elleran nodded as Scheln returned to his bed. "I will bring the ship around to the planet's acheron. It is in Hotrov, if I remember correctly."

"Hotrov?" Ya'ir said. "That's way out in Steria. There's an acheron in Tish, only a few minutes from Tercast by ascender."

"There are *two* acherons on Alvior?"

"Two? There are at least eight or nine."

Elleran's eyes widened. "Incredible. How does Rwenmar manage all of them? There must be *bi-mohs* now."

Zel cocked her head. "The acherons don't lead to Rwenmar, they go to travel hubs. I like the evelflips there. So heavenly. Like sorfdrops on Ulim."

The older woman smiled. "Travel hubs. Far more manageable." She rose from her seat. "Ya'ir, could you direct me to Tish? I am not familiar with that location."

He shrugged, rising to accompany her. "I can try."

They strode into the pilot's cabin, leaving Sam, Zel, and Scheln in the messy cargo bay.

Sam sat down, feeling defeated, and reawakened his connection to Kara. Her body was calm. Relaxed. In fact, he could feel a vague sense of boredom from her. That was a relief. He connected to Rose as well, who was likewise calm, though he sensed discomfort. Like Elleran had said, the three women seemed to be safe for the moment, but they were in hostile territory. Their safety could turn at any instant.

He wished they could speak to each other, the way Scheln and Tovas could. Why could they, but no one else? The pair had barely even started engaging with Sorcery on Tercast when it first manifested. Even with their abilities fully unlocked, the rest of the group could not achieve telepathic communication. It seemed to be reserved for the twins.

He turned to Scheln. "Can you feel Tovas at all anymore?"

Scheln lay motionless for several seconds while the craft accelerated, shifting the objects inside with inertia and causing Sam to stumble against a hose for support. He wondered at first if Scheln had heard him at all, and was about to repeat himself when Scheln suddenly blinked twice, his signal for yes. Then he blinked three times, his signal for no.

"Is that a 'sort of'?" Sam asked.

He blinked twice in quick succession.

"Well, I guess that's better than nothing. Is he okay?"

Scheln's face showed no emotion. He was challenging to communicate with when Tovas wasn't around to translate. He was more closed off from the rest of the world, again. Perhaps Sam could do more to work on communicating with him effectively. Finally, Scheln blinked three times, causing Sam's heart to sink.

"He's alive though, right?"

Scheln blinked twice.

"We'll do everything we can to get to him," Sam said, placing a hand on his shoulder. "And maybe Kara will beat us to him, knowing her."

The keglon trotted up to Sam and nuzzled his arm, clearly asking for attention. Zel had allowed them to wake and eat. Sam stroked its long, scaly snout. The animal was remarkably horse-like, with lizard skin instead of fur. Its flowing mane reflected rainbow light in a dazzling display.

"They're okay, but a little anxious," Zel said. "Like gillymungs in a yelish swamp."

"I didn't understand a word of that."

"Only an expression," she said absently. "Gillymungs are cute little arthropods from Olioneth. Their excrement glows a pulsing lightish bluish color like waves." She raised a hand. "I think the universe likes blue today. It could soothe. Upside down might do the trick too. Or nuumyun. Nuumyun is yummy."

Sam shook his head, struggling to follow the woman's bizarre train of thought.

After a few minutes of him stroking the creature's soft green scales, the vehicle slowed, causing the keglon to stumble. It quickly trotted back to Zel, who motioned for the animal to sit, and it settled next to the silvery wyvern.

Elleran and Ya'ir returned from the pilot's cabin.

"I've taken us into a forest just outside the city," Elleran said. "We should keep the ship and these artifacts hidden."

"What about the creatures?" Sam asked, gesturing to Zel and the animals.

"We should let them go. They are native to the planet, so they may be well enough here."

"But," Zelyra protested, getting to her feet, "keglons are native to Helenestia, not Oscertos! And caladrials are from Tolumofi!"

"They will be fine here, I'm sure," Elleran gently insisted. "We certainly should not take them with us."

They departed the vehicle into a forest bathed in warm evening air, lit by amber sunlight quickly fading under the horizon. Wide, twisting trees hung overhead, scattered with large diamond-shaped leaves of orange and red. They cast long shadows across a forest floor riddled with spindly brown bushes and tall yellow grass.

"I will stay with them. You go," Zel said.

"Zelyra," Ya'ir pleaded. "We can't. The Deia is probably still looking for stragglers from Tercast."

"Yes," Elleran said. "You should all stay with me until we can confirm it is safe. I know this is not ideal for the animals, but taking them with us will attract far too much attention."

After stalling for a considerable amount of time to give each of the animals a proper farewell, Zel gave the purple ulinko, a plaintive hug. Sam was sad to see the creature go as well. Tela, he remembered. That was the name Zel had given her. She had been their Tercast group mascot. The sight of the ulinko dashing across a field flashed in his mind, the fluffy white end of her tail whipping in the wind. He saw bubbly Niu and talkative Talanna getting into position on the field, preparing for a round of Elemorb. His vision blurred with tears at the memory. Though he had found their frequent chatter to be irritating at times, he missed it dearly now.

Kara and the others stuck on Uvlun *had* to be saved. Kara had pushed through ridiculous odds and rescued them at Tercast, so he could do no less.

After leaving the animals behind, they journeyed through the bright orange and red trees of the forest in relative silence. It had been late fall when they had departed Alvior before. So that would make it . . . spring? Summer? Probably summer, since Alvior years were shorter than Earth ones. Sam wondered what their latitude might be. Oscertos was supposedly a pretty large country. If they were closer to the horizon, there shouldn't be as much seasonal change anyway.

Just as enormous buildings peeked through the trees, Elleran turned to Scheln.

"I'm afraid we'll need to find some other way to transport you through the town. I'm glad Sorcery has allowed you the autonomy to move on your own, but you will draw far too much attention floating like that."

Scheln's thin, inert body turned to her, and Sam was surprised he hadn't thought of that. They had become so accustomed to Scheln floating about with their group that he hadn't even realized people would definitely find him alarming.

"You said you tried to cure him, right? During the unveiling?" Ya'ir asked Elleran.

She reached a hand out, and a boulder the size of a watermelon gently rose out of the ground in front of her, leaving a pit of dirt and organic debris in its wake.

"Yes," she said. The group watched in awe as the rock warmed to a glowing red. "I was wary to modify his neural biology, which would risk causing further irreparable damage." The rock glowed white as Elleran reached her hands around it and it re-formed into the shape of a chair. "Unfortunately, I am not an expert in brain physiology. If Sovereignty medical experts were unable to help him, I am highly doubtful I can do much better."

Some of the remaining volume of glowing lava formed into the rims and spokes of wheels, two large, and two small. Meanwhile, wet dirt from below the surface rose up and morphed into thin toroids, transforming into rubbery tires that slipped onto the ends of the rims.

"Rose said that his mind wouldn't respond to her attempts at treatment," Ya'ir said.

Several twigs, long since dead, split into long, thin splinters that weaved in and out of each other, forming a seat.

"Curious," Elleran mused. "I am unsure why that would be."

The seat moved onto the dull silvery surface of the rapidly cooling chair frame, and slipped onto the ends. Two footrests formed from the last bit of molten rock and attached near the front wheels, then the device gently settled onto the forest floor.

Sam glanced at the faces of his companions, who, like him, regarded the product with wide-eyed amazement.

"This should help," Elleran said. "Extremely rudimentary, but it should at least reduce interest in us."

"That," Zel said, "was amazing!"

Sam nodded emphatically, his mind a blur with countless questions. How did she heat the rock so quickly? How did she form it so precisely? How did she make the front wheels swivel like that?

"How the hell did you create a wheelchair out of a *rock*?" Sam exclaimed.

"And mud and sticks!" Zel added.

Scheln floated into his new seat.

"This is a relatively simple feat of Sorcery, and somewhat more difficult to perform within the oppressive Sources of the forest. Did the Tercast Masters not perform comparable acts of creation?"

"Nothing at all like *that*!" Sam said, pointing at the chair as if accusing it of the most heinous crime.

Scheln settled his feet into the plates designed for them, and Ya'ir offered to push Scheln's chair, which didn't look comfortable as it bumped against the roots. They soon emerged from the forest to the edge of the city, which rose to large buildings among tall, cultivated trees brimming with yellow leaves. Sam stared up at the imposing structures as they stepped past the end-of-road sign and onto the wide path between what appeared to be two residential buildings.

One lone silvery ascender zoomed into the distance, barely audible. The hard material he had stepped onto had that slightly springy feel to it, and Scheln's ride turned infinitely smoother. Only a handful of people were on the road too, walking in or out of the buildings. Thankfully, they didn't seem to regard their group with any undue attention.

As they progressed past the residential buildings, they reached an open parking lot of sorts, filled with sleek, angular ascenders. One was lifting off and pulling out overhead, while individuals clad in green clothing stepped out of another. Sam noted that most of the surrounding buildings were round, but a few were boxy. He wondered if they were older, and found his suspicions all but confirmed when he noticed a taller, sleeker building constructed atop a shorter, boxier one.

They stepped toward a nearby ascender, which opened for them, and dropped a slight ramp.

"So anyone can use these?" Sam asked. "You don't even need a Jit or a Nit?"

"Of course," Ya'ir said as he wheeled Scheln into the vehicle. "How would people get around otherwise if they lost their Jit?"

The rest of them, dirty white robes and all, followed into the clean, well-lit interior and settled down into the cozy bench seats that faced each other. Even with Scheln blocking two seats with his wheelchair, there was room for the other four to sit comfortably.

"City acheron, please," Ya'ir instructed.

"The Sovereignty has long held to the principle of universal access to transportation as a great equalizer," Elleran said as the vehicle smoothly lifted off.

"Equalizer?" Sam asked.

"Indeed. The inability to travel tends to hurt the people that need it most. I am glad to see the Sovereignty still holds to that principle."

They crested the tops of most of the buildings and weaved

among other ascenders which bustled about the city like a hive of bees.

"You thought they might have gotten rid of it?" Ya'ir asked.

Elleran shrugged as she scrutinized their surroundings out the large windows. "It is always a possibility. The benefits of egalitarian societies such as the Sovereignty should never be taken for granted. There will always be those who aim to see such social structures fall."

Sam's thoughts returned to Earth as he stared out at the sprawling urban landscape coated with yellow and orange trees, wishing he could see more green.

They landed amid a jumble of activity, reminding Sam of his and Kara's first trip to the Sovereignty. He quickly banished the thought, unsure if he could stand the heartache caused by her current absence. Elleran led them into the nearby building, and Ya'ir continued to drive Scheln's wheelchair among the sprawling crowd.

A blue-skinned mother and father with seven young children between them crossed their path. The children walked hand in hand, and one of the younger girls with a swaying blonde ponytail skipped along with her siblings.

The tantalizing scent of nuumyun, which Sam had experienced once before, caught his nose. Kara had said the snack was one of the most delicious things she had ever tasted, and he had never gotten to try a bite. Perhaps another time.

Soon enough, the enormous semi-circular acheron came into view, with crowds entering on the right and departing on the left.

"That is astounding," Elleran said, just loud enough for Sam to hear over the crowd. "I have never seen one so enormous. It must require a tremendous amount of energy."

Sam stared up at the massive device as they approached. He still didn't know how they worked. Maybe Elleran did? He should ask her if he ever got the chance to bombard her with the mountain of endless questions bursting from his mind.

They passed through into the space station, and Sam found himself stunned once again by the cylindrical surroundings.

Thousands of people walked around the interior, among various trees and shops, moving in and out of acherons. The view of a dull orange planet drifted in and out of the foggy windows, among the stars, showcasing the station's steady rotation, which provided a sense of gravity.

A bulky armored suit advanced toward them, causing Sam's heart to leap in his chest.

"Quickly," Elleran said, hastening her pace.

Sam and the others complied, until the armored individual sped out ahead of them and stopped. Elleran held her hand out in a halting motion, and a thick sense of foreboding fell upon them. Sam looked around to see two others flying toward them. The crowd began to scatter. A few stopped to observe the scene.

This was bad. *Really* bad.

"Elleran Laneum?" said a man's voice from the suit ahead.

She didn't answer. Her robes shifted with a nonexistent light breeze. The surrounding air tingled with tension.

"The Sovereign has instructed me to deliver this exact message: 'Respectfully, and urgently, I request that you report to the Razleh One travel hub's law enforcement station as an honored guest.'"

That was unexpected.

"They must come with me," Elleran said, gesturing to Sam and the others.

"Of course," the enforcer said.

Elleran's stance eased, and the tension in the air evaporated. She nodded, motioning for the rest of them to follow. Sam, in contrast, found his anxiety rising.

He shifted closer to Zel, who was characteristically aloof, glancing up across the station. "Did she trick us?" he murmured under his breath. "Has she been with the Deia this whole time? Did we just walk into a trap?"

Zel's attention returned to the situation at hand, then shrugged and glanced at the additional suits who arrived to box them in, preventing an escape. Onlookers gaped as they passed. Sam opened his Sorcery and felt his body, the mechanical floor beneath him, and his companions. Elleran was indeed calm. Her presence emitted no sense of fear, at least as far as he could tell. It seemed her connection to them offered her a clear view of everything, but the connection back to her was limited. She could be hiding things. Beyond several dozen feet of steel, pipes, wires, and other constructs, there was nothing but the vacuum of space.

Fighting their way out was highly unlikely to end well, so he decided that approaching her directly was as good a strategy as any in this situation, and jogged up next to her.

"What's going on?" he said in a harsh whisper.

"If the Sovereign is truly requesting this personally, I will comply."

"You trust them? You don't even know them! You've been stuck in a can for several lifetimes!"

She turned to him with a sober look. "If the Sovereign of Rwenmar is not worthy of my trust, the situation is more dire than you likely have the ability to comprehend."

Sam's eyes widened, and he distanced himself again, falling in next to Ya'ir and Scheln.

"What's going on?" Ya'ir whispered to him.

Sam shook his head. "I don't know, but I don't like it."

A door to a nearby building whisked open, revealing a break room of sorts. Padded chairs of various muted colors stood around several round metallic tables. Enforcers with their helmets off stared at the incoming group with fascination and interest. Their guide led them to another door at the side of the room, which slid open as they approached. This time the lead enforcer moved to the side, framing the rounded opening as Elleran led them through.

Inside, a young woman with warm beige skin and dark hair smiled at them as they entered. She wore a modest ombre dress that faded from dark at the top to sky blue at her knees, smiling at them as they entered. The woman stood between two tall, sleek, form-fitting suits similar to Kara's, though these had additional, unfamiliar engravings on the front of the breastplates next to the Sovereignty emblem. As Elleran stopped near the center of the smaller, otherwise empty room, Ya'ir gasped and dropped to a knee. Zel yelped next to him and dropped to a knee as well.

Sam glanced at them as the door closed with a light whisk. Why were they bowing? *She couldn't possibly be—*

"Sovereign Aiyla!" Zelyra said to the floor.

Sam's jaw dropped.

"Please stand," the woman said. "I appreciate your respect, but demonstrations of obeisance are most unnecessary." She approached Elleran, her guards following close beside her. "As for you." Her eyes became tearful, almost pleading "I cannot begin to express how pleased I am to see you."

She extended a hand, and Elleran took it tentatively.

"You know of me?" Elleran said.

"I gathered everything I could find about you within the past several minutes, after many high-priority detection alarms triggered with your name and face attached to them."

She tenderly placed her other hand on the back of the older woman's grip.

"Elleran Laneum, Zenith Sorcerer, Vivezan."

Sam gasped. "You know about Sorcery?"

Aiyla regarded Sam with a friendly smile. "Yes, Samuel. Select Sovereignty personnel have known of the existence of Sorcery since its founding."

He reeled at this new information. The Sovereignty *knew*. That meant they were knowingly keeping this knowledge from their own citizens. Why? To maintain power and authority? Prevent someone from becoming powerful enough to overthrow them?

The Sovereign sighed, turning back to Elleran with a frown. "Sorcery is actually what I wish to discuss. Oblivion is launching attacks against us."

Ya'ir and Zel both gasped at that. Scheln rose from his seat, prompting the suits to raise their arms defensively.

Aiyla reached out and pushed their arms down.

"Oblivion?" Elleran said.

Aiyla raised an eyebrow and let out a low whistle. "You truly have been living under a rock for generations, haven't you?"

"Pond, apparently."

"I'm sorry?"

"Nothing. Please continue."

"We believe Oblivion is likely a man who was once a close colleague of yours."

Elleran flinched. "Virahmgal is *alive*?"

"We think it's him. But we don't know for sure."

"If he has survived this long, he has surely surpassed my capabilities. I do not know what I can do."

"We have devised some ways to slow him down, at least."

"His abilities must have advanced to *astounding* levels."

"Don't undervalue your own abilities, Vivezan. I've read all about you. And we have someone else who may help."

"Who?" Elleran asked.

Aiyla smirked. "Another old colleague of yours who has decided aging isn't for him."

Chapter 19
Drones

Kara yawned, drowsy from hours of endless flying. Worse, she couldn't see anything, leaving her clueless and bored. While she liked returning to a state of blindness at times, she missed the ability to turn on sight when it was useful. Even her former faint sense of light and dark would be better than nothing at all.

She had tried to open her Sorcery again to feel her surroundings, or to feel Sam again, but the feelings wouldn't come. It was probably for the best. She didn't want to accidentally move something or change something and end up falling asleep. They were getting close to their destination.

From what Rose and Kula had described, what they could see of the landscape below was barren and lifeless. Nothing but rocks, dead trees, and air so dry it irritated their throats and eyes. The suit automatically tracked her elevation, moving her up and down according to the landscape below.

Her idle mind turned to Jeanette, still unable to comprehend her sister's actions back at the house. It was so utterly opposite to her character. Jeanette was there, at first, and then suddenly she wasn't.

What had triggered it? The mention of Delveton's death? The man who kidnapped her? The man who had murdered *hundreds* of people at Tercast? Tears formed in her eyes at the sudden memory of Olik lying on the ground of the courtyard, the picture of his family nestled into his neck near his scorched skin.

Welin Em Onii, she thought. He had honored his life and duty with love. She would never forget that.

"Kara!" Kula exclaimed over the oppressive gales.

Her heart jolted into action. "What? What is it?"

"There's a building! One that's intact."

"Put us down," Rose said.

"But we're getting close to the signal."

"Please, let's take a look."

Kara huffed, "Okay, okay."

They descended gracefully, and although it was not as helpful as sight, her suit's sensors did communicate some information about her surroundings to her Nit, so she had a vague sense of where objects were around her.

"Anything interesting?" Kara asked.

"A single giant dome structure," Rose said as she took Kara's hand. "Over here."

They walked around, circling the structure for what felt like ages.

"Is there at least any daylight yet?"

"No," Rose replied. "It's pitch black."

"There is no entrance," Kula said, bringing their attention back to the structure.

A sudden crack of thunder shook the air.

When it dissipated, Kara sighed. "I'll make an entrance. Stand back."

"No!" Rose said. "What if there are people in there? We can't just go smashing through walls."

"Can't you both just feel it out with Sorcery?" Kara asked.

There was a brief pause.

"I don't know why, but I can't," Rose said. "It's the same as the castle. I can't touch anything outside our bodies with Sorcery, except maybe a bit of the nearby air."

"I cannot f—"

An immensely loud, obnoxious buzzing echoed overhead, drowning out the relentless winds and Kula's statement. Thankfully, Kara's suit quickly adjusted and muffled the sound, but being effectively deaf to her surroundings left Kara disoriented. The buzzing pulsed in and out endlessly. A hand tapped Kara's suit, then pushed her head upward. It was above them, and Rose and Kula probably wanted her to do something about it.

She took off from the ground as another rumble of thunder briefly pierced the incessant buzzing, which grew slightly louder. It was reminiscent of perhaps the most annoying alarm clock she had ever heard. The sensors of her suit gave her Nit some clues as to where the thing was, but as she approached, it moved away, continuing its ceaseless blaring.

"Oh my god, shut up!" she yelled into the void.

Getting a rough fix on the object's location based on the sounds and her Nit, she shot forward and collided with something hard. The rigidity of her suit prevented her from discerning its exact size, but it careened off, continuing its barrage of maddening noise.

Kara extended her arm, activating the cannon. Could she tell the Nit to aim at it, even though she couldn't actually give it a visual target? She'd never tried that before. *Target source of the noise,* she thought toward her Nit. It gave her a subtle acknowledgment and her arm locked into position, so it seemed to work. She squeezed her palm, and a spray of projectiles rang out.

The obnoxious noises stopped. Kara's helmet adjusted, bringing the sounds of rushing winds back into focus. She had just began her descent when an earsplitting crack of thunder broke through the winds. She felt a slight temperature increase, which quickly faded back to normal.

It took her a little while to get her bearings, but the Nit helped her locate the structure, and she strode toward it.

"Kara!" Kula's yell broke through the gales. "Are you okay?"

"Yes, I'm fine. Why?"

"You were just struck by lightning!"

"I was? Neat."

There was no reply. An unfortunate side effect of blindness was the inability to see others' reactions. Even though she still struggled to understand many expressions, she'd had plenty of opportunity aboard the ship to start grasping annoyance. Kula was probably rolling her eyes or shaking her head.

A deafening low note pierced the sky above from several feet away.

"What was that?" Rose asked as Kara turned toward the noise. "Kara, can you shine your—yes like—"

"Move!" Kula yelled.

Something ran into Kara. Hard. It knocked her to the ground, and the suit automatically rolled and righted itself. She turned toward the source of the impact and sped toward it, activating her left arm cannon.

Distance fighting was so *annoying* without sight.

A projectile jolted her backwards, and she heard giant wheel-like mechanical noises. Some sort of tank? Another projectile jolted her. Whatever it was, it couldn't do much damage to the Ilkuth, thankfully, but she had no idea how to target the thing. So she aimed in a rough direction of where the mechanical sounds were coming from and squeezed her palm, sending out a burst of gunfire.

The mechanical sounds seemed unchanged.

Ugh. How do I target this thing? she asked her Nit.

Send data, her Nit subtly responded.

I don't have data!

Two more projectiles knocked her back slightly.

Rose's presence entered her body, directing her forward. *Good idea. You point and I'll destroy.*

Following Rose's lead, Kara shot forward toward the noises, until they were right in front of her. Another projectile smashed into her, scraping and reverberating off of her head as it sunk her suit into the ground up to her shins.

Some kind of robot maybe? Molkinar had some bots that were the size of tanks.

She pressed up against the hard surface, and punched it. The blow knocked her suit back, so she gave herself a large amount of forward thrust and ripped into the metal. She kept going, metal and components screaming as she pushed through to the other side. When she landed, an enormous wheel rolled over her and smashed her into the ground. It refused to lift, so she increased her anti-gravity completely, moving it off her. Apparently her previous move hadn't disabled it, so she aimed a little higher, crashing through more metal and gears until she emerged on the other side.

Heavy crashes against solid ground, coupled with the subtle sense of Rose's relief, indicated she had been successful.

"Kara!" Rose shouted over the winds.

Kara advanced toward Rose's voice, landing on the ground and tentatively moving forward.

A hand grabbed hers and pulled her, so she followed it.

The sound profile changed abruptly as they entered a structure, quieting the endless gales. A door then slammed behind them, which muffled the sounds further.

"Ugh, finally," Kula said. "Those winds are turning me to madness!"

From the echoes, Kara could tell the room was fairly large.

"What is this place?" Rose asked. "And who are you?"

Kara's heart leapt. There was someone else?

"I am Renoq. And we call this place the hell dome."

Chapter 20

Savior

Tovas sat against the cold stone wall of his tiny cell, shivering in his nakedness. Jeanette had removed his loincloth hours ago—much to his dismay—as part of her torment. He couldn't even figure out what she was after. It seemed she had simply wanted to torture him for her own amusement. How incongruent it was to observe such a beautiful person act with such cruelty. Lacerations, burns, and bruises stung his body. They were healing quickly, though. Perhaps a lingering effect of his fading Sorcery. He attempted to ignore the relentless pain by focusing his thoughts elsewhere.

There had been a brief commotion and thundering crash, followed by the arrival of more prisoners sometime later.

After fading in and out of restless sleep, his mind drifted to his remaining family back on Alvior. He and Scheln had left their mother and younger brother and their small community in the country of Steria. They had lost so much on Louron. Though his body was in pain now, nothing could compare to the agony of that loss at the hands of Oblivion. The Destroyer of Worlds had taken so much from the bi-mohs who had lived there.

Now an entity threatened his new family from Tercast. He missed them. Knowing Kara, he suspected they may attempt some kind of rescue mission, though he hoped they wouldn't. The Deia's Sorcerers were far more powerful than their group had ever been.

Jeanette's betrayal surely hit Kara pretty hard, though she was immensely driven and grounded. She would undoubtedly press forward, looking for some way to rescue them and snap Jeanette out of her bizarre devotion to the Deia. At least Sam might restrain her. He tended to be more cautious. Analytical. He was rarely impulsive.

"Hey, anyone there?" a woman's voice echoed in the dungeon.

"Yes," a man replied.

"Shh," another woman hissed. "They will come if they hear us talking."

"What does it matter? We're all dead, anyway."

"They're just trying to—"

"Please," the second woman sobbed. "They will just torture us more. Please be quiet."

Tovas didn't doubt her words. The others apparently didn't either, for they let silence consume the dungeon.

He wished he could reach Scheln and talk to him—see how everyone was faring. Every once in a while he would get flashes of his brother's presence, so he knew he was all right, but their connection was so faint now. His Sorcery was all but gone. He could rarely open it up to even sense his body anymore.

The sound of footsteps from the staircase came into focus, causing Tovas's heart to leap into his throat. It appeared the talking may have indeed caught their captors' attention. Scuffling echoed from the other cells. He moved to stand, but the pain of his injuries kept him on the floor. Instead, he wrapped his arms around his legs, covering his nakedness. The steps continued until they reached the floor.

Clang. Metal striking metal reverberated off the walls. Then again.

"What's happening?" a man yelled.

Two more clangs happened in quick succession. Tovas slid toward the bars and peeked through them with interest.

A woman wearing a sleek dark jumpsuit and heavy boots tossed bits of clothing to those in the cells.

"Put these on," she whispered. "Quickly."

"Divine above, we're saved!" the woman's voice from earlier said.

Their rescuer continued to Tovas's cell. She wore a mask and hood, showing only her striking gray eyes and light brown skin. He noted her belt, which carried a twin dagger to the one in her hand, and an array of small vials containing red liquid.

Health potions.

He backed away as she struck the lock of his cell, and the pieces fell to the stone floor. A gray pair of pants flew in through the bars, hitting his side.

"Put this on," she said.

He obeyed, thanking the Divine for some clothing to cover him. Her voice and features were unfamiliar. Had Kara and the others found a way to contact someone on Uvlun? Someone who could help?

Tovas opened the cell door and joined the others, pushing through the pain of his injuries, and approaching those who were congregating around the woman. Fita's eyes met his, his muscular torso and arms bruised and battered, though it appeared he had fared somewhat better than Tovas. He wore a similar set of pants, but in brown. Tovas locked forearms with him and gave him a warm smile. Fita returned only his usual intense, stoic expression.

The dark-skinned prisoner with wavy golden-brown hair stood nearby, one of the women they had attempted to defend from Urok. A pale, chubby man who had been in the room joined them as well. The other woman, middle-aged with fair skin and black hair, was a fresh face he didn't recognize.

"My name is Belze," the hooded woman said. "I will get you out. Follow me."

Only the light taps of bare feet on stone accompanied them as they crept up the spiral staircase. Once at the top, Belze led them down the extravagant, warm halls set with elaborate paintings and golden decorations. As they approached a three-way intersection, voices in conversation echoed around the corner. One of them was hauntingly familiar. Their rescuer crept past, and the group followed her. Tovas caught a brief glimpse of Jeanette talking casually with a shorter woman and Urok, who wielded an enormous axe.

Soon enough, they found their way to the double staircase of a grand entrance hall. Two men stood guard, one wielding a spear, the other with a bow and quiver full of arrows. That would be a problem.

"Stay close." Belze said. "We cannot avoid detection here."

"Is there no other way out?" Fita asked. "How did you enter?"

"This is the only entrance. Again, stay close. We must be quick."

She took off down the steps, and the group raced after her. The archer noticed them first. He called out, but before he could draw his arrow back, a directional shockwave of air erupted in front of their rescuer, throwing the two guards to the side. Tovas's eyes widened.

Belze was a Sorcerer. A powerful one.

A wave of her hand sent the enormous front doors of the palace flying open, sending icy winds into the grand hall. The middle-aged woman running next to Tovas tripped. He slid, then raced back to help her up. A glance toward the doors revealed the archer, who had recovered, aiming directly at them. Tovas dove onto the cold hard stone, attempting to shield the woman's body from the inevitable blow.

Clang.

Tovas looked back toward their attacker and found Belze standing between them.

"Go!" she cried.

Tovas helped the woman up. She brushed dark hair out of her face as they raced out to join the others in the pitch black, while Belze engaged the guard. The one with the spear roared, leaping in to help his companion. Clashes of metal, grunts and cries ensued, but Tovas didn't look back.

The winds became more intense when they crossed the threshold onto rock, whipping his companion's long hair about. The group turned right to continue following the elaborate palace wall. Their rescuer flew out from the entrance behind them, then hovered in the air. The doors slammed shut. A stream of intense light shot from Belze's hand and welded the entrance closed. After racing past the group, she motioned for them to follow her into the oppressive, stormy darkness.

As they sped farther from the eerie exterior lights of the palace, Tovas's eyes became nearly useless. He panted with exertion, unable to see his own feet, much less anyone else. The woman next to him unexpectedly grasped his hand. They raced to follow the steps ahead among the intense, frigid winds.

As seconds of ceaseless running turned into minutes, Tovas's feet screamed in protest. He coughed through the dry air. Clearly, there was a life-supporting atmosphere, but everything else seemed remarkably dead, and dark. Nothing but cold stone met his aching feet.

They must be on Uvlun, he realized, where Sam had suspected that Jeanette had been taken. Master Azeloram had called it a "dismal underworld." now experiencing the harsh, icy winds and suffocating darkness himself, Tovas would call that an apt description.

A flash of lightning briefly illuminated the few running ahead, as well as a surrounding grove of thick, angular trees, devoid of leaves. Hopefully, Belze knew where she was going.

Tovas collided with something soft. A body. They fell to the rough rock surface together, causing him to lose his grip on the woman's hand.

"Ow," a man's voice said through heavy panting. "Sorry . . . had . . . to . . . stop."

"Are you okay?" A woman's voice. Likely the one he had been running with. A smooth hand moved across him in the darkness and found his shoulder.

"Yes, I'm—"

"We must continue." Belze's voice. "It is not safe here."

"Can't . . . do . . . it . . ." the man panted.

"Very well," she said.

The soft hand on Tovas's shoulder helped him up. Another flash of lightning revealed Belze having lifted the much larger man over her shoulder—a feat that would surely be far less possible for a non-Sorcerer.

"Follow closely," she said. "We are nearly there."

The middle-aged woman grasped Tovas's hand again, and they raced on to follow Belze with Fita and their other companion. Belze didn't appear to be slowed at all by her additional burden. A sharp pain in Tovas's sides accompanied his throbbing feet. His breathing turned ragged. A brief rest would be wonderful, but thoughts of the horrid place they'd left behind gave him renewed stamina. No amount of rest was worth risking a return to the Deia's control.

Soon enough, the people ahead slowed. He nearly ran into another body, but a firm hand planted into his chest, stopping him.

"In here," Belze said from a few feet ahead.

As they moved forward, the winds slowed, blocked by an unseen barrier. Their heavy breaths echoed against a reverberant interior. A cave?

"Wait here," she said. "I will be back soon."

Tovas let go of the woman's hand and collapsed to the floor. His entire body screamed against the sudden, extended bout of physical exertion. Cold hard rock froze his back as he lay down, but at least it was smooth.

"Are you all right, Tovas?" Fita's voice. He seemed less winded than the rest of them, which wasn't too surprising given his sharpened physique and consistent training regimen.

"I am okay," Tovas managed to say between ragged breaths.

"Th—thank you, Tovas," his running companion said. She heaved with him. "My name is Wilen. Thank you for helping me. In the castle."

"Of course. Belze is the one we should truly thank."

"Your gratitude is appreciated but unnecessary." Belze's smooth voice echoed along with a clattering of wood.

A beam of intense light pierced the darkness and ignited the wood. It burst into a healthy flame, illuminating their rough stone surroundings. Tovas had to shield his eyes for a moment to let them adjust.

"What was that?" Wilen panted.

Belze's eyes lit up in the dim firelight. "A small portal to our nearest star, allowing me to use its energy. It is a Vitalization technique I have been exploring based on acheron technology." She raised a finger. "The trick is to prevent air from entering while it is open."

Fita, who was the only one among them standing, eagerly approached the flame. Putting his frigid limbs near a fire sounded glorious, but Tovas couldn't conjure the strength to move yet. The larger man Belze had carried scuttled over to the flame, as well as Wilen. Allowing himself a few more seconds to catch his breath, Tovas braced himself, then pushed his aching body toward the fire to join the others in putting his icy fingers near the exquisite warmth.

"So, I'm Wilen, and we know Belze and Tovas." The woman gestured to the others. "What are your names?"

"Gemald," the pale, chubby man said.

The dark-skinned woman with golden-brown hair raised her head. "Lelanna."

"I am Fitale."

"You two seem to know each other," Belze said, her intense gray, feline eyes settling on Tovas and Fita. She pulled her hood down to reveal a long ponytail of brown hair streaked with gold, and the mask continued to cover her mouth.

"Yes," Tovas replied, glancing briefly at Fita. "We have been friends for some time now."

"You met at Tercast?" Belze asked.

Tovas raised an eyebrow. "Yes. How did you know?"

"I sense the slight radiance from your persons. Traces of Sorcery."

"It has faded," Fita said.

"Indeed. The mysterious enchantment of Tercast fades quickly after you depart from its walls."

Tovas's eyes widened in realization. "You were once a study!"

"Yes. Many years ago now."

"You were banished?"

She nodded solemnly. "There was a time when all the inhabitants of Uvlun were those banished from Tercast. Now the Deia has brought many more."

"Tercast?" Lelanna said. "The so-called castle of magic run by old folk? It's actually magical?"

"It is called Sorcery," Belze explained. "The castle grounds imbue a limited unsealing of the potential in select individuals. When you leave the castle, it fades within a few standard days at most."

"Ours lasted several weeks," Tovas added, "but yes, it has almost entirely faded now."

"What of your Sorcery?" Fita said, nodding toward Belze. "It does not seem to be bound to Tercast."

"Indeed." Her gaze, dancing in the flickering firelight, drifted off into the distance. "A wondrous man unsealed my Sorcery some time ago." Tears formed in her eyes. "He was recently murdered. Taken from me."

Lelanna placed a hand on Belze's arm.

"I loved him."

Sorrow welled in Tovas's gut at the sight of her pained face. She had clearly been through much. Likely at the hands of the Deia.

"Is it possible for us to achieve this unsealing?" Fita asked.

Belze snapped back from her distant musing, and regarded them with her sharp gaze, then wiped her eyes. "Yes. We should proceed immediately. The sooner your Sorcery is unveiled, the sooner your skills will develop into formidable abilities."

"You can grant us this power . . . this Sorcery?" Gemald asked.

"Yes, I can unseal your Sorcery. It requires only that you trust me."

Tovas inhaled sharply. He never thought such power could be granted so freely. So easily. It raised many questions. The line of morality in the caves of Tercast flashed in his mind. Sorcery was potential. Potential for good, yes, but also potential for great evil.

Fita stood and clenched his fist. "I accept. I am ready to grasp this power again."

Before Tovas could attempt to restrain his friend's eagerness, Belze replied. "Very well, Fitale. You shall be the first." She stood with grace. "Come."

Perhaps he was being too cautious. If she truly had this ability, they could scarcely pass it up. They may *need* Sorcery to survive their current situation.

Fita approached her, standing only a few inches taller than the woman. With her gaze locked on his, she held her hand out, and he took it.

"It will feel strange, as if I'm trying to steal something precious from you. But you must open your Source to me."

Fita nodded, his face as emotionless as ever. After a moment, his eyes widened, and Belze eyes crinkled as she smiled behind her mask. He pulled his hand back and grinned—a rare sight indeed. His palm opened, and a small flame flickered above it, dancing in the stifled breeze.

The others gasped, but Tovas beamed at the marvelous sight. Fita had regained his Sorcery.

Thunder cracked as Fita dropped his hand and let the flame dissipate. He regarded Belze with uncharacteristic adoration.

"Thank you, savior. I will ever be in your debt."

"You and Tovas will regain much of your former strength immediately, and it will only grow stronger with time and study." She turned to the group. "For the rest of you, the initial unsealing is frequently accompanied by haphazard connections and unconsciousness. Do not be alarmed, for this is normal."

Eager to unlock the power of Sorcery in themselves, Gemald, Lelanna, and Wilen each engaged with Belze in turn. Gemald collapsed a moment after his unsealing with a sudden blast of air. Lelanna likewise fell unconscious after unintentionally scattering the wood of their fire across the cave. Wilen relished in the newfound sensations and managed to avoid any unintentional Vitalizations, maintaining her consciousness.

"Tovas, you have been remarkably patient. It is time."

He nodded, pushing his aching body up and around the fire. Belze held out her hand, and he took it, gazing into her mysterious gray eyes. Her presence entered his perception almost immediately. He had the impression of the presence attempting to enter a precious space. A holy space.

Tovas hesitated. Could he trust this woman? He knew nothing about her. Still, the offer was clearly enticing. Arguably essential. This should, in theory, reopen his connections with Scheln and Rose. He could learn of the others and keep in contact.

But at what cost?

There was something deeply sacred about this phenomenon she wanted access to. He felt he should not simply let it go so easily. Whatever it was, it was special. Something to be highly protected. While no ill will emanated from her presence, it still felt *wrong*. He tried to reason through how others would react to this. Would Scheln accept it? Would Rose?

Would Sam?

Perhaps not. Sam was cautious, skeptical. He would wait. Give her time to demonstrate her trustworthiness. Tovas suspected that her ability and disposition to free them from prison wouldn't be enough for him. What was her true intention? Why rescue them?

He slid his hand back, and their connection dropped.

"Tovas," she said, her brow wrinkled with worry. "You haven't accepted me. I haven't unsealed your Sorcery yet."

"I will, later."

"You need your abilities now."

"I'll do what I can without them."

"We depend on each other," Fita said to him. "You said we should use this power to help others. That is what we must do."

Wilen nodded her agreement. Belze's eyes pierced into him with a remarkable intensity.

"I'm sorry," Tovas said, "but I won't. Not now."

"You will almost certainly die without it," Belze said.

"That would be their choice, not mine."

"The unforgiving landscape can easily be enough to take your life."

True. Still, sacred things were not to be trifled with on a whim. He needed to know more first.

Her keen gaze drilled into his soul for another second, perhaps questioning his motives. Finally, she sighed and pulled a vial from the belt around her waist. "At least drink one of these to heal your wounds."

"Thank you," he said, taking the bottle and opening the lid, which swung on a small hinge. He downed its contents and sighed in relief as the pain of his injuries faded almost immediately. The intense throbbing of his feet subsided. A section of skin on his arm quickly closed over a red wound, leaving the surface unblemished.

Belze held her arm out, and Tovas returned the vial, which she replaced on her belt. He then headed back to his previous position on the other side of the fire.

Fita reached his bare hand into the flames to adjust the logs. "So, what is our plan?"

Chapter 21

Perception

Jeanette brushed hair out of her face. Again. At her Sorcerous command, her hair pulled itself back into a ponytail. She selected a clump of strands and wrapped them around the others, forming a makeshift tie. Not perfect, but it would do.

After finding Tercast abandoned, she had returned to Uvlun with the new selections from Verilar district. Then the Deia had performed the most critical part in the recruitment process: unveiling their Sorcery. While, in theory, any of those bound to the Deia could do it, her hold was supposedly stronger when she performed the task directly, so she insisted on doing it herself when possible.

Jeanette turned her attention back to the cave, where Belze sat with the five targets around a fire, reminding Jeanette of her first journey to the cave, where she herself had become a Sorcerer. The event felt like it had occurred a lifetime ago.

"The Deia really likes that cave, eh?" Urok said.

"It's where she and Del first escaped to," Tess replied. "It's special."

"That was—"

Urok cut his reply short. Jeanette felt it too: a subtle urge to advance.

"Here we go," he said, striding forward.

Jeanette followed alongside Tess. Two other men joined them, their steps coming up behind. When the group got within a few dozen feet of the cave entrance, the fire suddenly died.

"Now, Wilen, reignite the fire." The Deia's voice echoed across the ragged stone walls. Jeanette grinned, picturing herself on the receiving end of that command.

Urok's feet left the ground, and the rest of them followed suit, floating inside to avoid detection.

"I . . . there's too much," Wilen replied. "I don't understand."

"You must hold the impression," Fita explained. "Imagination is—"

He stopped mid sentence, letting the whistle of winds against the cave opening fill the void.

"What is it, Fitale?" the Deia asked.

"I sense something odd."

Jeanette raised an eyebrow, her heart racing in anticipation.

"This'll be fun," Tess whispered.

"Someone else is here!" Fita cried.

The logs burst into flame, lighting up the small enclosure. Urok smashed into Fita, throwing him down. Tovas rushed to Lelanna as Tess hurtled toward them, cloak flapping behind her. She clashed with Belze, who rushed to defend them.

Wilen was backing farther into the cave, terror written across her pale face. Jeanette brought her hand up and pulled a steady stream of flame from the fire in their midst onto a ball of air she transmuted into solid magnesium. That should be flashy and terrifying.

The fireball shot forward at Wilen among clashing weapons. She screamed, and a shockwave of air made Jeanette's ears pop. The fireball careened off course and slammed harmlessly into jagged rock. It shattered to the cave floor, cascading into shards that cast odd shadows across her opponent's features.

Her reaction had successfully deflected the projectile. Promising indeed.

Wilen's eyes quickly glazed over, despite her panicked state. There it was. Fatigue. Jeanette rushed forward and caught her as she fell, then slung her over her shoulder.

The rest of the cave was chaos. Tovas took a kick to the chest from Tess, which sent him crumpling to the floor. Fita clashed with Urok, having somehow stolen a sword from one of the other men, whose names she couldn't remember. He roared as he hammered Urok with blow after well-executed blow, ending the flurry with an upward strike that sent the larger man flying.

Tess, who had been clashing with the Deia, dove toward Fita and flung a barrage of darts in his direction. He expertly dodged the first and parried another, but took the third in his shoulder, causing him to drop his blade with a yell.

He crouched into a spin and grabbed the sword with his other hand just in time to deflect a blow from Tess's dagger. She spun with the motion and swept his feet off the ground, which sent him teetering to the floor.

His body hovered in the air, and Jeanette smirked. He was holding himself up with Sorcery. Impressive.

Tess laughed as she slashed his body before he could move out of her reach. A roundhouse kick knocked the blade from Fita's grasp, but he fell back and rolled into an upright position, gripping his injured side.

He yelled a battle cry and crouched for another strike, before an enormous fist struck his face from the side and sent him sprawling across the cave floor. Urok dusted off his hands with smug self-satisfaction, while Tess picked up Fita's limp body, and flung it over her shoulder.

Urok grabbed Lelanna and Tovas, hauling them out into the relentless winds of Uvlun. One of their companions lifted the Deia, and the other grabbed the last unconscious man, a chubby fellow.

"Quick and easy," Tess said.

"The woman shows real promise," Urok said, nodding toward Wilen, Jeanette's charge.

"And Fita," Tess added, pointing to his body over her shoulder. "He's got some serious skills with a blade. And even without. He could beat Jey any day."

"Hey!" Jeanette put a hand on her hip as chuckles echoed across the cave.

Urok laughed heartily. "From what I hear, almost anyone could beat Jey in a sword fight."

"It's true." Tess giggled as she strode to the cave mouth. "She's really quite terrible, despite all my training."

"As a matter of fact, I *did* beat him, thank you very much!" Jeanette said, following them out.

"You know we're just messing with you," Tess said. "Everyone knows you're more of a lover than a fighter."

"Is she, though?" Urok glanced over her body. "I haven't gotten a taste of that yet."

Tess slapped him. "That's because she's with *me,* dunderbrains! And don't you forget it."

"You can't keep her all to yourself if she wants to try someone new," Urok said.

"She doesn't want to try anyone new. Right Jey?"

Oh, now Tess cares what she thinks? Jeanette was curious about what Tess would do if she said she was interested in others. The Deia wouldn't mind. She seemed to encourage promiscuity among her subjects.

"I don't know," Jeanette said. "Maybe one day."

Tess's jaw dropped. "Hey!"

Urok shrugged. "Maybe the three of us can enjoy ourselves together sometime?"

"In your dreams," Tess exclaimed, turning on her heel and stomping off into the darkness.

Urok chuckled. "Anytime, Jey. Anytime."

He gave her a wink, then strode forward, muscles flexing across his enormous back under that tight black top. Jeanette wondered what a night with Urok might be like. His large, firm chest pressed into her face . . ."

A hand shot out to stop Jeanette. It was the man carrying the Deia.

"Wait," he said. "You take this one. I'll take her."

"Um, okay."

Jeanette handed him the woman from her shoulder, and he dropped the Deia's apparently unconscious body into her arms. He headed off into the darkness, but an impression told her to remain behind. When the others had faded from the dim light of the cave fire, the Deia's breathtaking eyes snapped open, and her graceful figure floated upright from Jeanette's arms. She strode back into the cave, motioning for Jeanette to join her.

"I heard you found some useful information from the things I brought back from Earth," Jeanette said as she approached.

The Divine woman pulled her mask down and grinned. "Oh yes! Among them was a text on the portal science behind acheron engineering, which is heavily protected information. It has proven remarkably valuable. But there is something else I wish to discuss."

She strode past the fire, clasping her hands behind her back and staring into the flames with a pensive expression.

"I wish to speak to you about Tovas."

"Oh?"

"He did not accept my presence. His Sorcery remains mostly sealed."

Jeanette furrowed her brow. "Really?"

"Yes. I would spend more time to sway him, but the Sovereign is on to our efforts. I cannot spare the time." She sighed. "I sensed profound moral conviction from him, as evidenced by his actions earlier. He likely has significant potential."

"What would you have me do?" Jeanette asked.

"Break him. Prepare him to accept me."

"What about the others?"

She smiled, the slight wrinkles around her eyes hinting at her true age. "Continue your work with them. Quade will continue to bring more Scelebriar recruits, and we should have potentials arriving soon from Tenrazka as well."

Jeanette considered the Deia's request. "I'm not sure how to handle Tovas. He's a devout Lomerian. Tess would probably be better."

The flames danced in the woman's sharp eyes as she paced, thoughtful.

"I need Tess to remain focused on Tenrazka. And this will be an excellent opportunity for you to strengthen your abilities. Help him understand this truth: perception is our reality."

"What do you mean?"

"The brain is an imperfect prediction machine, Jeanette—an organ developed specifically for inference-driven activity. It tends to *loathe* uncertainty. This often comes with the side effect of ascribing supernatural sources to gaps in our understanding, as well as to internal subconscious processes."

Jeanette stared into the flames, pondering the Deia's words.

"As a devout Lomerian, Tovas undoubtedly believes the Divine will occasionally communicate with him, especially when faced with moral dilemmas and suffering. Use that to your advantage. Test the limits of his convictions and the flaws of his beliefs will naturally emerge."

The Deia stopped, turning to face Jeanette with that piercing gray-eyed gaze, the gaze of one who knew and saw all. She placed a soft hand on Jeanette's shoulder. The woman's grace and wisdom were breathtaking, unfathomable. In her eyes, Jeanette saw the glory of infinity, the embodiment of one who was truly as Divine as anyone could be.

"Give them all time to deconstruct their beliefs. Especially Tovas," she said. "In time, they will all see the value of this period of agony, as you have. They will embrace my refuge. My unity."

The roaring fire extinguished, plunging them into the oppressive, endless night of Uvlun.

"My sanctuary from the darkness."

Chapter 22

The Alqesi Oasis

"I hope she agrees," Sam said.

"About what?" Ya'ir asked.

"About giving us a new ship so we can get Kara and the others."

"Oh, right. Yes, hopefully."

Sam reflected on the incredible meeting with the Sovereign as they sat waiting in the comfortable enforcer break room. A few officers ate at a table nearby. Their impressive suits, sitting lifeless in the room's corner, looked very similar to the suit Elysia had worn back on Earth. Scheln sat in his wheelchair next to Sam and Ya'ir, who were on one side of a circular table. Zelyra sat cross-legged on the floor, absently fiddling with her clothing. Sovereign Aiyla had wanted to speak to Elleran alone after their introduction.

"I can't even fathom the amount of power she holds," Sam said.

Ya'ir shook his head. "I don't think anyone can."

"Why would the Sovereignty put *anyone* above the law? That's a recipe for disaster!"

"The Aldan chooses each Sovereign. It looks for lots of distinct qualities to select a good person."

"How many of them have become overwhelmed with their lust for power and started destroying people's lives to further their own agenda?"

Ya'ir raised an eyebrow. "None, as far as I know."

"As far as you know," Sam repeated. "That could be exactly what they're counting on. The government could silence anything they don't want you to hear, like the availability of Sorcery, for instance."

"Wow, you don't trust anyone, do you?"

"Hey, that's not true. I trust you. I trust Kara. I trust several people. I just definitely do not trust leaders who lie to manipulate groups into doing what they want."

Ya'ir shook his head again. "I think you're wrong about her. She seems like a lovely person."

"People who seem lovely could secretly be the most ruthless people of all."

"You really think—"

The door to the small meeting room opened, and Elleran emerged, followed by Sovereign Aiyla and her two guards.

Sam stood, a shock of fear spreading through his body. Had she heard him?

"Elleran and I have determined the probable location of your friends."

Exhilaration replaced his fear.

"However," she said, her expression betraying sincere concern, "I cannot grant your request for a vehicle at this time. We need every acheron-carrying vehicle at our disposal to evacuate Oblivion's next target, and Elleran informs me that your friends are not in obvious, immediate danger. They will need to wait, I'm afraid."

"I'm sorry, Sam," Elleran said. "Even the vehicle we have been using is being hastily repaired to save lives in danger."

"But what about after this evacuation?" Sam asked. "Will you help us rescue them then?"

Aiyla nodded. "Yes, as soon as I can spare one, you will have a vehicle and some support to rescue your friends. It must strictly be a rescue, mind. I cannot justify the resources for an armed assault, particularly given their location and our lack of intelligence on it."

Sam sighed, feeling defeated, but he could understand it. Hopefully, Kara and the others could hold out until then. "Okay. I understand."

"You four are free to go where you wish," Aiyla said, "though Elleran has requested that you remain with us as we travel to the Alqesi Oasis."

"I'm going," Sam said. He didn't have anywhere else to go, anyway.

"Would you like a Nit implant, Scheln?" Aiyla asked.

Sam glanced at his motionless body. He blinked three times.

Elleran turned to Sam. "I believe that is a no, correct?"

"Yeah."

"Are you sure?" Aiyla asked Scheln.

Scheln blinked twice, quickly. A yes.

"Do you want to come with us?" Elleran asked.

He blinked twice again.

"Very well," Aiyla said.

Ya'ir scratched his head and sighed heavily. "I've actually been thinking . . . As long as it's safe now, I would like to return home to see my family."

Sam hid his surprise. *The family that pushed you to go to Tercast because they thought magic would cure you of "abnormal sexual attraction"? Why?*

"Of course," the Sovereign said. She turned to Zel. "And you, Zelyra?"

"Hm?" she said, shaking herself from deep thought and dropping the loose string of her garment she had been fiddling with.

"Would you like to accompany us to the oasis?" Aiyla asked. "Or you are free to return home if you wish."

"I will go with you."

"Excellent. Say your farewells. We must depart shortly."

Aiyla moved off to speak with the enforcers.

Sam turned to Ya'ir. "You really want to go home? Even after they—"

"Yes. You all helped me realize they shouldn't have treated me that way, but they really care about me, Sam. I'm sure they have been extremely worried since hearing about Tercast. I don't know how it will go, but I don't think I can handle this kind of conflict like the rest of you anyway . . ."

Elleran approached. "You are a gentle soul, Ya'ir Wenkat. The universe needs more men like you. I wish you well."

He smiled. "Thank you, Elleran. That means a lot."

"Please take great care to avoid spreading knowledge that you are a Sorcerer, for your own safety and the safety of others."

"I will," he said with a nod.

He embraced the woman, followed by Zel and Scheln. When he turned to Sam, his eyes went misty.

"I don't think I ever apologized for that awkward confession in the Tercast hallway."

Sam shook his head. "There's nothing to be sorry for, Ya'ir."

They embraced.

"I'll miss you," Ya'ir said. "Take care, all right?"

"I will."

They released their hug as Aiyla approached with an enforcer at her side. She handed each of them a small tear-shaped device that gave Sam a surge of excitement. "These new Jits will reconnect you all to the Sovereignty network." She smiled at Ya'ir. "It should help you get back home swiftly, Ya'ir."

"Thank you so much, Sovereign Aiyla," he said with a slight bow.

"The rest of us will travel with my personal shuttle. Please follow me."

Sam and Ya'ir shared one last wave before he took hold of Scheln's wheelchair and followed the rest of them out. The Sovereign's shuttle had shown up right next door, a sleek but rather unassuming vessel that looked much like a typical ascender. Sam was astounded to find it no more elaborate than the other ascenders he had taken, though it was slightly larger. He parked Scheln's wheelchair and sat between Zelyra and Elleran, across from the most powerful leader in the known universe and her two guards.

"Samuel," Aiyla said as the vehicle smoothly accelerated. "I hope you can forgive my eavesdropping, but I appreciate your critical eye for government oversight. It is people like you who make my job easier."

Sam raised his eyebrows and his heart raced. He was unsure how to respond. The all-powerful leader had heard him discuss how she might be a horrible dictator? His life expectancy may have just dropped to near zero.

"I'm quite serious," she continued. "In a perfect universe where no one ever misuses their authority, I would have almost nothing to do as Sovereign. As it turns out, our universe is far from perfect."

"So what *do* you do as Sovereign?" Sam asked.

Outside the thick glass windows, the view of the cylindrical station interior abruptly shifted to a small corridor, with embedded silvery lights.

"My main duty is to act as the utmost moral authority," she said, leaning in and placing her elbows on her thighs. "I spend most of my time rooting out internal corruption where I can, providing guidance on high-profile disputes, and directing the military. After the disasters at Enck and Tercast, the developments with the Scelebriar rift and their opponents have become a significant focus recently."

"What is happening with the Scelebriars?" Elleran asked.

Aiyla sighed, sitting back. "Many of them have organized against the government, calling for the destruction of my office in favor of a monarchy led by a mythological figure they call the Deia."

"The Deia?" Sam asked. "Kara said Delveton had mentioned that name just before they attacked Tercast!"

After a brief pause, the corridor outside shifted to a brilliant view of the nearby galaxy, as billions of colored stars swirled in bright clouds.

Aiyla's brow furrowed. "Indeed. His deception and despicable misuse of the Gilmar Company has cost us much. You see, Sam, your critical view of government and my efforts can help root out dishonesty and corruption, which can be devastating."

The ship passed through a portal, arriving instantly in a new sea of stars and nebulae.

"Trust is the foundation on which every society operates. As trust erodes, instability rises."

"So that's what's happening with these Scele-something-or-others?"

She nodded. "The Scelebriars primarily, yes. There are records of Sorcery being used to perform various kinds of mind-control in the distant past, but we've never seen those under control have command of Sorcery themselves, which you said may have been the case with Jeanette. Quite an unsettling development."

"Concerning indeed," Elleran added. "I did not think that was possible."

"The Scelebriars have other political allies in their movement as well. Unfortunately, their opponents, mostly various skeptic and anti-religious organizations, are becoming increasingly problematic as well."

"In what way?" Elleran asked.

"Both sides desire to erode our long-standing secularism. While the Scelebriars want a religious dictator, their opponents want an anti-theistic government. They want to remove the protections religious organizations have from government intervention and oversight, particularly after the tragic events at Tercast."

"Well," Sam said. "I can't say I blame them, having seen firsthand what the leaders were doing and the destruction there."

The ship moved into a blue atmosphere, which steadily obscured the view of the brilliant galaxy.

"How did Ilius gain control of Tercast?" Elleran asked. "I'm sure it was being monitored."

The Sovereign rubbed her temple. "Now that was a mess. My predecessor, Sovereign Thalus, had only recently begun as

Sovereign when Ilius discovered Tercast by accident. He was notified, but the developing situation with the Molkinar Empire delayed his response until it was too late. Ilius formally claimed that Divine intervention had led him there and was therefore its new rightful owner. Since the ruins had been uninhabited for many years, the law allowed his claim. Thalus could have removed them, but that would have raised tremendous suspicion, and he thought it risky to draw attention to the castle. He allowed Ilius's claim, as long as he agreed to certain restrictions."

"Seems like it got plenty of attention anyway," Sam said.

Tall columns of deep orange cumuli rose in the distance, illuminated by the fading sunlight. Down below lay an endless desert.

Elleran shook her head. "Virahmgal never sought them out?"

"Thalus wondered if that might happen, but Oblivion never came for them. It's one reason we're not sure it is actually him."

The sea of large, scraggly rocks cast long shadows against the loose sand. The vehicle settled among them, stopping without so much as a bump.

Sovereign Aiyla leaned forward again with a plaintive expression. "Whoever Oblivion is, he has brought about so much devastation. That is why we are hoping we can finally stop him."

The door opened, and Aiyla motioned for them to exit. Sam followed Zel out onto the dirt, eyes wide. Before him stood the most enormous trees he had ever seen, with trunks that must have been nearly a hundred feet wide, stretching far into the sky. Healthy hemispheres of deep green leaves sprung from their tops, and vines streamed from the branches, tapering down toward the lush forest floor where a variety of other colorful plants leapt up to reach for them.

"An oasis indeed," Elleran said with awe, pulling Scheln's wheelchair out with her.

"Come," Aiyla said. "We need to get his attention."

Scheln rose from his wheelchair, and his nearly inanimate body floated up next to Zel. *I should probably help him learn anti-*

gravity, Sam thought. *Then he wouldn't have to use as much energy to get around.*

The group followed the Sovereign and her two guards toward the edge of the massive forest, which stood as a stark wall of vibrant green in the vast brown sea of sand and rock, with a smattering of yellows, reds, blues, and violets among the shrubs and smaller trees.

A low roar rang out from the tree line, just before a giant scaly creature emerged—a quadruped. Elleran rose over the group's heads, and the two guards pulled ahead of the Sovereign.

"Don't harm it!" Aiyla cried. They crouched as the animal charged. Sam thought it looked almost like a ram, with large, curling horns that framed its enormous round head, which it lowered in preparation to strike a guard. The suit threw its hands out, grabbing the creature's horns and stalling it in place.

"Watch out!" Zel yelled.

A gray blur swooped in at a tremendous velocity, knocking over the suit with a loud clash and freeing the large dinosaur-like creature to kick at the other suit, which narrowly dodged the blow. Another bird dove toward them from the tree above at incredible speed. Sam reflexively connected to the sand nearby, raising it as some kind of shield. It disappeared with a tremendous gust of wind from Elleran's position, which shoved the bird from its target.

Dozens of other animals emerged from the dark bushes, comprising a variety of enormous cat- or bear-like beasts, and more scaly dinosaur-looking creatures, growling and spitting. Two more birds plunged from the trees, which Elleran and Scheln forced away with additional gusts of air.

In an instant, the animals stopped, calmed. They turned back and disappeared into the forest while the birds ascended back to the branches of the enormous trees overhead.

From behind a shrub with wide, spade-shaped leaves strode a short, muscular man with tan skin, long brown hair and a short beard. He was stark naked.

Sam averted his gaze, catching Scheln's wide-eyed look. Elleran descended in front of the two guards, between them and the newcomer.

"Ellie?" the man said.

"Duriel!" she scoffed. "Put some pants on!"

He looked down at himself as if his nakedness were a surprise. A few of the fallen leaves from nearby rose to create a makeshift skirt around his waist.

Another Sorcerer!

Duriel rushed forward and embraced Elleran. Sam strode with Zel and Scheln behind the Sovereign as they approached the pair.

The two guards rose into the air and drifted behind the group, while Aiyla approached Elleran and the mysterious man. The two aged Sorcerers broke their embrace.

"Welin!" he said with tear-filled eyes.

"Welin." She grinned as she eyed him up and down. "You look amazing for someone who is grohs of years old!"

"So do you!"

"I was trapped in near-suspended animation. What have you been doing?"

He glanced up at the surrounding trees, and gestured to them. "This."

Elleran's gaze turned upward with an expression of awe. "You cultivated this?" She shook her head in disbelief. "You have truly honed your skills into something extraordinary. This is incredible."

"Duriel Tardep, Vivezan," Aiyla said. "I am Aiyla Covenmoor, current Sovereign of the Intergalactic Sovereignty of Rwenmar. I apologize for the intrusion on your long-undisturbed sanctuary, but we request your help."

"No," he said.

"It is—"

He shook his head. "I know what it is you ask, and I cannot help you. My place is here."

"It's Virahmgal," Elleran said. "We need to stop him."

"Virahmgal is Oblivion?"

"We think so."

Duriel looked at his old friend with a pained expression. "Oblivion approached me, some time ago—threatened to destroy the oasis. In exchange for staying free of the conflict, the being promised to let us be. I must not get involved."

"We cannot let him do this." Elleran put a hand on his shoulder. "I likely cannot stop him alone. We need you."

"If it truly is Virahmgal, he has become more powerful than you can imagine, Ellie." He gestured to their surroundings. "And I must care for the oasis. This is not a wild habitat, it is a garden. I must tend to it."

"Please," Aiyla said. "Eventually, he will come for your sanctuary as well. Please help us stop this destruction. He has already launched the beginnings of his next attack, which will threaten all life of an entire world."

"Aiyla is right. He will not let you be indefinitely," Elleran said. "You know this, Duriel. By remaining here, you are only delaying the inevitable."

Duriel glanced down, his brow furrowed in thought. Sam, feeling suddenly weary, glanced at the incredible sunset-lit shrubs and plants, teeming with the noise and atmosphere of life. The oppressive presence of the surroundings significantly limited the reach of his Sorcery. He could barely feel the air beyond his own body.

The man slowly rose, hovering in the air. "I will consider," he said, before speeding off into the trees. His makeshift clothing fell, drifting back down to the forest floor, which was darkening with the waning sunset. The background chirps and clicks of forest critters settled over their small group.

"What do we do now?" Sam asked.

"We wait here," Elleran said. "Give him time to consider. I am confident he will join us before Oblivion's strike. For now, we should rest."

Chapter 23

The Survivors

Rose sat behind Kula and Kara within the interior of the survival dome, eating from her can of rather bland rehydrated beans and trying to avoid attention as her companions recounted their tale to the two occupants, Renoq and Sheylana. The group sat in one small compartment of the larger dome, which was open above the walls. A single bright light, off-center from the dome peak, was their only source of illumination, casting deep shadows across the area.

"Kara flew us toward the signal until we saw this building, which is when the drones attacked and you helped us inside," Kula said.

Renoq listened with rapt attention, occasionally taking a gulp from his own can of rehydrated beans. Sheylana glanced up briefly from her tinkering between a curtain of black hair. She was bent over the drone Kara had shot down earlier, tools and parts spread out around her. They were both several standard years older than Rose, Kara, and Kula, and wore ragged, faded T-shirts and pants.

After another gulp of beans, Renoq shook his head, causing his thick, curly brown hair to bounce. "Well kads I'm ecstatic you gals aren't with the Deia," he said with his non-rhotic accent. "When you all first showed up, I thought she'd found us."

"I'm still not convinced they're not," Sheylana said, with a similar but more glottalized manner of speech, keeping her eyes fixed on the drone part she held up and scrutinized. "She thrives on deceit, after all."

"If we were here to take you out," Kara said through a mouthful of her own beans, "we would have done so already." She had taken her helmet off, but she still wore the rest of her Ilkuth armor, sitting on a makeshift chair with one leg crossed over the other.

Renoq chuckled. "Now *that* I believe. You can't fathom how glad we are to have more parts from those drones you took down, though."

"What are you using them for?" Kara asked.

"Shey's been workin' on a transport. Won't get us off world, mind, but it'll let us get further. We're hopin' we can find another ship left behind somewhere."

"So," Kula said. Having finished her beans, she lay on the hard concrete floor, her sword and bow within reach. "How did *you* end up here?"

"Well, Shey and I were both exiled from Tercast, o' course. I came—what was it—?" He turned to his partner. "A few years after you or so?"

Sheylana didn't respond.

"Anyhoo," Renoq continued. "King Walnon was a right kook. Didn't trust anyone after what had happened with Delveton, Belze, and their entourage, who had left the castle with some stolen items. We were all just resigned to gettin' by. Completely reliant on Walnon for water and food. Leavin' the castle was a death sentence, or so we thought. Walnon'd sit around in his library all day, while the rest of us mucked about with piss-all to do."

"Didn't you all have Sorcery from Tercast too, though?" Kula asked.

"Meh, it'd linger for a little while, but became almost useless within a day or so. It rarely works well on Uvlun anyway. Walnon somehow got unsealed. Never said how, and only shared it with his family and a few close friends. Even then, can't do anythin' outside our own bodies and a bit of air, just like you found, before the Tercast Sorcery faded to nothin'. Anyway, sure enough, Del and the others came back"—he raised his hands dramatically —"with a functionin' ship! Belze started callin' herself the Deia, asked people to join her. Many did. Unlike us, she could touch the landscape with Sorcery somehow. Shey and I and others stuck with Walnon, and he finally wizened up, sharin' Sorcery with us. We tried to fight 'em off, which didn't go so well. About a half doh of us ran off after the attack. Did the best we could out in the winds."

"Seven," Sheylana said.

"Yeah, seven. Goralo, Walnon's son, was a skilled Sorcerer, and he tried to keep us alive. Two of us died on the way here. Crushed by a flyin' piece of debris or whatnot when the winds got real bad. None of us had much skill as healers. We found the dome, but them drones found us as we were tryin' to find a way inside. Second most frightenin' thing I've ever seen. Goralo found the circuitry for the hidden entrance and gave it a little juice while we tried to fight off the death machines. Shey here got it open, and four of us made it inside, includin' Goralo." He sighed. "Unfortunately, the others didn't make it."

"What happened to the other two?" Kula asked.

"Ah, Bren, poor soul." He furrowed his brow. "She got sick. Real sick. Nothin' we could do. There are supplies in here, but we're not physicians. Goralo went mad tryin' to help her. Couldn't figure out what was wrong or how to fix it. She couldn't keep any food or water down. Her body couldn't take it.

"Goralo took his own life soon after."

Renoq hung his head, then sniffed. "Anyway, I s'pose they may be better off than we are. This hell's no vacation."

"About that," Kula said. "What happened to this place? Why is there no sunlight?"

"We haven't been able to put all the pieces together. But we do know this was once Molkinar territory. Maybe it still is. We're on the edge of a city, which is out that direction"—he pointed off toward the wall—"I think. And there were Sorcerers at war, out in the open. Found some writings. Said they were tryin' to save the planet's oceans. Seems that didn't go well since I've never seen a drop of natural water here."

"Where do you get your water, then?" Kula asked.

"Initially by transmutation. Then Shey fixed the water recovery system, so we've been able to recycle it pretty well."

"You can Vitalize your surroundings?"

"Only the air a bit, like I said. Dunno why. Belze and her gang seem to be able to Vitalize everythin' somehow. We had no chance against 'em."

Rose's attention turned to her own Sorcery, with which she had the typical, detailed sensations of her organs. Her lungs pulsed with her breath. Her heart thumped normally, circulating life-sustaining blood throughout her body. She strained to reach outward and, like before, could only get a faint glimpse of the surrounding air.

"Do you have weapons?" Kula asked.

Renoq nodded. "Yeah, we've got the ones we took with us after the battle at Evamune. Got a nice set of enchanted boots too."

Sheylana glanced up with a sour expression. She didn't seem to be happy with how freely he was sharing information.

"Well," Kara said, putting down her can of beans and pulling the helmet from her waist, "I bet this signal I've had ringing in my head is somewhere in the city you mentioned, so I want to go figure out what it is. Maybe we'll find another ship or something that can help us get Tovas and Fita out of there."

Rose stood. "Kara, we should wait. Rest awhile. We don't even know what that signal is."

Sheylana and Renoq both glanced at her, and her cheeks burned with their unfamiliar attention.

Kara shook her head, clearly unaware of Rose's sudden discomfort. "We don't have time. I can't just sit here while they're suffering who knows what. I have to *do* something."

"You still need to practice your Sorcery too, Kara," Kula said. "It will be advantageous in our next fight."

Kara's brow furrowed in thought.

Rose, fighting with her brain, surprised herself by putting her hand on Kara's shoulder, almost by reflex. "You . . . you need rest." She tried desperately to ignore Renoq's and Sheylana's stares. "Your body needs . . . needs rest. And Kula has a good point."

Kara raised her eyebrow. "What's up with you? Why are you so frightened all of a sudden?"

Rose kept her grip firm and found that she couldn't answer.

Thankfully, Kara shrugged it off. "I'm fine, Rose. No one else needs to come with me."

Kara moved to leave, but Rose strengthened her arm and pressed her body forward against the massive weight of the deceptively small suit, stopping her. "Please. I don't think it's a good idea to go yet. You should rest. We *all* should stay and rest. Like Kula said, you also need to get a handle on your Sorcery to be more prepared."

Kara laughed. "You think you can keep me here?"

Her cheeks burned again. She cursed them. "I . . . I can try."

"We can't wait. They need help."

"Your friend's right," Renoq said. "You should rest awhile. No good tryin' to help others if you're barely standin' yourself."

"Don't worry about me, I've got the Ilkuth. I'll be fine."

Rose stumbled back as Kara's powerful suit moved to leave.

"Kara, please! You need to rest."

She grabbed the arm. Each swing of Kara's gait pulled Rose forward, past a large steel pillar. Rose enchanted her muscles and bones with as much strength as she could muster and grabbed the column as they passed.

Surprisingly, the Ilkuth strained against her fingers with a powerful whine, and halted. Then the pain hit. The tissue of her hands was being crushed by the ridiculous power of the suit.

Kara's head turned. "How are you doing that?"

Tears of pain clouded her vision.

"Just stay. Please."

"You can't make me."

Rose poured more Vitalization into her arm, willing it to pull, and it scraped Kara's feet along the concrete floor. Her body screamed with the strain. "I can try."

"Nice, but I really don't want to fight you." Kara reached over and grabbed Rose's hand, attempting to pry it off her arm. Rose tried to maintain her grip, but the suit was too powerful. Kara pried a single finger off, and Rose gasped as the rest of her hand went painfully with it.

No.

Rose flung herself downward, gripping the suit's armored leg while wrapping her legs around the large steel pole behind her. She had just enough reach to lock her feet around its circumference. When Kara moved, the suit whined. Rose's elbow popped, but miraculously she held the suit in place.

Kara sighed with frustration, then backed up and sped forward. Despite the spike of crushing pain in her hands and feet, Rose's grip held.

"This thing ripped through a freaking *tank* a little while ago. How the hell are you doing that?"

"I don't know," Rose admitted. Indeed, she had never enhanced herself to such a level of strength and durability. It was quite remarkable. Perhaps an effect of Elleran's full unveiling.

Despite that, fatigue set in. She couldn't hold the suit for long.

"That's right impressive," Renoq said.

"Rose understands the human body like no one else I've ever known," Kula said.

"Ugh." Kara put her hands on her hips, and the suit left the floor, pulling against Rose's grip into the air. "Yeah, okay it's impressive, but can you let me go now? I'll be back before you know it—I just want to check out that signal."

"You're not going alone," Rose said.

Sweat began to run down her face as Kara slid her body upward along the pole.

What could she do? If she lost her grip, Kara's gallantry could get her killed. Just like—

Her mind turned to Tercast, to Talanna's horrific scream, to the electric blast that had marred her pure white hair with blood. She saw Niu's face pierced with a flaming dagger. She felt Relon, in her last few moments. Her fear. Her surprise. Then a blade crackling with electricity pierced her skull, cutting Rose's connection. She saw that figure emerge from the hallway.

A suit of Ilkuth.

"Ahh!" Rose let out a burst of energy into her body and threw the suit downward with all her might. It slammed into the concrete floor with a resounding *crack*.

Rose stumbled from the pillar and fell, landing next to the small crater. Thankfully, they hadn't lifted too far off the ground.

Kara groaned, shaking her head. "What the f—"

"I'm sorry!" Rose said, panting. "I . . . I didn't mean to hurt you."

Kula approached with visible concern.

"H-how?" Kara asked as Rose's eyes drooped with a wave of colossal fatigue.

"I . . . don't know," Rose said. "But . . . you better . . . stay."

She closed her eyes, unable to keep the enticing void of sleep away any longer.

Chapter 24
Choices

Tovas sniffed the bowl that had been placed on the floor of his cell, and immediately regretted it. It smelled of spoiled olviguck and vagath seeds. However, driven by ravenous hunger, he downed the foul meal as quickly as he could. A thick greenish liquid filled with unknown brown and yellow chunks traveled down his throat and settled in his empty stomach. As soon as it was finished, he placed the bowl on the stone floor and wrapped his arms around his shivering legs to preserve as much warmth as possible.

He rotated his left shoulder, which ached from sleeping on it earlier, and wished he could speak to Fita. They would frequently take prisoners away for a time—with force, if necessary—returning them bruised or bloody, with haunted looks. Curiously, they had let them keep the clothing Belze granted them.

Urok had come down briefly to taunt Lelanna a few hours earlier, much to Tovas's distress. His outburst during the event had only gained him a personal visit from the large man, and a painful knee to the gut.

Divine above, he prayed, *I know I am weak. I am powerless to protect thy people. But thou knowest all, and art all-powerful. Please. Please deliver us, according to thy will. For Life, Agency, and Virtue. Amen.*

He had prayed with similar sentiment frequently since his capture. They didn't deserve this.

At the thought, Scheln's response to those words echoed in his mind: *If I could smack you, I would. Life is what it is. Deserving has nothing to do with it.*

Life is what it is. A reflection of classic Lomerian teachings to appreciate what you had, no matter how minuscule those things seemed.

He hoped Scheln was well. It had pained him to see his brother losing his autonomy because of their weakening Sorcery. He was likely bedridden now, unable to move. Again. Trapped due to the attack by Oblivion years ago.

The Masters at Tercast had told Scheln that Sorcery would cure his condition, but it never did. He had gained control of the Elements, but never regained the natural control of his body. Why? Even Rose could not cure him. Perhaps his brain had simply suffered too much damage to—

Light footsteps descended the staircase, echoing along the walls. The sound profile told him it was almost certainly not Urok, but his heart quickened anyway. He heard a subdued gasp from one of the other cells. Whoever was coming, he desperately hoped they would not harass the others. Hopefully, they were only picking up the bowls. As they came into view, Tovas kept his gaze on the stone floor, hoping to avoid any chance at eye contact with the newcomer.

He could tell from his peripheral vision that they were wearing feminine clothing, which flowed with their gait. The figure strode past several cells, causing Tovas's heart to thump more frantically in his ears. He kept his face fixed, attempting to appear uninterested. A pair of thin, woven sandals stopped at the gate of his cell. The squeak of the latch brought up a wave of dread that threatened to expel the foul contents of his stomach.

"Hello, Tovas," Jeanette's distinctive, cheerful voice said. "Come with me. I have something for you."

That couldn't be good. However, she certainly would not accept refusal and easily had the power to force his compliance, so he rose, feeling the ache in his bones and the frigid air on his skin. He glanced up at her eyes for a moment and thought they looked almost empathetic.

As she led him past the other cells, he gazed through them for a sign of Fita but didn't find him. They must have taken him out or set him up somewhere more secure, given his abilities. The remaining prisoners appeared as he felt: demoralized and defeated. Hopeless. He sighed, sorrowful that he could not catch a comforting glimpse of his friend.

Tovas watched Jeanette's alluring pink slip dress ripple as she ascended the steps ahead of him. Air turned less frigid once they reached the palace hallway. Bright colors danced along the corridor, and elaborate paintings adorned its walls. The transition from crumbling cold stone to lively decorations was jarring. Jeanette turned left, and Tovas had a brief thought of attempting to run as he stepped in line behind her. *It would never work. Perhaps if I was as skilled as Fita, Kula or Kara, there might be a shred of hope.*

She opened a door for him. "You didn't even try to run," she said with a smirk. "Such a good little doggy."

He walked through the threshold, wondering what a "doggy" was. Clearly something derogatory.

Inside the small room he found a man tied to a chair. On the stone floor in front of him was a long dagger. He looked up at Tovas with wide eyes full of fear. Jeanette closed the door behind her, and the man struggled against his bonds and the gag in his mouth.

"So," she said. "It's simple. Kill this man for us and you'll get a proper meal, a real bed to sleep in, and some better clothes."

"No," Tovas said.

"Wow, you won't even think about it?" She moved around him, standing near the wall between him and the seated occupant. She raised an eyebrow. "He's going to die anyway, you know. He's a criminal. A horrible man who has caused much suffering. If you don't kill him, I will. The only difference is that you get some benefits if you're the one who does it."

"No," he repeated.

Protect my people. The words radiated through his mind, giving him confidence.

The knife rose from the floor and into Jeanette's hand, where she gripped the blade and held the hilt toward Tovas, waving it around. "You sure? Either way he's dead. Why does it matter?"

It matters because I refuse to be a tool of your destruction. Outwardly, he remained silent, staring defiantly into Jeanette's beautiful yet cold eyes. The man in the chair watched motionlessly.

She sighed, dropping the dagger to her side. "I used to think like you do, you know—that life is inherently precious. Turns out life is just like anything else in this universe: ruthless and manipulable. Life is competition. All that matters is how powerful you become with the life you have, and who you choose to fight for."

"And you have chosen this Deia?"

"*The* Deia. She is the Divine. Or at least as Divine as any being can possibly become. She empowers me."

Tovas shook his head. "She controls you."

"No, I am free!" she shouted, taking a step forward and raising the dagger. Tovas stepped back. "I am more free than I have ever been." She lowered her hand, but the weapon remained in place, floating in the air between them. "I have control." She folded her arms. "Last chance. Will you kill him? Or not?"

"No."

She shrugged. "Okay."

Tovas reached out and took the blade before Jeanette had a chance to move it. "You may have power, but you can't control me."

Jeanette rolled her eyes, then snatched the dagger from him and kneed him in the stomach in one fluid motion. He grunted at the pain in his gut, falling to a knee. He looked up helplessly as

Jeanette tossed the dagger toward the man struggling against his bonds. It pierced through his forehead, and his struggling ceased. His head slumped, revealing the tip of the bloody weapon protruding from the back of his head.

Tovas remained on his knee, praying for the Divine's acceptance of the man's soul.

"Time for round two!" Jeanette said as she walked to the door and opened it. She called out, "Bring her in."

Tovas's heart raced. *Not another.*

A tall man brought in a fair skinned woman with reddish-brown hair, then hurled her bound figure onto the stone floor next to the dead man in the chair, blood dripping from his wound. The gag in her mouth stifled her cries as the guard carried out the chair with the body.

"Thanks Wollark," Jeanette said with a grin.

"Always a pleasure, Jey!" he called back.

The door shut of its own accord. Jeanette then slid another dagger from her waist. The prisoner writhed on the floor, wearing nothing but thin rags. Her wrists and ankles were bound behind her back, which prevented significant motion. Her eyes grew wide as Jeanette hefted the dagger and smirked at her.

"Okay," she said, turning to Tovas. He stood, panic rising. "Now that we're clear that I am a woman of my word, what about her?" She gestured to the prisoner on the floor. "And this time, I have a different proposition." She held the hilt of the dagger toward Tovas once more. "You can either give her a quick, relatively painless death. Or,"—she raised her free hand and a flame burst from the air above it—"I'll burn her alive. Far more painful."

Tovas glanced at the woman, who looked at him with tear-filled eyes. He couldn't do this.

"Same offer as before. You'll get a nice bed. Clothing. Only difference is you would be killing her with mercy rather than letting her suffer in agony. What do you say?"

She waved the dagger around again. Tovas felt sick to his stomach. *Divine above, what shall I do?* He couldn't do this—

wouldn't do this. They were trying to force him to take a human life, but why?

"Please, Jeanette," he said, voice cracking, "don't do this. This isn't you. What would Kara and Sam think?"

She laughed, twirling the dagger. "They don't know me anymore. I don't care what they think. And stop stalling. I will not wait around all day."

He glanced again at the woman, who was motionless but for her quiet sobbing. She squeezed her eyes shut, tears streaming onto the hard floor which pressed into her face.

Jeanette raised a finger. "Or . . ." She trailed off briefly. "How's this, I'll even sweeten the deal. All you have to do is have sex with her. No torture. Just pleasure."

Tovas's insides went cold. "Just take me instead. Do whatever you will with me. Let her go."

Jeanette shook her head, lowering the dagger. "Not how this works. Kill her, or bang her, or do nothing and watch her burn. Those are your options."

Divine above, help me. He could bolt forward, tackle Jeanette. And then what? She was a Sorcerer. She could overpower him easily. He could use the dagger to free the woman, but what would he do after that? Try to help her escape while he distracted Jeanette?

"Stop trying to think of a way out of this, Tovas. I've given you your options, and I'm getting impatient." She turned to the woman. "Wouldn't you rather have sex with him than be burned alive?"

The woman twitched, then nodded with her face still pressed against the stone.

"See? She's even consented to it. Probably even excited by it. Hurry and choose, I have other things to do."

It was wrong. All wrong. Giving in to her wishes would mean even worse things, and he had no reason to trust her word. It could all be some kind of trick. He couldn't risk—

Jeanette turned and stretched a hand out, from which white-hot flames erupted, consuming the woman's body.

"No! Stop!" Tovas leapt toward her, but the dagger in Jeanette's hand shot forward and pierced his shoulder, embedding into the stone wall behind him and anchoring him to it. He struggled against the searing pain in his arm as the woman's stifled screams and the scent of burning flesh rose from the inferno. Tovas coughed at the smoke, his head swimming.

The flames abruptly died. Against the blackened stone lay the woman, her skin red and charred. Small flames danced on what remained of her hair or clothing as she writhed against the floor. Jeanette turned and pulled the dagger from Tovas's shoulder, and he fell to his knees, tears streaming down his cheeks. A few drops of health potion escaped one of her vials and shot into his wound, which healed rapidly. The pain in his shoulder vanished, but the agony in his soul only grew stronger.

"Well, hope you're happy with your moral high ground," Jeanette said, opening the door. "I'll leave you in here for a few minutes to reflect on your choices. Someone will be around soon to take you both back to your cells."

After she slammed the door behind her, Tovas hung his head and wept.

Chapter 25
Instruction

Sam awoke to the brilliant white interior of the Sovereign's portable abode—something of a highly advanced mobile home, complete with plumbing, electricity, and extremely comfortable bedding. Though only sparsely decorated and rather utilitarian, it had a warm, homey feel. His face felt a little stiff, probably due to the dry desert air. Elleran, Scheln, and Zel were still asleep.

Soft flooring met his feet as he stepped from his bed. He entered the restroom, or lav, as they liked to call it, then recoiled at his reflection in the mirror. Dried red lines made circles around his eyes and a false tongue on his chin. They looked reminiscent of the berries they'd eaten with dinner. He raced to rub them with water, and to his relief, the marks came off readily.

"Scheln, you knucklehead!" he whispered, wiping the last streaks off his chin. "I'll get you back for that."

After changing into his field robes, Sam stepped out of the floating structure, wincing in the sunlight. Enormous trees cast horizontal rays of golden light through the colorful surroundings, which were alive with the sounds of life. Leaves rustled in the gentle, warm winds. Birds and other animals chirped and called in the distance. He relished in the wildlife. Ignoring his rumbling stomach, he touched a plant with bright blue spear-shaped leaves, his hands becoming wet with cool morning dew.

He found Aiyla inspecting the orange leaf of a tree. She stood in a light blue blouse and white business-like pants, her dark hair now pulled back into a tight bun. The leaf she was studying came out to five points, reminding Sam of maple leaves from Earth, though they were larger, and splotched with yellow, as if someone had tossed a bucket of paint on them.

He walked toward her, watching his feet to avoid tripping over a root or tree branch, when his shoulder met with sudden, alarming resistance.

"He's fine, Emerat," the Sovereign said.

The resistance disappeared. *The suits could cloak?* Sam invoked his Sorcery and found a mass of fuzzy absence floating away. It blended with the oppressive obscurity of the surrounding forest, confirming his suspicions.

"Remarkable, isn't it?" she asked.

"Being threatened by your superpowered body guards?"

She smiled. "I was referring to this oasis."

Sam smiled back, nodding. "It is. I'm surprised you're still here, though. Don't you have other places to be?"

"Convincing Duriel to help us is the most important activity I could be engaged in at the moment." She tapped the back of her head. "I can fulfill most of my other duties remotely." Her eyes settled on Sam. "What do you think of him?"

"Well . . ." He considered his surroundings. "Given this place, and that he's as old as Elleran, he seems like a pretty powerful Sorcerer."

"As a person. What do you sense about his intentions?"

He shrugged. "I . . . don't know. I mean, we only saw him for a few minutes. He definitely cares a lot about this place, and appeared genuinely happy to see Elleran. Seems like a decent guy to me, from what I could tell."

She returned a single nod and a kind smile.

"So, what's happening with the Scele-whatevers?"

Her smile faded, and her gaze turned distant. "Continuing to worsen, I'm afraid. Some groups are becoming more violent, clashing with anti-religious groups. The enforcers are having difficulty allowing the protests to continue while ensuring the surrounding public is not at risk."

Sam picked up a small twig off the forest floor and fiddled with it, keeping his fingers busy. "So, why not impose more restrictions on religions? Prevent them from doing this kind of thing?"

The Sovereign raised an eyebrow. "Are you suggesting I suppress government criticism?"

He raised his hands, dropping the twig. "No, no. Of course not! What I mean is, why don't you restrict religions from brainwashing people?"

Aiyla gave him a curious look. "I can empathize with your point of view, considering the history of Earth. Belief systems *can* cause harm. However, the Sovereignty, at its core, values respect for liberty and the experience of life. To restrict belief is to restrict liberty at its most fundamental level."

Sam found it remarkable that she knew anything about Earth's history.

"But what if they themselves are the ones restricting people?" he asked.

"An excellent question. Such preventive measures are always a challenging balance of freedom and security, and the Sovereignty legislature is constantly debating and adjusting laws on the matter, as they should."

She cupped a leaf in her palm and inspected a small luminescent bug crawling its way up the stem. It appeared similar to a caterpillar, with a long cylindrical body, though it had no distinctive head that he could see.

"What if you don't like those laws?" Sam asked.

Her eyes met his. "Ideally, I, as the Sovereign, never adjust laws. With the rule of law, my primary role is to ensure the democratic process executes as intended."

"But you could pretty easily twist the narrative toward your own preferences, right? You could make it *seem* like you're impartial but be suppressing certain information behind the scenes to suit your own ends."

Aiyla nodded. "You are right. And my actions should never be above scrutiny. Our society hinges on our trust in each Sovereign and, by extension, the Aldan."

Right, the computer system Alice had told him about.

"So, given that you're aware of Sorcery, why don't you have it? Why don't you have a team of Sorcerers?" He raised an eyebrow. "Or do you?"

Aiyla turned her attention back to the glowing critter.

"The Sovereign may not exert any command of Sorcery, either directly or through the military, though Vivezan and the Sovereignty military would often work together in the past. The founders always considered the combination of absolute political power and Sorcery as too great a risk. Vivezan have historically been a hidden line of defense against a corrupted Sovereign, if that catastrophic situation were to take place."

Sam picked up another stick the length of his forearm as he considered her explanation. It was somewhat comforting. To most inhabitants, the Sovereign would be seen as all-powerful, but there was, in theory, a secret group of Sorcerers who could pose a serious threat to that power if needed to keep it in check.

She turned to him. "Do you miss your family?"

The question caught him off guard. Truth was, he hadn't thought about his family much since departing Earth. He had never contacted his mother like he'd promised. Guilt gnawed through his stomach at the thought.

"Yeah. Somewhat."

"Given your background from Earth, I'm curious to know: What are your impressions of the Sovereignty so far?"

"Heh, where do I start? It's incredible! Especially the technology. I still want to learn how all the physics work at some point."

Aiyla smiled again, sweet and genuine. "I'm glad to hear you say that."

"I'm not sure why you're waiting so long to talk to Earth, since the technology could do so much good there. You could prevent all kinds of horrible things from happening."

The Sovereign frowned, her gaze turning distant again. "Unfortunately, it is not in the inhabitants' best interest for us to become publicly involved in the planet's affairs. Our subtle efforts to nudge it toward progress have been fruitful, though. There are good people there doing remarkable work, and we do our best to support Earth's development without exposure or undue control."

A large red bird soared by overhead, catching their attention.

"In fact, your friend Kara's parents were two such individuals."

"They were?"

"Yes. They volunteered for their assignment to the planet and had requested that location for their home. Clearly, they had ulterior motives that we were unaware of."

Sam nodded. "Right. They must have found out about Elleran and where she was while they were at Tercast." He tossed the stick back onto the forest floor, where it splashed into a pile of star-shaped leaves. "What was their assignment?"

"It is best I do not divulge the specifics, but know that they saved many lives." Her eyes filled with poignant sincerity. "Their loss was a tragedy. But through their efforts, they may have saved us all."

Steps approached, crunching against the forest floor. Sam turned to find Elleran and Zel striding toward them, with Scheln hovering behind.

"Lively morning," Aiyla said.

"Lively morning," Elleran returned, handing Sam's mace to him. "Samuel, to make use of this time, I would like to give the three of you some instruction in Sorcery."

Excitement rippled through him.

"Yes!"

"It was a pleasure speaking with you, Sam," Aiyla said.

"Thanks. You too."

She smiled, then strode past him back toward the abode. Zelyra and Scheln bowed their heads as she passed.

"Come," Elleran said.

Sam froze at the realization that he had engaged in a rather mundane, personal conversation with perhaps the most powerful person in the universe—politically, anyway. Could anyone truly have all that power and *not* use it for their own gain? Could a computer system really determine altruistic intentions? What if those intentions changed? Despite his skepticism, he liked Aiyla. She seemed genuine and trustworthy. Time would tell if she followed through on her promises.

Elleran led them past the edge of the forest, back into the desert. This time, Sam noted the drastic change in humidity. He wondered how much of the oasis was being preserved by Sorcery. Could such immense vegetation possibly exist on its own in the middle of the desert otherwise? Elleran tied her curly gray hair back into a ponytail, then turned to face them.

"First, what have you learned at Tercast about combat?"

"Not much," Sam said. "They claimed to be anti-violence. Their instruction was all based on the four Elements, and most of their lectures toward the end were just religious preaching. They spent a lot of time talking about how 'Land is the Element of stability' and 'Water is the Element of change', and how everything in existence is one of the four Elements."

Elleran shook her head and lifted a hand, where pebbles from the surrounding landscape gathered above, swirling in remarkable patterns.

"Unfortunate," she replied.

"We learned deflection," Zel said.

"Oh, that's true," Sam admitted. "They did teach us how to deflect projectiles for protection. I guess that was something."

"Excellent. Enchant yourselves."

Sam, heart racing, connected to his skin, trying to remember how to achieve it. It was a sense of velocity change—reflecting fast-moving objects across the skin's surface. Elleran's presence entered his body as well.

Tiny stones flew at them. One reflected off Sam's forearm. Then his other forearm. Then his hand. The fourth broke through the limit of his enchantment, piercing his wrist with a small splatter of blood. Sam's eyes widened. He felt no pain, and the wound healed almost immediately. Scheln and Zel each looked over their hands with equally surprised expressions.

"Excellent. Your enchantments varied in strength, but each of you executed it quickly and properly. Well done."

Her feet left the rocky floor, and she backed away from them in the air.

"Hit me," she said.

Sam glanced over at Scheln and Zel, who seemed as stunned by the request as he was.

"Attack me," Elleran said. "It will be a splendid exercise for me, and will allow me a decent gauge of your abilities."

Scheln was the first to respond, blasting wind toward Elleran, which picked up dust and small rocks. She remained casually upright, the dust and pebbles splitting around her.

Can't do any harm, right? Sam figured. *Even if we hit her, she can heal herself easily.* He hefted the mace and connected to a rock near her right side, throwing it toward her, where a smaller stone sprung up to deflect it off course. Scheln's wind faded.

"Scheln, your command of the air is quite impressive. Sam, the distance of Vitalization from your body weakened your strike." She smiled. "Don't hold back. Show me what you can do."

Sam glanced over at Scheln and Zel, whispering. "Let's surround her so she can't see all of us at once."

Scheln blinked twice and floated off to the side. Sam fixed his eyes on Elleran, who locked her eyes on him. He lifted his body from the ground with antigravity, pushing around to the opposite side from Scheln. Reaching out with Sorcery, he found a boulder about as large as his body buried in the sand. Scheln sent out another burst of wind and Sam lifted the massive stone. His Sorcery-powered impact sent the boulder flying toward its target, where it was deflected.

A low shockwave sent him flying back into something hard, winding him. In a panic, he connected to his body, realizing he should have enchanted himself again for protection, and found that Elleran's lingering presence had already protected him from serious damage. The impact still hurt, though, and he struggled to regain his breath.

Scheln hovered in the air, his listless limbs trailing around awkwardly. He shot a ball of fire toward Elleran, but a column of water appeared out of nowhere to douse it.

Sam pulled himself upright, his aching body still floating with antigravity. He accelerated toward Elleran and tried to think of something that might catch her off guard. *A laser! It's just a beam of photons. A beam of light. I should be able to do that.* He concentrated on the tip of his finger, imagining an intense and focused beam of energy, and pointed it toward Elleran. For a moment he couldn't tell if it was working, until a spot of sand near her began to darken and smolder.

She was reflecting it!

Boom.

A blinding flash struck the air. Sam's left leg screamed in pain, spiking his adrenaline. A glance downward showed him that his shin was smoking. He felt Elleran's presence, which eased the pain and healed the damaged tissue, but his heart continued its frantic pace.

"Okay," she called out. "Come back."

Sam and Scheln floated toward her, and Sam tentatively allowed his body to be bound normally by gravity once again. He tested his injured leg and found that it could bear his weight without pain. Ragged breaths escaped him from the adrenaline rush, his back and shoulders still aching from the impact during the fight.

"Excellent work varying your attacks. Always remember that one of your most important tools in any conflict is your ability to be unpredictable. How is your fatigue?"

Sam, panting, took inventory of his mental state and exhaustion. "It's okay. I'm feeling a bit tired, but I think I've still got plenty of energy left."

He and Elleran glanced at Scheln, who blinked twice, indicating that he felt the same way.

"Marvelous," she said. "We will go over some basic principles and I will teach you a few specific techniques. Then we can try—"

"Wait," Sam said, looking around. "Where's Zel?"

Chapter 26
Peculiar

So vibrant! So gorgeously spectacular!

Zelyra ran through the trees and bushes of the Alqesi Oasis, in awe with every step, her gray field robes hugging her like a warm blanket in the light, humid breeze—a stark contrast to the dry heat of the desert now several steps behind her. Birds sang to each other all around. Trees rustled their comforting music. Why would anyone ever choose to practice fighting over *this*? How ridiculous. Fighting was stupid. This was life like she had never seen before!

Having reached the base of one of the massive trees, she touched it eagerly and marveled as the enormous plant positively glowed to her perception. However, it *resisted* her connection. She felt something akin to fear emanating from it. It wanted her to stop. As she lifted her fingers from it, it turned dark to her perception once more.

She had established a connection with a few plants at Tercast, but nowhere else. It was likely an effect of the castle's special aura. No other plant, at Tercast or elsewhere, had actively resisted her, though. This oasis, and the beings within, didn't seem to trust her. How tragic. Heartbreaking even. She held her Sorcery back, stretched her arms out, and gave the tree a hug. It was like hugging a wall.

"Why won't you trust me?" she said. "I just want to explore your incredible life here! You must be sooo old."

She released the tree and skipped farther into the forest, her attention pulled every which way by the sheer variety of resplendent plants. Movement on the branch of a bush caught her eye, and she approached it with interest. A small inchworm-like creature glowed softly, shifting from a bright pink at the head to a neon green at the anus. It inched across the branch, repeatedly bringing its rear prolegs forward and then propelling the rest of its body. Zel gasped with excitement.

"Hi, little one!" she cooed.

The insect stopped and rose up on its prolegs, then swept and bobbed its head around as if searching for something.

"You're probably looking for food. What do you like to eat, hmm?"

It returned its forward legs to the branch and continued propelling forward, where it would run into the spear-shaped leaves of the bush soon. Breakfast.

Zelyra backed away from the tree and heard the faint rushing of water, so naturally, she headed in that direction, skipping along the way. Water always had interesting creatures. Like willivongs! They were so cute. Would she find them here? Not likely—

A root caused her to stumble, but she caught herself and continued on cheerfully. What was an adventure without a few stumbles?

After pushing through a thick cluster of bushes, she found a small, shallow creek, perhaps twice as wide as she was tall. The water ran crystal clear across the variety of gray and brown rocks underneath. She knelt at the water's edge and dipped her fingers in. The cold sensation sent pleasant shivers up her arm. The water was visible to her Sorcery, so she connected with it, lifting a small column of it into the air against the force of gravity. She ran her fingers through the floating liquid, delighting in the sight of sunlight reflecting through its amorphous, shifting volume.

She let the water fall, giggling at the splash that added to the bird calls and rustling trees around her. Movement caught her eye farther out, where she found small, round water creatures twisting around each other among the rocks. Not willivongs, but beautiful all the same. Like almost all other life, they were dark to her perception through Sorcery—fuzzy blobs of absence.

As bird calls sang in the distance, Zelyra idly spun her fingers through the cool water again. She missed the animals from Tercast dearly—especially Tela, their sweet purple ulinko, who would so often curl up in her lap and enjoy chin scratches and back strokes. Her connection to the creature persisted, similar to her connection with Rose and Elleran, though it had diminished because of their distance. She was currently sleeping. Balon, the keglon, calmly grazed. They were presumably still on Alvior where she had left them.

A tear fell from Zelyra's eye and into the creek with a light plop. Maybe when she returned to the camp, she would ask Aiyla if she could return to Alvior and find them. She couldn't bear to leave them in the wild.

What she had thought at first to be a bird call, part of the backdrop of the forest, now sounded more urgent—more like a whimper, a cry for help. Zelyra stood up and strained her ears, attempting to pinpoint a direction. Another cry came, distant, faint. *There!*

She took off her shoes and lifted her clothing as she stepped barefoot through the cool water. The stones were smooth and slippery, forcing her to move carefully. Frigid water caressed her legs as the water rose past her knee, deeper than she had expected, then receded as she approached the other side. She stepped up onto the sandy bank, letting her pants fall over her wet legs, when another cry came. It sounded desperate. She dropped her shoes and ran toward the sound.

Most of the forest floor offered a remarkable cushion for her feet. Velvety grasses and mosses caressed her soles with every step. The bleating steadily grew in volume as she ran. The distant sound of rushing water pierced the air as well, and the foliage of the canopy above blocked out more and more sunlight, darkening the forest floor. Bushes and shrubs gradually gave way to large fungal structures, which grew to branching bulbous heads that glowed soft blues, purples and greens, providing soft illumination to the surrounding life. A swarm of tiny lumincus insects buzzed past her. The ground beneath her feet became moist, causing her feet to sink with each step. She slowed to a walk, her heart pounding with the exertion of her extended jog.

The rushing water and animal cries grew louder. She moved past a cluster of smaller pink and purple fungi and found a large pool, where water fell in from a cliffside. Large, sprawling trees with bright, multicolored flowers stood at the sides and top of the cliff, spreading sparse petals into the water below with the passing breeze.

Another wail reached her ears, emanating from the side of the cliff near the waterfall. Within the crags, a four-legged, reptile struggled, whipping its pointed head around, on which a single curved horn poked from the crown. It appeared to be stuck.

Zelyra strode into the crisp, cold water, not bothering to spare her clothing this time. More small spherical creatures weaved around each other in the water, and scattered as she approached. The surface beneath quickly dropped, forcing her to tread water and then swim toward the creature in slow breast strokes. It bleated again, moving its head about haphazardly, then its gaze settled on her. The creature stilled, watching her progression.

"It's okay," she said, the end of her words garbled as her mouth dipped below the surface. "I just want to help you."

Reflective scales emerged from the creature's skin, coating it in a layer of vibrant armor. Spikes protruded from its spine. It panicked, flailing around and calling out with distressed urgency.

"Please don't be—ah!"

Something that felt like wrinkly, solid slime gripped her foot and pulled her under. In her panic, she pushed the water away from her body with Sorcery, submerging a bubble of air from the surface. She dropped to the smooth floor of the pond and was met by a creature with a bulbous, round body and three long tentacles. Having let go of her leg, it darted away, into a darker corner of the pool.

Zelyra released the heavy pressure of water, letting it crash into her, and she propelled herself to the edge of the cliff, where she climbed onto a rock.

She'd never exerted that much force against water before. This new Sorcery Elleran had given them was fantastic!

A large feline with black fur and turquoise stripes jumped out of the tree overhead, landing between her and the scaly creature. It snarled. She put her hands up, connecting with her body. Her heart thumped. Her lungs pulsed. Her muscles tensed. She enchanted her skin against penetration, pushing it to be unyielding.

The feline pounced. Zelyra yelped and clung to the rock wall, narrowly avoiding the creature. It lost its footing on the wet surface and slid into the pool. Turning her attention back to the scaly creature, Zelyra moved toward it, where it continued to call out in distress. Once she cleared the crags, she noticed its body was partially suspended. The tail had gotten wedged between a narrow section of rock, where the downward pull of the creature's weight jammed it tight. She strained her mind, but could not reach the area with Sorcery. It was too close to the creature's influence.

She tentatively approached, hand outstretched. Glancing back at the water, she found the feline pulling itself out of the pool. There wasn't much time. She reached a hand toward the creature's tail and it cried out again before sinking its teeth into her shoulder.

Zelyra gasped at the pain. The creature's bite was powerful, and its teeth sharp. Too strong for her enchantment. Blood seeped into her top, mixing with the water. She pressed her other hand forward, touching the rock and finally finding the connection. She caused its internal bonds to release, and it crumbled into sand, releasing the creature's tail and allowing it to pull itself away from the rocks. It released its bite from her shoulder—evoking a reflexive scream of pain—then jumped out of the crag, splashing into the pool below.

Zelyra grunted as she pressed down on her wounded shoulder, connecting to it with Sorcery. Something collided with her back, sending her forward into the rocks. She rolled over and found the feline snarling above her. Claws swiped against the forearm she instinctively brought up to her face, but they failed to pierce her skin. She rose, then covered her head as she moved around to the opening while the animal slashed at her repeatedly. Her foot slipped against the slick surface, and she tumbled, smashing her hip against another rock before the water swallowed her.

As she reached for the surface, a slimy appendage gripped her ankle, and pulled her under again. Panic threatened to overwhelm her, and her Sorcerous perception dimmed significantly. Her heartbeats thumped in her flooded ears as she flailed against the creature that was drowning her.

She was going to die. Become one with the universe. *It likes pink today. That's a wonderful color, at least.*

As she found peace with her imminent passing, the perceptions of Sorcery returned. She connected with her body and gave it a powerful push upward. She broke through the water's surface, and the creature's grip slipped from her ankle. Arms flailing against the warm wind howling in her ears, she willed her bones to be strong against the coming impact. The ground rose quickly, and she met it with a damp splat.

Zelyra rolled onto her back in the mud as she slid, until her body slowed to a wet, sloppy stop. She was dazed and lightheaded, but alive. The screaming pain of her shoulder suddenly came back into focus, so she connected to the tissue there, willing it to close up. Rose was much better at healing than she could ever be, but her work should stop the bleeding, at least.

The thought of Rose brought her into vague perception through their shared bond. She opened the fuzzy connection to her, hoping she would notice.

Rose's presence soon entered her body, pulsing with concern.

The tissue closed, covering the wound, but didn't seem as clean of a healing as Rose's usual work. Her Sorcery was probably weaker because of their distance, but it was certainly a better healing than Zelyra's own amateur attempt.

Thank you, Rose. What would we do without you?

Chapter 27
One with Nature

After taking a deep breath, Zelyra sat up, peeling her hair and clothes from the sticky mud. As she wiped muck and grime from her body, the reptile she had rescued emerged from a cluster of mycelia, having returned to its unarmored, bumpy skin, which reflected the glow from the bulbs nearby and the sparse light cascading through the giant trees overhead. It reminded her of the dragons of Yolfan, though smaller and without wings. It had two small stubs poking up from its body where wings might be, though. Those dragons also definitely didn't have retractable scales, as far as she knew.

Shoulder aching, Zelyra moved slowly, putting her hands up and rising. The feline rose from the pond behind the dragon-like creature, watching from a distance.

"I just . . . wanted to help you," she said, a wave of fatigue washing over her. Apparently she had exerted quite a lot of Sorcery already. If she did much more, unconsciousness would undoubtedly take her.

The scaly creature approached slowly, sniffing the air near her.

At least it didn't seem fearful anymore. In fact, it seemed curious. Its bright blue eyes searched her.

"You're beautiful," she said, keeping one hand out toward the creature, which stood several paces in front of her. She let her other hand drop slowly to her side.

It approached cautiously and brought its spade-shaped head forward, sniffing Zelyra's fingers with wide-eyed curiosity. Her heart raced. The creature truly was magnificent, standing just a little shorter than a keglon, with a long neck, broad body, four muscular legs, and a long tail with a bulbous tip. Part of the tail appeared injured, dripping dark, oily blood, which reflected a dazzling array of subtle secondary colors.

The angular head brushed her fingertips, and she gasped as the creature's body came alight to her perception. She felt its magnificent internal organs. A strong heart pumped blood. Dense muscle fibers ran throughout the being, connected to sturdy bone structures. Lungs inhaled, pulling in the warm, moist air, and then slowly exhaled. She wanted to reach out and embrace it for all its beauty, but feared startling it again.

It retreated from her touch, but her vision of it remained. They had established a connection, similar to her connection with the animals from Tercast. Tears formed in her eyes, and she moved forward to touch its snout again. She connected with the damaged tissue of its tail, pushing with her might to close it up to stop the bleeding. The tissue was immensely strong and difficult to move, but it responded.

As she worked her way along the wound, the large feline crept toward them with a curious look. Its bright orange eyes scanned Zelyra. She tried to ignore it and focus on her task. It came within a few feet, then stopped, maintaining a hard gaze.

After the wound closed, Zelyra glanced at the feline, which crouched and gave a low growl. The dragon-like creature turned to regard it, and she instinctively backed away.

The feline pounced, and she yelped, raising her arms against the oncoming claws.

A soft thud disturbed the air, causing the creature to hit the ground with a splat. It slid into a cluster of glowing green fungus. Her new dragon friend swung its tail back and gave a light roar, while the feline pulled itself up from the mud, struggling to find its footing. The dragon charged.

"Wait!" Zelyra called, holding her hand out. "Don't! I think it's just scared."

The dragon stopped, cocking its head. Growls met Zelyra as she approached the feline, and it swiped at her again. Lines of mild pain ran across her arm, but her skin remained unbroken. She connected to her skin, ensuring that her enchantment remained strong and unyielding.

"You stop it!" she commanded the feline.

The creature stilled. It stared at her and cocked its head.

She steadily reached out toward it. "I just want to help."

As her hand approached its head, it cried and swiped her arm with a powerful paw full of claws. Though pain still rippled along her skin, her enchantment held, preventing it from breaking.

"Can't hurt me," she said. "Let me help you."

The creature's ears flattened as her fingers approached its head. A fear response?

She touched it tenderly, and its body came alight to her perception. She noted male anatomy. His muscles tightened. He was indeed afraid. While non-human animals rarely understood speech, she'd previously had some success communicating to the Tercast animals with emotions. With the feline, she tried to communicate a sense of affability. Understanding. A desire to help. He stared at her with those bright orange eyes.

Zelyra released her fingers from his furry head, and his body became a fuzzy hole of emptiness to her perception again, unlike the dragon, which approached slowly.

The feline, thankfully, accepted her help out of the mud pit he had slid into, then stepped up beside the taller dragon.

She sighed, looking down at her damaged, terribly uncomfortable, mud-filled clothing. That wouldn't do.

Zelyra undressed, cringing at the profound discomfort of peeling off muddy, abrasive clothes, and dropped them at the edge of the pond, then jumped in. Her body reeled against the sudden cold, but soon savored the immense satisfaction of mud dissolving off her skin. As she broke the surface, a large splash announced the dragon following her. The feline jumped in soon after.

She smiled and decided she should name her new friends. Jivax. Yes, that sounded nice. Jivax for the dragon, since she had never seen one before. She couldn't reliably determine the creature's sex, finding its anatomy quite unusual. And the feline could be . . . Mewigath. It was the name given to a neighbor's derlag growing up. A good name. He could go by Mew for short.

After they all enjoyed several minutes of swimming and bathing themselves, Zelyra climbed back onto the shore and stared at her clothing. She could try to wash and patch them, but the thought had no appeal. She felt rather free without them—more in tune with the music and ambient energy of nature. Human society enjoyed clothing, but she was never great at society anyway. Nature was always more interesting.

Jivax and Mew followed behind as she trotted happily to the rocks and climbed them toward the stunning multicolored trees at the top of the waterfall, fighting her irritating fatigue. *No time to rest. Too much to explore!*

At the top of the cliff, she found a completely new mix of dazzling plant life. Long, thin yellow pole-like plants shot up into the sky, reaching toward the branches of the titanic trees overhead, among vast changes in elevation. More light passed through the canopy overhead, casting shimmering beams of light to the surface. The ground sprung up in tall, lively plateaus. Small green grass-like plants with soft branching heads sprung from rich, red soil.

As she was inspecting a fascinating insect with large colorful wings on one of the pole plants, a group of plump gray creatures with white spots and thin, birdlike heads darted past. Mew chased after them. He struggled to keep up as they twisted and turned expertly through the plants, using their smaller size to squeeze through where Mew could not.

Zelyra's breath caught as a small one slipped and smacked into a pole plant, squealing madly. Surprisingly, Mew ignored it. A large, older one stumbled soon after, and Mew pounced on it, ripping its throat cleanly and quickly with a swipe of his claws.

After gathering some fallen sticks and bits of dead pole plants, Zelyra started a fire near Mew's kill. Jivax settled down next to it, enjoying the warmth. As Mew engaged his meal, Zelyra approached. She stroked his head, feeling his body light up to her perception once more, and scratched his ears. He seemed to enjoy it. When she lifted her hand from him, his body continued to glow to her perception, bringing a grin to her face.

Her stomach grumbled. While she would love to gather some fruits or plants for food, that was risky. Wild plants were often poisonous. Meat was probably safer.

Her feline companion didn't seem to mind when she took a few raw pink pieces of his kill and stuck them on a spike to cook.

Thank you for giving us sustenance, she thought toward Mew's kill.

Once she seared the pink flesh to a delicate brown, she took a bite. The meat was incredibly tender, reminding her of murvolue meat. Some seasoning would be nice, but it was satisfying.

After eating, she and Mew drank from the nearby river that flowed toward the swampy area below.

As Zelyra washed refreshingly cool water over her face, Jivax flinched and bolted upright. Anxiety flared within her, and she scanned the rocky landscape and trees overhead. *A threat? What did you hear?*

Jivax took off at a run, and Zelyra followed, not knowing what to expect. The creature led her between several tall plateaus, where the plant life transitioned to bundles of red ferns jutting out of the ground. The enormous trees overhead became more sparse, letting even more sunlight through to the surface. Mew followed close behind. Rushing water accompanied another waterfall over a stunning cliff face. They ascended a gentle path up the side, weaving their way ever higher. She marveled at the sight of their previous locations from above, admiring the pole plants and colorful trees, beyond which she could make out some of the dim glow of fungus plants, past the lower cliffside below.

The path veered underneath the waterfall, where an enormous cave led into the mountain. Jivax continued ahead, casually trotting into the darkness. Curiously, Mew stopped at the entrance. Zelyra wondered if she should wait with him, but her curiosity got the better of her. She followed Jivax into the dark. Small agaric fungi sprouted in clusters along the walls and between rocks. The humidity increased, and the temperature fell. Zelyra rubbed her shoulders, and considered warming her body with Sorcery, but that would cause her mounting fatigue to worsen. As the daylight faded behind her, the agaric glowed a pale blue, offering a small amount of illumination. She created a point of light in the air above her anyway, to light her way into the misty depths.

After they rounded a rocky turn, the cave opened up to an enormous room filled with glowing fungi and plants of all varieties along the floor, walls, and ceiling. In the middle lay a much, *much* larger version of Jivax, with enormous, magnificent wings. Zelyra gasped at the sight and stopped, watching Jivax approach the giant creature. It did, in fact, resemble the dragons of Yolfan, though certainly much larger. It had two long, curved horns sprouting from its head, with smooth, scaly skin, brighter than Jivax's.

A stark naked Duriel strode out from beyond one of the marvelous wings. Zelyra yelped as he glanced in her direction, and she covered herself, suddenly feeling far too exposed. He would probably be angry that she had intruded on his sanctuary.

To her surprise, he smiled.

"Come," he said, beckoning her forward.

She approached tentatively, continuing to cover herself as much as she could.

"This is Velara." Duriel stroked the scales of the massive dragon. "Thank you for helping one of her young. This one is always getting into trouble."

"She's beautiful," Zelyra said, unable to resist reaching out. The creature's scaly skin was smooth and warm.

"I am sorry the creatures attacked you. We are quite defensive against outsiders."

"It's okay. I understand."

"What is your name?"

"Zelyra."

"You are unique, Zelyra."

"Oh?"

He gestured to Jivax, who was snuggling up against Velara. "It is difficult to win their trust."

She grinned. "I'm grateful."

"Why are you not with Elleran?" he asked.

Zelyra gave a slight shrug. "They are training. I don't like fighting. I'd rather be here." She gestured to her surroundings. "These creations are amazing!"

He frowned. "Invariably, conflict is sometimes required to preserve the balance of life."

She considered his words, then continued to marvel at her glowing surroundings. "How is all of this even possible?"

His gaze settled on her—poignant, searching. She felt self-conscious about her nakedness again, but his gaze never drifted from her eyes, as if he was evaluating her soul.

"Give me your hand," he said, holding his palm up.

She studied his rugged, bearded face and wondered if she could trust him. Curiosity won out, and she tentatively placed her hand on top of his.

Zelyra gasped.

Besides his body, the entire oasis around them became alive to her perception. Every being, from the smallest insect to the massive trees to the dragon lying next to her, became perceptible through the supernatural connection of Sorcery. Tears fell from her eyes as the beauty and immensity of the entire oasis overwhelmed her.

"I will show you."

Chapter 28
New Vision

Kara let out an impatient breath, which reflected off the limb in front of her face. An itch on her back begged to be scratched. Unfortunately, it was inaccessible, pressed motionless against the leathery exercise mat she lay on somewhere in the reverberant survival dome. The faint smell of old rubber lingered while Rose and Sheylana hovered overhead.

"Stop moving. You're making it harder," Sheylana said.

"I'm not moving."

"Your eyes. Stop moving your eyes."

Kara sighed. "Sorry, it's really hard to keep them still."

"I'm almost there—trying to reconnect the energy supply. Can you double-check the optic nerve connections to see if they look okay?"

"Yes," Rose replied. "They seem okay, as far as I can tell. I don't know how the connections work, though."

"As I mentioned before," Sheylana said, "I am familiar with some of the basic components, but these are far more advanced and tiny than anything I've worked with before. I'm making a lot of guesses. Thankfully, the damage wasn't too severe."

Something clicked, an almost inaudible sound, and two fuzzy, colorless faces faded into Kara's perception. A point of harsh light shimmered between their heads. The image slowly increased in focus and color. The light was farther away, on the domed ceiling above. She took in Rose's kind, freckled face and the one next to her, which was new. Sheylana's black hair cascaded down her fair face, scrunched in concentration.

"Hey!" Kara said. "It worked! I can see again!"

The women smiled.

"Brilliant," Sheylana said. "Now we just need to do the other one."

"Ugh," Kara said. "Do we have to? One eye should be fine, right?"

Rose rolled her eyes, giving Kara a sense of satisfaction. She knew it would be useful to have both, but complaining about it made her feel better. Sheylana didn't react. She only shifted, her dark brown eyes gazing at Kara's face.

"Oh, by the way, Kara," Rose said. "I connected with Zelyra a while ago."

"Did something happen?"

"I only had a fuzzy sense with our distance, but she was injured pretty badly. Some kind of animal bite. I helped heal her up as much as I could. She seems okay now. Excited, in fact."

"Think they're coming to get us, then?"

Rose shrugged. "I don't know. I'm sure they would if they could. They may not be able to. How would they find us?"

A rough outline of Sheylana's face appeared from Kara's left eye. She closed her right one, expecting color to fade in like the other, but the image remained fuzzy and monochrome.

"The second one sort of works now," Kara said, "but I'm just getting fuzzy outlines. No color."

"Okay, hold on," Sheylana said. "I think . . ."

She trailed off, while the image faded to nothing, leaving only the vague light sensation through Kara's closed right eyelid. It reappeared a moment later, still a blurry outline, which color faded in to fill. The image sharpened a moment later.

"It's back!" Kara said with a grin. She sat up, and Sheylana and Rose backed away to give her space. "Ready to go?"

"Kara, slow down," Rose urged. "Let's not rush into another dangerous situation."

She sighed. "We've already rested plenty. I don't want to sit around here twiddling my thumbs while Tovas and Fita are in trouble, and my brainwashed sister needs a good kick to the face."

"You plan to get her out?" Rose asked.

The image of Jeanette plunging a knife into her chest flashed in her mind, bringing a brief wave of sorrow.

"She's not herself."

"If she has fallen to the Deia," Sheylana said, "her mind is gone. The sister you knew is no more."

Kara shook her head. "No. I can't believe that. I wont. I'm going to do everything I can to get her back. She'd do the same for me."

"Hey, ladies," Renoq said as he approached. "Inventory's done." He turned to Sheylana and frowned. "With the five of us now, we've only got doh-ish days' worth of food left."

His unfamiliar tawny face broke into a suspiciously fond smile as he eyed Rose, though. It was probably nothing. Kara's interpretations of expressions were likely still way off the mark.

"Guess that means it's about time for all of us to go," Kara said.

"You need training," Kula said, rising from her seated position on the floor nearby.

Kara stood from the mat. "I've got plenty of training. Years of martial arts, and basic training in the Sovereignty's Armed—"

"With your *Sorcery*. You need to exercise your new power with the Elements."

"Yes," Rose agreed.

Renoq and Sheylana nodded with them.

"Not a bad idea," Renoq said. "We could use all the help we can get."

Magic powers would be useful, no doubt about that. While the suit was powerful, Rose had proven earlier that Sorcery could overcome the advanced technology. Kara's own Sorcery *would* be an important edge against the enemy.

"Okay, fine, some magic training it is."

"Besides," Sheylana said. "A working vehicle will help us all get around faster. Then we can go together. You can't carry all of us, after all." She gestured to the mess of disassembled wires and metal components nearby. "With these new drone parts, I think I finally have what I need. Renoq and I would like nothing more than to help get your friends out and escape this rock."

"How long will that take?" Kara asked.

She shrugged, standing from her seat on a battered crate. "I don't know, I should be able to get it working within a few days." She stretched, then strode toward her workshop.

"Sounds like a plan, then."

Kula led Kara to a more open area of the dome. Various containers of parts or garbage, neatly organized, surrounded them. Renoq chatted quietly with Rose as they moved the junk to the cubicle walls, clearing a space. She seemed to be unusually uncomfortable around him. Kara had a thought to go tell Renoq to buzz off as she was finishing the last barrel of cables, but before she had a chance—

"I'm with Kula!" Rose shouted.

Breathing heavily, she strode over to a remarkably wide-eyed Kula and locked arms with her.

"Oh," Renoq said, sheepishly scratching his head. "Uh . . . all right then. I'll, er . . . see you gals around. I should probably help Shey anyway."

He shuffled off.

Kara walked to the pair with a grin, covering her mouth to force down the laughter threatening to burst out. Kula glanced at Kara with a horrified expression, while Rose let her arm go, clearly relieved. A snicker escaped Kara's lips.

"Shhh!" Rose's cheeks flushed a bright red.

"What was *that*?" Kula whispered. "We're not—"

"I know, I know!" Rose said. "I just couldn't stand him approaching me like that. So . . . so . . . yeah."

Kara laughed heartily, unable to contain herself any longer.

"The look"—she turned to Kula, tears of mirth dripping from

her eyes—"on your face. I am *so* glad Shey fixed my sight just in time to see that."

Kula scowled, while Rose bit back her own nervous chuckle.

"Sorry."

Kara's laughs subsided to a heavy sigh as she followed Kula to the center of the room and wiped her eyes. Rose seated herself on a lidded metal container in the corner while Kula stretched her legs, pulling her long blond hair back into a ponytail. She then unfastened the sash at her waist and tossed it into the center of the room.

"Lift the sash without touching it," she instructed, folding her arms.

Kara raised an eyebrow. The woman was probably just getting back at her for laughing. "Seriously? No further instruction? Just 'do this impossible task' and that's it?"

Rose giggled. Kula smirked.

"What?"

"That was the same reaction Sam had when the Tercast Masters started teaching us," Rose said.

"Ha! Well, as much as I hate lectures, I feel like I need some kind of instruction before diving into this."

Kula shook her head. "There truly isn't much to instruct. It is impossible to explain adequately. You must get a feel for it."

Kara raised an eyebrow again, this time directing it at Rose.

"Kula is right," Rose said. "There really isn't too much we can say because everyone experiences it a little differently. I would say it's a feeling of connection and directed imagination."

Kula nodded. "For some, entering a state of meditation is helpful."

"Sam and I both struggled for days to get it at Tercast," Rose added, "but you are also fully unveiled, unlike we were, so it might be easier for you."

Meditation. Some of her martial arts instructors over the years had included meditation as part of their training. Kara always hated it. She'd rather be doing something—*anything*—than sitting around and stewing in bored silence.

"Meditation isn't really my thing. What else you got?"

"Is there anything that gets your mind into a state of calm focus?"

Kara thought for a moment. "Sparring maybe."

Kula grinned. "Is there a larger mat in here?"

"Hmm," Rose said, "not exactly a training mat, but the thing we slept on might work."

She slid from the container and led them to another cubicle with various bedding supplies. Inside was a large, soft surface which appeared to be designed for communal sleeping. They brought it back to the open area and spread it out. Kara stepped onto it with her bare feet, stretching in her Sovereignty uniform. It was indeed soft. Too soft. Not ideal for sparring, but it would at least be safer and more comfortable than rolling on the concrete.

"Pay attention to any new sensations," Kula said, readying herself at the other end of the mat.

Kara took a deep breath and turned her eyes off. She always felt weird sparring with sight. The visuals were distracting, and often weren't helpful with her fighting style anyway. She crouched into a wide stance.

Breathe.

Focus.

Something new entered her perception. She could feel her heart thumping, its pear shape shifting with rhythmic contractions. She perceived the thick, striated muscles in her thighs tightening, keeping her body upright. Around her, a fluid moved, dancing, disturbed by her breath. The air.

"I can feel things," Kara said.

"Good. Find the sash," Kula replied.

Kara attempted to sort through the sensations around and within her. Bone. Muscle. Skin. She found fabric, but it was the wrong kind, dense and strong—the uniform encircling her body. Cloth. There it was, thin and light. What had Kula said? Lift it somehow.

Lift, she thought, and she turned her eyes back on. The sash remained on the floor.

"It didn't work," Kara said as the sensations faded.

"Use your imagination."

"What, like, pretend it's happening, even though it's not?"

"Imagine the sash lifting," Rose explained.

"Oh, got it. So it's not like controlling a Nit?"

Kula thought for a second, then shook her head. "No, not really. You don't give it commands. Imagine what can happen, in a directed, concentrated way, and the Elements will follow."

"All right, I'll give it a shot," Kara said, turning her eyes off once more.

Breathe.

Focus.

While the sensations returned for a moment, they drifted away. She couldn't get them to return.

She sighed. "I can't get the feelings back. This is—"

Steps sounded toward her position, and her instincts kicked in as she threw her arms forward. She collided with a leg, then reached out and grabbed an ankle as she fell to the mat. The cold fabric of the soft surface dragged across her face as Kula pulled. Kara failed to get free of her grip. Swinging her legs around, she connected with the Kula's other leg, and the blow brought her opponent to the floor.

Kara pounced toward Kula's upper half, taking the brunt of a strike to her own shoulder. Her hands found an arm, and she slid naturally into side control, connecting her arms underneath Kula's neck and shoulder. Her opponent continued to swing one arm for impact while the other attempted to push Kara off.

"How do you *do* that?" Kula panted.

Kara smirked. The sensations unexpectedly floated past again. Blood. Bone. Muscle. Fabric. Kula moved her hand to Kara's face, pushing up against her jaw. When she connected, the woman's body came alight to Kara's perception. Her opponent's heart thumped a few inches from her own.

The sash. She found it, sensing it's light, smooth surface. Her mind strained to imagine it rising. She turned her eyes on, and saw Kula's frustrated expression behind long, golden strands of hair that had slipped from her ponytail. The sash was still on the floor nearby. Unmoved.

Kara furrowed her brow. "I tried moving it again. It didn't work."

Kula continued to strain against Kara's hold, trying unsuccessfully to reach her with her feet.

"Did you sense it?" Rose asked.

"Yes."

"Use your imagination?"

"Yep."

"You sure you were connected with it?"

"Connected?" Kara asked. "What do you mean?"

"When you sense it, you should feel a kind of subtle connection to it."

A frustrated sigh left Kara's lips.

Taking advantage of the distraction, Kula slid a knee up under Kara's chest, and pushed her away with her feet. Kara tried to regain control, but Kula was too strong, pulling her into a roll where she came out on top. Kara got one leg inside to protect herself, but her opponent had the advantage now. It felt remarkably odd to observe her movements visually while her body instinctively executed them against her opponent.

She turned her eyes off again.

Sensations flowed around her. The sash entered her perception once more. She needed to connect with it somehow. Kula breached her guard, pulling up past her legs and pushing Kara's arms against her face. Kara's focus remained on the sash, relying on her subconscious training instincts.

As she held on to the sensation of the sash, something clicked. She could feel the tension in its fibers, the force of gravity pulling it downward. It *did* resemble some kind of connection. She imagined it rising, and exhilaration pulsed through her as she felt it comply.

After flicking her sight back on, a slight roll allowed her to see past Kula. One side of the fabric lifted into the air.

Rose clapped, and Kara beamed as Kula pinned her left arm while pulling on her right, applying painful pressure to her elbow.

"I yield," Kara said, the material rising higher off the floor and into the air.

Kula let go, and sat up with a satisfied grin. Once the sash was positioned right, Kara let her connection go, and it fell onto Kula's head, cascading across her face.

"Also, I win."

Chapter 29

Restraint

A freezing splash of flowery-smelling liquid woke Tovas with a start. Adrenaline pushed him up from the stone floor, but his hand slipped, causing him to smack his cheek against hard stone. As awareness roused his blurry vision, he heard another splash, followed by a woman's shriek. He lifted his swirling head, and the familiar squeak of his cell gate sent another wave of adrenaline through his system.

A large, powerful hand grabbed his upper arm and hoisted him up with a laugh.

"You're all smellin' up the place," Urok's deep voice echoed through the dungeon as he dragged Tovas, vision still foggy, across the dungeon hall. "You and Lelanna can wash each other off."

He chuckled against the squeak of another cell's gate, then threw Tovas against a new set of cold stone. He slid across the slick surface into something soft. A thigh. A foot pushed against him, and he struggled to sit upright.

"Enjoy!"

Urok closed the gate and strode back toward the stairs to the main level, whistling a merry tune.

Tovas turned to the woman, Lelanna, who stared at him with terror through a mess of wavy shoulder-length hair, which was dripping with soapy water. Her brown body shivered against the bitter cold, wearing the purple jumpsuit Belze had given her. He shivered with her.

Tovas held up a shaky hand. "I . . . I'm sorry. I won't harm you."

She continued to shiver, her teeth chattering, as she moved into a corner and wrapped her arms around her legs.

"I know it sounds terrible," Tovas said, gesturing to the small water spigot to his left, "but we should wash this off."

Lelanna eyed him suspiciously. He couldn't blame her for being apprehensive.

He sighed. "I'm sorry. I don't think there's anything I can do to help, but I'm going to turn around and stare at this corner until you tell me it's okay not to do so."

Tovas spun and crawled into the far corner, staring off and trembling furiously. He wiped soap from his brow, attempting to keep it out of his eyes, as his mind slowly drifted elsewhere. He wondered where Fita and the others were. The two cells next to his own, across the dungeon, appeared to be empty. It was possible the occupants were simply sitting quietly or asleep outside his view. It was also possible that the Deia's people had taken them to endure their next round of torment.

Why were they doing this? Was it just their preferred method of torture, or was there something deeper to it—something more nefarious?

The squeak of a valve, followed by trickling water on stone, interrupted Tovas's thoughts, and he fought the impulse to turn around. Lelanna had decided to wash herself, and to do so effectively, she likely removed her clothing.

He shook his head slightly, pushing the thought of her undressing from his mind. She was a woman. A person. A human being. Not an object to be ogled for pleasure. He must respect her.

A single, almost triangular stone in the corner stood as the target of his intent gaze.

Self-restraint is the foundation of all respect for life.

A central Lomerian proverb. One often quoted by leaders in the faith. A principle he had determined to live by a long time ago.

The sounds of trickling water disappeared momentarily, then crashed with a splash against the stone. Tovas, suddenly aware of the crusty parts of his skin and hair where soap had dried, ached to be under the water himself. The other areas of his body remained an unpleasant mess of cold, slimy wetness.

A tiny stream of water crept past him on the floor, running through the cracks between stones and settling in the low points, always taking the path of least resistance.

A part of him wished he would take that path.

His situation would be far more pleasant if he stopped resisting, no doubt about that. It would be easy to harm others for his own comfort. To catch a quick glimpse of an attractive woman as she bathed. To give in to Jeanette's—the Deia's—demands. It would be natural for him to look after his own interests, to seek his own pleasure. But he believed in a better path. A harder path. One that led to the glory of the Divine, who watched over all existence with infinite wisdom and power.

Streaks of red appeared with the clear stream of water. Blood? It wasn't a large amount, but upon further inspection was almost certainly blood. She was likely injured, perhaps from a recent tortuous experience at the hands of the Deia's Sorcerers.

Squeaks resounded with the closing of the valve. Trickles and splashes against stone continued to echo across the small cell for a few more seconds, then eased, returning the cell to frigid silence.

"You can bathe now," she said.

Tovas tentatively turned his head and found her naked body in the far corner again. Drenched, curly hair cascaded over her shoulder, with her body curled up sideways against the wall. An arm covered her breasts, and her right leg bent toward the ceiling, achieving as much modesty as was feasible.

Tovas directed his eyes to hers with a slight smile. "Thank you."

He uncurled from his ball, then crawled toward the spigot. Lelanna, shivering furiously, fixed her leery gaze on him as he moved into position.

"I am going to undress."

"Okay," she said through chattering teeth.

She turned her face to be in line with her body, staring at the ceiling above. Glancing at her from the corner of his eye, Tovas pulled the sopping pants off his body. Though it made him even colder, the dry air on his skin was a welcome change from the uncomfortable chafing of slimy trousers.

He twisted the valve handle of the spigot, and water trickled out from the pipe opening, pattering against the wet stone below. Droplets chilled his feet. He let the water wash briefly over a finger, testing it, then moved his head under the stream, letting the water soak his half-dried hair. Freezing trickles ran down his cheeks, neck, and chest. He involuntarily gasped as he turned and let it hit his back.

From the corner of his eye, he noticed Lelanna's eyes fix on his naked body. He avoided meeting them, pretending not to notice as he continued to wash the slick residue from his skin.

When he'd rinsed the last of the soap away, he grabbed the trousers and ran them under the water as well.

"Would you like me to wash your clothing too?" he asked.

"That would be wonderful," Lelanna said, removing the arm covering her breasts as she twisted. Tovas averted his gaze, and her garments landed near him a moment later. He placed the thin purple jumpsuit under the spigot until it ran clear of the frothy substance.

Once the clothes were washed, he began laying them out at the other end of the cell, where the stone was dry.

"Thank you . . . er . . . what's your name again?" she asked.

"Tovas," he said, unfurling the legs of his pants against the floor. "It's a pleasure to meet you, Lelanna."

"The pleasure is mine," she said. "Though I suppose we technically met in the cave."

"Indeed."

Lingering water dripped from the stopped spigot.

Lelanna subdued her voice to a whisper. "How is your Sorcery? Have you been able to regain any significant power?"

Tovas furrowed his brow. "I'm still sealed. I . . . didn't accept Belze's offer."

"*What?*" she said with a harshness that made Tovas flinch. "Why?"

Tovas shrugged. "It didn't feel right."

"That seems like a terrible reason to give up Sorcery."

"Hm," he said with a slight smile. "I suppose it does."

"Maybe if you had it, you could have helped Belze fight them off, and they wouldn't have captured us again."

"Doubtful. The Deia's people are skilled, and powerful."

Silence settled between them, allowing the futile struggle of that escape attempt to mire his mind and sink his empty stomach. Having Sorcery certainly wouldn't have helped then, but it may have improved his current situation.

"You must be an Escalar priest with that level of restraint," Lelanna said.

Tovas shook his head. "I'm not a Scelebriar."

"You're not? I thought all the prisoners were."

"No. I'm Lomerian."

"Ah, okay. It's a branch of Scelebriar religion isn't it?"

Tovas moved his aching legs into a cross-legged position and leaned back on his arms. "Actually, the other way around. Lomerianism is much older. There was a schism called the Great Lomerian Dissent, where Scelebriars parted from Lomerians."

"Oh, right, right. Now I remember. Something about same-gender sexuality and firearms."

"Yes, that's right."

"How can you possibly claim to be a true respecter of life? Those things actively prevent life from thriving."

"While we also discourage these practices, we also hold to the fundamental principle of liberty. People should be free to choose their own path. We don't believe in imposing our religious convictions on others."

"Evil thrives when good people do nothing."

"I agree. We do not believe in doing nothing. We believe in being examples, and letting the Divine touch the hearts of others through our influence."

"Heh," Lelanna said. "And how's that going for you? I heard your religion has been declining for ages."

Tovas shrugged. "It rises and falls, I think. We are only loosely organized, so I think it is not unexpected."

"Lomerians are too passive. The Divine requires large-scale action and influence to save humanity. Those who divert from the ways of the Divine will only cause destruction and death in the long run."

Tovas turned his head, bringing Lelanna's naked figure into the corner of his vision. "One of my best friends is a man who is attracted to other men. He has now embraced that attraction. He is perhaps the kindest, most wholesome soul I have ever had the pleasure of encountering, and has more respect for life than most who claim a devotion to the Divine."

Lelanna's blurry head shook. "Not so. Kindness doesn't make up for a lack of respect for the natural reproduction of human life!"

Tovas turned his head forward again, sighing heavily. It would likely be useless to argue the point with her. She clearly had strong convictions.

She gave a sigh as well. "Sorry, I didn't mean to insult your friend. Natural childbearing is the highest honor of the Divine, though."

He considered her words. It was true that the bearing and raising of children was a great honor, but Tovas believed there were plenty of other profound ways to honor the Divine's gift of life. Who was he to judge one's chosen path over another's? Only the Divine could gauge the true impact of one's life.

"Do you have children?" Tovas asked.

Lelanna shifted. "No, but I want to one day. When I find the right partner."

"I do as well," Tovas replied.

A slow drip of the spigot punctuated the icy silence.

"I'm mostly dry, except for my hair," Lelanna said. "But it's freezing."

Tovas became painfully aware of his own shivering. "Indeed."

"Perhaps . . ." she trailed off. "Perhaps we could warm each other up."

Tovas's eyes widened at the thought. Only a few minutes ago, Lelanna had been fearful of exposing herself.

"I don't think that's a good idea."

"The Divine will forgive us, given the circumstances. I'm sure of it."

Tovas shook his head, actively pushing the image from his mind.

"Tovas," she said with a trembling voice. "I am already defiled. It will not matter."

He lifted his head, and he spoke with sudden fervor. "You are *not* defiled. Never think that. No one can defile you, as a person or as a woman, against your will. They only defile themselves."

"You misunderstand," she said, her voice soft. "I . . . I gave in. I . . ."

Tovas's head dropped in sudden realization. The sight of Jeanette's fire consuming a human being flashed through his memory.

"I . . . didn't want to do it . . . but they would have done something worse. What else was I supposed to do?" she said, breaking down into sobs.

Tovas turned to find her naked back facing him, and a lump formed in his throat at her sobs. He crept toward her, and placed a hand on her shoulder, finding it slightly warmer than his fingers. She didn't respond, and only continued to weep. Though their nakedness made proximity a risk, he felt she needed human connection.

"'For it has been said: In sin, those who dwell below cannot know the heart, but only the Divine above, who understands the heart, and perceives all capacity.'"

Lelanna wiped her eyes and turned her head toward him. "How is *that* supposed to help?"

"I've always thought this scripture was about grace," Tovas explained. "I cannot judge you, because I cannot understand the whole context. The circumstances of our actions are *always* relevant. Our state of mind. Our sobriety. Our ability to control our impulses. We are only morally accountable for our physical and mental capacity to choose the correct course of action."

"But . . . I still chose wrong. I chose wrong to save myself from torment. I was selfish."

"The human mind can only take so much. You have suffered greatly. Endured horrors. It doesn't excuse conscious immoral behavior, but I believe it counts for something."

Lelanna sniffled and wiped her nose. Her shivering had lessened.

Tovas stared at the stone wall ahead with fierce intent. "There is *always* a path to redemption."

After a brief pause, Lelanna grasped his hand with her own, and her shivering stopped momentarily. She wiped her eyes again.

"Thank you, Tovas. I needed to hear that."

Footsteps from the stairway reverberated against the stone walls. He and Lelanna flinched and turned in unison. Tovas shifted to the other corner, hoping not to arouse suspicion as the steps approached the cell.

Jeanette, wearing a modest red dress and long white gloves, appeared through the bars. She placed a hand on the gate, stared at both of them for a moment, then smiled.

"Urok said he washed you, but I didn't know he also threw you in it together. I hope you had plenty of fun with each other."

She unlatched the gate, causing Tovas's adrenaline to spike. *Please don't. Leave us be, Jeanette. Please.*

"Tovas," she said, causing his heart to drop. "You're coming with me."

He pushed himself back against the wall, unwilling to comply.

Jeanette's cheerful smile quickly faded to a frown, and she strode toward him, rolling her eyes. "Oh, come on. Your last test wasn't even *that* traumatic."

She grabbed his arm and pulled him up with a powerful grip. He could refuse to walk. Make her drag him. But what was the point? She was a Sorcerer. It would be a minor inconvenience.

He did it anyway, letting his naked body slump against her grip as she dragged him out of the cell.

"Ugh. You're such a child."

He closed his eyes, trying not to let the memories of his last encounter with her flood his mind as she dragged him up the stairs to a door. His shoulder ached from the awkward position of his body's weight against it.

Tovas was pulled inside a room and thrown against a stone wall, knocking his breath out of him. As he was about to fall, Jeanette grabbed his left wrist and lifted it so his feet left the floor. A cold metal clasp encircled it. His eyes squeezed shut as the same happened to his right wrist, and his body stayed suspended. Metal clenched against his ankles, completely binding his limbs, bringing back panicked memories of his first torture session.

A brutal impact to his gut sent pain rippling across his organs. He fell into a coughing fit.

"Hang around for a little while, 'kay?" Jeanette said. "I'll be back soon."

After his coughing finally ceased, Tovas's watery eyes drifted downward. His mind searched for comfort.

Self-restraint is the foundation of all respect for life.

Chapter 30

Energy

A small, comfortable interior came into Sam's perception. Sunlight trickled through the trees and into the window of the Sovereign's mobile abode, creating a pleasant cluster of glittering, yellowish spots on the gray wall in front of him. When the realization of his consciousness sunk in, Sam jolted into a sitting position, eyes wide.

Practice! I need more practice.

He glanced briefly at the other beds as he rose from his own. Scheln and Elleran were still fast asleep. Zel's bed remained empty. Though Elleran assured them Zel was fine exploring the oasis, Sam still worried about her. Why hadn't she come back?

The door whooshed out of his way as he approached, and let him onto the forest floor. He connected to his body, and enchanted it against gravity, allowing him to fly up and over the floating structure, toward the desert. His stomach grumbled, but food could wait. He needed space for Sorcery.

Flying through the edge of the oasis brought back the recent memory of soaring through the trees near Kara's home, dragging with it an intense ache for her presence—one far stronger than his empty stomach's grumbling. He let his body settle against the dirt at the edge of the forest and stared out at the torrid desert landscape. The rising sun, already exuding a blistering, dry heat, cast long, shadows against the crags and boulders, striping the scenery. He reached out to Kara, finding his connection to her fuzzy, due to their great distance from each other. She seemed to be sleeping. Sam's insides twisted as he imagined himself there with her, wrapping an arm around her softly, holding her body close to his as he received a faceful of her hair.

He pushed aside his longing for her. He had things to do. Techniques to master. When he would finally be free to get to her, he needed to be at peak ability to rescue *her* this time, in addition to everyone else trapped on Uvlun.

Sand blew up from the ground as he exerted himself with Sorcery, spinning the granules around himself as a warm-up. Stones whirled about his body, and he tried to synchronize them in nice even patterns. Elleran had told him more precision would be a great initial focus for training.

At Sam's command, an igneous rock about the size of his head pulled itself from the ground and stopped a few feet in front of his face, where beads of sweat ran down his skin, leaving trails of tickling relief in the arid breeze. His brow furrowed with concentration as the rock's temperature continued to rise. A deep red glow emerged below the surface, rising steadily to a brilliant orange. The rock began to liquefy and bubble.

Responding to his imaginative will, a point on the left side of the amorphous, glowing blob extruded, pulling the substance of the rock with it and forming a sharp point. He focused on the other end, pushing it inward and flattening it, then rounded out the bubbling sides to form a cone.

He relaxed his Sorcerous concentration on heat, and the thick liquid quickly cooled. It faded back to a deep red and then a smooth, glassy black. As his gravity-defying force of Sorcery diminished, the cone slowly fell toward the sand below, and Sam spun it, letting it land on the flat surface. It settled into the sand with a soft puff, and he grinned, unable to resist reaching a hand out above the sharp tip, where the heat rising from the former rock washed over his skin.

"Well done."

Startled, Sam whirled his head around to find Elleran's smiling face.

"Here," she said, holding out a large orange fruit that resembled a squash. "The Sovereign informed me that you haven't eaten yet."

He took the offering without a second thought. "How did she know?"

The sand before Elleran lifted and hardened into a simple stool, and she sat on it gracefully, her usual gray robes falling around her. "She's the Sovereign. There is little information she does not have access to."

Sam took a small bite. Though the exterior was firm and smooth, the interior was like gel and had a slightly sweet, nutty flavor.

"Mm. This is really good. What is it?"

Elleran spoke as she chewed her own piece of the delightful fruit. "I do not know. Duriel brought them to us. They are delicious indeed."

"Duriel came? Was he able to find Zel? Is she all right?"

"Yes, yes. Zelyra is quite well. She has been vigorously exploring the oasis." She chuckled. "I think Duriel's reclusive character was wearied by her curiosity."

Sam laughed. "I'm so glad she's all right."

Elleran tilted her head toward his handiwork as he took another bite. "I'm glad to see you practicing more precision."

"Is that how you plan to defeat Oblivion? With precise counter-moves?"

Her eyebrows slowly scrunched into a thoughtful or worried expression as she ate. "In truth, Sam, I do not know. I am confident we can stop his attack from destroying the planet, but I am not sure if we will be able to destroy him. I think the most likely outcome is that he will retreat after we thwart his attack."

"You think he'll retreat?"

"Yes. If it really is the Virahmgal I once knew, he will be exceedingly practical. He will not waste time or energy fighting us unless he feels it is necessary. I believe he will retreat, then strike again when a clear opportunity arises, which should give us time to prepare."

"What is he after?"

Elleran's expression turned grim. "According to the Sovereign's intelligence, he appears to desire the destruction of all life."

A chill ran down Sam's spine.

"But *why*? What's his motivation?"

"I cannot know for certain."

"You were his closest colleague, so you must have some idea." He threw the last of the fruit into his mouth.

She sighed, her eyes full of melancholy. "We were more than colleagues. We were great friends. I have given the Sovereign my theories. Perhaps the simplest explanation is that he wants to expa—"

A rock smashed into Elleran's head with a crash, shattering into pieces around her. Sam recoiled, then looked up to find a floating Scheln by the rock's origin. A pillar of sand rose toward Scheln's listless body, spinning around him. A beam of tiny projectiles then shot toward Elleran with a blast of wind.

"Ahh!" Sam jumped back, pushing himself off the floor and floating backwards out of the line of fire. The beam of sand collided with Elleran, who continued to eat her meal, giving no attention to the unexpected barrage.

In a moment, the sand and wind quieted, and Scheln approached her. His movements were smoother and more graceful than usual, thanks to the anti-gravity lesson Elleran had given them the previous day. That should save him a great deal of energy. Sam moved forward as well, touching down and walking toward the two.

Elleran turned to Scheln with a smile and swallowed the final bite of her meal. "Thank you, Scheln, that was excellent." She then turned to Sam. "My apologies for the interruption. I had asked Scheln to attempt a surprise attack on me this morning."

Sam blinked in pure astonishment. "How did you possibly respond that quickly? Were you enchanted?"

"No."

"Then how? That was so fast!"

The older woman stood, looking remarkably frail for someone who had just shrugged off a propelled boulder as if it was nothing.

She dusted off her robe. "Awareness, knowledge, and precision. Almost any Sorcerer with experience can destroy an incoming rock. The key is to destroy an incoming rock that you weren't expecting in a way that minimizes your energy expenditure." She held a finger up for emphasis. "Remember," she said, glancing at each of them with intensity. "In any engagement with Sorcery, efficiency is just as important as power. Draining yourself too much for any one strike or defense could mean the difference between life and death."

Elleran stretched her hands out, and the sand rose between them, melting instantly into a bright yellow ball of molten heat. In only a second or two, it formed into a perfect sphere and cooled. To Sam's astonishment, several intricate weaving indentations formed patterns across its surface.

"As in all things, study and exercise yield skill and efficiency."

The symbols across the sphere's glassy surface stretched as the object expanded. Sam's jaw dropped as he realized the smooth rock still appeared to be cool. He connected with it, and Elleran gave him the slightest hint of a smirk as he analyzed the material. Disorder. Speed. Causality. She was changing the substance at a molecular level. He watched as she flattened it into a semitransparent disk with legs, and it settled onto the sand between them, creating a table.

"Today I wish to discuss the acquisition of knowledge in more detail. When you wish to learn something about the physical world, what is an effective way of doing so?"

Sam let his connection to the glass surface fade, and he leaned his elbows against the table, considering her question. "Probably by studying scientific experiments. Reading and researching."

Scheln's head nodded awkwardly in agreement.

Elleran smiled. "Indeed, learning from the experiences and observations of others is certainly valuable. However, there is another way that is even more effective."

She let the unasked question hang in the air, and Sam wondered what she might be referring to. Personalized instruction? Logical reasoning? Those were other decent ways of learning.

"First-hand experimentation," she answered. "Knowledge is always most pure and valuable when it is gained directly."

Her words rang true, bringing back lectures from his high school physics teacher, Mr. Nowell. The older man had often echoed the same sentiment as he encouraged them to learn the material in his class—and get their lab work done on time.

"Every experiment begins with a hypothesis," Elleran said. She turned to Sam. "Where are the limits of your understanding? What is a testable question into the unknown?"

Hypothesis? I have about a billion questions, but I don't know about any hypotheses. He racked his brain to find something he could conjecture about. What were the limits in his under-standing of physics?

"Oh! Quantum mechanics."

She raised an eyebrow. Scheln looked at him with a blank expression.

Right. The Sovereignty probably doesn't use the same terms.

"What I mean is, the most fundamental particles of existence," Sam explained. "I think we'd call the groups fermions and bosons, and there are particles like up quarks, down quarks, and electrons."

Elleran continued to stare at him blankly.

"If I understand correctly, you are hypothesizing about the foundational components of the universe. Particles, you say, from which all things exist. Is that right?"

"Yes! Exactly."

"Could you be more specific? Perhaps an illustration would help."

He nodded eagerly, and connected to several golf-ball sized pebbles nearby, then raised them up to float at eye level.

Let's see. Hydrogen is the most basic atom, but it doesn't have any neutrons in its base form, and I should probably include them, so maybe I'll start with helium. He had only four rocks currently, so he'd need two more to show helium. He found more stones on the ground and raised them up with the others. Brow furrowed in concentration, he clustered the four together into a nucleus, then caused the two remaining stones to orbit the cluster. It was challenging to keep their motion regular.

"So, considering this as a basic atom, we have two protons, two neutrons, and two electrons," Sam explained. "The orbiting electrons are already fundamental particles, but the protons and neutrons"—he caused two rocks to break of from others in the nucleus, and let the others fall gently to the table—"are composed of fundamental particles, we called quarks. Three of them, I think." He caused the connective bonds to rupture in a Y-pattern within the two rocks, splitting them into three parts each. The two particles he had used as electrons floated up to join the others. "So together, these constitute the most fundamental particles in the universe."

Elleran brought a hand to her chin and considered his explanation, then nodded. "This is the chemical structure for helium, I suppose?"

"Yeah, exactly!"

"Very well. How do you propose we test this hypothesis?"

Sam massaged his forehead and strained to recall if he had ever read anything about the discovery of subatomic particles. They probably involved complex machinery. Could they create one? What would they measure? How would they measure it? He didn't know enough about how they worked, but maybe Elleran could help with that.

"Well," he said. "On Earth, I think scientists would use particle accelerators. I think they would speed up these particles to high energy, smash them into atoms, and then measure the results, but I don't know enough about the details."

Elleran smiled. "Might I suggest a simpler approach?"

"There's a simpler way?"

"Of course. A benefit of Sorcery is that we can connect to and observe the universe directly."

Excitement surged through Sam as he recalled his first successful attempt at changing the universe with Sorcery. "Right! About a week after I gained Sorcery, I connected to atoms or molecules directly to split their bonds apart in a bar of clay."

"Unlikely," Elleran said. "The smallest constituents of the universe are profoundly challenging to observe without significant experience, or aid from an experienced Sorcerer. It is likely that your imagination of those particles and their bonds assisted in your manipulation of the substance."

Sam furrowed his brow in thought. The mark he had first created in that bar of clay was tiny, but still visible. Individual atomic or molecular bonds were infinitesimally small. There was no way he could see a rupture of even thousands of them with his naked eye.

"Fair enough. So how do we sense things that small?" he asked.

Her presence entered the cut stones he was lifting. She pushed some of them downward, against Sam's force keeping them suspended from gravity, and he let them fall gently to the table before releasing his connection. One remained, floating between them.

"Scheln, please connect to this piece with us," she instructed. Scheln complied, and his presence entered with theirs. "Concentrate on keeping your connection to the material intact. I will systematically annihilate sections of the substance, attempting to reduce it to its most fundamental facets."

She turned to Sam. "Samuel, what do you predict to observe?"

"I . . . don't really know. I suppose I might feel something like bits of energy interacting with each other. Some orbiting the others."

"Good." She stretched a hand out toward the floating pebble. "Pay very close attention to your sensations."

A part of the object disappeared suddenly with a clap. He kept his focus on the remaining section, and another chunk disappeared with a lighter clap. The third disappearance, as well as its accompanying clap, was barely perceptible. Sam could hardly even see the speck that remained.

"Well done. You have maintained your connections so far," Elleran said. "Now, to continue, we will need to create an isolated environment for the substance, and remove all other sensory distractions. You should close your eyes. I will nullify your other senses."

Sam shut his eyes, concentrating on the rigid substance and internal interactions of the speck of rock as his sensation of the passing wind and the pressure of his weight disappeared. The distant rustling of the oasis faded to silence. A brief sense of vertigo accompanied a surreal feeling of detachment from his body, as if he had been pulled out of it and poured into the rock.

Elleran continued to remove sections of the stone, where they vanished mysteriously. He wondered how she could simply remove matter from existence, but stifled the question. Right now, he needed to concentrate. Each time she removed part of the substance, his connection became more tenuous. He felt the sensations slipping from his grip, but maintained his focus. The once-rigid substance turned foggy. He furrowed his brow, willing the connection to remain in tact.

Soon, he felt it: a hazy energy, surrounded by another blur of energies. An atom? The energies separated rapidly, dispersing into a spread of odd sensations, which then faded into a background of haphazard ripples.

Sam opened his eyes, and he found himself within his body once more. Nearby, Scheln also opened his eyes. A stiff, warm breeze caressed Sam's skin once again. Silence gave way to the sound of rustling trees.

Elleran smiled. "Excellent. You both did well. Now, Samuel," she said, turning to him, "please give us your observations, as objectively as possible. What did you sense?"

His brow furrowed in concentration as he reflected on the

experience. "Well, when it got really small, it became blurry. Hazy. It didn't feel solid anymore."

"Did you perceive separate components of the substance, or did it feel uniform?"

"I *think* I felt different components. It's hard to describe . . . It was more like different types of fog mixed together, that separated before they disappeared."

Elleran nodded. "Anything else? How did the experience match up with your expectations?"

Sam tapped his chin, trying to think of the right words to describe his otherworldly sensations. "It was different. It didn't really feel like unique bits of something, for instance. Even blurry ones. It was all more like . . . like fuzzy bits of energy overlapping each other. I *did* feel like one kind of energy was surrounding the others, but I didn't really sense any type of orbit. It was more like a cloud, but denser on some parts compared to others. I figured that could have been the atom I was describing."

"Anything you would like to add, Scheln?"

Sam turned to Scheln, who looked back at him with his unreadable expression. Two words made of light flashed over his head: *distinct medium*.

"Distinct medium?" Sam said. "What does that mean?"

"I believe he may be referring to the fog you were describing as occurring within separate, clearly distinct mediums or channels. Is that right?"

Scheln blinked twice.

"Hmm." Sam considered the words. "It was like each cloud was part of a larger space, so I guess that makes sense."

"If you were to update your model, Sam, how would it look now?" Elleran asked.

His eyes lit up as he connected to grains of sand nearby and brought them flowing above the makeshift table. He needed different colors. The rocks separated into five clumps. He then enchanted each to reflect more strongly in a particular spectrum, turning them red, green, yellow, purple, and blue. With a flourish, the grains spread out into clouds, where clusters of them faded outward near other clusters, overlapping each other. He took the yellow one, deciding it should represent electrons, and moved it out farther to create a cloud of dust surrounding the others in the center.

"Something like this, maybe?" he said.

Elleran smiled broadly. "Excellent. May I make a few adjustments?"

"Of course."

Her presence entered next to his. The red and green clumps separated into smaller groups of three, with one red and two green clumps, or two green and one red. The yellow and purple split into an array of other colors, spreading through and gathering around other parts of the model. They flickered in and out rapidly, appearing like clouds of colored sparkles. Sam's jaw dropped, stunned at the remarkable depiction of what he had recently experienced, and finding it profoundly accurate.

"To summarize," she said, "at its most fundamental level, the universe appears to be a set of discrete energy fields, which interact with each other in remarkable ways, only some of which are highly predictable." The electron cloud morphed to form unique patterns around the center cluster, which morphed as well into multiple sparkling clusters. "Base elements are formed with stable interactions among these energy fields."

The clumps of sand dispersed into a uniform cloud of colors, moving about each other haphazardly.

"The universe is constantly changing," Elleran explained. "Ripples of excited energy, at certain discrete levels, constitute all of our observable existence."

The randomized cloud of sand fell to the table, and Sam found himself hungry to know more. There were so many more questions.

"But how did this energy come into existence?" he asked. "Where does it all come from?"

Scheln turned toward him, and Sam held his hand up to stop him.

"I know what you would say, Scheln: the Divine. Well, I'm

sorry, but I don't find that explanation to be very compelling. Let's say the Divine *is* the source of existence—that *still* doesn't really answer anything. *How* does it come from the Divine? What does that actually mean?"

Scheln stared back blankly. Sam turned his attention back to Elleran, who smiled at him with a twinkle in her eye.

"So," he said. "Is there an answer?"

"What do you think, Sam?"

He thought for a moment. "Well, an old teacher of mine used to say that science doesn't really give us answers. Science gives us results. It's up to us to decide what those results mean."

"Hmm." Elleran's gaze turned outward, thoughtful. "An intriguing perspective."

Mr. Nowell's following words rang in Sam's mind:

Perception is not reality.

Chapter 31
Attraction

Rose emerged from the lav, her thoughts dwelling on Tovas and Sam. She jumped with a gasp as Renoq stood over her wearing only a towel.

"Heh, sorry, Rose. I didn't mean to startle you." He moved past her with a grin, and she glimpsed the desire in his eyes before he closed the door behind him.

She stared at the door for a moment, shame threatening to rise within her. He still seemed to be interested in her.

Rose turned and continued down the half walls, her thoughts racing. *Why? Why does he have to be interested in me?* A pang of guilt hit her for lying to him about being in a relationship with Kula. But he didn't understand. The attraction of others had *always* caused her anxiety to spiral out of control. Well . . . almost always. Somehow, Vurkil had breached it. By some unfathomable means, the blunt, imposing giant had slipped past her subconscious mind's impenetrable fortress. And she had fallen for him. Hard.

Now he was—

She shook her head, dislodging the agonizing thoughts from her mind. *Can't think about that.* She pivoted her focus back to

Tovas, who she still received brief, foggy impressions of through their connection from time to time. He was in pain, but alive. *Hold on for a while longer.*

She turned the corner and nearly collided with Kara.

"Sorry, Rose!" Kara said through heavy breaths.

A stream of fire shot toward Kara's face, and Rose backed away out of reflex. Thankfully, Kara redirected the fire off course and onto the concrete floor. Kula, its source, smirked.

"Hey!" Kara shouted. "You singe my hair, I'm gonna beat the snot out of you!"

"Come try it," Kula taunted.

Kara shot forward with a remarkable jolt of acceleration into their training area. Rose followed her through to find them colliding at speed. They fell to the mat, each struggling to subdue the other. Rose, moving to sit on a nearby barrel, connected to each of them to inspect their vitals.

"Ahh!" Kula yelled as Kara pinned her arm. After a moment, the arm pushed upward with unnatural strength, shoving Kara's body clean off her.

Rose watched with interest as the two continued their super powered dance of dominance. They seemed to be evenly matched. Kara had an edge on Kula in grappling skills, whereas Kula had more experience and power with Sorcery and long-range attacks. If she could keep Kara at a distance for most of the fight, she could potentially come out on top, but Kara was very good at closing that distance.

After pulling herself free of Kara's attempted locks, Kula rolled upward into a fighting position. Kara rolled up a moment later, and the two faced each other, sweaty and panting heavily. Kula threw a kick forward, but Kara was prepared for it, grabbing the leg and using its momentum to throw Kula back to the floor. They wrestled for control for several seconds, during which Renoq entered and walked to Rose, chewing on a snack. Anxiety flared in her chest once more. With a remarkable gravity-defying bend in Kara's back, she threw her thigh across Kula's neck and pulled her arm into submission. After a sharp inhale, Kula tapped her opponent's shoulder, conceding the fight.

Wanting desperately to move away from Renoq, Rose stood from her seat and approached the women. Renoq clapped. Kula saw her coming, glanced over at Renoq, and displayed a Fita-like scowl as she stood. Rose pulled her into a hug. She was sweaty and smelly, but surely that would only solidify their relationship in Renoq's eyes.

"What are you—"

"Just hug me back," Rose whispered. *"Please!"*

"Ugh," Kula said, returning the embrace briefly, then pushing one of Rose's arms free and straightening her clothing. Rose kept her other arm firmly around the taller woman's waist, as she and Kara heaved heavy breaths and grabbed their towels, which had floated to them in the air.

Rose turned with a cheerful smile. "You're getting a lot better with Sorcery, Kara. That was impressive!"

"Thanks, Rose." Kara returned a quizzical look, glanced over her shoulder at Renoq, then subdued a chuckle as she resumed drying the sweat from her body.

Renoq popped another piece of his snack into his mouth and left the room. Rose exhaled a sigh of relief, and let her arm drop from Kula's waist.

"Why do you have to bring me into this?" Kula whispered.

"Sorry! I . . . I just can't deal with that. This is the easiest way to keep him away from me."

Kara smirked as she wiped sweat from her forehead. "I dunno, Rose. He may not be convinced. You should probably kiss her next time to remove all doubt."

Rose's cheeks burned.

Kula rolled her eyes. "I'm surprised he hasn't approached *you* yet."

"Oh, he has," Kara said, trying to reorient her skin-tight uniform properly. "But I didn't have to lie when I told him I'm already with someone."

"Has he approached you?" Rose asked Kula.

"Not really. Mostly, I sense an aura of jealousy from him. He likes *you*, Rose."

"I really wish he wouldn't . . ."

"At any rate, I'm exhausted," Kara said. "This Sorcery fatigue is something else. I'm going to take a nap."

"Aren't you going to bathe first?" Kula asked.

Kara shrugged. "Yeah, I probably should."

She turned and strode out of the area. Kula headed toward the other end of the room, and Rose followed.

"Have you connected with Fita recently?" Rose asked.

Kula shook her head. "No. I can't feel him at all anymore. I fear the worst. Perhaps we *should* go."

Sorrow formed a knot in Rose's throat. "As much as I hate to say it, we shouldn't go back yet. We're not ready. Sheylana needs to finish that vehicle of hers to give us any kind of real chance."

Kula furrowed her brow. "By then it may be too late."

"Maybe . . . but remember, we need to have a way to escape. It won't do any good to get them out of the palace and have nowhere to go from there."

Kula nodded solemnly as they moved through a gap in the half wall into the smaller food storage area. She grabbed a can of isko beans and handed Rose a packet of savory loorith crisps. When touching the packet, Rose once again attempted to connect with the material, finding a remarkable resistance to her Sorcery, accompanied by a sharp sense of loss and sorrow. What could have possibly caused this to befall an entire planet?

The pair ate together in silence for several moments, while a few clangs or screeches of steel echoed from Sheylana's work area. Rose felt compelled to say something.

"I . . . I'm sorry for roping you into this, by the way."

"You are referring to our fictional relationship?"

"Yes. Thank you for playing along."

Kula shrugged and spoke through a bite of her beans. "It is fine. If it were real, this would be my first romantic relationship."

Rose's eyes widened. "Really?"

"Yes. I am likely not a great actor. I have no experience playing the part."

"You're fine," Rose said with a smile. "You're beautiful. I'm surprised you've never been in a relationship before." She threw a handful of crisps into her mouth.

"Some have shown an interest in me. I have never shared their feelings, however." She smirked. "Some were also likely intimidated by Fita and gave up their interest in me rather quickly."

Rose chuckled. "I could see that. So, you've never been interested in anyone?"

Kula chewed through several seconds of thoughtful silence, then swallowed. "Not romantically. In fact, I do not think I have ever felt a romantic or sexual attraction to anyone."

Rose's brow furrowed in thought. "It's interesting how our experience of that can be so different. Mostly, people being interested in me makes my anxiety explode, but when I was with the right person, it was also one of the most incredible sensations I have ever experienced."

Kula gave her a tentative look, sending her heart into a panic. The conversation had taken a dangerous turn.

"It's true. You seemed quite euphoric when you were with—"

She stopped herself. Something on Rose's face must have betrayed her inner turmoil.

Kula hung her head. "I am sorry."

As silence settled over them again, leaving only the distant sounds of Sheylana's work to accompany their meal, Rose forced her thoughts toward the questions surrounding Uvlun: the endless winds and lack of water were likely all connected somehow. As she pondered that, her heart gradually returned to its banal rhythm.

After finishing the last bite of her meal, Kula expertly tossed the empty can into the barrel they were using as garbage. "Perhaps I should check with Shey and see if she could use assistance."

"I'll join you." Rose threw the last few crisps into her mouth as they entered the hallway leading to Sheylana's work area.

They found her with arms locked onto the sides of an enormous fan while she pressed a foot into its housing, which stood several inches taller than her.

"Hello, Shey," Kula said. The woman's head turned. "Is there anything we can do to help?"

"As I've mentioned several times now," she said with a strained breath, "if I need help, I'll—"

Her foot slipped in deeper, and a metal bar shot out from the opening, smashing into her leg with a soft thump. She toppled over with a cry of pain.

"Shey!" Rose leapt forward, but Sheylana lifted an arm in a halting motion and shook her head.

"Rose can help!" Kula said. "She is a healer."

Sheylana kept her hand up. Rose considered ignoring it and helping anyway.

"I . . ." she said, her eyes teary. "Don't . . . I'm okay." She struggled to get the words out, clearly in agony.

"Please, let me help," Rose said.

"No." Shey took in a deep breath and let it out slowly. "I am"— she winced—"okay. Give me a moment."

Kula and Rose waited in silence as Sheylana gradually recovered and stood.

"Now . . ." She wiped her tears and exhaled a heavy breath. "Why are you distracting me?"

"We just wanted to see if you needed help," Kula said.

She winced again, then scowled. "If I need help, I'll ask for it. As none of you have any knowledge of mechanics or electronics, you'll simply get in the way otherwise."

"At least let me bring you something to eat," Rose said. "I know you haven't eaten in a while."

Sheylana sighed, her expression softening. "Oh, all right. I could probably use a break."

Rose smiled and strode back into the storage area, where she grabbed a can of sliced root plant called quetao and cut the lid open with a knife. Back in the work area, she found Sheylana sitting on a box of components and Kula leaning against the half wall nearby.

"Thank you," Sheylana said as Rose handed her the can. "What about you two?"

"We just ate," Kula replied.

Sheylana nodded, pulling open the cut lid and grabbing a round slice of purplish tuber.

"So. How long have you two been together?"

She threw the slice into her mouth while Kula shot a look at Rose.

"Well, uh," Rose said, her insides twisting uncomfortably. "Not very long, I guess. Renoq told you?"

Sheylana smirked. "Yeah. He fancies you, Rose."

"I . . . I'm aware," she said, her insufferable cheeks reddening.

She turned to Kula. "Your girl is quite the shy one, isn't she?"

"You have no idea."

Can we change the subject? Please? Rose's mind raced for something else to talk about.

"How is the vehicle coming along?"

Sheylana swallowed her next bite before answering. "Getting there. Probably another day or two. So, how did you two meet?"

Rose's cheeks burned again. "We met at Tercast."

"Love at first sight, then?"

Rose moved closer to Kula. "I'd rather not talk about it."

Sheylana shrugged. "If I didn't know any better, I'd say the whole thing was a fabrication."

"Excuse me?"

She looked into Rose's eyes with a knowing gaze. Rose nearly buckled, but she needed to maintain the illusion. Sheylana and Renoq had been stuck together for a long time. She would surely tell him if she knew.

Rose put her arm around Kula's waist. "Why do you think we would make up such a thing?"

"Only a feeling." Sheylana glanced at Kula, who appeared to be faltering.

Keep it together, Kula. Don't give up on me now!

Kula looped her arm around Rose. "Rose is a stunning, beautiful woman. I am simply awkward with relationships, so that is probably why you feel that way."

Rose smiled. Regardless of Kula's true feelings, she found the woman's words flattering—mostly because Kula was far more attractive than she could ever hope to be.

Sheylana continued to glance from one to the other as she ate, then shrugged with a genuine smile. "Well then, I'm happy for you two. Being together probably makes this hellscape easier to deal with."

Rose nodded.

After finishing her meal, Sheylana placed the can down and stood with a small gasp. She was still in pain. If only she would let Rose help and heal the damaged tissue. The woman's reluctance was understandable, though. Rose needed to gain her trust first, which, admittedly, may not be going so well.

"Well, I'm going to get back to work. Thanks for the meal."

"Of course!"

Sheylana turned and limped back to the contraption.

"She got hurt pretty bad," Kula said under her breath. "I wish she would let you help."

"Me too. I can understand her hesitation, though. She hasn't known us for very long."

Rose let her arm drop and took a step back from her "partner". She gazed into Kula's bright eyes, which contrasted with her lovely dark skin and long golden hair. In a universe where she felt any attraction to women, perhaps she could see herself actually wanting to be with her.

"What?" Kula said.

Rose shook her head. "Oh, nothing. You caught me off guard is all, calling me beautiful. You're infinitely more beautiful than I am."

"Preferences vary widely. Clearly Renoq favors you, for example. Besides, I *do* think you are beautiful. Perhaps cosmetics could accentuate your natural features, if you wanted to increase your confidence in your own beauty."

They turned their heads at the sound of footsteps in the doorway.

"Shey," Renoq called out, causing Rose's body to release a surge of adrenaline.

As he crossed the threshold, Rose panicked. Without thinking, she grabbed Kula's face and engaged her in a hasty kiss, shutting her eyes.

An instant later, Kula broke it off, staring at Rose with utter astonishment.

Rose turned away, her cheeks burning. Renoq's eyes were as wide as Kula's, and he spun and left.

"Why does everyone keep interru—" Shey said, pulling her head from the device. She turned to Rose and Kula with a raised eyebrow. "Where did he go?"

Rose shrugged.

"Well, tell everyone to leave me alone for a while, all right?"

"Okay."

Rose glanced up at Kula, who looked back at her with an unreadable expression. Shock? Arousal? Fear? Disgust? She couldn't tell. Connecting with Sorcery would probably reveal more, but Kula might find that intrusive at the moment.

Rose strode from the room, with Kula close behind, and put a hand to her forehead in exasperation.

Roseliavelirosara, you're a mess.

Chapter 32

Grit

A massive arm swung around, smashing against a golden blond head of hair. Jeanette watched through glass as Fitale fell with the blow, dexterously rolling upright a few steps away on the stone floor of the experimental chamber. Though his nose bled and his bruised body was clearly fatiguing, the man displayed remarkable grit. This was his third consecutive one-on-one bout with other loincloth-clad initiates.

"He's really skilled," Bellanna said.

The stout, umber-skinned woman had taken over responsibility for Fita's integration, along with several others who had been under Tess's oversight before the Deia decided to keep Tess on Tenrazka full time. Jeanette didn't even get to say goodbye.

"Yes, he is," Jeanette agreed.

The larger, pale man, Gemald, one of Jeanette's more recent charges from Alvior, threw a blow forward, which Fita skillfully deflected. His body spun into a fluid counterattack, catching the man in the ear. Gemald stumbled, but remained upright, though clearly disoriented. Fita panted, bruised muscles tightening across his alluring figure. He bent forward and rested his hands on his knees.

His opponent leapt toward him, throwing his knee out. Fita moved to block, but the blow was too powerful. It sent him sprawling onto the stone floor.

Panting, with blood running from his broken nose, Fita seemed to relax.

"Do it then," he said calmly. "Finish it."

Gemald looked up at Jeanette. He had surprised her with his fighting skill, despite his size. She raised an eyebrow at him. Would he go for the killing blow? His brow furrowed as his attention turned back to Fita's heaving but otherwise motionless figure.

Gemald spat, then lifted his arms triumphantly. Jeanette sighed and rolled her eyes.

"Figures. Disrespectful, but still unwilling to take a life. He probably has only mediocre potential, at best."

"Yeah," Bellanna said. "You could use him as fodder for one of the others."

Jeanette tapped her chin. "Hmm. Maybe for Tovas. I'm putting together a plan for him."

"He's the Lomerian right?"

"Yes. The guy has remarkable integrity and misplaced devotion. If I can get through to him, he'll probably be *amazing*."

"I think Fita will be great too," Bellanna said with a smirk. She eyed him with a thirsty look.

"Yes, I'm sure he will. If nothing else, he's an excellent fighter."

With a sly smile on her face, the woman's eyes brightened. "I have an idea. I'd like to surprise him in his room. Can you bring him by?"

"Sure." Jeanette pulled the cord on the wall down between the observation rooms with Sorcery. The door lifted.

Bellanna turned and left in haste, her long, forest-green dress billowing behind her. Jeanette entered the observation room and yanked Fita up, then draped his muscular arm over her shoulder.

His golden hair nearly matched the color of her flowy blouse. "You did well. You've earned yourself a bit of relaxation."

"You," he breathed. "Betrayer."

"Come on, Gemald," Jeanette called out, ignoring the comment.

Fita was wise enough to submit as she carried him past the other two men he had pummeled into submission. He had shown remarkable restraint and respect, hitting pressure points and breaking limbs in a non-life-threatening way. He likely *would* make a significantly powerful Sorcerer under the Deia's care. Tess had suspected his potential weakness for attractive women. Perhaps Bellanna planned to exploit that.

The hallway was sparsely active. A pair of individuals conversed outside one room, while a group turned the corner ahead. Fita's breathing slowed as they made progress down the corridor, and Jeanette carried him to a room near the end of the hall. Inside, Bellanna lay on a bright pink mattress on the floor, head propped by a hand. Only a semi-transparent rose-colored cloth covered her nakedness. She idly fiddled with a small vial of health potion in her free hand, while she aimed a salacious grin at Fita.

Jeanette rolled her eyes before glancing at Fita. He stared at the woman with his mouth open in astonishment.

Looks like Tess was right.

"Have fun!" Jeanette said, leaving him in his dumbfounded state. She let the door shut softly while Gemald strained to peek inside.

Jeanette sighed. The man was mostly a disappointment, but he had defeated a wounded and heavily fatigued Fitale, so she supposed he deserved something for that.

"Come on," she said. "You may join me for dinner."

They entered the dining hall, where several people were pulling plates of food from the long table at the other end. Round stone tables with soft pillows for seats were arranged throughout the remaining space.

Each time she entered the extravagant room, the memory of

her first entrance flashed through her mind. She had been in chains. A woman had lain on the floor, dead and defiled. Jeanette had fought another human being for the first time in her life, and had miraculously survived.

The memory always brought with it an odd mix of feelings. It had been a terrifying experience, but she appreciated it now. The fight had caused her to rise to her convictions. It had prepared her for the Deia's subtle influence to teach her—prepared her to embrace the unity. In the end, devotion to the Deia was all that would truly matter.

She allowed her charge to approach the table, where a recent devotee she didn't recognize pinched his behind as she passed by, causing Gemald to spin. The brunette woman laughed as she strode from the hall with a plate full of food.

Jeanette grabbed her own plate and began filling it with the spoils of the table, entrées procured from the team's expeditions to the Sovereignty. As she looked about for an open seat, she glimpsed a familiar dark face she hadn't seen in a long time. She smirked as she dropped her plate onto the table and sat on the open pillow next to the man.

"Hello, Yester."

He flinched, turning to her with wide eyes and distancing himself. The two others at the table, a man and woman who Jeanette couldn't name, watched them with interest.

"Maven Jey!" he said, absently dropping his pastry, which plopped against the stone table. "Uh, lively day to you! It has been so long."

"It has." Jeanette pulled the bread from her plate and took a bite. The flavor was reminiscent of garlic bread from Earth, though it was denser and more substantial, with a subtle gingery aftertaste. "I see the Deia still keeps you around for some reason," she said through her chewing.

Yester picked up his pastry, and glanced at the others at the table, awkwardly scratching his chest through his elaborate coat, which was similar to the one he had worn the first time they had met. "As you well know, I have many connections throughout the Sovereignty which the Deia finds valuable."

Jeanette shrugged. "They can't be *too* valuable. I think Tess was fully hoping I would kill you when you pulled your little dominatrix stunt."

The pair at the other end of the table chuckled.

Yester scowled. "Tess encouraged me! She said you wanted it."

Jeanette swallowed her bite, then laughed. *She would. Tess knew it would send me over the edge.*

"I certainly found no interest in *you*," she said, looking him over and tossing the rest of the bread into her mouth.

"I am the bes—"

"You're a saphead, and a worthless Sorcerer," Jeanette said flatly. She gestured to the man's right hand. "You probably didn't even heal that. Had to get a potion or someone else to fix it for you."

Yester's scowl deepened, and his lips tightened. Jeanette grabbed a stick of sweet, tangy kaluka meat and took a bite, locking her gaze with his bright hazel eyes.

"Well," he said, tossing the pastry back onto his plate of scraps. "It seems I've lost my appetite." He stood from his pillow, rubbing his right hand. "Farewell."

As Yester left the room, Jeanette realized she had lost Gemald. Her gaze darted about the room as she chewed. She found him brushing the long curly brown hair from his smiling face as he chatted with a woman with bluish skin and blond hair seated next to him. She looked vaguely familiar. Evanya? Velanya? Something like that. Jeanette couldn't keep everyone's name straight. The Deia had amassed quite the collection of devotees, which grew steadily, thanks to their recruiting efforts.

Yester's plate lifted from the table of its own accord, placing itself in the hands of an attractive young man, one of those assigned to kitchen duty today. The other pair at the table chatted quietly. Jeanette largely ignored them, keeping an occasional eye on Gemald and the woman next to him as they laughed and flirted. He was clearly winning her affection. Charming and witty and all those things Jeanette's boyfriends back on Earth had been, surely. They always ended up breaking her heart. Selfish bastards. In the end, Kara was right. She had been far too nice. Too forgiving. A pushover.

A sneer crossed her face as she considered what those men would think of her now. She could probably break them in half with little more than a thought. And might consider doing just that if she ever saw them again.

Having finished her meal, Jeanette approached Gemald and his newfound interest.

"I always loved the wildlife on Yolfan! So many—"

"Meal's over," Jeanette cut in. "Time to go back to your cell."

"Oh, come on, Jey, just a little longer?" the woman pleaded.

Jeanette wanted to call her by name, but couldn't be confident enough in her memory to try it. "You can come by and play with him later if you want."

She grinned. "I'd like that."

He smiled naively at her.

"Come on," Jeanette prodded, and the man rose.

She and the woman walked together into the hall, Gemald following close behind. The man had no clue what he was in for. He had momentarily forgotten his place in the levity of the dining hall. They would well remind him of it soon enough, then his life may or may not be over shortly afterward.

She took him to the room they had thrown the other less promising candidates in, which he entered without protest. Jeanette shut the door and locked it, then checked the room's enchantment that should keep any of them from manipulating their surroundings easily. It remained strong.

Jeanette turned to head toward her bedroom, then stopped. Perhaps she should check on Tovas. She had asked several others to pay him a visit and was eager to see the aftermath.

The hallways of the palace were moderately active as she made her way down the twists and turns to Tovas's room. One pair she passed discussed a looming attack from Oblivion. Apparently, the powerful being was targeting a Sovereignty world. As their voices faded away, Jeanette felt sorrowful for the many who would likely lose their lives.

Why couldn't they see? The Deia was the only being that could effectively protect them from such a foe. All they needed to do was accept her into their minds—embrace her unity.

Muted snaps of electricity found her before she crossed the threshold into the room. Tovas, naked and bound by the metal clasps on the wall, writhed against the wand held by Suni, a voluptuous devotee who wore nothing but a set of lacy undergarments. She had brought a friend Jeanette didn't recognize, also wearing undergarments, who watched casually from the floor.

The sparks of the wand stopped as Suni acknowledged Jeanette's entrance.

"Oh, hello, Jey!" she said cheerfully. Tovas's body slowly relaxed next to her, eyes closed and head bowed, while Suni pouted. "He refuses to play with us. Maybe you can help us change his mind."

Jeanette laughed. "Oh no, thank you. I just wanted to check on him."

She approached Tovas, noting the bundle of colorful dresses on the floor next to him. His body was littered with bruises and burns. A slight cut on his foot dripped blood. Tilting her head to get a good look, she found they had left his face unscathed. In that moment, she found his light stubble and angular features quite handsome.

"I'm sad you're not being more courteous to your guests, Tovas."

He gave no response. She had the urge to grab his neck, or other body parts, but stopped herself and placed her hands on her hips instead. "Stubborn and witless as ever, I see. Tell me, do you feel loved by your Divine?"

He remained motionless. Still defiant. He'd need a bit more softening before the last trial.

Jeanette turned and strode toward the exit with a satisfied smirk. "Carry on, Suni. He's obviously enjoying himself."

The woman and her companion both grinned. "Okay!"

A new crackle of sparks and low grunts drowned out as Jeanette shut the door softly behind her. It was time for some rest. She'd carry on letting others torment him between periods of silence, preparing him for the final blow—which would be his undoing.

She was certain of it.

Chapter 33

Streams

A tingling rippled across Sam's skin as his hair stood on end. Through Sorcery, he manipulated the dry, desert air—creating a mounting imbalance. He quickly traced a path a few feet from his position, pushing electrons away, effectively ionizing it.

Boom.

An unusually straight bolt of bright light struck the rock he'd aimed for, forcing his eyes closed. A heated shockwave washed over his skin a moment afterward. Ringing pulsed in his ears. He opened his eyes to the landscape lit by evening sunlight, revealing a dark spot of charred rock. He nodded, satisfied with the results.

Scheln hovered in the distance, his lanky figure moving in an awkward walking motion. Sorcery offered him a way to control his movement, but Sam didn't yet find it a convincing simulation of normal muscular behavior—something most people, like himself, took for granted. Scheln was getting better, though.

He sighed, turning toward the oasis. He wished Elleran was available for training or for answering more questions. Unfortunately, Sovereign Aiyla had requested her presence. Sam and

Scheln had continued their practice and experiments without her, honing their Sorcery under Elleran's loose curriculum.

Exhaustion was mounting. He wouldn't be able to do much more before the risk of unconsciousness grew too high. Perhaps he'd soar around for a while longer with the energy he had left— explore the oasis. He had mostly been avoiding the wildlife, because of its oppressive impact on his Sorcery, but if he wasn't reaching outside his body, that shouldn't make much of a difference.

"Scheln," he called out. "I'm going to go fly around for a bit. Want to come with?"

Scheln's head moved in an abnormal back-and-forth motion. A clear no. He probably wanted to continue improving his walk.

"All right, see you back at the abode."

Scheln nodded as he moved into a sort of moon walk. Sam chuckled before peppering his bones, muscles, and other tissue with dashes of anti-gravity, lifting his weight and pushing him into the sky. The cool wind against his face and stunning elevated view of the surrounding landscape never ceased to make his stomach surge with exhilaration. When he was about halfway up the height of the giant trees at the edge of the oasis, he returned some of the anti-gravity in his body back to normal, until he leveled out to an effective weightlessness. A modest force on his hip, and steadying forces on his upper back, sent him soaring into the trees at a relaxing speed.

He admired the colorful landscape below that surrounded the Sovereign's tent. It grew somewhat less resplendent as he progressed past a small stream into the dense, darkening forest. The flora transitioned to a fascinating array of bulbous pink and purple fungi, some of which emitted a soft glow. The swampy terrain led to a cliffside, and the white noise of a distant, unseen waterfall rang with the ever-present backdrop of singing birds and buzzing insects.

As he moved past a cluster of fungi, the waterfall came into view, cascading magnificently across the rocks into the shimmering pond below. Twinkling flower petals spanning the color spectrum rained down from trees at the top. Beyond it were large pole-like plants that reminded him of bamboo, but with bright yellow trunks and small clusters of spear-shaped leaves. He continued his current trajectory past the falls, following the cliff side.

The swamp to his right abruptly transitioned into a grove of sprawling trees with dull red-brown trunks and enormous orange vines. Hard sunlight streamed toward them past the massive trees overhead, which had become sparser. The glittering fan-like leaves of the reddish trees were a familiar dark green. A stream caught his eye through the grove, weaving gently through the terrain. Orange-and-white birds took off from a nearby tree, heading farther inward.

Something sparkled in the corner of his vision. He turned and yelled as a gush of water sprayed him, sending him tumbling into a spread of those fan shaped leaves he had been admiring. Heart racing, he pushed himself off, wiped his eyes, and scanned the ground frantically for a sign of the threat. Freezing water dripped from his doused robes. He reached out for anything, but the wildlife's oppressive presence prevented him from sensing much of anything besides the air and water just beyond his body.

Soon, a figure appeared from behind a tree. A woman. A naked woman. With a familiar face.

Sam's eyes widened. "Zelyra?"

He tentatively lowered himself toward her position, then rubbed his eyes again. Sure enough, it was her. He forced himself to keep his eyes on her face, though he found the feat somewhat difficult.

She giggled. "Hi, Sam."

"Uh, hi," he said. "You, uh, do realize you're naked, right?"

"Yes," she said with a wide grin. "Isn't it wonderful?"

Awkward was more like it, but she certainly seemed at ease about it.

Shifting the anti-gravity gradually from his body, he landed softly on the grassy forest floor.

He scratched his head, turning his gaze toward the nearby tree. "So, uh, what have you been up to?"

"Up to?" she asked.

"Oh, sorry. Force of habit. I mean, what have you been doing? Just exploring the oasis?"

"Oh, yes! It is most incredible. Duriel has allowed me to help him nurture the different biomes."

A large black tiger-like creature with turquoise stripes sprung out from a nearby bush with a roar. Sam flinched, falling back reflexively. The beast moved in front of Zel and lowered into a threatening position, continuing a low growl.

Zel reached forward, placing a soft hand on the creature's head. "No, Mew! Sam is a friend."

"Mew?" Sam said, heart thumping in his chest.

Thankfully, the tiger's stance softened, and it rubbed affectionately against Zel's body.

He shook his head with a slight chuckle. "I should have expected you to have found a new animal friend already. You certainly have a way with them."

"We are all animals, Sam."

He tilted his head in concession. "True."

Mew approached, causing adrenaline to rush through him again. If the beast attacked him, could he defend himself? Most objects outside his body were beyond reach. He could electrify the air, perhaps. Shock it. Or just fly away.

Zelyra snickered. "He's curious. He won't harm you."

Sam raised an eyebrow. "How can you be sure?"

"We're connected."

Mew sniffed at his wet clothing. Up close, the subtle differences between this creature and the tigers he had seen back on Earth became clearer—besides the unusual turquoise stripes. Mew's bottom jaw was larger, and his eyes had square-shaped pupils, rather than the characteristic round or vertical slit pupils of Earth's felines.

"Like with the Tercast animals?"

"Yes!" she said.

Sam shook his head. "How? How does that work?"

Zel thought for a moment, then shrugged. "I don't know. I just connect with them. Similar to my connection with Rose, but different." Mew casually trotted back to Zel, where she scratched his head. "We're all one, after all."

"Our connections to each other all seem to depend on Sorcery though. Why not with them? Why are other animals different?"

"I don't know," Zel said in her usual airy tone. "All creatures are not the same. All variety and threads of life's oneness. The cute creatures of the oasis and those from Tercast are special. I think they are accustomed to the colors of the universe."

Sam blinked. Was she referring to Sorcery, in some abstract way? Possibly. As often happened with Zelyra, he couldn't quite tell whether she was completely out of her mind or saying something oddly profound. Either way, he knew from experience that asking her to expound on her statements would only confuse him further.

Zelyra turned and crouched next to the stream, swirling the water around with her fingers. "You are still playing with rocks?"

"If you're referring to practicing, then yeah. Elleran has been teaching us a lot of incredible things out in the desert, where we can work."

"Boring."

"Not in the slightest!"

"Is to me."

"Fair enough. *I* love it." He sighed, staring off at the massive trees in the distance. "I really wish Kara and the others were here, though."

At the thought, he connected with Kara, aching at the sensation of her fuzzy figure, which appeared to be sleeping or resting. She was safe, at least. Rose was likely nearby—a quick connection told him she was sleeping as well—and Kula should be with them. Hopefully, this situation with Oblivion would be over soon so they could get everyone off Uvlun.

Zel stood, and ambled toward him with a furrowed brow. "I am sorry, Sam. I know she means a lot to you."

Before he could protest, she hugged him around the waist, pressing her unclothed body against his sopping wet robes. As a flushing sensation crept up his face, Sam kept his arms out, unsure of what to do with them for a moment, then lightly rested his fingers on the back of Zel's shoulders. Thankfully, she broke the embrace and returned to crouch at the rushing stream, which now reflected orange sunlight that shimmered below the gigantic trees in the distance. Mew settled beside her, lying in the typical relaxed manner of a cat.

Sam idly turned his attention to the trees and grass for several minutes as Zelyra continued to tinker with the water. He gazed at one of the yellow vines hanging from the tree, admiring its wavy pattern and the crimson seed-like sprouts. The plant life was exotic but somewhat familiar. He wondered whether life on all planets somehow shared a single origin, and how that might have happened. Alice, the AI he had spoken with back on Earth, had said there was no widely accepted answer to the question.

He took the vine gently in his hand, and his stomach growled, protesting the fact that he hadn't eaten since breakfast. The small red sprouts of the vine looked rather tasty, but he wasn't foolish enough to eat a random plant. It would be best to get a full meal from a trustworthy source.

"Well," Sam said, letting the vine go. "I'm going to head back to the Sovereign's tent for some dinner. Want to come with me?"

Zel shook her head. "No. The oasis is my home now. I was always meant to be here."

"What about Alvior? Your family?"

She shrugged. "They will not miss me."

Zel rarely talked about her home life, but she didn't seem to be close to her family. That was remarkably depressing. Even though Sam had distanced himself from them, he still missed his parents and sister. He felt a slight ache of guilt again at failing to contact them. He committed to doing so after these situations with Oblivion and Uvlun were settled.

"Well, your Ulinko family will definitely miss you."

She turned to him with a warm smile. "Thank you, Sam. I hope you all visit from time to time."

"How does Duriel feel about you staying here?"

Zel gazed into the distance past the water, then shrugged. "He said he is okay with it."

"Well, I'm glad you are happy here," Sam said with a grin.

She returned his smile.

"Take care, Zel."

"You too, Sam."

With a little dash of Sorcery, his body rose off the ground and accelerated back toward the camp. A yellow vine abruptly reached out and curled into a large circle in his path. He sped through it, glancing back with wide eyes at the impossible sight. Zel held a hand to her mouth, giggling, as the vine moved back and dropped to its normal position.

Turning to face forward again, Sam wondered how the vine could have possibly moved in that way. It was almost as if Zel had something to do with it, but she couldn't possibly have connected with the trees and vines, too. It was impossible.

Wasn't it?

Chapter 34

Fabrications

"That's part of your peritoneum."

"My what?" Kara asked.

An unusual, somewhat unnerving but subtle sensation of movement in her gut accompanied the tissue's movement. She observed it through the bizarre sensations of Sorcery—telesthesia, Elleran had called it. Rose's presence stayed with her, and she was likely probing the tissue directly. The thin, folding membranes of tissue hugged her intestines underneath her abdomen.

"Your peritoneum," Rose repeated.

"What does that do?"

"Several things! It mechanically supports your abdominal organs, hosts major blood vessels, elum pathways, and nerves; and secretes lubrication to reduce friction between organs." The folds of tissue twisted slightly, causing Kara to wince at the odd sensation as they bunched up against the left side of her abdomen. "If you have an abdominal injury, it will migrate and move to protect—"

"Okay, okay," Kara said. "That's enough of that. How did we get there, anyway? I was asking about my muscles. You said I can strengthen them mainly by enhancing the filaments inside?"

She opened her eyes to find Rose's pale, freckled face before her in the poorly lit bedroom area of the dome.

"Yes. But keep in mind that changes done with Sorcery only seem to be permanent when *restoring* tissue to the way it was before. Healing, for instance. Any kind of change from the norm reverts after the enchantment fades."

As she sat up Kara furrowed her brow. "Why, though? Isn't that weird?"

Rose shrugged. "Sam and I discussed it aboard the ship, though we never really found out much about it. It's like our bodies have a natural 'default' that they spring back to."

"So, cosmetic surgery via Sorcery is off the table, huh?"

"Seems so."

"Bummer."

"What would you change? I mean, you mentioned muscles, but what would you change cosmetically?"

Kara pursed her lips, wondering if she should reveal such a thing to Rose. She was essentially her doctor, but also a friend, so that could make things a little awkward. Oh well.

"Maybe my height."

She glanced at Rose, who didn't seem fazed by the answer. Instead, her face reflected genuine curiosity as she cocked her head. "Why?"

"I dunno," Kara said, looking down at her chest. "I'm really short. Might be nice to be a few inches taller."

"If you really wanted to, surgeons in the Sovereignty could make that happen. If you ask me, though"—Rose smiled—"I think you are wonderful the way you are."

Kara chuckled. "Don't start ogling me now."

Rose's cheeks reddened, and Kara smirked, leaning forward and draping her arms loosely across her bent knee.

"I heard what happened in Shey's workshop. I didn't know you were really into her."

"I'm not!" Rose said, her cheeks becoming even warmer as she turned her head downward.

Kara laughed. "I was joking when I said you should kiss her, but you really took that to heart, didn't you?"

"No! Really! I . . . I just can't handle Renoq's interest in me right now. Not after . . . after . . ."

Her face crumpled, and Kara's teasing transformed to guilt.

Damn it, Kara. You messed that one up.

Not knowing what else to do, she wrapped her arms around Rose. "Hey, I'm sorry. I'm sorry . . . I . . . was trying to be funny and failed miserably."

Rose hugged her back. Though she wasn't crying, Kara sensed she was holding back her emotions. A change of subject was in order. She pulled out of the hug and locked eyes with Rose's, which were misty—on the brink of something terrible.

"You know," Kara said, "a few years ago I wondered if I might be bi."

"Bi?"

"Bisexual? You don't use that word or something?"

"Oh, you wondered whether you were attracted to women?"

"Exactly. Anyway, it became pretty clear to me soon afterward that I don't swing that way, but I did question it for a while. I thought I might have had a crush on a girl at my school." She giggled at the memory. "Got physically closer to her one day, though, and bam, the feeling vanished. Never felt that way toward another woman since. I don't think there's anything wrong with it. It's just definitely not for me."

Thankfully, Rose smiled.

"Anyhoo," Kara said, standing up. "I'm going to go see if Kula's up for another spar before bedtime."

"Okay."

Kara left her in the room to return to her reading. It was too bad she didn't still have her parents' copy of *Pride and Prejudice*. Rose had been casually perusing some journals left behind by the dome's former inhabitants while Kara napped, even though Shey and Renoq had already told them a summary of their writings. As she moved through the "rooms," a heavy clanking from the direction of Shey's workshop echoed across the interior. Kara found Kula right where she expected her to be: the exercise room. She fired an arrow from her bow, then spun and slashed with Renoq's sword.

"Hi, Kula."

Sweat rolled down the woman's elegant face. Her golden hair whipped about as she finished a flurry of strikes, then caught the arrow she had fired as it returned to her position. She had been working on enchanting the arrows to come back to her, since she had only a handful left. While Kara didn't feel a romantic attraction toward her, she did find Kula to be a strikingly beautiful woman.

"You up for another spar?"

Kula finished one last lunge, then relaxed and turned to Kara, wiping sweat from her brow. "Yes, after a brief rest."

"Sure."

Kula strode to the half wall, leaning Renoq's sword against it.

"How is Rose?" she asked as she sat on a crate.

"She's all right." Kara plopped onto a barrel nearby, scratching her head. "I . . . uh . . . may have accidentally touched on a sore subject, though."

Kula's brow furrowed. "Vurkil."

"Yeah." She sighed. "She mentioned how she pushed into this whole situation with you and Renoq because she can't handle another guy being interested in her."

"You didn't see them." Kula's gaze turned downward. "They were wonderful together. His death was profoundly tragic."

The emotions of that fateful night at Tercast played briefly in Kara's mind. The immense unease. Olik. The giant. Countless others, including her own parents. Killed at the hands of that despicable man, Delveton, and his deceptions.

"Welin Em Onii," she whispered.

Kula's head perked up. "What was that? I believe I've heard it before."

"It's the Force's unofficial motto. It means 'for life, duty, and love.'"

Kula gave a respectful nod, letting a solemn silence take hold before she spoke.

"I have completely lost my connection to Fita."

"You did? When?"

"I don't know exactly ... It seemed to happen while I was asleep." Her head dropped in sorrow.

"What about Rose? Can she feel him?"

Kula frowned. "No, she cannot connect to him either."

"This is why I didn't want to wait. We should—"

"No. We don't know for certain, but his Sorcery may have simply vanished again. And Rose is right. Charging in now could make things worse. We need a transport."

Approaching steps caught their attention, and Renoq entered.

"Hey, ladies," he said, brushing his thick hair back. "Enjoy the sword?"

"Yes, thank you." Kula picked the sword up from against the wall. "It has a fascinating enchantment."

"Yeah," he said, chuckling. "Name is Tham-Hammer, so it goes."

Kara raised an eyebrow. "It's a sword."

Renoq took the blade from Kula, gripping it tenderly. "Meant to be deceivin'. When the blade strikes a surface it can't penetrate, it throws a concussive blow at it." He reached into a barrel of scraps and grabbed a thick, warped metal plate. "Watch."

He stepped back and tossed the plate up, then lightly batted it with the sword. It hit with a loud clang, louder than Kara had expected. The plate flew across the room, smashing into a nearly empty crate, which splintered and spilled its contents of empty canisters onto the ground.

"Whoops!" He hurried forward.

Kara and Kula both stood from their seats and moved to help.

"Anyway," he said, picking up the splinters of wood. "You get the idea. Works somethin' fierce on armored opponents."

"You think it could harm someone in Ilkuth?" Kara glanced at her suit in the corner as she bent to pick up a few pieces of the crate.

Renoq shrugged. "Dunno about that." He eyed the suit himself for a moment. "That's pretty advanced stuff. Maybe if I hit it right."

"I would not recommend testing that," Kula said.

The weapons they had used at Tercast to defend themselves seemed to have been effective. Granted, Kara was pretty sure Delveton had sabotaged the suits to make that happen. They should not have been that easy to take down.

As they were throwing the last of the junk into a pile where the crate had once stood, Renoq stiffened.

"Rose! Apologies if I disturbed ya. Was showin' them the sword's enchantment."

"It's . . . it's okay," she said, approaching timidly. "Renoq, I've been thinking about this a lot, and I . . . I need to tell you something."

Kara met Kula's eyes.

Renoq glanced briefly at Kula as well, scratching his head awkwardly. "If it's about you 'n' Kula, I apologize about that. Shouldn't have pushed it." He put his hands up. "Promise I won't be tryin' to come between you two."

"Renoq," Rose said, her cheeks reddening. Kula's face was remarkably stoic. "We . . . aren't really together. Not romantically."

Renoq blinked, glancing between Rose and Kula, clearly perplexed. "But—" He stopped, putting a finger to his cheek. "Why?"

Rose faltered and her gaze turned downward. The tense silence made Kara's bones quiver. She was about to speak up when Renoq finally broke the silence.

"Ah. You know, if you don't find me attractive, that's all you gotta say."

"That's not . . ." Rose trailed off.

Kara rolled her eyes and opened her mouth to speak, but Kula beat her to it.

"She is in love with another."

Renoq nodded. "Ah, someone else in the group you were separated from?"

Rose retreated inward even more. This was dangerous territory. She clearly wasn't ready to confront that again. Not yet.

"So to speak," Kara said. "It's a really sensitive topic. We shouldn't talk about it."

"What about you, Kara?" Renoq said. "Are you actually with someone or was that a fabrication too?"

Kara smirked. "No, that's the truth. Sam's *my* guy."

Renoq smirked himself. "Think he'd fight for you?"

The question intrigued her. Would Sam fight for her? He wasn't really the fighting type.

She folded her arms. "Depends on what you mean by that."

"Would he fight me for your affection?"

Kara laughed. "I'm perfectly capable of beating you down myself, thanks."

Renoq gave a hearty chuckle. "So you're the man in the relationship, eh?"

Reflexive anger coursed through her veins. So much was wrong with that statement, she didn't even know where to start with a rebuttal. Then realization set in.

He was baiting her.

Kara stepped toward the mat with a grin. "All right, Renoq." She widened her legs and lifted her arms into a fighting pose, then turned off her eyes.

"Let's see what you've got."

Chapter 35

Fita

Tovas awoke from his brief nap, which he had managed only out of sheer exhaustion. Aches and waves of agony washed over his entire body. Cold, metal clasps bit into his wrists and ankles, suspending his body above the stone floor of the small, otherwise empty room. Despite his attempts to stop it, the dryness of his mouth and throat caused him to cough, bringing a spike of pain along the bruises and burns on his legs and torso. Several people had come in occasionally to inflict more punishment or give him food and water, though he had been alone for several hours now.

Divine above, give me strength. Do I deserve this? Is this my fate for failing to protect Tercast? For failing to save souls from Jeanette's wrath?

Death would offer a welcome relief.

Tovas quickly smothered his longing for it. He couldn't think like that. Suffering was an inevitable part of life. He must honor life.

What was it Scheln had said? *Life is what it is. Deserving has nothing to do with it.*

Scheln knew suffering. He had endured so much. Tovas could do the same. He had to.

He wished he could sleep more. Fatigue gnawed at his mind, but the pain of his injuries and shackles refused to give him rest. His physical body surely couldn't take much more punishment. Despite how quickly his wounds seemed to heal, if they kept pushing with this intensity, his body would eventually give up, releasing his soul to the Divine.

As minutes of agony ticked by, Tovas wondered how everyone else was faring. Jeanette had said Kara had come to Uvlun. Was she all right? Had she found a place to hide? Jeanette likely would have mentioned if they had captured her. Were the others with her? Perhaps they were all waiting for the right time to strike. Or perhaps they had taken the chance to escape, finding the castle too difficult to penetrate.

Given the power he had observed in those under the Deia's command, he could understand that course of action. His friends stood little chance of executing a successful rescue. Sam was reasonable. He might convince them it was impossible, that trying to save Tovas and Fita would be a worthless endeavor.

A man's muffled voice echoed in the hallway outside Tovas's door. He only caught a few words. "—permitted down here, the Deia—"

The man screamed along with the sound of sizzling. Tovas flinched, and a spike of pain from his injuries rippled through his body. A moment later, the door burst open from a powerful kick, thrown from its hinges. In the doorway stood Fita, his long golden hair disheveled. In his right hand he gripped a familiar sword, glowing with radiated heat that distorted the surrounding air.

Tears of joy fell from Tovas's eyes at the sight. He wanted to call out to him, but the ache of attempting to speak held his tongue.

"Tovas!" Fita said, rushing to him. "Hold on."

The blade burned hotter, and he struck the chains binding Tovas's ankles. Tovas gritted his teeth as the metal singed his skin, but the metal melted quickly and released the tension on his legs. When Fita freed the ones holding his wrists as well, Tovas collapsed to the ground, finding himself too weak to support his own weight. Pain shot through his body as Fita pulled him up and slung an arm around his shoulder, holding Tovas up.

"I . . . I'm too weak," Tovas said through pained breaths. "I won't make it. You go. Get out."

"No. Take this."

Fita pulled out a bottle of red liquid and popped the lid. Tovas wondered for a split second how Fita could have possibly gotten his hands on a health potion, and his sword, but decided he didn't care. The man poured the heavenly liquid into Tovas's dry mouth, and the pain across his body faded, offering wondrous relief. With the new comfort afforded by his healing wounds, Tovas felt a renewed longing for sleep; fatigue weighed on his mind, suffocating him, but Fita kept him upright.

"You're coming with me," he said, grabbing Tovas's pants which had been brought in earlier. "Put your clothes on."

Fita helped him dress, then assisted Tovas through the door into the hallway, which was thankfully empty except for the body on the floor with a charred hole in his chest. Tovas attempted to contribute some to their escape, but Fita did most of the work. Despite being healed, Tovas found himself still subconsciously avoiding movement for fear of pain, and the weight of his fatigue pressed ever downward.

Two female voices echoed around the corner. Fita pushed hard to the side, throwing them into a small storage room containing boxes, buckets and cleaning supplies. The women rounded the corner and passed by the door, their jovial chatter continuing down the hall.

"Let me unveil your Sorcery," Fita whispered.

"Let's get out first," Tovas said wearily.

"No, *now*." He pulled Tovas's arm off his shoulder. "Before it's too late."

He held open his palm, staring at Tovas with stoic determination. Tovas tentatively placed his hand on Fita's. If his Sorcery was still working, he knew he could perceive his friend's body. Fita was likely experiencing that remarkable sensation himself.

Again, like with Belze, his presence sought entry into something sacred. Something holy.

Tovas withdrew his hand. "I'm sorry. It doesn't feel right. I don't want to rush this. Let's get out of here first."

"Tovas, this is serious. You must accept."

"I will not. Not now. I'm too fatigued to assist you, anyway."

"I cannot take you with me without it."

Tovas furrowed his brow. "Then go. Get out. I will attempt to find my own way. If I am captured again, then so be it."

"NO!" Fita slammed a strengthened fist into the stone floor, creating a small crater. "Why are you acting like this? You know you can trust me! Let me in so you can have your power back."

"Fita." Tovas placed a hand on his friend's shoulder. "I do trust you. Truly. I simply don't feel right about this. I fear that rushing into it without precaution may do more harm than good."

"It is Sorcery! You have already had it. I am only revealing its full potential."

"Not now."

"Argh!" Fita grabbed Tovas's arm in frustration and hoisted him up, then barreled out of the room. They turned the corner and, to Tovas's horror, came face-to-face with Jeanette. She wore a chilling smirk.

"Hello, Tovas," she said.

Fita pulled Tovas's arm off him and raised his sword. Numbness overtook Tovas's limbs. Fear gripped his stomach, making him feel sick. Could Fita best her? He was unsure. His friend had clearly regained his grasp on Sorcery, presumably from Belze. Perhaps he could hold her off long enough for—

A stiff, unexpected force shoved Tovas forward, and he fell onto his arms. He turned, looking for the enemy. To his surprise, he found only Fita, whose arm returned to his side.

"He wouldn't accept," Fita said.

Tovas's jaw dropped as he stared up at those familiar dark features. Fitale? He couldn't. He *wouldn't*. The man was steadfast, loyal. Adamantly so. It had to be some kind of trick.

Jeanette approached, and she sighed. "You said he would trust you."

"I thought he would, but it appears that was not enough."

Tears welled in Tovas's eyes. He watched him say those words, but he couldn't believe them.

"Fita," he said. "How could you? What would Kula—"

"The unity!" Fita said, lowering his sword. "I didn't understand before. It's *all* about unity. We are one with the Deia. She guides us. We preserve the—"

"I've already tried reasoning with him," Jeanette said. "It doesn't work. He doesn't listen to reason." She grabbed Tovas's shoulder and lifted him up with a powerful arm. "Come on, let's put you back in your room."

Tovas stared into the face of his former friend as Jeanette hoisted him up, still hardly believing it was him. His mannerisms. His expressions. They were certainly his, though. Fita's light eyes were harsh but pitying, sorrowful. He seemed genuinely upset that Tovas continued to resist.

Somehow, the Deia had taken him.

Jeanette unceremoniously dragged Tovas down the halls, past the man Fita had killed in the supposedly false rescue, and tossed him back into his room. The door flew back to its position from the floor, and the hinges repaired themselves.

Jeanette stopped in the doorway. "When this is over, you will understand, Tovas. You will thank us for opening your eyes."

She departed into the hall, and the door shut and locked itself behind her.

Tovas remained on his knees, and warm tears ran down his cheeks as he prayed for Fita's soul.

Chapter 36
Metaphysical Oppositionism

Sand and stones flew, propelled against a powerful late afternoon wind. Sam focused on as many as he could, and sent them on new trajectories. They whizzed past his ears, crashing into sand or rock nearby. Another eye-watering blast came through, carrying more. He found them all quickly, and shot them in different directions until one, about the size of his fist, smashed into his leg and sent him tumbling to the ground.

The winds subsided, and their Source, Scheln, descended. The pain in Sam's leg quickly subsided with Elleran's presence. She approached, hovering in the air.

"Good," she said, "but a great number can easily overwhelm your ability to focus on them one by one. Once you see a pattern, set up an enchantment on your body, or the surrounding air, to counter it."

"We learned to enchant our bodies against projectiles at Tercast," Sam replied. "I definitely should have thought of that."

Ribbons of light appeared above Scheln's head, spelling the word *tired*. He then floated off toward the camp.

"That blast took a lot out of him," Elleran said. "He's going to need rest."

"Sounds like a good idea."

Sam dusted off his thick Tercast field robes, wondering if it was weird that he kept wearing the same outfit every day. He'd bathed, he'd cleaned them, and they were fairly comfortable. There didn't seem to be any reason to change them. Clothing was best ignored, anyway. He had far more important things to do.

"Is now a good time for me to ask more questions?"

Elleran's aged face turned back to him with a smile. "Yes, but let us go to the peak. It has a better view."

Sam lifted his body with antigravity and propelled himself forward after his instructor. He and Scheln had been practicing and learning for the past two days under Elleran's patient and experienced guidance, significantly advancing their skills. She had even described her understanding of the physical mechanisms behind antigravity—concepts that Sam still struggled to fully comprehend.

They settled onto a flat peak of a nearby hill, giving them a distant view of the beautiful oasis amid otherwise endless desert. Elleran sat with her legs crossed, and Sam joined her, excitement building within him.

"Did you try the experiment last night?" she asked.

"Yes, I tried. I couldn't quite get the causality shifting to work, but I think I was close."

It was something Rose had some experience with. Perhaps he could discuss it with her after they rescued everyone from Uvlun.

Elleran smiled. "I am sure you will have success. Persevere. Remember: Learning from books or from others is second-hand knowledge, communicated through imperfect language, and will always be inferior to direct, first-hand experimentation and observation."

Sam nodded, suspecting that Mr. Nowell would quite like Elleran.

"That said, what is on your mind today?" she asked. "I will answer to the best of my ability."

"The temples. Each one was a test focused on a different physical category, right? Mechanics for Land, electromagnetics for Air, thermodynamics for Fire, and biology for Water?"

"Yes, broadly speaking."

"So." Sam stood up and began pacing, unable to keep himself still. "Why was the Water temple different from the others? Why did it try to kill us?"

"I can guarantee you that if the original Tercast Masters enchanted it, any danger was illusory."

Sam brought a hand to his chin in thought as he paced. "But it was the only one without a timer. The chamber flooded completely. We would have drowned if it wasn't for Rose."

"Hmm. That sounds like a test for more advanced studies," she said, idly drawing in the dirt with her finger. "They would frequently use the temples for lessons targeted to more experienced groups. I suspect they simply left the chamber in that state. I am certain it would not have let you truly drown. The Masters took safety seriously."

Sam stopped for a moment and stared up at the bright blue sky with only sparse wisps of distant clouds. "Okay, so what about that last chamber? The one with the Tercast symbol above it? We guessed it was a lesson on morality. What was that all about?"

Elleran nodded, stopping her drawing and bringing her hands gracefully into her lap. "Your conjecture is correct. Their presentation has several flaws, and was always too presumptuous for my taste, but yes, the Tercast Masters always emphasized the duality of Sorcery as a means of moral instruction."

"So morality *does* have an impact on Sorcery? Good and evil, so to speak?"

Elleran smiled. "What do you consider to be either good or evil?"

He stopped and placed his hands on his hips. "I don't really believe in good and evil. My stance has been that morality is made up by society, until I saw that room at Tercast."

"A logical conjecture," Elleran said, to Sam's delight. "But surely you believe that some behavior, according to your own judgment, is morally praiseworthy, while other behaviors are reprehensible. Is that right?"

"Well, yeah, of course. I'm a part of society, after all."

"What distinguishes these sides of morality according to your personal view?"

Sam continued his pacing, turning his gaze toward the ground. It was a good question. What *did* he think created the distinction between right and wrong behavior?

"It's fuzzy, I think," he finally said. "But I would say it's probably suffering. Causing suffering is immoral. Relieving suffering is moral."

"That is quite hedonistic. A common philosophy."

He stopped and turned to her. "What do you mean?"

"Tell me, Sam. Considering that Kara's parents likely had the option to cure her condition as a child, was it morally wrong for them not to have done so?"

The unexpected question took Sam by surprise. If Kara had been sighted, her life would have been profoundly different. Easier. She likely would have endured less suffering. But Kara had *embraced* those difficulties. They had become a key part of her entire personality. Without them, she could be a completely different person now. Would he change that to save her from suffering?

"I . . . don't know," he admitted. "Maybe, but I don't know."

Elleran grinned. "An excellent answer."

Sam raised an eyebrow. "But it wasn't an answer."

"'I don't know' is always an excellent answer, when given honestly, especially regarding judgment. It means you acknowledge the limits of your understanding. I believe there is great wisdom in a reluctance to pass moral judgment."

"So, if suffering isn't the line between good and evil, what is?"

Elleran's gaze turned distant, pensive. "Objectively, many traditional views of good and evil are so nebulous and subjective as to be almost meaningless."

He spread his arms wide. "Ha! That's what I said." He pointed into the air. "Tovas wouldn't have it, though. He always insists that good and evil are just as real as anything else."

"He is Lomerian, yes?"

"Yeah. He also believes that the Divine gave him a revelation through that staff of his."

"The Staff of Dreams?"

"Yes. When he first touched it, he believed he received a revelation from the Divine saying 'protect my people.'"

Elleran rubbed her chin in thought. "According to history, the staff's original owner was an immensely powerful Sorcerer. He claimed the object had been enchanted by Divine will, and not by his own hand, though I doubt those claims. Tovas is likely falsely ascribing supernatural sources to the staff's powerful enchantments."

"That makes sense." Sam was sure Tovas would take issue with that deduction, but it certainly made more sense than Divine intervention. "What do you believe in, then?"

"Like you, I consider myself a skeptic. I embrace uncertainty. While I consider supernatural explanations plausible, I also consider them unlikely. Based on my understanding of the universe, I would say the closest thing to religious belief I adhere to is metaphysical oppositionism."

Sam furrowed his brow. "What does that mean?"

She gestured to their surroundings. "All that exists in this universe appears to be based on an underlying principle of opposition. Matter and antimatter. Positive and negative charge. Clockwise and counterclockwise momentum. The principle holds true in the realm of experience as well. Sweetness and bitterness. Pleasure and pain. Happiness and suffering."

"But not good and evil?" Sam asked.

"As I said, good and evil are often too subjective and ill-defined to be useful. While I believe one side of Sorcery is 'right' and the other is 'wrong,' objectively speaking they are necessary oppositional manifestations of the natural world."

"In the context of that room at Tercast, you mean the bright side and the dull side, right? What exactly do those refer to?"

"The division of Sorcery appears to be one's intent toward the experience of life," Elleran said.

"As in . . . appreciation for one's own life?"

"In part. A reverence or respect for *all* life, including one's own. The Sovereignty holds fast to this principle."

"So, the protection of life?"

"Again, in part. Perhaps it would be helpful to answer the question: 'What is life?'"

Sam looked down at her, but she didn't go on, staring up at him expectantly. It was a question best left to someone like Rose, not him. Could he come up with an all-encompassing definition of life? He doubted it.

"I don't think I know enough to say."

Elleran's eyes crinkled with her grin, and her gaze turned to the oasis. "In truth, I suspect Duriel could answer that better than either of us, but my favorite definition of life is that of an entity engaged in intentional self-preservation."

Sam nodded as he studied the oasis with her, observing the massive trees hanging over vast changes in elevation where colorful plant life sprung from the surface. He considered Elleran's definition, and couldn't think of any immediate exceptions.

"The principle perhaps most associated with life is that of balance," she mused.

"What do you mean?"

"The balance of oppositions. Too much order and you have an inert rock. Too much disorder and you have a chaotic tempest. Life is the balance: homeostasis. A blend of rigid structure and disorderly motion. Diversity. Harmony. To honor life is to honor all aspects of balance."

The words rang true to Sam. There was something almost poetic about the idea of life as a balance of extremes. A balance of heat and cold, rigidity and flexibility. Perhaps also of pleasure and pain, as she had mentioned.

"Okay." He resumed his slow pacing on the rocky peak. "So, thinking back on that room at Tercast, what you're saying is that a greater respect for life results in greater power of Sorcery on the light, colorful side of the spectrum, correct?"

"Yes."

"Then what corresponds to the other side? The dull gray?"

Elleran smiled. "What is the opposite of life?"

Of course, she would turn the question around on him.

"Uh . . . death?"

"No. Death is the *absence* of life. Not its opposite."

Sam furrowed his brow, unsure.

"The opposite is that which, when met in equal force with life, results in its absence. We Vivezan have historically called that concept 'uvlun,' which is another piece of Sorcery vocabulary Ilius and his followers seemed to have misunderstood."

"Oh, so *that's* why you said you were pretty sure the planet's name was not Uvlun."

"Indeed. Uvlun is not a place. It is a state of mind. A state of intentions that are anti-life."

Sam raised an eyebrow. "Like murder? Genocide?"

"Think broader," Elleran said, turning her gaze back to the oasis, which reflected deeper orange rays as the sun settled on the horizon. "If life is balance, what does that make anti-life?"

"Imbalance," he said, considering the implications. "So it's an extreme?"

She nodded. "In human interactions, it usually manifests in the extreme imbalance between the vital concerns of individual freedom and security of life, which is why the Sovereignty places such emphasis on those principles."

"You mean letting everyone be free, but only so far as they don't infringe on the freedoms of others?"

"Precisely. Well said. It is a most challenging balance to strike. Uvlun is often exhibited as an extreme in either direction. Anarchy results in chaos and death. So does ruthless unification. Gestalt consciousness is the objective of the Molkinar Empire, which is why they have opposed the Sovereignty since their inception."

That aligned with what Kara had told him about the empire.

"And you said power is based on intent?" Sam asked. "Not action?"

"Correct. I am impressed you caught that distinction. Sorcery appears to depend entirely on whether the user's intentions truly respect the balance of life or seek to drive an imbalance. Importantly, the actual life-or-death consequence of their actions has little to no impact on Sorcery."

"So the path to hell *can* be paved with good intentions? Or uvlun, as it turns out."

Elleran tilted her head. "Possibly." She held up a hand. "But remember that knowledge is also a key component. *The* key component. The greater one's knowledge, the greater the possibility the results of one's actions will align with their intentions."

Sam tapped his chin. "So the transparent figures in the middle of the line, those are people who lack knowledge?"

"In part. Those who are ignorant are effectively impotent with Sorcery, since knowledge is the primary driver of a Source's power. Those who are indifferent toward life, or who cultivate relatively benign but selfish inclinations, are also fairly impotent."

Sam stared at the clouds, which were also turning a deep orange. The annoyance of hunger gnawed at him, but he couldn't eat at a time like this.

"So why does the Sovereignty keep Sorcery a secret?" he asked. "Why not just tell everyone and let this natural process entice people to gain more knowledge? Seems like that would be a good thing."

Elleran raised her eyebrows. "A drive for knowledge is good, yes, but tell me honestly, Sam. If everyone had immense, universe-driven incentive to embrace either balance, selflessness, and respect for life, or some form of uvlun, what do you think would be the result?"

He thought for a moment, then shrugged. "It's probably better than mass ignorance."

She shook her head. "Not if you value life. Historically, ignorance has been safer. Sorcery drives all toward either side of the conflict. Addiction. Narcissism. Manipulation. All these things drive imbalance. Humans are often hypocritical. When forced to confront their own hypocrisy, many will choose to embrace an imbalance. The Masters of Tercast always prophesied a day when the secret of Sorcery could no longer be contained, resulting in a great conflict between Sorcerers. Many would surely perish in such a scenario."

She raised a wrinkled finger pointedly. "To preserve the secrecy of Sorcery is to preserve life."

"So that's what that whole fight at the end was, between the colorful side and the dull side," Sam said. "Where they were attacking chains? Their prophesied fight between life and anti-life?"

"Between Vivezan, Sorcerers who respect life, and Mortezan, Sorcerers who embrace uvlun. Yes."

He thought of Jeanette's frightening anger. Kara, lying on her back porch with blood pouring from her chest. A horrifying scene he still couldn't quite believe he'd witnessed.

"People can change sides, though."

Her gaze turned distant. "The line gives an inaccurate impression of slow progress one way or the other, but yes. It is possible for one's so-called standing on the spectrum to change. Those who initially maintain respect for life can plunge to the other side, embracing uvlun. The path back to respect for life is typically far more arduous. Few have made that transition."

"Is there any difference in strength?"

Elleran gazed up at the clouds. "Not significantly, but there appears to be an underlying difference in the mechanism of action between Vivezan and Mortezan. Both typically cannot Vitalize the same material simultaneously."

"So when a 'good' Sorcerer"—he made air quotes as he paced—"enchants something, a 'bad' Sorcerer can't reach it?"

"Not typically at a distance. Physical touch often pierces that barrier, however."

"But not always?"

She traced a finger in the dust. "If an opposing Sorcerer is in proximity, that can prevent even physical touch from allowing a Sorcerer to Vitalize materials under their control. Powerful, long-term enchantments often block opposing Sorcerers as well. I fear this is likely what prevented my Vitalization of the area through the portal."

"But then the reverse is true too, right? For instance, even though they have that powerful staff, they can't really use it?"

"Somewhat. It bears a powerful enchantment, which a Mortezan cannot immediately use, but the enchantment can be . . . Usurped, so to speak, over time."

"Okay, so what about after this prophesied battle? At the very end, a single figure came into the middle. They seemed extremely powerful, like they had control over the entire universe."

"Ah," Elleran said. "The Transcendence. There have been archaic accounts of Vivezan who claimed to have momentary power over all of existence. Tercast religion took those accounts literally, giving the event a kind of holy significance."

"Sounds like some kind of Divine ascension," Sam said.

"Indeed. They are almost certainly myths designed to encourage ethical behavior. Privately, I know many of the Masters of Tercast believed this to be the case."

"Yeah, all of their interpretations around morality and power sound like a lot of conjecture."

Elleran gave him a piercing look. "Remember, Sam, that the presentation in that room is a metaphor. A model of what is. While models can be useful, at some level they are always wrong. That includes models derived from objective scientific thought and inquiry."

Perception is not reality. The words rang in his mind.

He nodded, moving to resume his pacing. "So, what was the deal with the choosing rooms at Tercast? Those gems? Couldn't they be used to grant Sorcery to anyone?"

"Gems?"

"Yeah!" Sam held out his fingers, estimating the size to be

about equal with his palm. "They were about this large. Glowing. They gave us Sorcery."

"Oh." Elleran chuckled. "No, those are nothing more than enchanted light sources. The limited unveiling of Sorcery is a property of the Tercast area, not any object."

He stood still for a moment. "As in, the *ground itself* is enchanted?"

"Yes. The walled area of the castle is under enchantment."

"How does that Tercast enchantment choose who to unveil?"

"I don't recall the details, but I believe it will eventually unveil everyone on its grounds who has respect for life, given enough time. If memory serves me, it depends on aspects such as the candidate's emotional state."

"You're telling me it just depends on how you're feeling that day?"

Elleran shrugged. "Somewhat. Emotion is a volatile factor in the manifestation of Sorcery."

"Ah, right. Strong emotion seems to increase power pretty significantly."

"Yes. Never underestimate the power of emotions. They can seem to break the normal rules of Sorcery in profound ways. Very challenging to research."

"Emotion can do more than just enhance your power?" he asked.

"Yes. However, Sorcery driven by intense emotion is always a significant risk. It will often leave the Source drained of energy, resulting in unconsciousness."

"What about—"

Elleran flinched, her eyes widening. Sam's heart leapt with a surge of adrenaline. He spun in alarm to glance behind him, looking for a threat, but found nothing but blue sky.

"I'm sorry, Sam," she said as she stood. "The Sovereign is requesting us immediately. There appears to be a development."

He sighed. He still had so many more questions.

Air rushed past his ears as they flew back toward the edge of the forest, where the enormous trees, darkening with the evening light, expanded to consume them as they approached the Sovereign's white tent. Aiyla strode toward them from the entrance in a simple pale blue top and black pants.

"Duriel, Vivezan, keeper of Alqesi," she called out. "Please answer. We have no more time to wait."

"Oblivion has launched the attack?" Elleran asked once she landed next to her.

"He launched many, as he always does. But we now know which are decoys and which is his true intended target. We have already begun evacuating the planet."

Evacuating an entire planet? Sam thought incredulously. *How is that even possible?*

"Duriel, please," Elleran called to the oasis.

Something large approached through the forest, rustling the leaves and bushes. To Sam's immense surprise, a magnificent white dragon appeared, its enormous wings beating gales through the trees before it landed nearby. Sam wondered how a creature that size could even fly. Duriel and Zelyra slid from the creature's back, both of them stark naked. Leaves rushed up from the forest floor to cover their nudity as they approached the group.

"I will go," Duriel said with conviction. "As long as Zelyra remains behind to tend to the oasis."

"Wonderful!" the Sovereign exclaimed. "She has my full support to remain here."

"What is the attack?" Duriel asked.

"An asteroid heading straight for Naleren. It will strike the atmosphere in less than six standard hours."

Chapter 37

Sky Raft

Knives flew in all directions. A familiar, low, booming voice cried with anguish. The massive force of an enchanted hammer collided with an impenetrable suit of armor. Lightning struck, sending a shockwave across a destroyed courtyard.

Rose woke with a start, gasping as she found herself on a cot inside the survival dome. Her frantic heartbeat thrummed in her chest. Kara and Kula were already up, having left their sleeping spots in a disheveled state. Through the opening to their small "room," she found Kara seated on the floor in her uniform, with her plasma rifle disassembling itself in the air nearby. Rose smiled at the sight. Kara's skills with Sorcery had come quite a long way over the past few sleep cycles.

Rose sat up and rubbed her eyes, then strode into the larger area with the rest of the group. This breakfast would be one of their last, since supplies would run out soon.

"Morning Rose," Kara said. "How did you sleep?"

"Lively morning. Okay, I suppose."

"Grab some berries we hydrated. I think it's our last can."

Rose continued past the group toward the lav. "No, thank you. I'd really like a bath."

After using the lav, Rose entered the washroom, which contained a single standing tub and a shower, the door to which had been broken off.

Rose approached the tub and found strands of brown hair scattered about the white interior and peeking up from the drain. She picked up the hairs with Sorcery and threw them in the nearby garbage bin. Kara was lucky Rose was the next user. If Kula or Sheylana had come in, she would have received a mouthful. Again.

A turn of the dial sent water gushing into the tub—purified water which had likely circulated through human bodies many times. A fascinating thought. Once it was full, she undressed and heated the water before testing it with her hand. Not quite warm enough. She gave it more energy, warming it until steam visibly rose from its surface. Water always seemed to take more energy than her intuition guessed, likely due to its high specific heat. She felt it again, satisfied with the temperature.

Rose immersed herself in the steamy liquid, relishing the intense heat that melted the endless chill of Uvlun, and settled into a comfortable position. She felt as if she could almost go back to sleep. As her body relaxed, she checked on the state of her connections. Elleran, Sam, Scheln, and Zel were anxious, but healthy. Ya'ir appeared to be sleeping. Kula and Kara were rather well. She would now only rarely get brief, fuzzy glimpses of Tovas. He was in pain, and her connection was unfortunately too weak to do anything about it, but he was at least alive. Fita's connection was still unreachable. She feared for him.

Using the nearby box of soap powder, Rose cleansed herself. She soaked for a few more minutes before telling herself she had to get up, then stood, feeling the chill wash over her. A clean towel from the nearby rack flew to her through the air, and she let the tub drain into the water reclamation system as she dried. Once empty, she refilled it partly with cool water and dashed in a bit of powdered detergent, then scrubbed her field robes, wishing she had something new to wear.

Talanna and Niu would be appalled that they wore the same clothing all the time. The pair had been horrified enough at the idea of wearing the same robes every day at Tercast, but at least they had changed into sleepwear for the night. No such luck now.

A tear dropped down Rose's cheek. She missed them. Missed their endless bubbly chatter. Relon may not have minded the clothing situation as much, or at least wouldn't have been vocal about it. Rose missed watching her from the sidelines during their Elemorb games. The woman was a natural athlete. Often quiet, but fiercely competitive. Another tear fell into the tub with a light plop.

Rose let the water drain, wrung out her clothing, and placed them into the ancient dryer that Sheylana had fixed. She could use Sorcery, but it might be best to save energy. As she sat waiting for the cycle to complete, Rose saw to her other hygeine, cleaning her teeth and tending to her nails. The cycle completed with a loud ring.

As she was pulling the clothing out, the door to the washroom flew open. Rose whipped around, draping the robes over her front, cheeks burning.

"Do you mind?"

"Sorry, Rose," Kara said, striding in with purpose. She wore her shiny Ilkuth armor without the helmet. "Sheylana has finished her vehicle. We're heading into the city today to see if we can find something that can help us get off this rock."

"Oh. That's good. I'm worried about Fita."

"I just hope we're not too late."

Rose nodded. "Me too. Now can you *please* let me get dressed?"

Kara chuckled and turned to leave. "Okay, okay. Just wanted to let you know."

Relieved, Rose dropped the clothing and began dressing. As she pulled the pants up to her waist, Sheylana burst in. Rose grabbed her top and held it to her chest, blushing furiously once more.

"Why is everyone walking in on me?" she cried.

"Oh," Sheylana said, turning around. "Sorry, I thought since . . . Kara just . . ."

Rose donned the rest of her clothing, then addressed her unwelcome guest. "Okay, what is so important you have to come barging in like this?"

Sheylana turned and strode toward her with an odd expression. Shame? Guilt?

"Sorry again for coming in, but I wanted to catch you alone."

Fear spiked in Rose's chest. Her cheeks burned, and she cursed them. What could this be? Was *Sheylana* going to confess a romantic attraction? *Please no.* More drama was the last thing they needed as they prepared to wade through the dangers of Uvlun.

"I know Renoq and I will want to share a connection with you, as you are by far the most effective healer we have, but I want to do mine privately, since it may come as a surprise to you."

Oh. Just some unusual anatomy or something. That's a relief.

"Okay. I'm ready whenever you are," Rose said, holding out her hand.

Sheylana placed her hand on Rose's, and her body came alight to Rose's Sorcery. Curious as to what Sheylana was concerned about, Rose inspected her organs. She found the unique features of every human body quite enthralling, and enjoyed seeing how each person differed in both subtle and profound ways. Sheylana's anatomy seemed fairly typical. A healthy heart thumped in her chest. Lungs expanded and contracted, pressed by a strong diaphragm. Her muscles had experienced some atrophy, likely from suboptimal nutrition. Digestive organs were working properly, currently digesting her breakfast before it would move into the small intestine.

Roses eyes widened as her perception reached lower, into the pelvis. Something was missing. Ovaries. Additionally, she had partially developed male anatomy. Sheylana stared back with apprehension.

"You're ven!" Rose said.

She nodded. "Yes, I'm vengale. Though I prefer to present as a woman, since that's how my body mostly appears."

"Male hormone insensitivity?" Rose guessed.

"Yes."

"Why do you seem ashamed of it? It's nothing to be ashamed of."

"I'm not ashamed, just embarrassed."

Rose smiled. "It's nothing to be embarrassed about either."

Sheylana raised an eyebrow. "Says the woman who just got upset about others walking in on her while she was dressing."

Rose's cheeks burned again. "Fair point."

"I'm comfortable with my body. Could have always had surgery, you know, gone one way or the other, but this is how my body naturally developed, and I see nothing wrong with it. The . . . uh . . . Tercast Masters were *not* happy when they found out, of course."

"They banished you here? For that?"

She shrugged, then pulled away, but her body remained alight to Rose's Sorcery. "I technically lied, since I told them I wasn't ven. Otherwise, they wouldn't have let me in. Poor decision in retrospect."

Rose didn't know what to say, so she stood there awkwardly.

"Thank you," Sheylana said with a smile.

"For what?"

"For listening. It feels good to talk to someone about it, but I'm always afraid people will start asking probing questions or, worse, ask to *see it* because it's uncommon, you know? That's why I prefer to remain a woman as far as society is concerned. It's nice to blend in."

"Of course."

"Renoq already knows, by the way," Sheylana said, turning to join Rose as they headed toward the exit. "The man can be insufferable sometimes, but he's all right."

The pair emerged to find Kara braiding Kula's long golden hair as she sat on a plastic chair. A mirror leaned on a crate in front of them.

"You two ready to go?" Kara said, maintaining her focus on her fingers, which worked the hair with precision. "Renoq has almost finished loading everything into the—what do you call the thing, Shey?"

"I haven't named it. I've just been calling it the 'vehicle.'"

Renoq entered the main area. "Hey, ladies. I'm almost done loadin' Shey's masterpiece." He hoisted their last box of food and headed back the way he had come. "Should be about ready to go."

Rose surveyed the open area for anything else they might want to bring. Most of what remained were crates filled with junk. In the corner stood Kara's Ilkuth, with the Maul of Ruin and Kula's wind bow leaning against the half wall next to it. The sight of the maul threatened to bring memories to the surface, so she moved her attention elsewhere, focusing far more intently than necessary on a crate filled with all kinds of cables and wires.

"Done!" Kara said.

"Have you done that a lot?" Sheylana asked.

"God, no. I've always been terrible at braiding."

Kula rose from her seat, twisting her body in front of the mirror, admiring her look with a smile. "It looks wonderful. Thank you, Kara."

"Thanks for teaching me!"

"Helps when you can see."

"Definitely. Now you'll look all pretty for any robots or Sorcerers we need to smash up."

The two laughed together as Kara donned her helmet, and Kula picked up her bow.

Kara hefted the maul, and the four women headed into the sizeable area next door, where the typical background scent of grease and ozone became far sharper. Inside sat the vehicle, encircled by crates filled with mechanical and electrical parts. It was slightly smaller than an ascender, consisting of a large U-shaped metal housing compartment containing various parts, with an open section in the middle for passengers. Two large circular humps stood embedded in the rear housing, with two smaller humps on the sides, each with shiny fan blades within.

Sheylana lifted a box of parts and tools, likely bringing it so she could make repairs if needed.

Her mechanical skills awed Rose, having constructed the vehicle from the parts scavenged from drones and the dome. Renoq's upper torso became visible for a brief second as he worked to secure their cargo with cords.

"Kind of like an airboat," Kara said. "Reminds me of an inflatable raft from back on Earth, but backwards." Her eyes lit up. "We can call it an air raft!"

The others groaned.

"Ugh, no," Kula said.

"Whaaat? It fits!" Kara insisted as they approached the vehicle.

Sheylana shook her head and sighed. "I guess we can call it a sky raft."

"I still don't like it," Kula said, climbing onto the open middle section.

Rose chuckled. "Sounds better than 'air raft.'"

"What's that?" Renoq said, reaching his hand out to Sheylana. "You're calling this an air raft now?"

Sheylana took his hand and climbed aboard. "Sky raft. Kara's insisting on a name, so that's what we'll call it."

"I like it!"

Kara remained behind as the rest of them climbed aboard. Rose took Renoq's hand and stepped onto the craft, maintaining her grip on him after lifting herself. His body came alight through the perceptions of her Sorcery.

"Renoq, let me connect so I can heal you from a distance if needed."

"Yeah. Good idea."

A moment later, he released her. "All good?"

His body remained visible to her, his organs shining amidst the dim, barely perceptible air of the dome. "Yes."

"Ready for me to cut our exit?" Kara said.

"Hold on," Sheylana said, fiddling with the controls at the back of the sky raft. "Let's get this thing off the ground first."

She tipped a rocker switch upward, and the metal of the craft groaned until it left the ground, holding them up in the air.

"All of us add significant weight, which worries me. Kara, make sure you don't put too much weight on this when you get aboard."

Kara put her hands on her hips. "You calling me fat?"

The group chuckled, Renoq's laughter bellowing out above the rest.

"I'm *saying*," Sheylana said through her own laughter, "that suit of yours can easily destroy this thing. Be gentle!"

Kara returned a thumbs up. Humming crescendoed from the rear of the craft, accompanied by the whirring of large fan blades. It was followed by two more brief, higher-pitched hums from the left and right sides, corresponding to the smaller blades there.

"Everything checks out. I don't know how far it'll get us, but the power supplies should last a good long while."

"I don't care," Renoq said. "I'm ready to get out of here."

"Sounds good," Kara said. "Ready for our exit?

Sheylana nodded.

Kara's suit left the ground, then flew straight through the wall, breaking the thick concrete and steel reinforcements with ease. Cold air rushed into the dome, where the winds immediately scattered dust and small parts everywhere. She dove back and forth several times, crashing into the wall to create a few feet of extra clearance for the craft. Sheylana fired up the rear blades, which were scarcely audible over the winds of Uvlun.

The craft eased through the opening, and the headlights engaged, illuminating the rocky ground through the oppressive darkness. Dry winds whipped Rose's hair across her face, and she wrangled it into a bun, while Kara flew gracefully into the spot they had left for her in the vehicle.

"Following your lead, Kara" Sheylana yelled over the gales. "Where are we headed?"

Kara pointed off to their right. "The signal is coming from that direction."

The craft turned. Once they aligned, the whirring behind them screamed and the sky raft sped into the darkness.

Chapter 38

Olorus

As the rocky landscape of Uvlun flew by beneath them, Kara's thoughts turned to Jeanette, Tovas, and Fita. She was glad they were finally leaving the dome. Hopefully, they'd find something that would help them complete the rescue and get off the planet.

Upon reflection, she was grateful Rose had insisted they stay in the dome. Navigating Sorcery was an incredible experience, and would certainly be useful in a fight. She opened herself up to it, relishing in the fleeting emotions of her body, her suit, and the air as they passed through her perception. It was reminiscent of finding her surroundings with blindness, relying more on the feel of herself and her environment rather than the visuals. She wished she could feel more than the air, though. Uvlun sucked.

Their vehicle crested a scraggly hill, and Kara's eyes widened at the sight of crumbling buildings. Jagged edges of concrete and steel reached out to the suffocating darkness in all directions, surrounded by piles of windswept rubble spread by Uvlun's endless winds. The haunted structures grew in size and number, and Sheylana navigated between them, taking them several feet over the destroyed roads in between.

What happened to this place?

"Keep heading in that direction," Kara said, pointing toward the source of the signal.

It could have been anything: nuclear war, some kind of natural disaster, or maybe Molkinar had quelled an uprising and torn the planet to shreds. Whatever the reason, the planet was dead. They needed to stay focused on rescuing Tovas and Fita. The planet's history didn't matter at the moment.

"If you see something that might be useful, call it out," she said. "And Sheylana, this road is veering off from our target." She motioned toward the signal again.

The vehicle crested the single standing wall attached to the side of a building's skeleton, taking them in the direction she had indicated. As they were now flying higher, the ground below became less visible. Kara turned the lights of her suit's wrists on and focused them down on the surface, providing much better illumination.

"Look!" Kula called out.

Kara glanced up and saw a lit building. Her helmet displayed the source of the target signal right on top of it.

"It's that building! That's where the signal is coming from."

A drone emerged from a nearby structure, a spherical device about the size of a watermelon, shining its own spotlights at the rubble below. Kara quickly aimed and fired, shredding the device to pieces.

"What was that?" Renoq said.

"A drone. Didn't want to let it detect us."

As they approached the building, they found more drones, which Kara disposed of as soon as she saw them. They swarmed around their target like a hive of insects.

"Land over here." Kara pointed to an area behind a standing wall. "We don't want them to see us."

Sheylana complied, landing the vehicle where Kara had indicated.

"What are you planning to do? Go in there?" Renoq asked.

"Yep," Kara said, rising from the raft. "It's being guarded for a reason. Hopefully, we'll find something useful."

Kula gestured to the maul she had left behind. "Aren't you going to take this?"

"No. Honestly, I don't think it helps much. My suit has more than enough power to smash things. That thing just gets in the way."

The others followed her out, and they gathered near the edge of the wall separating them from their destination. Kara waited for a drone to pass by, then raced toward the large, well-lit building. The drone turned when they neared the doors, and Kara aimed her arm cannon at it, centering the target reticle on its spotlight as Rose threw the door open, easily destroying the locking mechanism. The drone's spotlight shone on them.

As Kara was about to pull the trigger, the drone turned and rushed off without alarm.

"Come on!" Kula said in a harsh whisper.

Kara kept her eyes on the departing drone, her skin crawling.

Something wasn't right. It didn't sound an alarm like before. Why?

Kula continued to beckon, so Kara turned and followed her inside. A steady clanking of gears and motors echoed within the metallic walls. After passing through the dimly lit entryway, she and Kula headed toward the others, who stared out over a massive room. Kara's jaw dropped at the sight of giant machines connected by a mess of conveyor belts. Each carried parts of various drones. Semitransparent pipes filled with black or blue fluids ran along the walls, connecting to some machines.

It was a factory.

"What are they building?" Rose asked.

Kara zoomed in on one belt that looked like it had a more completed part with several components.

"Drones. Molkinar-ish drones. But they don't look right."

She followed the progression of the belt through the mess of other machines and components, and it led to a point where the belt split in two directions, with an arm that swept the parts one direction or the other. Every piece was being pushed down the rightward path, which led to machines that pulled the components apart and sorted them onto other conveyors.

"I don't get it," Kara said. "It looks like it's constructing them and then taking them apart again."

"I think one or more of the machines is defective," Sheylana said. "See all the maintenance drones over there?" She pointed below them, where small round machines with several arms worked. "They're trying to fix it, but it looks like this assembly line has been malfunctioning for a long time."

"Well, the signal is a few floors up," Kara said. "Anyone see an elevator?"

"You mean a lift?" Renoq asked.

"Yeah."

"I think that's one over there." He motioned to another section of destroyed wall, through which they could see gated platforms.

Kara led them down the hallway, past the section of destroyed wall, which turned to follow the edge of the factory floor. Around the corner, the left wall had been knocked down, revealing the interior of a conference room. Chairs, some lying sideways, circled a large table, that was missing a chunk at one end. A spherical object floated through it, with small glowing lights. A drone. Kara aimed at it, but it ignored their group, floating away to the hole in the right wall that led into the factory.

They reached the platforms and found that they were indeed some kind of lift. Curiously, instead of being enclosed in the typical Sovereignty glass, this lift was more like a cage, surrounded by metallic bars. As they approached, the gate opened with an ear-shattering screech. Thankfully, Kara's suit compensated almost immediately to dampen the noise, but the others slammed their hands over their ears.

"Ow. Looks like a platform," Renoq said. "How do we control it? Can you connect with your Nit?" He strode onto the platform.

Kara queried her Nit for a lift. *No lift found,* it responded.

"I don't think so. It can't find it."

"There are buttons here." Rose gestured to a small panel on the side of the cage. "Should I try it?"

"Sure," Kara said.

Rose pushed one of the upper buttons, and the platform jolted upward with an angry whine. Jerky oscillations eventually settled into a slow, squeaky rise.

"Whoa, this thing clearly hasn't moved in ages," Renoq said.

"It does move, though, which is remarkable," Sheylana added.

Kara's patience quickly wore thin as the platform screeched its way upward. She could easily fly through the elevator shaft on her own and make her way to the signal much faster. In fact, she probably didn't even need to use the shaft or hallways; her suit could rip through the floor and walls like nothing, but it would cost more energy. A glance at the power on her helmet display showed only less than a sixth remaining. She'd want to preserve that. Unfortunately, with no sunlight in the dome, the Ilkuth had received no chance to recharge. In hindsight, she should have flown it into the upper atmosphere to recharge at some point, or plugged it in at the dome. Oh well, she should at least have plenty of charge for the rescue. That's what mattered.

"Are we there yet?" Rose asked.

"No," Kara said, eyeing the marker showing the source of the signal. "Keep going. I think it's just a few more floors up."

Door after painstaking door gradually passed by, but soon enough the marker got close to leveling off.

"Next floor up, I think."

Rose nodded. When the platform came to the next set of doors, she let go of the button, relieving them of the obnoxious squeal of the lift. The metal doors opened, then stopped after only a few inches. It emitted an irritating buzzing noise—likely because of some kind of error. Kara strode to it and forced it open.

Darkness.

She turned on her helmet lights, illuminating the area, and came face-to-face with an odd sight of clean destruction.

The steel walls and sections of the floor and ceiling had been met with devastation. Lines of bullet holes littered the remaining pieces of infrastructure. But the remaining floor was spotless. There wasn't a single piece of debris in sight. Kara cautiously walked into what used to be a hallway.

"What happened here?" Renoq asked as he followed her out.

"A fight, clearly," Kula said, joining them.

They strode down the dark interior toward the source of the signal. The passage opened up into a large circular hall, where cleaned gashes marred the steel floor.

"Almost there," Kara said. "I think it's right up—"

The unexpected sight of a shriveled humanoid figure stopped her. Her heart leapt into her throat, and she lifted her arm cannon, scanning the area. There were several more figures lying on the floor ahead, but nothing else.

The group gasped at the sight. Kula readied her bow. Rose rushed forward, and a point of light appeared near her head, illuminating the bodies. Kara continued to scan the area for threats, the sense of dread looming like a dense, ethereal fog. Thanks to Rose's light, Kara could see that thick metallic bonds tied three bodies to a circular pillar in the center of the room; perhaps five or six others were scattered about.

"They died ages ago," Rose said. "The bodies are exceptionally well preserved."

"That pillar thing in the center is the beacon," Kara whispered.

"Looks like some sort of trap," Renoq said.

"Seems to be. Doesn't look like there's anything else here. We should get moving."

Rose threw out a hand. "Wait. This may give us clues about what happened to the planet." She touched one body tied to the center pillar. "If I can just—"

An earsplitting alarm blared overhead.

Kara flew toward Rose. "To Rose!" she called to the others. "Stay together."

Drones poured into the room, firing at the group. Kara aimed her cannon, but there were too many of them, and she had limited ammunition. Kula let an arrow loose, which rippled through a powerful air current, striking an unlucky target and sending several other drones colliding with each other. She sent another arrow flying, and a new gust carried it through another group of drones.

I need to identify the biggest threats, she told her Nit.

Red indicators popped up over a few of the drones on Kara's display, startling her. *Whoa! I didn't know this could do that.*

She fired a few bursts of her arm cannons, taking down a cluster. The machines continued to barrage the group with gunfire that ricocheted off Kara's armor and the others' skin. She kept her focus on the biggest threats with her arm cannons, which she noted locked on to a particular weak point with perfect aim, requiring only a single bullet per drone. Metal scraps quickly piled onto the floor. She would be fine in her armor, but eventually the enchantment protecting the others would weaken, and they would be vulnerable.

Two bright red indicators turned her attention to giant steel doors on either side of the room. They opened simultaneously with a thunderous roar, revealing enormous bots. Each one's upper torso was a large turret and other weaponry sitting on a body with six wheels on each side. Her display highlighted sections of the machines in transparent orange: weak points. They resembled some of the Molkinaran units she'd learned about in training, though more blocky and rugged. The one ahead of her fired a rocket, and Kara flew to meet it head-on. A brief bump and increase in temperature accompanied the ensuing explosion. She continued straight into the "head" of the machine, bathed in orange, and ripped through it. Her momentum brought her straight through the wall, into another destroyed yet clean hallway.

She shot back through the lower half of the machine, noting that Renoq and Sheylana were hitting the other "tank" with their weapons, tearing it to pieces. Kula remained with Rose, firing her air-splitting arrows ceaselessly at the surrounding masses, which returned to her after wreaking their destruction.

Kara flew through the clusters of drones nearest her, firing precision arm cannons as she went, and smashing a few of them by hand for good measure. Within minutes, they reduced the remaining enemies to scrap metal. A mountain of mangled parts and curved metal bodies littered the enormous room.

"Is everyone all right," Kara asked as she landed near Rose.

"Yes, everyone is fine."

"I actually quite enjoyed that," Kula said with a smirk.

"Kara," Sheylana called out.

"Yeah?"

"If the bodies have a Nit, you may be able to retrieve data from it."

Kara groaned. "Do we really need to?"

"Yes!" the others said.

"Fine, but I'm not touching any dead bodies. Nooo, sir."

Sheylana didn't seem too keen on touching them either, despite her suggestion. Rose, Kula, and Renoq carried on, inspecting the bodies for anything of interest.

"These don't have any," Rose said, referring to the ones tied to the pillar.

"This has one!" Kula pointed to a body near the center of the room, but not tied to the pillar.

The group gathered at her location.

"Your suit should have an uvo connector," Sheylana explained.

Kara queried her Nit about an uvo connector. *External uvo connectors are located in each wrist*, it replied to her mind. She requested to use them, and a tiny, thin cable popped out near the palm of her right hand.

"Got it," she told the others.

Sheylana took the cable, which only stretched a few feet out, and pulled Kara toward the body. She recoiled at the sight of dried flesh, and tried to focus her attention elsewhere.

New device detected, the Nit told her. *Identifier 8J199E449A497. Decryption in progress.*

"I'm connected."

"Find anything?" Renoq asked.

"It's decrypting."

"Shouldn't take too long," Sheylana said.

Data corruption.

"Says there's data corruption," Kara said. "Seems like the more recent data is okay, but the further back the data gets, the more unreadable it is."

She didn't want to be stuck here all day.

Read the interesting parts of the most recent entry out loud for the group, she instructed her Nit.

Her suit's confident female voice echoed across the room:

"Reading sections of entry one doh three five nine with the highest likelihood of value. Common language detected. Data corrupted. Unreadable sections will be replaced with inferred language where possible.

"'[CORRUPTED] continues the war on water, sending [CORRUPTED] of it into the upper atmosphere. We've transmuted enough to stay alive, but our grip on the planet is failing as plant life continues to die rapidly. [CORRUPTED] and some of the other Vivezan are working on a solution, but we have little time left.

"'I miss Raina. I hope she and Emiloy are okay. We don't dare send out broad communications though, or they'll find us.

"'We have received a distress signal from Ren's team in the remains of Olorus, so we're heading in to get them out of the city. Word is they were trying to get to the hangar again. We [CORRUPTED] the explorers to get off planet, but they're far too heavily guarded. Drones are everywhere, replicating like a virus. We can't [CORRUPTED].'"

The group shared looks as they processed the sparse account.

"Well, that's terrifying," Renoq said.

"What are Vivezan?" Kula asked.

The others shook their heads or shrugged. Kara queried her Nit.

"My Nit says that Vivezan were religious volunteers who occasionally worked with the Sovereignty military on peace-keeping efforts."

Kula frowned. "Sorcerers?"

"Maybe."

"Can you search for Olorus?" Sheylana asked.

Kara asked her Nit for any planet in the Sovereignty with a city named Olorus. She received dozens of results.

"There's a ton. Doesn't exactly narrow it down."

"What about any *formerly* inhabited planets?"

She modified her query, and it returned a single result.

"Got it! The planet was called Icalron."

The others gasped.

"*This* is Icalron?" Renoq said. "No way."

"What's Icalron?"

Rose spoke, her eyes wide. "According to history, Icalron was the very first planet Oblivion destroyed."

Chapter 39

The Final Trial

Tovas awakened groggily, finding himself immersed again in the nightmarish agony of his cold, stony, sparsely clothed reality. A few unfamiliar faces had visited after his encounter with Fitale, and the memory of their torment encumbered his thoughts. He slowly sat up from the stone floor, new bruises, burns, and cuts accenting his misery. After using the corner bucket, he drank from the keg of water they had left and idly longed for death before catching his subconscious musing.

No! Life is precious.

Was it, though? Was all this suffering really worth it? It could end easily. All he had to do was comply the next time they returned. Killing himself would prove difficult, even if he allowed himself to attempt it. They would surely revive him and torture him more. The only option was to obey. Then he could be free.

But no, that wasn't right. By complying, he would disrespect his life. All life. He would be unworthy of ascending to the Divine —of being reunited with his faithful family. That was what he believed. It was what he had always believed.

Divine above, give me strength. Tears fell from his eyes. *I cannot do this alone. I am weak, and they are powerful, but thou art all-powerful. I need thee. Please. Help me escape this.*

His memory of that deep, peaceful feeling he had experienced when first touching the Staff of Dreams entered his mind, comforting him: *Protect my people.*

How could he possibly follow that guidance? He couldn't protect himself, much less anyone else.

The door to his room opened, and his body instinctively backed against the opposite corner.

Jeanette.

She stood in the doorway wearing a long-sleeved square-neck top with subtle chevron patterns, embroidered white gloves, and a skirt showing plenty of thigh. Attractive, yet terrifying. An icy chill settled in the pit of his stomach. When her eyes rested on him, her lips twisted into an ominous smile.

"I trust you have been well, Tovas."

He stared back in silence, acutely aware of the way his heart was bursting to escape his chest.

Her shoes clacked against the stone as she entered the room and approached. The chill in Tovas's gut rose into his throat. He had nowhere to go. No way to fight her. He was powerless.

When she came within arm's length, she grimaced. "Ugh, it smells in here." She hoisted him up with a powerful grip. "Come. I have a *new* wonderful surprise for you."

Her words sent shivers of terror across his skin.

She pulled him down the hall by his upper arm, a few others they passed greeting her with a smile. A tawny-skinned woman with dark hair gave him a salacious look as they walked by, making him feel too exposed without a top on. Jeanette led him through a set of large double doors. His eyes widened at the unexpectedly familiar surroundings—the place where he had found himself when he first awoke inside the palace, what now felt like a lifetime ago.

Windows on the far wall gave him a view of two smaller rooms. One had several occupants pacing or sitting against the wall, wearing rags. They didn't seem to be aware of his and Jeanette's entry. A fine white powder coated the room's walls and drew haphazard splotches on the skin of those inside. The other room contained a single occupant.

Lelanna.

She sat against the far wall, head hung low. Jeanette waved her hand in front of the window, and the tone of the glass shifted. Lelanna seemed to notice it, lifting her head and flinching when she saw Tovas.

"We're going to play another game!" Jeanette said. "I made it myself. You'll love it, I'm sure."

Tovas squeezed his eyes shut as she dragged him across the room. *No. Not again.* The memory of a woman being scorched alive flashed in his mind.

"More moral dilemmas! With fire. I like fire. So transformational! Anyway," she said, pointing to a thin white cord leading from the center of the area to a levered switch box that split into each of the smaller rooms. "One room is coated in highly flammable powder." She tossed some in the air, and a spark ignited it, exploding into a burst of white-hot flames that spread across the floor. "That's where the fuse will go unless you take action." The flames dissipated. "There's only one way to stop the inferno."

She gestured to a crystal attached to the ceiling in Lelanna's cell, only partially visible through the window. "That's a special enchantment of my design. When hit with a spark, it'll transmute all the air in the room into pure nitrogen. She'll go unconscious in seconds, and her brain will fail soon afterward. A nice, peaceful death."

Lelanna placed a hand on the glass, staring at Tovas with pleading eyes. *Please, end it,* her lips said, though he couldn't hear her voice. She pointed to her chest. *I'm ready.*

"Oh, look at that," Jeanette said. "She's eager for it."

Tovas regarded Jeanette with a pained expression. How could she have fallen so far? How could she be so removed from the suffering of others? How could she desecrate the sanctity of life to play these terrible games?

"Don't do this Jeanette."

She laughed. "Oh, Tovas. Soon you will see what I'm trying so hard to teach you. Besides, this is the easiest decision ever. Flip the switch, and painlessly end Lelanna's suffering. The other five get to live on."

"The Divine will—"

"Ugh. Do you *really* think some almighty, otherworldly 'Divine' exists? And that they deeply care about life? Tell me, Tovas, if that's the case, where is this 'Divine' when people suffer? Why doesn't the 'Divine' actually save those who desperately need saving?"

"Sam once asked me the same thing."

"Heh." Jeanette crossed her arms. "So what did you tell him?"

"Opposition is essential," Tovas said, hoping that by keeping her engaged in a discussion, it would at least delay her disgusting game. "The Divine allows us to experience the consequences of our actions, and the actions of others."

"So that's it, huh? This 'Divine' cares so much about everyone and everything that They leave existence to destroy itself?"

"They are not inactive. They guide us. And we are only good inasmuch as we resist and conquer evil. Evil must exist to be resisted."

"And that makes me 'evil,' right?" Jeanette ignited a flame above her finger.

"No," Tovas said, causing her to raise an eyebrow at him. "*You* are not evil, Jeanette. Kara and Sam know you. The real you. This is not you. This is a version of you twisted by the Deia. You can always come back."

She let the flame die as she folded forward, laughing. When she straightened up, she wiped a tear from her eye. "Wow, you *really* think I would change after all this?" She gestured emphatically. "The Deia *is* Divine. She grants us power. Control. Unity. I'd never give that up to be the weakling I was before."

"I didn't know you, but I find it difficult to imagine you could be weaker than you are right now."

"Don't patronize me. You're trying to get me to change my mind about letting you decide who to kill. It won't work."

She raised her fingers, and the flame reappeared above them.

Tovas's heart thumped in his chest. *Keep her talking!*

"Wait!" he yelled, reaching out to grab her arm. "You can—"

"No more talk," Jeanette said as she bent down and ignited the end of the fuse. "Time to choose."

Tovas watched helplessly as the spark traveled down the line. He looked around the empty room for anything that might douse it. But there was nothing.

Jeanette stepped back, giving him space to panic.

He stepped on the spark, finding only pain as it burned the sole of his foot. He jumped down ahead of it and bit the fuse, but it was far too strong. Turning his gaze forward, he followed the line all the way to its end in the small room, where people sat or paced.

Five lives. About to die. Or one, if he decided it.

Banging caught his attention. Lelanna's hand pressed against the glass.

It's okay, Tovas, she mouthed as she pointed emphatically at herself and the room next to her. *Free me. Save them. I'm ready.*

He shut his eyes, where tears formed. No. He wouldn't kill her. He wouldn't play Jeanette's game. There *had* to be another way.

Divine above, help me save them. Help me protect them. All of them.

He opened his eyes to an implacable ceiling. Then insight. Comfort. He noticed the cord between rooms, hanging from the ceiling, and his eyes traced its mechanical connections. It controlled the doors. By pulling the lever, he could let them free. The prisoners could flee to the larger room. While escape from the palace was nearly impossible, it was a chance. Jeanette was powerful, but her power still diminished with his presence. He could tackle her. Delay her. Give them a chance to get out. It would at least thwart her horrifying game.

Hope warmed the icy chill in his gut.

Sweat rolled down his neck as he turned to regard the spark, which was nearing the switch. Jeanette leaned against the far wall with crossed arms, watching with apparent boredom.

She was complacent. Unsuspecting. It would work. The Divine had made him aware of the cord. It had to be for a reason.

His perception of Sorcery flared momentarily, confirming his thoughts. It was his chance. He connected to the muscles of his legs, giving them all the force he could muster.

Just as the spark was about to reach the switch, he launched himself upward, gripping the end of the cord and pulling it down with his weight. Exhilaration surged through him. He had made it. The Divine had—

An unexpected flash caught his eye. A flame, falling behind the window. Time seemed to slow as he watched, in horror, as the ember fell. To his surprise, an identical ember fell in Lelanna's room. She backed away, staring at the falling flame with surprise. When it hit the floor, an explosion of heat knocked him from his grip on the cord.

Screams.

Shrill voices echoed across the stone.

Broiling air washed over him.

Tovas fell to his knees. He forced his eyes open to find the partially open doors falling shut, blocking the intense heat. Though the brightness was painful to look at, he stared through the glass where the five were moments before.

They were burning alive.

On the floor, the spark continued to travel toward their room. His empty gut twisted as Lelanna too screamed, her body bathed in flame rising from the floor beneath her. A weak scent of burning flesh made him gag.

Unable to watch further, Tovas collapsed to the floor, squeezing his eyes shut. Tears streaked from them as his mind failed to fully comprehend what was happening. The clacks of Jeanette's shoes approached, and Tovas wished desperately for her to end his life. End his misery.

He had failed. Again.

His actions had only made it worse.

Two firm hands pulled him up and dragged him away from the flickering brightness.

Jeanette clicked her tongue. "Even if you had done nothing, at least Lelanna would have been spared this suffering." She waved a hand, and the flames in Lelanna's cell faded. "Don't worry, though. I won't let her die needlessly."

He kept his eyes closed, unwilling to open them. The desperate screams dissipated as Jeanette threw him up against a wall.

"Look at me," she said.

Without thinking, Tovas complied, finding her graceful figure partially blurred through his tears of agony.

"You believed your idea to pull that cord was Divine inspiration, didn't you?"

He couldn't answer. The lump in his throat made it impossible.

"Thought so," she said with a nod, pulling him from the room and into the cool hallway.

Tovas's bare feet dragged against the plush carpet, while doubt and confusion swirled within him, threatening to consume his soul.

Chapter 40
Allure

After bringing Tovas back into his room and binding him to the wall, Jeanette closed the door, taking one last peek at his defeat before the crack closed completely. Excitement surged through her. She had gotten through to him. She could feel it. He was finally understanding the ridiculous absurdity of his beliefs—how they controlled and manipulated him.

Soon he would be one with the Deia.

She let out a heavy breath, then released the door handle and strode down the hall toward her room, content with her own ingenuity. It had worked out better than she could have hoped. She'd taken care of five rejects, Lelanna had received a heavy dose of torment at Tovas's hands, and the experience seemed to have finally pulled him out of his own head. She'd let him stew on his thoughts for a while before coming back to finish his transformation.

Around a corner, she found Urok and Fita engaged in conversation, leaning against a large painting of mountains in the hallway. Both of them were shirtless and wearing tight black-and-blue trousers with thick belts lined with health potions. She suspected they had recently returned from the Deia's chamber.

"Hey, Jey!" Urok said with a grin. "How did it go?"

Fita turned to regard her with his emotionless beauty.

"Really well, actually," she said. "Fita, you were right about those protective instincts of his. He didn't even consider playing by the rules. Went right into trying to find some way around it to save everyone."

"As I said, he is convinced of his Divine purpose. 'Protect my people.' Break that illusion and you break Tovas."

"He seems to be deconstructing, so it's only a matter of time. I'll come back to finish him in a few."

"You look beat," Urok said. "Why don't we find a room and—help you relax a little." He raised his eyebrows suggestively.

Jeanette blushed at the thought of having these two powerful, muscular bodies pressed against her own, overwhelming her senses with ecstasy. Her skin tingled.

She giggled awkwardly. "Maybe later, boys."

"Aw, come on," Urok said.

"I need to finish Lelanna. Then I need a bath."

"We can all take a bath!" Urok suggested.

Fita nodded.

It was a tempting offer, but she couldn't bear the thought of what it would do to Tess. Jeanette was nothing if not loyal. She couldn't do it behind her back, even if it would be sanctioned by the Deia.

"No," she said firmly. "Not now. Maybe later."

"Jey," Urok said, approaching her. The man's large chest approached her at eye level, flooding her body with primal desire. "You *know* you want it."

"She said no," Fita said, throwing his arm in front of Urok.

"But her eyes say yes."

So presumptuous. His disrespectful insistence caused her body's natural yearning to dissolve. What remained was distaste.

"Thank you, Fita." She frowned upward at the broad, bearded face. "Get out of my way, Urok."

The man glared at her with lust, and the scene of the first fight for her life in the castle flashed through her memory. He was large, and strong, but Jeanette likely had more potent Sorcery. She could push him aside, and Fita would probably help. She returned the glare, letting him know she would not yield.

He sighed and turned aside. "Fine." A weak chuckle left his lips. "Suit yourself."

Jeanette continued down the hall to the rejects room. A brawl was taking place as she opened the door. When the participants noticed her, they stopped, shying away into the corners. A woman in the middle, bloody and bruised, shuffled back on her hands and knees. Tense silence followed. The prisoners' eyes twinkled in the dim illumination of the single overhead light. She strode into the room, and they backed farther against the walls.

Where was he? Light brown skin. Short black hair.

She found her target's beady eyes staring from between two darker individuals. E-something. Errol? Ernie?

She pointed straight at him, and he yelped, along with those next to him. They scrambled away as if she'd struck him with a terrible contagion. His face went pale, then he leapt up to hide with a group. They had packed themselves so close together that he couldn't get around them. A woman kicked at him, shoving him away.

Jeanette rolled her eyes, then grabbed his shoulder with her gloved hand.

"No, no, no!" he cried.

Once she dragged him out into the empty hallway, she sighed, and slammed the door shut behind her. "No need to be so dramatic. Besides, this might finally be your day."

He whimpered, stumbling along as she pulled him with her.

"What's your name, again?"

"E-Enol."

"That's right." She had been close.

Their "experiment" room was only a few doors down, where the lingering stench of burning flesh hit her with force. She tossed the man to the wall and clasped his wrists with chains. The windowed test chamber of the five rejects Tovas had burned still had some remaining flames amid the oppressive smog. The other room with Lelanna was relatively clear, and dark. Jeanette swished her wrist while raising the door, an unnecessary but gratifying performance that revealed a writhing figure on the floor. Angry red patches and blisters marred the woman's dark skin.

Jeanette stepped through the threshold and knelt down, softening her voice. "It hurts me to see you like this, Lelanna. Tovas had a choice to end your pain, but gave you more agony instead."

The pitiful woman looked up through a tangled mess of singed hair. Tears streaked down her face.

Jeanette pulled off the glove of her right hand and reached forward. "Here, let's finish this. Let's end your torment."

Lelanna's dark eyes steadied on the outstretched hand. Wary. Untrusting, but spent. Broken. In that moment, her face again reminded Jeanette of her old friend Amy. Stubborn, dutiful Amy. But Lelanna's stubbornness seemed to have finally evaporated.

She took Jeanette's hand, and her body came alight to Jeanette's Sorcery. A few touches to the severe burns eased Lelanna's pain, but she avoided a complete healing. That would wait. The woman stood, clearly relieved.

The pair emerged from the testing chamber, and Lelanna flinched when she saw the chained figure, her abuser from the dungeon. She shot a sharp scowl at Enol as they strode toward him.

Jeanette smirked, and pulled a dagger from her waist. Enol stared at it with wide eyes while Lelanna let go of her hand and backed away. Jeanette tossed the dagger in the air and grabbed the blade, then held the hilt toward her.

"You have suffered enough. It's time to grasp your potential."

Lelanna, her face still marred with burns, gripped the weapon tenderly. She turned to the man on the wall with a familiar, thrilling emotion behind her eyes.

Wrath.

She was ready.

"I—I was only doing what they forced me to," Enol said, eyeing the dagger. "You know I didn't have a choice!"

"There is always a choice!" Lelanna yelled.

She plunged the dagger into his chest. He grunted as she pulled it out and stabbed him again, and again. The women backed away to avoid the spray of blood as he coughed and sputtered. Lelanna maintained a rigid gaze on the man. Blood dripped from his body to the cold stone below. Soon enough, his gagging and coughing subsided, and his head hung low. Motionless.

Lelanna's gaze remained rigid, though it had softened. In her eyes Jeanette recognized another familiar emotion: shock. She had likely surprised herself with her own ferocity, her own power. She had finally escaped the cage of her naive, false morality, just as Jeanette had done.

A beautiful sight.

Lelanna's wounds slowly closed, replacing sores with smooth, dark, flawless skin. Jeanette felt a sudden kinship with the woman now that she had completed her journey.

A sweeping blade glinted in the dim light, causing Jeanette to flinch. Lelanna shoved the dagger toward Jeanette's face. She was fast, but not fast enough. Jeanette brought a hand up, gripping the blade firmly. Though her hand flashed with pain, the blade stopped. The woman's look of fierce determination quickly faded to utter astonishment.

Jeanette grinned. "Welcome to the Deia's unity."

Lelanna's brow furrowed. She turned to the man against the wall again with a distant, astonished look on her face.

"Well," Jeanette said, pulling the blade from Lelanna's grip. "I desperately need a bath." She sheathed it to her waist while closing the deep gashes in her right hand, then replaced the glove she had removed and wrapped an arm around the shorter woman. They strode from the room and into the empty hallway. "You must be starving." She pointed down the hall to her right. "If you go straight that way, down the stairway on your left, and then take a right, you'll find the dining hall. Enjoy!"

Jeanette turned and strode off in the other direction, leaving Lelanna to herself. She'd be fine. Just needed a bit of time to get used to everything.

The path down to her room was sparsely populated. She nodded with respect to the few devotees she passed. Once in her room, she headed straight to the attached bathroom, the comfortable stone interior lit by flickering candlelight along the walls. The standing bathtub's faucet could draw a slow, steady stream from the reservoir atop the castle tower, but that would take forever. What she wouldn't give for a nice hot shower. She could probably manage one with Sorcery, but it would require consistent concentration. Not very relaxing.

She connected to the air above the tub and transmuted it into water, which fell and splashed into the tub at once. The glimmers of water thrown out of the tub were easily redirected back inside. Then she heated the water to a steaming temperature as she undressed. After testing the water with a finger and feeling satisfied with the warmth, she settled inside, exhaling with pleasure.

Sure, time with the boys would have been fun, but a nice steaming bath after a long day of tortuous, but satisfying work . . . Now *that* was ecstasy.

Jeanette lay in the exquisite water for several minutes, soaking her mind away. The Deia's presence entered briefly, startling her. Was she needed? Did she have a new task? Had they shipped a new batch of people from Alvior already? She received a subtle sense of delight, then the soothing presence departed.

She must be pleased that I'm taking time to rest. Smiling, Jeanette settled back into the tub, letting her body release tension. She wondered idly how Kara was faring, somewhere across the barren landscape of Uvlun. Perhaps she had found a cave to hide out in. Eventually, she and her friends would return to Evamune, and they would see just how powerful the Deia was.

A distant sense of sorrow pressed on her mind. The rival

within. It still lingered. Perhaps she should ask the Deia about it the next time she spoke with her. It was a rare occurrence lately. The Divine woman was so busy.

The door to the bathroom burst open, and Jeanette jumped, spilling water over the edge of the tub. She gasped at the figure in the doorway.

"Tess! You're back!"

Tess threw her hands out and rushed forward. "Jey!"

She embraced Jeanette, soaking the long sleeves of her low-cut blouse.

"I missed you. How is everything? Did you crack Tovas yet?"

"Almost." Jeanette lowered herself back into the warmth of the tub. "I think I finally got through to him. He just needs one final push. Lelanna is ours, though."

"Ooh, nice." Tess put her hands on her hips. "I heard Fita's on board now too."

Jeanette laughed. "Yeah, he and Genalla both broke a little while ago. Both are pretty traditional by nature, so the idea of unity and honor really appealed to them once it clicked. Bellanna also took him to bed, so that surely helped."

Tess laughed. "I'm sure she enjoyed that."

"How about you? How are things going on Tenrazka?"

"Amazingly well. We had a breakthrough several days ago, which is why I needed to stay there. With the Scelebriar situation building, we had grohs of people joining up."

"That's wonderful!" Jeanette said.

"Yeah. I'm absolutely exhausted, though. Talking science and politics gets so tiring."

Jeanette laughed. "I bet."

Tess glanced over Jeanette's body with hungry eyes. Jeanette raised an eyebrow. "Can I help you?"

Tess smirked, throwing her clothing off with a few dramatic waves of her hands. Jeanette smiled and rolled her eyes as Tess stepped over the edge of the tub and lowered herself into the warmth. Splashes echoed off the walls as water fell over the edges. Jeanette ran her fingers through Tess's hair as she laid her head on Jeanette's chest.

"Yes."

Chapter 41

Defense of Naleren

Sam stared out the window of the Sovereign's mobile space station hovering above the moon of Naleren, thankful for the brief lapse in chaotic activity since they'd left the oasis. Plain, clean and well lit, the station had a faint aloe-like scent, with plant life tastefully placed along the walls among comfortable seating.

A few military personnel stood at the center of the room, examining a vast semicircular array of screens displaying views from various drones on the surface. Civilians were being hurriedly shepherded into acherons by bulky enforcer suits similar to the one Elysia had worn back on Earth. The anxious activity of the Sovereign's team as they coordinated planetary evacuations was overwhelming, so he had excused himself to the window to allow his nerves to settle. He actually found the reduced gravity of the moon relaxing—a literal weight being lifted from him.

Come to think of it, why *did* all the life-sustaining planets he had visited seem to be so similar? Earth-like gravity. Earth-like atmosphere. And human beings. There was *no way* that was all a coincidence; no way life just casually evolved the same way on hundreds of planets. Tovas would undoubtedly point to Divine creation, but Sam found that explanation unimaginative and unsatisfying. Portals were a thing. Maybe humans had discovered them millennia ago. Maybe they had even *engineered* these worlds. Inhabited them. Then something went wrong. War, or sickness, or some other major event had wreaked havoc on the interplanetary system. Cut off, the worlds then fell into chaos, some of them—perhaps including Earth—becoming primitive.

He could turn around and ask someone, or query his Jit to investigate it, but he felt content enough to consider the possibility for now.

A tap on his shoulder turned his head, and he found Scheln floating in clean field robes.

"Hey, Scheln. Enjoy your shower?"

He nodded.

The word *ok* followed by a question mark appeared briefly above his head.

"Yeah, I'm fine, thanks," Sam spun back to gaze out the window once more. "Just so much commotion with the evacuation, and there's not really anything I can do. My head needed a break, you know?"

Scheln settled into his wheelchair nearby and pulled up next to Sam, joining him in his appreciation of the incredible view of the blue planet. Sam could hardly fathom how this entire world could be threatened by a single being. A Sorcerer. If one person could wield that kind of power, maybe it really was a good idea to keep Sorcery a secret.

"Sam, Scheln."

They both turned. Elleran wore silver robes, ancient Vivezan clothing that Aiyla had procured, and which apparently bore powerful protective enchantments. Duriel had on a similar set and seemed quite uncomfortable in it, tugging at the material of his top. "It's time. Duriel and I are heading to the surface."

Sam regarded her, worry clouding his mind. She was confident in their success, and powerful. Extremely powerful. There shouldn't be much to worry about. He wished he could go down with them, help them, but his abilities were far from theirs. He would only get in the way. Besides, he had to go get Kara and the others out as soon as this was over. They needed him.

"Don't die down there," he said. "I still have a giant list of questions for you when you get back."

Her warm smile melted his anxiety, and she placed a hand on his cheek. "Oh, Sam. Whatever happens, any answers I can give you will be infinitely less adequate than your own discoveries. I foresee you will take Sorcery and our understanding of the universe to fascinating new heights."

She turned to Scheln, and touched his cheek in turn. "Scheln, I am sorry we have not yet rescued your brother. If he is anything like you, he must be a strong, remarkable individual."

She released him, and her eyes flared with determination. "If Duriel and I survive this encounter, I promise I will do everything I can to help your friends."

"You mean 'when,' right? When you survive. You can't leave us."

She smiled again. "Certainty is a luxury I cannot abide, Samuel, but I am confident Duriel and I will save this planet from Oblivion's wrath. He will then most likely retreat, and we will return safely."

Duriel approached. His silver robes cast a subtle distortion of light around the edges, which Sam found intriguing.

The words *Divine bless you* appeared near Scheln's head.

"Good luck," Sam said.

"Thank you both," Elleran said. "Be mindful and analyze our encounter. I'm sure there will be much you can learn."

"Come." Duriel put a gentle hand on her shoulder.

Her affectionate gaze settled on them both for a few more seconds. Sam wanted to say something else, but couldn't find the words.

She and Duriel turned and strode off past a pair of sleek black suits that had exited the Sovereign's private quarters. They entered special ascenders docked to the side of the tiny space station. A screen focused on the craft as it sped off toward a circular acheron, no doubt leading to the planet's surface.

Sam fell into a slow, anxious pace as they waited. He occasionally glanced at the screens, which continued to show various sites where civilians were rushing through acherons. Some wore backpacks. Many carried different kinds of suitcases. A few had nothing at all. Sam noted people of all ages, and groups of families. He turned his gaze to the soft floor, hands clasped behind his back as he paced.

So many people. Children.

Gasps came from others in the room. Several screens focused on a rugged asteroid spinning toward the planet's surface, sending adrenaline rushing through Sam. He and Scheln moved toward the images to get a better look, along with other personnel around the station. Had that been there before? Where had it come from? A few screens zoomed in on a tiny speck following the asteroid against the backdrop of space, revealing, to Sam's amazement, nothing but a plain black cloak.

His eyes widened. *Oblivion?*

The black cloak gave the figure the appearance of death incarnate.

The Sovereign strode out of her quarters. "He saw us. Elleran, Duriel, are you ready?"

"Yes," Elleran replied, her voice echoing crisp and clear from an overhead source. "How close are the nearest civilians?"

Sam found Elleran and Duriel on one screen, hovering near a coastline lit by dawning sunlight, with a mountain in the distance. Elleran was reaching up toward the massive rock. Winds picked up around them, and the view zoomed out, showing the atmosphere and water swirling around their position. The air steadily turned violent, turning up trees, houses, and anything else on the ground, and dimming the morning light.

"Over three moh kilometers away," the Sovereign replied.

Sam's eyes widened as light distorted around the pair, followed by an enormous pillar of water, which spun around them.

"Rhea team, engage," said a male voice overhead.

"Welin Em Onii," Aiyla said quietly. Several others repeated the words.

On a different screen, a craft fired projectiles toward the asteroid. The cloaked figure sped into a portal that opened in the vacuum of space, and a side of the craft instantly burst open, spraying atmosphere and debris into the void. Sam found the cloak, speeding along the craft's surface as it ripped apart like tissue paper. A group of armored individuals sped toward Oblivion, firing a round of plasma in unison. The light encircled him, and a massive section of the ship shot toward them, smashing into the group. Four green squares next to the screen, which Sam had barely noticed before, turned red.

A bright light from Elleran and Duriel's video feed caught Sam's attention. The view had fallen back to a wide angle, showing billowing clouds of frost swirling across the atmosphere. A closer, shaking view caught Elleran in its midst, stretching her arms upward with a strained expression. The leading edge of the asteroid, visible from another screen, blazed with terrifying, otherworldly fire. Then, a pillar of ice shot up into the asteroid's surface. One view followed it into the glowing depths.

Duriel?

Oblivion had engaged another ship and was ripping it to pieces. He stopped suddenly, then entered a portal and disappeared from view.

"Where did he go?" Sam asked.

"Elleran, Duriel, he has noticed you," Aiyla said, her voice betraying a sense of fear. "Be ready."

"We are ready," Elleran said with confidence.

"Almost there," Duriel said.

The cloak appeared off the coast, outside the swirling vortex pressing against the giant flaming object.

"Now!" Elleran screamed.

Duriel let out a yell, and the screens went white. Sam's heart raced. *What happened? Are they okay?*

The views returned to reveal that the asteroid had shattered. Flaming rocks smashed against the water and coast nearby, sending fiery shockwaves across their surfaces. Sam scanned the views for Elleran but couldn't find her amidst the chaos. Oblivion remained in position, explosive waves of fire flowing around the eerie figure as if an invisible shield surrounded him.

Sam, and others in the room, let out a sigh of relief as Elleran reappeared, floating up against the boiling water.

One of the other views shook as citizens were being hurriedly shepherded through an acheron. Shockwaves spread across the landscape, originating from the horizon. People screamed. Some panicked and pushed forward. The enforcers quickly intervened, helping to restore an orderly progression. A young, frightened couple walked down the designated path, holding each other as they stood next to a mother and father with three little girls. The youngest clung to her father's neck as he stared off toward the source of the explosions, pressing with the crowd toward safety. Anxiety gnawed through Sam's gut at the sight.

They will be okay. They're almost there. They will be okay.

Sam took a deep breath, and turned his attention back to Elleran, heart still racing. Duriel had joined her, and the remaining rocks fell with less force. Crater-speckled molten slag now made up the coastline behind them, but they were alive, staring at Oblivion with determination. Sunlight cast an ominous orange glow underneath the clouds of blackness billowing through the sky above. The dark cloak of Oblivion approached slowly, while clouds swept away unnaturally, allowing the light to pass through. The overwhelming thunder of impacts subsided to steam, followed by the crashing of waves.

"Virahmgal," Elleran said with emotion, her voice piercing through the lingering sounds of destruction. "It is over. This planet will not yield to you."

"Do we strike?" the male voice from earlier asked over the channel.

"No," Aiyla said. "This encounter is between Sorcerers."

The cloak turned to face Duriel, and a chilling, deep voice rang through the overhead source. "After the Queen of Minds falls. Your paradise will burn."

A spout of water shot up toward Duriel, then burned through the air as it arced toward Oblivion. The air in front of the cloak became solid as glass, screeching as the stream of water broke against it. Elleran flew sideways, moving to surround the enemy. Lightning lanced toward it with a thunderous crash. Sam couldn't follow what ensued, only that a massive column of steam rose from the aftermath.

The cloaked figure shot upward, and boulders flew up from beneath the water to orbit him, blocking more attacks from the pair. Sam found himself transfixed, barely able to comprehend what was happening as elements of nature clashed in impossible ways. Light distorted. Beams of energy and fire shot between them. Lightning struck again. How could human beings wield this kind of power? It was unfathomable.

This was the strength of *gods*.

A boulder near Oblivion cracked into tiny pieces, which became millions of streaks of white fire sent toward Duriel. Many were deflected, shooting off in various directions.

Sam held his breath as he regarded the weariness on Duriel's face. Another column of water shot up toward Oblivion as Elleran blasted him with lightning and air from the other side.

More streaks, now of blue-white fire, smashed into Duriel. His expression turned to wide-eyed surprise, then emptiness. He fell. Elleran cut through the air at sonic speed, creating a visible shockwave as she raced toward him.

His body hit the cooling black rock of the coastline, and the room gasped. Some turned their heads away from the image.

"No," Sam whispered.

Elleran stopped, then turned toward Oblivion, her brow furrowed in anguish.

Light consumed her body.

The mountain behind her, decimated by the blows from remaining asteroid chunks, flew from its position toward a glowing Elleran. It became a beam of white toward Oblivion as she rose higher, pushing her target into the water, which spread out wildly from the force of impact.

Water arced toward Elleran, deflected off course by a massive wind. The very atmosphere around the pair swirled into a tempest of chaotic activity as the two godlike beings threw Elements at each other at impossible speeds. The very fabric of reality seemed tenuous between them, warped with unnatural intent. Rock. Lightning. Fire. Water. Nature screamed through the tempest, clashing with extraordinary force.

"Elleran!" Aiyla yelled.

Half a dozen white-hot streaks appeared through Elleran's glowing body from all sides. The air stilled. Torrential rain poured into the turbulent waves below. Boulders, which had been flying against gravity by unnatural forces, fell, plunging into the watery depths.

The ethereal connection Sam shared with Elleran severed abruptly, sending a chill of anguish down his spine.

"No!" Sam yelled, his eyes filling with tears. "NO!"

The tempest calmed. As clouds of dust, debris, and steam parted, Elleran's body appeared, her curly hair flowing through the air as she fell.

Her body smashed into the ground, the sound inaudible next to that of raining debris. Sam could almost feel the weight of the impact himself. She had landed only a few dozen feet from where Duriel lay.

The terrible figure of Oblivion hovered above the water's surface and approached the pair, head bowed as if in reverence. Two points near the hood glowed, then erupted in beams of fire, incinerating the bodies.

Two streaks of glowing, molten rock were all that remained.

Chapter 42
Shattered

"What do we do?" asked a woman's voice over the channel.

"Wait," the man's voice said.

"Yes," Aiyla agreed, her voice cracking. "We wait to see what he will do next."

Oblivion remained motionless, staring toward the destroyed landscape and the two cooling red scars, where the bodies of human beings had lain just moments before.

Sam, shaking with existential tension and sorrow, suddenly noticed Scheln hovering next to him. Tears streamed down the man's pale face. Sam numbly put an arm on his shoulder, remembering that Oblivion had destroyed the twins' home planet years ago, and the turmoil had resulted in Scheln's disability. Sam could scarcely fathom the terrifying memories he must be reliving, and the emotions he was going through.

Hot, glowing lava shot up from beneath Oblivion, consuming him. One view dove into the heat, following him, while the external view remained. The source stopped, and Sam watched the hot, smoking magma reach a remarkable height before falling back to the surface.

What was that? A portal?

"He's heading toward the core," a new man's voice said over the channel. "We've never seen this before."

"If he's heading for the core, why didn't his portal reach it?" Aiyla asked.

"The unique gravitational effects and pressure near the core make it very difficult to project a portal in that environment. He's likely conserving energy."

"Get me projections," Aiyla said with harsh determination. "I want to know what he's planning. How long until he reaches the core, assuming that's his target?"

The camera that had dived into the lava caught up to Oblivion, his robes flowing past a sea of intense, fiery red that parted for him. The terrifying Sorcerer could certainly destroy whatever device followed him, so why didn't he? Perhaps he *wanted* a show. He *wanted* the Sovereign to see how powerful he is. He wanted them to fear him.

"Slightly over seven standard minutes."

"We may be able to get ahead of him," the man's voice from earlier said overhead. "Rhea Seven has a prototype that could make the jump."

"Put a ship under the surface?" a uniformed man with blond hair said near Sam. "That's madn—"

"Our analysis suggests he most likely intends to destabilize the planet's magnetic field, or use it as a weapon to wreak havoc on our systems. He may also—"

"Send all the projections to the ground teams," Aiyla said. "Let them know what to prepare for."

"Sovereign. Rhea Seven is ready to jump."

She gave a light nod. "Do it. Every second we can delay him saves lives."

One screen, which had been displaying refugees moving through an acheron, switched to the view of an angular, shimmering vessel against the backdrop of a stunning galaxy lit by its nearby star. A large round acheron flew out ahead of it. Glowing yellow gobs of lava exploded out of the portal, drenching the ship. It fired something into the mouth, which sent out a wave that pushed away and cooled the molten rock, slowing the flow for a few brief seconds.

Sam's jaw dropped as the space vessel pressed into the acheron, bearing the intense heat and pressure of the planet's internals. The portal severed abruptly, leaving the back fifth of the ship behind in space with the floating gobs of magma. A new view took its place from inside the cargo section of the craft, where the crew, wearing sleek, black suits, floated around a large egg-shaped device

"Didn't have enough power," the low voice said, "but the team is in position. We've prepared the claustra."

Claustra? Sam wondered

"He's nearly there," Aiyla said. "Welin Em Onii, Rhea Seven," she added.

The group of floating suits on-screen saluted with thumb, index and middle fingers extended across their chest.

"Welin Em Onii," everyone repeated.

Some personnel in the room, including the man near Sam and Scheln, returned a solemn salute.

A new screen displayed an incredible cross section of the planet. It highlighted Oblivion's position with a red diamond, progressing toward the core, and the ship's position with a blue circle. They were almost on top of each other.

The top side of the giant egg—apparently called a claustra—split open and lurched upward. A moment later, the dark blur of Oblivion parted the ceiling of the vessel, smashing into the device, which fell through the floor as the opening collapsed, trapping the Sorcerer. The suits followed it.

"Got him!" a woman's voice said over the channel.

A burst of energy ripped a small hole through the side of the shell, and a suit quickly moved to cover it.

"Surround it!" the deep voice said.

The suits encircled the claustra as more bursts of light shot out of it. They pressed inward, trying to keep the shell together for as long as possible. Sam glanced at the screens of people shuffling quickly through acherons, frightened but unaware of the team of heroes stalling their enemy.

The shell burst open with a violent explosion.

Personnel indicators next to the screen turned from green to red, leaving two a deep orange. The cloak of Oblivion emerged from its midst, and white-hot magma shot into the interior of the spacecraft, cutting through the material. The two remaining suits flew toward the figure, firing streaks of plasma from their arms to no apparent effect. Slices of magma solidified, smashing into the suits with tremendous force, sending shockwaves across the collapsing structure. The two orange indicators turned red.

The team had given their lives for precious few seconds of delay.

Oblivion shot downward, and the camera followed. Sam trembled as he and the others watched anxiously amid the Sovereign's ongoing directions for evacuation while the cloak continued to dive into the depths. Families and individuals on the surface pushed hastily through the acherons. Vehicles rose into the air, heading into the atmosphere—an attempt to escape the imminent magnetic disruptions.

"Oblivion has reached the core," Aiyla announced.

The figure stopped, then turned toward the camera. Blinding white matter illuminated his surroundings, an incredible contrast to the cloak's impenetrable darkness, as if light had little effect on it at all. No face was visible under the hood.

The view cut to black. Low rumbling came from overhead, echoing from an unknown source.

Alarms blared. A circle of white rippled out from the center of the planet on the cross section.

Sam felt the blood drain from his face as he scanned the views of people escaping through portals. This couldn't be good. Quakes? Volcanic activity?

The Sovereign put a hand to her face, and Sam and the others watched in horror as the solid ground underneath the refugees lurched upward. He caught sight of a mother holding her young boy, only inches from the gate before the view went white.

The video feed cut off. Over half the screens went dark. Rock, bathed in red and white, flew apart in every view that remained.

Heart racing, Sam rushed to the window to stare at the planet he had idly gazed at not long ago. Tears distorted his view of the once-blue sphere, which had cracked into horrific drifting pieces of red and black, split by an expanding cloud of white.

A planet full of life, lost to the void.

Chapter 43
A Way Out

Faith. Revelation. Divinity. Was it all delusion?

Tovas once again hung in the room of his demise, the same one Jeanette had locked him in many days ago. Icy chains bit into his wrists and ankles. The dark stone interior, barely lit by the single point of light in the center of the ceiling above, was otherwise empty.

His mind was a turbulent blur of unrest. Could it truly all be illusory? The Divine wouldn't have prompted him to pull those levers if it would have caused such loss of life, such anguish. But he had been so certain. Could everything he believed in be false? Was he any different from Jeanette? Was his faith in the Divine nothing more than subconscious deceit? Would he be able to tell the difference if it wasn't?

A conversation from a Tercast storage room flashed in his mind: *When you speak to a deity, that's one thing. When a deity speaks to you, that's madness. It's all in your head!*

Sam's words struck much harder as Tovas reflected on them now. Had Sam been right? *Was* it all in his head? The revelation had seemed so powerful, so magnificent. Were the miracles he had witnessed nothing more than his inclination to ascribe good things to the Divine based on his upbringing?

His family had always believed. Half of them were gone. Many had said they would all be together again in the afterlife. Was that simply a lie to soften the sting of loss? Were they inserting the Divine only because it was comforting to think benevolent Creators were out there, watching over them all?

The thought of his family brought the agony and sorrow of their deaths back to the surface. He pictured the beautiful face of his younger sister Zoya and remembered how happy she had been when he said he would play her new game with her after her studies that day, before Oblivion had struck.

Tovas squeezed his eyes shut, restraining his tears. If only he had Scheln's comforting presence. His brother had always been better with words. His faith seemed to remain resolute, no matter what he was facing.

At the thought, Scheln's presence settled over him. It was ever so slight—nothing more than a delicate, comforting touch amid the torrential storm of his racing thoughts. It appeared he still had enough Sorcery to sense a frail trace of his brother.

Tovas recalled the day he had first felt their connection at Tercast. It had been so subtle and unusual, but now he recognized it for what it was: Scheln was trying to reach him.

And it was working.

After a few moments, Scheln's presence returned with greater force. A new sensation accompanied it this time, as if he was trying to enter the holy space within Tovas's soul—the place Belze had attempted to reach.

Tovas knew beyond doubt he could trust Scheln with his soul. He opened himself, and gasped.

Scheln's presence entered, and the oppressive shroud smothering his Sorcery lifted, causing the glorious sensation of his body to return with brightness. Though his surroundings remained dark, the passing impressions of his body and organs filled him with exhilaration.

"Tovas!" Scheln said.

Scheln! Tovas cried. *You reached me!* Tears streamed down his face. *How did you—*

A sense of Scheln's intense fear, anguish and sudden exhaustion crushed his elation.

"It's him!" Scheln said, before a sense of overwhelming fatigue consumed him. His presence left.

Scheln!

Tovas connected to the fibers of his muscles and the skin of his body, relishing in the feeling of ethereal connection once more. He caused them to strengthen, and pulled against the metal bonds on his hands and feet, breaking them more easily than expected. His body collapsed painfully to the ground. The tight muscles of his arms and legs screamed as he rose, his mind settling on Scheln's words and the fear behind them.

Oblivion. It had to be.

The realization rippled across his skin. Oblivion was about to strike. Or had already done so.

Protect my people.

The revelation echoed in his mind, and he yearned for the Staff of Dreams.

Rose's comforting presence entered his body, stunned, ecstatic. She healed his wounds and soothed his aching body. He was glad to know she was well.

Kara, he remembered. Jeanette mentioned her sister had attempted a rescue but had left the castle. He should leave. Try to find her.

Tovas strode toward the door, clenched a fist, and enhanced it with unnatural mass and resilience. He pulled back as he approached his target, preparing to meet a host of enemies on the other side, which he could hopefully evade in his escape through the castle. Then he threw his fist forward.

Jeanette.

He stopped his fist mid-swing, pulling him off balance. As his arm leaned against the stone, he pressed his forehead to the cold, rough surface.

He couldn't leave. Not yet. He needed to face her again, one last time.

After a deep breath, Tovas pushed off the wall and strode back toward the clasps that had held him moments before. His body lifted with Sorcery, and he spread his limbs back into their previous positions. Though invisible from a distance, when he touched the metal, they allowed a connection. With it, he felt a curious remnant of suffering and loss. The clasps closed around his wrists and ankles, binding him to the wall once again. Once he let his weight fall, they painfully pressed against his wrists and ankles once more.

Tovas bowed his head and prayed.

Chapter 44

The Hangar

"Kara! Kara!" Rose yelled out as soon as the suit was in view.

The small, shiny figure turned toward the sky raft and flew up alongside it.

"What?" she asked.

"It's Tovas!" Rose cried, excitement bursting from her. "He's okay! Somehow he has his Sorcery back. I can reconnect with him!"

"Sweet! We need to find this hangar *now* so we can go back and get him. Did he escape the castle?"

"Hang on." She reconnected with Tovas. Cold pressed on his skin, but his muscles were not engaged. The weight of his body pulled against his wrists as if he were hanging. "No, it seems like he's still a prisoner in the castle. He might be waiting for us. Maybe it's too risky for him to try escaping on his own. I'll let you know if anything changes."

"Okay, I'm going to keep scanning. The guy's notes said the hangar was somewhere around here. We've got to be close."

Rose nodded, then realized Kara may not even be able to see her reaction in the dim light. Her suit veered off to continue the search elsewhere. Rose's attention came back to Tovas. Why was he still hanging? Did he not have enough Sorcery to enhance his strength? She connected to the muscles of his arms and back, finding the waning, residual effects of a previous strength enchantment. She added a touch of her own, surely giving him enough power to free himself.

Tovas shook his head. He wasn't trying to escape. Perhaps he was simply conserving his wakefulness. That could be smart. As she had mentioned to Kara, he was probably waiting for them to arrive. The Deia's people likely didn't know he had his powers back. He could use the surprise to give them an advantage in their escape. She let her connection to Tovas drop so she could focus on the landscape and help locate the warehouse.

"I'm so glad he is okay," Kula said as she scanned the darkness below.

"Me too."

"If he's still alive, 'it's cause the Deia wants him," Renoq said. "They may use him as bait."

Rose frowned. "I don't think so. He's staying where he is by choice. I think he's waiting for us."

"Then let's find a ship so we can take him and get off this rock," Sheylana said.

Rose agreed, redoubling her efforts to scan for any building that was still remotely intact. Almost none were. Their spotlights found nothing but the shattered remains of civilization. Kara had said the bits and pieces of the man's journal had mentioned a warehouse containing exploration vessels—spacecraft with acheron-carrying ships—but that a massive, impenetrable swarm of machines guarded it. Many had supposedly attempted to enter, only to lose their lives as drones overcame them.

If the drones were anything like the ones in the factory building they had found, they may get through. Kara could likely take out a whole horde single-handedly with her indestructible Ilkuth and some Sorcery enchantments.

"There!" Kula called out. "What about that one?"

Sheylana veered the craft toward the building Kula was

pointing at. It appeared to be relatively intact, though had clearly suffered some damage. Piles of drone remains lay around the exterior.

The group grabbed their weapons and hopped out of the craft. Kara landed next to them.

"Good find," she said. "This looks like it could be it."

She moved to the front of the group and entered the building through a large hole, illuminating the area with her helmet spotlight. Rose followed the others inside to what seemed to be a hangar of some sort. It was empty.

"Bust," Renoq said. "Guess we should keep—"

"Wait, look." Sheylana approached a circle of red light on the wall. "This building has power."

"If that's so, where's the lights?" Kara asked.

"Seems like something tripped a breaker." Sheylana located a panel and flipped a small switch. Streams of light along the upper edges of the walls lit up the mostly empty hangar.

At the far end of the long interior stood the remains of a vehicle, long and cylindrical. It looked vaguely like it could be some kind of exploration vessel, but it was clearly in disrepair.

"Hey!" Renoq said. "That could be our ride."

"Looks to be in pretty awful shape." Sheylana pointed to a sleek black box next to the breaker. "There's a working security system. It's really old, but it might still work. Kara, maybe you can plug in and see if there's anything useful?"

"Sure," she said, floating over to the box and pulling the connection cable out of her wrist. Sheylana found the port, and Kara linked the suit to it.

"Says it's decrypting . . . and done. Looks like there's a lot of captured video events."

"Can you pull up the most recent one? And project it so we can all see, please?"

"Uh, sure. Just a sec."

After a few moments of silence, Kara's helmet projected a video onto the wall. She took several steps back, as far as the cable would let her, to expand the projection and allow them all to see clearly. Lightning filled the display of the building's exterior, frying a massive swarm of drones that fired at a target beyond view. Many of them collided with each other, propelled by an invisible force.

After a minute of nearly endless waves of drones getting destroyed by electricity, rocks, and parts of other drones, it seemed the last of them had finally fallen. Onto their corpses trod a figure wielding a sword. The wearer pulled a dark hood back, revealing a pale face with a short pointed beard.

"Delveton," Kara spat.

Rose's heart leapt into her throat. The man who had destroyed Tercast. The man Kara had stopped. The man who had murdered Talanna, Niu, Relon, and—

She recoiled, then reflexively glanced back through the hole toward their sky raft, where the edge of the long handle of an enchanted maul was visible. Rose squeezed her eyes shut, unwilling to let the thought continue.

When she reopened her eyes to return her focus to Kara's projection, she watched as a woman approached Delveton, short and pale with dark hair, wearing a cloak over an outfit with swirling silver patterns. A second woman, with darker skin and long brown hair streaked with gold, followed. Their attention turned abruptly to their right, and bullets ricocheted off their bodies, peppering their surroundings. Delveton and the pale woman took fighting stances, while the other simply stood there. Drones sped toward them, and lightning arced from Delveton's sword, destroying large swaths of them. The pale woman stretched a hand out, and a shockwave blasted several drones in all directions. One came straight at the view and smashed into it, ending the video abruptly.

"One of those women was probably the Deia," Kara said.

"Yeah, Belze," Renoq said. "She's the one with the golden streaks in 'er hair. One ruthless human bein'. The way she can get so many people to worship her like some kind of goddess is downright terrifyin'."

"They must have taken the vessels," Kara said. "*That's* how they've been traveling from Uvlun. It's how they must have . . ." She paused, seemingly overcome with emotion. "How they must have gotten to Earth and kidnapped Jeanette."

"We should check the other vehicle," Kula suggested. "Just in case."

The group made their way down the hangar to the remaining vehicle, which was a wretched sight. Twisted metal scraps littered the floor beneath it, and wires and framing hung at odd angles. Sheylana jumped aboard through a torn-open side of the hull, inspecting components while the rest of them grimly inspected the exterior.

"They used these to take down the castle," Renoq said. "Ruthless bastards."

"Why even come back to the castle at all?" Kara asked. "Why wouldn't they just escape this hellscape and go back to some comfortable corner of the Sovereignty?"

"The library. Supposedly had some real unique knowledge in there. Things you can't find on the open networks."

"She'd come back to this hellscape for *books*?"

He shrugged. "That's what Goralo said."

"The ship is trash," Sheylana said, poking her head out from the side of the vehicle. "They stripped it for parts. Even if I had all the components to fix it, I'm certainly not an expert with these kinds of craft. There's no way I can repair this."

"Well," Kara said. "Worth checking anyway, I guess."

Sheylana jumped down to join them.

"How is Tovas?" Kara asked.

Rose found him in the same state—hard objects digging into his wrists and ankles under the painful pressure of his hanging body.

"He's where he was before, but there's no telling how long he'll be able to wait there for us."

"What about Fita?"

Unable to utter the words, Rose shook her head, noting Kula's sudden interest in a crooked sheet of rusty metal. She wished she knew for sure, but it was just unclear. Fita's Sorcery may have simply faded completely.

Or he could be gone.

"They've been waiting far too long," Kara said, clenching her fist. "And this mission has been a complete waste of precious time already.

"Let's go kick this Deia's ass."

Chapter 45

Through the Darkness

Jeanette woke with a jolt of adrenaline, finding Tess's wide eyes staring back at her. The Deia had awakened her too. Something was happening. Something big.

She sat up, pushed by a powerful need to move, and jumped out of bed.

"What is it?" Jeanette said, heart racing as she grabbed the first set of clothes she saw.

"I don't know. Maybe the Sovereignty found us."

The thought sent a shiver down Jeanette's spine. That would be terrifying. An army of powered suits could almost definitely overwhelm them. She threw on a jumpsuit and put on her belt, which held her daggers and six small bottles of health potion. Tess wore her favorite black outfit with swirling patterns and did the same with her belt, which carried her darts and a pair of short steel swords.

The hallway outside was a mess of activity. People were gathering weapons and rushing toward the entrance. Jeanette and Tess joined the throng, racing through the vibrant, colorful hallways until they reached one side of the double staircase leading down into the grand entrance hall. A sparkling chandelier cast rays of light over the room.

The Deia was instructing a group near the entrance, the strands of her hair shimmering as they cascaded down her dark byzantium-colored dress with gold embellishments. Heads bowed quickly, and the group rushed out the door into the howling winds of Uvlun. The Divine woman grinned at Tess and Jeanette, motioning them to her and encouraging the others surrounding them to continue onward.

"Oblivion has decimated another world," the Deia said with glee. "The Sovereign is calling an emergency meeting of all leaders to discuss the event, giving us the perfect opportunity."

The woman's joy radiated through Jeanette like a wildfire, melting the tension. They weren't under attack. They were preparing to strike!

"Yes!" Tess said.

The Deia placed her soft hands on Jeanette's shoulders. "Where are you with Tovas?"

Oh, right. Tovas.

"He's so close. I think I finally got through to him."

The Deia pulled her arms back and tapped her lips thought-fully, her gray eyes gazing into the distance. After a moment, they settled on Jeanette again. "I'd like you to finish your work with him. He has great potential. Give him one last chance to embrace my unity. I will reach him through you, if he is prepared. If he refuses, kill him. I'll leave one ship here for you so you can join us afterward."

"Can I stay with her?" Tess asked. "Please?"

"Yes, of course. But allow her to finish her work with Tovas alone."

"Of course."

The Deia gave them a smile of matchless beauty. "This is the moment we've been waiting for. I want you both by my side as soon as you are done here."

Jeanette bowed her head, unable to stop beaming from excitement. "It will be done, Deia."

She brushed their cheeks, then rushed out the door with the last of her other subjects.

Tess turned to her. "I'll go get our ride ready. Go finish with your boy toy so we can go!"

Jeanette nodded. "Okay. Be there soon."

She strode with purpose through the now-empty halls. Oblivion had destroyed another world. How did the being achieve such incredible power? Could Jeanette ever possibly reach that level of might? The thought sent a tingle across her skin.

At last she reached the door to Tovas's room. She had forgotten to send anyone to feed or water him as she had slept. Oops. The guy was probably dying of thirst. He should still be alive, though, if nothing else.

She pushed the door open, pleased to find that his head hung low with apparent despair. His face remained down, giving her only a clear view of his dirty sandy-brown hair and stretched body as she approached him.

"Had enough time to figure things out yet?"

Tovas didn't respond. Was he dead? He shouldn't be, unless he killed himself. It would be anticlimactic, but at least it would make this easy. She watched his chest. It moved steadily with his breathing, confirming that he was alive.

Jeanette shrugged. "Oh well." She turned to leave. "I thought you might finally be ready to face the truth, but I've got somewhere to be, so—"

"Wait." Tovas's voice came out raspy. He cleared his throat. "Wait."

She turned again to face him, and he lifted his head, looking at her with tearful eyes. Her hands went to her hips.

"So," she said. "Out of your own head yet? Realized the ridiculousness of your beliefs?"

"I believe in the Divine."

Jeanette rolled her eyes, feeling disappointment eat through her insides. She really thought she had gotten through to him.

She sauntered toward him. "Why? I know you thought what

you felt was Divine inspiration. Don't tell me you didn't. And it killed people. Why do you cling to these ridiculous ideas?"

She stopped, now standing mere inches from his face. She could see it in his eyes. The doubt. The questioning. There was uncertainty swimming around that head of his. Then his eyes locked with hers. Determined. Decisive.

"Because I choose to."

Before Jeanette could respond, his hand flew forward, breaking effortlessly through the steel clasp that had been holding it, and grabbed her exposed arm. His body lit up to her perception. She felt his racing heart. His pain. And his power.

He had somehow unsealed his Sorcery.

A flurry of imaginative thought and movement whirled the dagger from her waist into her right palm. She plunged it into Tovas's chest. He gasped, wide-eyed, and pain signals erupted through his nervous system. She tried to pull her arm back to release his grip, but it remained firm.

She twisted the knife, and blood poured from the wound. Tovas writhed and grunted with pain, his eyes fixed on hers and his grip unyielding. Through their physical connection, Jeanette felt a baffling sense of *attraction* from him. Compassion. He actually cared for her. The orchestrator of his torment.

"I . . ." Tovas cringed at the pain of attempting to speak, but continued anyway. "I . . . forgive you."

Jeanette furrowed her brow. His presence pressed on her mind —attempted to reach the private space that Belze had once opened to grant her Sorcery.

He was trusting her to change. To join him. To free him.

She smirked, feeling a surge of sudden understanding. He had inadvertently given her everything, the power of the universe at her fingertips. The Deia had taught her that Sorcery's potency was proportional to one's dismissal of their former misdirected convictions. After she discarded Tovas's genuine, relentless benevolence and naive altruism, the strength of her abilities would multiply tremendously.

She would be a god—a superlative instrument of the Deia.

Her power would be unfathomable.

With a simple thought, the other dagger at her hip rose into the air and aimed at his head. She pushed his body back and strengthened her own body to prevent him from making any sudden movements.

"Goodbye, Tovas."

The rival within her mind suddenly burst forward, clinging to Tovas's presence. Its identity became clear:

It was herself.

Jeanette gasped.

Thick fog enshrouded her senses, suffocating her. Subduing her. Shreds of ethereal darkness sloughed away as she ascended through the darkness, freeing her thoughts from veils she couldn't so much as perceive a moment before. She shuddered as stunning, illuminating clarity pierced through her obscured awareness. The floating dagger fell, clanging against the stone floor.

Enchantments. In her brain.

They faded completely with the lifting fog, along with the Deia's oppressive presence, bringing the horror of her actions into intense, crushing focus.

She had manipulated.

She had tortured.

She had murdered.

Tears flooded her eyes as the surging mountain of guilt became overwhelming. She couldn't live a moment longer. Tovas yelled as the other dagger ripped through his chest. Jeanette flipped it around and thrust it toward her right eye.

Tovas released her arm and grasped the other with blurring speed. The weapon waited a fraction of an inch from its target.

"Jeanette," Tovas said softly with a weak smile, wincing from the pain.

She gazed through the blur of tears into his hazel eyes and paling complexion, which radiated a ludicrous gentleness. The dagger fell from her grip and landed with a cacophony of ringing.

"Tovas, I . . . I . . ."

"I know."

Metal snapped as he broke his other arm free. Jeanette stepped back while Tovas let go of her arm. His ankles were freed, causing him to collapse in a puddle of his own blood.

Jeanette fell to her knees, grabbed a potion from her belt and held the vial up to his mouth. He drank eagerly. The wound in his chest quickly closed, returning his frighteningly white skin to its typical state. She helped him to his feet, and he wiped sweat and blood from his face.

"Thank you," he said. "I think the others are coming."

"Kara?"

Tovas nodded.

Jeanette, shaking from the experience of her world turning upside down, held his warming face in her lap. "T-Tess is waiting for me out front. We'll need to find another way out."

"There's one thing I need first."

"What?"

Tovas rose slowly, testing his balance. Jeanette rose with him, horrified at the stains of blood wetting their clothing. Teetering against the stone wall, he pulled himself upright, then turned to her with a look of resolve.

"The Staff of Dreams."

Chapter 46
Freedom

Tovas ran behind Jeanette through the brightly colored halls, feeling tremendously lightheaded but joyful. He didn't know exactly how he had done it, but somehow he had reached her. The real Jeanette.

Rose's presence remained with him, conveying her irritation, anger, and intense concern. She had reached out to him just before Jeanette's intervention with the potion, which may have saved his life. Rose was immensely skilled, but he was unsure if she could have repaired the tremendous damage done.

The pair turned a corner, and Jeanette threw open a set of double doors. Tovas crossed the threshold with wide eyes. A mess of weapons, shields, and clothing covered the spacious interior.

"They took most of the weapons in a rush, but left a few. The enchantments on most of these are weak."

Tovas scanned the scattered remains of those left behind, hoping desperately that they hadn't taken his—

He saw it, a rod of silver and gold. Plain from a distance, with delicate plantlike etchings that were only visible up close. He raced to it, grabbing the object and marveling at its brightness through his Sorcery. He felt its Divine purpose flow through him once more.

Warmth. Hope. Protection.

"Here," Jeanette said, tossing a bundle of clothing at him. "It has an enchantment to help your digestive system or something. Not much, but it's better than nothing."

"Thanks."

He watched her curiously as he placed the staff on the ground and unfastened his pants. She turned around, giving him privacy. He donned the new trousers and tan lace-up shirt as quickly as he was able, then hefted his staff.

"Let's go."

They sprinted down the hall, the pale green of the halls shifting to yellow as they turned back down the corner they had arrived from. Jeanette threw open a door to her right, which led to a simple bedroom. Tovas stopped in the doorway, raising an eyebrow.

"What are you doing?"

Jeanette turned, shaking. "I . . . Tovas . . . I don't know if I can use Sorcery right now. I can't feel it and honestly don't even want to try. I *think* this is an exterior wall. Can you break through it?"

"I'll try," he said, rushing to join her at the far wall.

The stone surroundings were invisible to his Sorcery. Even when touching them, he sensed remarkable resistance, with that lingering sense of agony again. Sorcery could not control it, but perhaps his body could break through it. He connected to the muscles of his arm, enchanting them with strength. Rose's perception persisted, and he felt her curiosity perk up. He connected to the skin of his hand, willing it to become unbreakable. Then he punched the wall as hard as he could.

The impact threw him backwards. His work had created a small chip in the wall, but caused no significant damage. Then pain exploded in his fingers. The skin remained unbroken, but the tissue underneath began to bruise and swell.

"Ow." He shook the injured hand and flexed his fingers with difficulty.

"You need more mass, more momentum," Jeanette said. "Not just strength."

Rose's annoyed and concerned presence focused on his hand, and the injured tissue healed, significantly easing the pain. She connected to large portions of his body—likely enchanting them for additional protection.

"Okay, let's try this . . ."

He threw his fist forward. It crashed into the wall of solid stone, scattering shards of rock and breaking through to the other side. The wall was nearly as thick as his entire arm. He pulled his hand back into the room with difficulty. Darkness and winds howled through the opening.

"I don't think this is going to work," he said. "It's too thick."

"The only other exit is the front door."

"Then that's how we get out."

"Tess will see us!"

"I'll likely fall unconscious before we break through this."

Jeanette sighed, then led them back out of the room and into the hallway. They raced past beautiful paintings and elaborate decorations—a remarkable contrast to the repulsive activities of the palace's inhabitants—well lit by golden beads of light at the top of the tall ceilings. Tovas nearly tripped over himself as they tore down the wide double staircase of the main hall and made their last dash toward the enormous front doors. He was finally leaving this wretched place.

Jeanette reached the handle of the door and pulled. Tovas assisted, and the enormous door opened, letting in a burst of turbulent, frigid air. He followed her through the opening into the darkness, where powerful winds whipped her long hair around. Lights from a small vessel in the distance stood out against the suffocating darkness, illuminating the edges of several curious pits in the black landscape below. The pair shot to the right, taking only a few steps before a familiar voice called out.

"Jey!"

Tess. She was there, in the darkness somewhere. A light appeared, revealing her pale face and dark hair. Silver patterns swirled along the shoulders of her dark cloak and leathery bodysuit. Lighter designs of silver laced her long gloves and thigh-length boots.

"What happened? The Deia is worried!"

"Tess," Jeanette said, visibly shaken. "I . . . I can't . . ."

The woman turned to Tovas with a fierce glare. "It was you. *You* did something to her."

Tovas lightly gripped Jeanette's shoulder and moved in front of her, standing between her and Tess. He raised his staff defensively.

"Jeanette is no longer the Deia's."

Tess's furious gaze gave way to genuine sorrow as she looked at Jeanette. "He has taken your Source?" Her attention returned to Tovas, and she pulled something from her waist. "You're *dead*, Lomerian!"

Sharp objects hurtled at his face with blurring speed. Impressions from the staff flowed through him, and his body obeyed, deflecting the projectiles harmlessly off course. He had hardly processed that the attack was coming before his body responded. Another flurry flew at him, and he deflected those as well.

Divine above, give me strength.

Tess let out a cry of frustration, leaping forward with drawn swords. Tovas let the staff's enchantment flow through him, disconnecting his mind from his body. He fell into a dream-like trance, only vaguely aware of his body's movements as the staff moved with remarkable precision, deflecting Tess's whirl of blows with minimal effort. Rose's enchantments for protection and strength were still working as well, enhancing his effectiveness.

"Tess!" Jeanette called out.

Despite the woman's increasing frustration and ferocity, he felt calm. At ease. Each cut or jab rang or scraped against the metallic surface of the staff, diverted just enough to prevent any injury. When she cut inward from both sides, he raised the staff to his neck, pressing up and out with enough force to send Tess stumbling backwards.

She dropped the swords and fell to her knees, screaming

through tears. The ground shook beneath their feet. Boulders rose up from the dirt, then shot toward Tovas with terrifying speed. The staff moved his body masterfully, creating the perfect amount of force to send the rocks away harmlessly. Jeanette had collapsed to the ground, her eyes wide with either amazement or fear.

Tess, with tears spilling down her cheeks, flew toward Tovas with a cry of pure agony. Gloved hands reached for his neck. He grabbed her upper arm, touching the bit of exposed skin between her gloves and cloak, then twisted, forcing her to the ground.

With their physical touch, the woman's body came alight to Tovas's perception. He felt her desperation, her genuine affection for Jeanette.

Jeanette appeared by his side, subduing Tess's other arm. Her presence appeared, reaching into Tess. It appeared to focus on the woman's Source, the point from which her entity originated, as Tovas had done with Jeanette only moments ago.

"Tess," Jeanette cried over the winds. "Let us help you. Come with us! We can do this together."

Tess writhed. "No! The Deia. She is coming. She is the Divine! She—" Then her eyes softened. Lightened. They locked onto Jeanette with sobered shock and wonder. Jeanette was reaching out to her. She was coming to grasp her manipulated state.

"*NO!*" Tess screamed.

A shockwave blasted Tovas and Jeanette backwards. He landed painfully on his back, but maintained a firm grip on the staff.

After rising, he assisted Jeanette to her feet. They gazed over at the woman on the ground, who now lay unconscious—most likely from an overexertion of Sorcery.

Tovas's aching body twirled the staff reflexively, deflecting an arrow off course. He stared into the darkness, wondering where the projectile had originated.

A flash of lightning revealed a large group of Sorcerers pouring out of a new vehicle ahead and advancing toward their position. Jeanette stared out with wide, fearful eyes, and her voice trembled.

"She's coming."

Chapter 47

Overpowered

Breathe.

Focus.

Wind screamed in Kara's ears. She opened her eyes to the endless rocky landscape of a destroyed world flying beneath her, determination flowing through her veins. After Rose exclaimed Tovas had nearly died, Kara had shot off ahead. The Ilkuth was far faster than the sky raft could be, and she would let no one else die. Not if she could stop it. Tovas and Fita had endured enough.

It was time to act.

This could bring her face-to-face with Jeanette again. She didn't know how that would go, but it needed to happen. If Jeanette needed a beat down, Kara would deliver. They could capture her. Tie her up and try to get the Deia's brainwashing out of her head.

The power gauge had fallen more after their engagement in Olorus, but it should be enough. Thankfully, her Nit had recorded exactly where they had arrived through the portal. Estimated arrival time was less than two minutes. She would undoubtedly need to fight the Deia's horde of Sorcerers to get them all out, but she looked forward to it.

Everyone was getting off this wretched planet if it was the last thing she ever did.

Sam's presence returned. He had been reaching to her frequently lately. Worried. Anxious. She connected with his body as well, noting that he seemed a little less fuzzy than before. Odd. She wished she could get more from their connection, or that they could speak to each other somehow, but Sorcery could only convey emotions. Except with the twins, of course. Sam was the scientist, right? He should be able to figure out how that worked. Make it happen for the rest of them.

Through Sorcery, Kara connected with the entirety of her suit, sensing its dense plates, fabrics, and mess of electrical pathways. She enchanted the ensemble, imagining it to be steadfast in structure and function. In truth, the weak enchantment probably wouldn't do much beyond the suit's incredible engineering, but it couldn't hurt.

Flashing lights appeared above a rocky hilltop in the distance. She was nearly there. Her eyes zoomed in on the location, stretching her sight as far forward as possible. The view was shaky, making it difficult to see clearly, but she didn't dare slow down. Flashes illuminated the front side of the enormous castle, and several pits in the dark rock near it. As she approached, she zoomed out, maintaining a little more stability and giving her a clearer view of what was happening.

Tovas, with his staff, was deflecting weapons that spat fire and lightning. He was defending someone. A woman. When her face was finally in view, Kara gasped.

Jeanette.

Tovas was defending her against the other Sorcerers, backed up against the front doors of the palace. That meant she must have come to her senses. She must have changed.

Jeanette was her sister again.

Elation and adrenaline rippled through her veins at the sight, and she willed the suit to go faster, though it was already at maximum speed. Tovas whirled the staff with incredible precision, deflecting every blow from sword, spear, arrow, and knife coming at them. Jeanette constantly pivoted to stay behind Tovas, avoiding attempts to grab her from the sides. The Sorcerers were trying to take her back.

Tovas's face betrayed increasing weariness. He couldn't keep up his defense forever.

Show me the biggest threats to Tovas and Jeanette, she commanded her Nit. Red indicators popped up on her display, but it was difficult to make out exactly who they were pointing to. *Give me outlines instead of markers. And how about a gradient of red to show their degree of threat?* The view changed according to her command.

How far are they?

Decimal numbers appeared next to the highlighted targets, decreasing rapidly with her approach.

Kara took aim at the reddest target on her display: a thick-bearded man with a curved longbow. Bow Guy's brown cloak fluttered in the relentless winds, and he stood among the Sorcerers, readying an arrow for another strike.

The distance closed quickly, and she gritted her teeth. He lifted his bow, pulling the drawstring back as the group gave him space and prepared for a coordinated strike. Her suit shot toward her target at a steep angle. The shiny metal of her forearm rose in front of her face as she prepared for impact, making herself a human projectile.

Kara had a split-second glimpse of surprised faces and blood flying as she smashed into the man. Then rock. The suit screamed against solid ground. She directed it against its momentum, until it stopped. Anti-gravity raised her suit off the black rock, glowing with the heat of friction. The group of Sorcerers turned toward her with looks of astonishment within their outlines, lit up somewhat by her helmet spotlight.

She shot toward the closest one while whipping the plasma rifle from her back. Her enemy launched a spear at her. It ricocheted harmlessly against her helmet, and she unloaded the rifle into his chest with a brilliant, electrifying flash. She kicked his body for good measure, sending him flying into the darkness. The other Sorcerers surrounded her, cracking various weapons harmlessly against the impenetrable Ilkuth.

Kara reattached the weapon to her back as she spun with a low kick, tripping two of her assailants. With so many enemies, the rifle's recharge time was going to be a problem.

While her suit moved upright, she pushed it toward the first outline she saw and swung a forearm into the face. The woman's dark robes fluttered in the turbulent air as she tumbled. The blade of an enormous flaming axe then crashed right into the narrow slit above the Ilkuth's left neck guard with enough force to topple Kara's balance. She swept a leg out, tripping the blond wielder, and the axe scraped against her suit as he fell. Diagnostics on her display told her the suit had, thankfully, suffered no damage.

A giant boulder shot toward her out of nowhere. Kara raised her arms, unable to dodge. It crashed into her, and the suit pushed forward against the larger object, which scraped and crumbled around her.

Angry, concerned faces surrounded her. One said something to the others that Kara couldn't hear, likely because her suit had decreased the volume to protect her hearing from the earsplitting clashes.

Raising her arm cannons, she fired a continuous spray of projectiles at the group. Predictably, the shots deflected off them, but all the Sorcerers reacted, either retreating or advancing on her. A glance toward Tovas showed that two Sorcerers with spear-like weapons were still giving him trouble.

Someone grabbed Kara from behind. She halted her spray of gunfire and twisted her body, taking both of them to the floor. Getting into a position of submission was remarkably easy, and Kara snapped the man's arm in the wrong direction. He screamed in response.

As she rolled to stand, more Sorcerers piled on with remarkable force, pushing her down. The suit strained against the pressure, meaning they must be changing things with Sorcery.

Well, *she* could play that game now.

Kara closed her eyes and realized the indicators were still visible, so she turned them off. Impressions of her body flowed through her among the sea of imperceptible bodies. Bone. Muscle. Armor. Air.

The air. Not in her lungs. It was just outside her suit, flowing around the areas where the Sorcerers touched metal. So wispy and free, moving with endless turbulence. She connected to a small bit of it and remembered that first occurrence with Elleran, when pushing the air away had made her lurch forward. Pressure. She had decreased the pressure in front of her, creating a force that pulled her in.

She had learned something about that in Mr. Nowell's class. What was it? It was—*Sam, help me out here*—pressure something. Pressure and volume. And T. What was the T?

Temperature.

Understanding settled in her mind. Changes in pressure could come from changes in volume and temperature. The faster the change. The bigger the force.

Kara's arms continued to strain against the powerful bodies of Sorcerers pinning them down. She calmed her mind, connecting to a portion of air in front of her chest, keeping it steady against the surrounding air, which strained to push it away from her. Volume. She needed more air. Hot air. A *lot* more.

She focused with intensity, imagining the fluttering bit of air she held becoming a scorching, mountainous column.

Boom.

The deafening blast threw her attackers off, freeing the suit from their abnormal weight. While her opponents were recovering, she sent them all flying with superpowered blows from her fists and legs.

Fighting a sudden wave of fatigue, Kara found Tovas, who was still warding off the others. She pulled out her rifle as she approached, then gave one a clean, roundhouse kick. The other received a blast of plasma to his chest, followed by a superpowered jab with the butt of the rifle, throwing his body into the oppressive darkness with a rag doll tumble.

Tovas smiled, leaning against the staff and panting. "Kara it . . . it is so . . . so good . . ."

"Catch your breath first, dude," she said, putting the rifle back. She pulled off her helmet and was hit by the unpleasant cold, dry air of Uvlun. Her focus was on Jeanette, who stared at her from behind Tovas with the most pitiful, teary-eyed gaze she had ever seen from her.

"Kara . . ." The familiarity and sincerity of her voice tied a knot in Kara's chest. "I'm sorry . . . I'm so—"

Kara rushed forward and embraced her sister—careful to avoid crushing her with the suit's power. The warmth of their embrace vanquished the chill of their surroundings. Everything was right in the world.

Jeanette was herself again.

"I . . . really hate . . . to break this up," Tovas said, still panting. "But we should leave . . . while we can."

The sisters released their embrace, and Jeanette wiped her eyes. "Yes. Let's take the ship." She pointed off into the darkness. "It can get us off Uvlun."

"God, yes."

Kara donned her helmet again, which lit their way toward the vehicle. It appeared to be empty, but Sorcerers to the right and left, who had been thrown back by Kara's powerful blows, were stirring.

Damn magic cockroaches.

Kara looped her arms under Tovas and Jeanette, lifting them off the ground with the suit and soaring toward the vehicle against the turbulent winds. Lights descended from the sky from two sources. *More of them?*

A ball of white-hot flame smashed into their escape vehicle, exploding it in a fireball of metallic debris. Kara hastily turned around and dropped Tovas and Jeanette, laying her body out in the air to block as much of the blast as possible. Unfortunately, her small frame was ill-suited for such work. Tovas swung his staff, swatting away a few flaming pieces of wreckage that passed around her.

Jeanette flinched as something struck her head, and Kara's heart leapt into her throat at the sight of blood streaming by her ear. Her sister quickly put a vial to her lips, and the wound closed.

Thank God for magic potions.

After the flying debris settled, Kara shifted upright and turned around, eyes widening. The two other ships had landed. Sorcerers were pouring out and rushing toward them, the sight causing her heartbeat to thump in her ears. They were sorely outnumbered. She could only handle so many at once. Tovas was clearly reaching his limits, and Jeanette needed to stay away from them at all costs.

A cluster of arrows, sparking with electricity, rained on them, bouncing off Kara's suit and Tovas's staff.

"It's her," Jeanette said, her voice trembling, barely audible over the gales.

A sudden burst of powerful wind sent several Sorcerers into the air. One had an arrow pass straight through his neck. War cries rang out from their right, and two familiar figures engaged the enemy with a burning ray of light and a sword that swatted enemies away with uncanny force. Another gust accompanied an arrow that sent a man tumbling. Renoq sliced at him, spraying blood.

Kara crouched and yelled with them, raising her arm cannons and firing at the small army of Sorcerers that descended on her, with flowing cloaks and ancient weapons attacking from all directions.

Rose peeked over the rock they had parked the sky raft behind, watching as her friends battled an overwhelming force. Rocks flew. Kara smashed heads. Renoq, Sheylana, and Kula, all empowered with Rose's enchantments and their own powerful weapons, fought valiantly, trying to prevent the Deia's devotees from surrounding the trio. The Sorcerers pushed forward with determined and remarkable coordination, striking in simultaneous bursts that caused Kara to stumble. She swung the limbs of the powerful suit around, taking out swaths of enemies that just kept coming.

Tovas was defending something. No, *someone*. Who was she? Another captive?

Rose turned her attention back to the rest of the group, which she had a connection to. All of them were okay. No major injuries yet to heal. Her enhancements of strength and durability were holding for now.

A sight caused her eyes to widen. Dark brown hair streaked with gold.

The Deia. She was standing at the rear of her group, with a look of intense concentration.

They were in serious trouble.

Panic spiked in her gut. What could she do? She wasn't a fighter. Yes, she could enhance strength, but she had no actual skill to speak of. She was a healer, an expert on physiology.

Which could be effective.

If she got close enough to touch the woman, she could connect with the Deia's body and destroy her from the inside. They certainly wouldn't expect that. How would she get close enough, though? She'd need something to get through the horde of Sorcerers protecting her.

Rose glanced back at the sky raft, where the handle of an enormous maul glimmered in the dim lights of the battle raging from afar. She approached slowly, and tried desperately to stop herself from thinking too much about what she was doing. She gripped the handle, feeling the weapon's immensity, and its purpose. Momentum. Density. Destruction.

Images from horrid memories she had blocked for weeks burst through her mental barrier, flooding into her mind. Talanna's stark white hair tainted with blood. The heartbreaking sensation of Niu's and Relon's bodies disappearing from her perception. The roar of righteous anger from a man she loved. A magnificent, well-aimed leap. An explosive impact.

Then enormous fists, enchanted with every bit of strength Rose could pour into them, smashed into an impenetrable suit of armor, which stumbled but remained upright. Blow after blow of shockwaves rippled through the air. A face shield cracked. A drawn sword rang. And, with a horrid crack of lightning, the titan fell. The titan she loved.

Vurkil was dead.

Tears streaming down her face, Rose found herself halfway to the mass of armed Sorcerers, several of which guarded the Deia.

Vurkil was dead. And the Deia was responsible.

Rose let out a furious scream, connecting to her own body and enforcing an increase of causality that made the world slow around her. The momentum of her run carried her forward, and she spun wildly, with the energy of the maul flowing through her. Human bodies, no doubt enchanted, smashed against the solid, flat face of the maul's head. They flew away, reduced to mangled bags of bone and flesh, one after the other.

Rose let the maul drop toward the ground as she slid her spin to a stop. One person remained between her and her target. The large, pale man hefted an axe.

"Heh. Come, girl," he said. "I'll show you a—"

She swung the hammer with incredible ease, and it arced through the air. He barely had time to react, only beginning to bring his arms up before the weapon obliterated him.

She rushed forward, throwing the maul down once more at her distracted target. The Deia moved at the last moment. She was fast. Too fast.

An unexpected kick knocked Rose back, and she lost her grip on the maul. Golden strands fell out of a long ponytail on the evil woman's head. Rose pushed her body forward with Sorcery and stretched a hand out with enhanced speed, gripping her target's neck with a hand enchanted with superior strength. The body came alight to her perception, and she wasted no time aiming for the Deia's brain.

She couldn't connect to it.

Instead, Rose connected to the heart and lungs, tearing whatever she could. They repaired themselves immediately.

Dizziness hit.

Rose, alarmed, checked her own body, which was a mess. Her brain appeared to be unharmed, but her heart had been torn to pieces. Brutally destroyed. Complex neurotoxins raged in her bloodstream, though she managed to stop them from entering her head. Maintaining oxygenation with Sorcery, she stared up into the cold gray eyes of perhaps the most dangerous person in the universe. Rose's iron grip on the woman's neck met with unbreakable resistance.

She had made a terrible mistake. The Deia was more than a powerful Sorcerer, or cunning manipulator. The woman was a *master* of the human body, with skills surpassing her own.

Rose was going to die.

Chapter 48

Starlight

Kara spun, taking out two of her attackers with a leg sweep. She had expected another well-timed blow to catch her again, but it didn't come. The man behind her swung his abnormally powerful club once more, and it knocked her back. She sent a blast of arm cannon fire into the man's face, which ricocheted but caused him to look away briefly, giving her an opening. She kicked out, catching the man in the chest and sending him flying past Tovas and Jeanette.

The rest of the Sorcerers surrounding her gave way, having somehow lost the ridiculous coordination of their attacks. She was glad for a moment of relief, where their blows weren't all landing perfectly to knock her off balance.

As she punched through a stream of fire, catching a woman in the face, lights appeared overhead. Kara's heart dropped.

Damn! Not more of them . . .

The spacecraft appeared to be landing on the opposite side of the other two ships, surrounding them. Kara spun, flying toward Jeanette and the others and knocking another Sorcerer aside. Tovas glanced upward at the new vehicle with a furrowed brow as he continued to deflect the never ending onslaught of arrows, knives and swords. He heaved with exhaustion.

They needed to get out of here. Now.

"Run!" Kara yelled, and the group raced off, fighting Sorcerers as they went, which slowed their progress. The ship maneuvered ahead of them. As Kara aimed at it, she noticed that her cannon ammunition was nearly empty. It wouldn't do much against that armor, anyway. The rear of the ship opened, and she prepared herself to face off with a squad of fresh enemies. Her heart did a somersault at the unexpected sight of Tercast field robes.

Sam.

"Get on!" he yelled.

Pure joy pulsed through her as she picked up Jeanette and flew into the opening. A fireball smashed into Kara's back as she put down her sister. She turned, looking over the chaotic field of downed Sorcerers. Behind them was their leader, the Deia. Somewhere. Kara had caught a glimpse of her earlier.

When she spotted her, she zoomed in and gasped. Rose. Her ashen fingers gripped the Deia's throat, her eyes wide, terrified. What was she doing there? She was supposed to be hiding!

Through her connection, she sensed Rose's desperate panic and fading consciousness.

She was about to die.

"Rose!" Kara screamed, turning and pushing her suit forward as fast as it would go.

She sped straight into a woman wielding a scythe, who grunted at the impact, but Kara kept her eyes dead set on the Deia. Jagged stone, painted with blood, passed beneath her as the distance to her target closed, but not rapidly enough. She reached out with Sorcery, moving air aside before it hit her, giving her more speed.

The Deia regarded her briefly before shoving Rose away, and then crossing her arms. Kara slammed into them, pushing the woman far backwards, away from Rose. Remarkably, she remained upright, digging grooves into solid rock with her sliding heels.

Satisfied with the distance, Kara set herself down on the hard ground. The Deia lifted her bare feet from the rock and narrowed her eyes with a look of pure hatred.

Yeah, that's right. I killed your man Del. And I'm gonna take you down too.

The woman flew forward and struck at her with astounding speed. Training took over, and Kara grabbed the arm, using the Deia's momentum against her and bringing them both to the ground. Kara rolled herself into a dominant position, with her armored leg over her opponent's face, gripping her arm. She let the full weight of the Ilkuth fall, and the woman struggled. Kara pulled with her might, snapping the arm back.

The Deia's leg twisted into an unnatural angle, and she pressed powerfully against the suit, squeezing her broken hand out of Kara's grasp. Both women righted themselves, and Kara glanced over to find Rose's body in another Ilkuth's arms. The suit leapt into Sam's vehicle. Kara turned her attention back to her target, surprised to see the Deia's arm fall back into its natural position.

She can heal. Gotta hit her where it counts, then

Kara raised her anti-gravity, then shot into the air. The Deia remained below, staring up with that burning scowl. When she felt she'd gained enough height to do the trick, Kara let her full weight fall again, her stomach lurching as the Ilkuth pushed with all the acceleration it could muster. She cut a path through the air with Sorcery. Dirt and rocks from the landscape below formed into a circle around her target, presenting a perfect bullseye. Her fall aimed straight for the woman's head.

Intense bright light appeared out of nowhere.

The expected impact never came.

Kara fell.

And kept falling.

Tremendous heat baked her feet and hands, then gradually cooled. An alarm buzzed in her helmet. All that lay below her was a sea of shifting, dazzling light. She looked up and found nothing but darkness above. After she presented her back to the light, her eyes eventually adjusted to the darkness.

A sea of magnificent starlight filled her vision. Clouds of

sparkly purples, reds and every color in between flowed across the breathtaking image. Streams of wispy bluish gas arced in her peripheral vision, emanating from the impossible brightness behind her.

Pure bewilderment stunned her for several seconds. Then slowly, a chilling realization settled over her.

A portal? To somewhere in space?

She willed her anti-gravity to rise, but it only moved slightly. Her battery gauge pulsed red, even though it still had some amount of power remaining.

Danger, the Nit communicated to her mind. *Insufficient power. Gravitational field exceeds parameters. Unable to maintain vital temperature.*

"There's plenty of power!" Kara yelled. Heat had returned to her backside, which was facing the incredibly bright light. A sun? A star?

Send me back! she thought desperately to her Nit. *Send me back!*

Invalid, it replied.

What can I do? she asked it.

The device failed to respond, causing anxiety to twist in her chest.

I'm going to die?

No response. The alarm continued to blare, and the heat on her back kept rising. The sound of her anxious breathing echoed in the claustrophobic space of the helmet.

No. She couldn't die. There was far too much to do. Too much to see. Sam's presence entered her, and she grasped at it, sensing his concern. She couldn't leave him. Couldn't leave any of them. She needed them, and they needed her. Death was not an option.

Sweat poured down her face. Her back burned.

What could she do? This was an enemy she couldn't fight. Or could she? Kara Jones versus an unbelievably massive celestial body. She could take this. Right?

She reached out with Sorcery and felt only her body, the suit, and distant particles. The turbulent surface of the star was terribly far away. She could barely sense it.

So, so hot.

Power! She just needed power. She connected to the suit as sweat trickled down her face, trying to find out where the energy was coming from. What had the suit mentioned when she had first worn it? *Power cells. On the . . . upper back?*

She found the ring and connected to it, desperately trying to feel it out. Something was going on, but she couldn't quite tell what. The technology was far beyond her comprehension. No matter, she just needed electricity, right? She willed a charge to build as she eyed her gauge, which refused to move.

"Budge, you damn thing. Move!"

Nothing happened. The bar drained slowly, despite the enormous source of energy behind her. It must be spending far more energy trying to keep her alive than it could gain.

Through the building pain and dizziness, a revelation calmed her mind. Even if she could somehow charge or move the suit, she couldn't possibly escape before the heat overcame her.

It was so hot. She *was* going to die.

Kara hissed, inhaling sharply through her teeth at the mounting pain on her back. Dizziness threatened to overcome her. Sam's concern spiked. Perhaps he sensed it too, the inevitability of her situation.

At her command, her eyes shut off, returning her to a comforting lack of visual stimulation. Tears mixed with her pouring sweat. Her breath, ragged and shallow, reflected off the helmet, less than an inch from the void of space.

"I'm . . ." She found it difficult to speak through the pain spreading across her backside. "I'm sorry, Jeanette. I'm sorry, Sam."

Kara imagined his handsome brown face and morbid eyes with clarity, bringing a slight smile to her lips. She wished she could have kissed that face one last time.

"I love you."

Chapter 49

Broken

Sam gripped the sides of the passenger bay of the Sovereign's provided Thalas-class vehicle amid the roaring turbulence of Uvlun's thick, tempestuous clouds. Wet gales beat against the hull. Eyes wide, he stared past the metallic interior, filled with friends, into the abyss, where Kara had disappeared to. Where she was in intense pain. Where she was dying.

Her presence faded from his perception.

"We *need* to get to her!" Sam yelled again, tears streaming down his cheeks. "Now!"

"Unable to set destination," the ship responded again.

He hung his head, letting tears drip to the steel floor. The Deia had opened some kind of portal. To intense brightness. The ship couldn't locate Kara afterward.

The others held his gaze with their tense stares. Rose was the only other one with a connection to Kara, and she was unconscious. He had tried his best to cool Kara's body with Sorcery, but the heat was tremendous. There wasn't much he could do.

His connection to Kara abruptly severed.

"No. No no no no no no. *No.*"

He couldn't reach her.

"No no no no no no."

She was gone.

"KARA!"

Sam connected to the rear door of the passenger bay and pressed it. The door ripped from the hull, depressurizing the interior. A suit fell out, but everyone else held to their anchors. Lightning struck as tempestuous rainwater doused them.

Sam let go of his handhold, but a firm hand grabbed his. He turned to find Jeanette looking back at him with tearful eyes. They were the last thing he saw before unconsciousness took him.

Jeanette kept a tight grip on Sam as his unconscious body flailed in the furious winds and ice-cold rain.

"Sheylana!" yelled the dark-skinned woman with blond hair, who looked remarkably like Fita. She reached toward the opening, where the severed door reappeared. "Help!"

A male-shaped suit that had fallen out of the vessel slipped in past the door. The woman with olive-colored skin across the bay let go of her handhold and fell toward the door. She caught another anchor near the Fita-looking woman, and the pair lined the door up to its former position along the hull, dampening the noise of the thunderous hurricane outside. The edges welded to their surroundings and blocked the rest of the noise.

The blond woman fainted, no doubt exhausted from her use of Sorcery. After the person named Sheylana finished her work welding the door, she slumped to the floor but remained conscious. The suit grabbed both of them and took them farther inside. Tovas, holding on to his staff and handhold, was awake, though dazed. His consciousness held on by a thread. After the suited man bound the blond woman to keep her secure, he took Sam and bound him as well.

Everyone panted against the muffled sounds of the maelstrom outside, including Jeanette. In the pilot's cabin, the other suit was tending to an unconscious freckled woman named Rose. Bruises and concerning deformities littered the visible portions of her body. No one spoke. Unable to look at anyone around her, Jeanette stared numbly at the cold metal floor.

Belze. She had—

No. It was *impossible*. Kara was resilient, unstoppable, a force of nature. She had saved them all.

She couldn't be dead.

"She is a hero," Tovas said, his voice cracking with emotion. "May the Divine welcome her with open arms."

Fresh tears welled in Jeanette's eyes at his words. Something about them felt real. Her mind was probably just grasping at any chance of comfort, but she desperately wished it was true—that Kara's soul was out there somewhere. Happy. Free.

A vision entered her mind: Kara, cane in hand, walked into a Divine re-creation of their childhood home. The wooden front door swung open to reveal her father grinning with his dimpled, controlled smile. Her mother stood next to him, spreading her arms wide with excitement. The three joined in a heartwarming embrace of tears. Her father kissed her forehead. They held the joyful embrace until the vision faded, leaving Jeanette in the cold, dark, uncomfortable wetness of the passenger bay, where tears fell onto her waterlogged jumpsuit.

If there is a joyful afterlife, I don't deserve it.

The turbulence outside waned steadily to peaceful quiet. Then several minutes of uncomfortable silence passed while the ship took them to an unknown destination.

"We're here," the suit from the pilot's cabin said as he entered the passenger bay.

"I'll open it," Sheylana said. She touched the edges of the hastily welded door, which fell outward with a soft thud, revealing a bright sky with massive columns of cumulus clouds over a grassy field.

Groups of people moved about through clusters of small buildings in the distance. Many stood in lines. Several were crying, or tense. Refugees.

Jeanette released Sam's restraint and took his hand in her own, connecting to his body once more and removing the enchantment on his blood she had used to put him under. Her Sorcery's potency had surprised her. He stirred, woozy at first. When his eyes locked onto Jeanette, they became sharp, focused. He rushed toward the opening. The suited soldier attempted to get his attention, but Sam brushed past him.

"Sam!" Jeanette called out, following him out onto the grass. He stopped, keeping his gaze forward, and his dark curly hair shifted in the stiff breeze. Jeanette halted a few steps behind him, unsure how to proceed.

A comforting hand settled on her shoulder. It belonged to Tovas.

"Sam," he said. "There was nothing you could have—"

Sam spun with a look of tearful vehemence, causing Tovas to flinch. He then turned back and began striding away.

"Sam, please," Jeanette cried. "You shouldn't be alone. Stay with us. Please."

He stopped again, motionless for several breaths while people bustled about in the surrounding distance. Finally, he turned his head slowly, regarding Jeanette with tear-filled eyes. The eyes of a broken soul.

He shot into the air with a resounding shockwave of force, attracting a few looks of curiosity.

Jeanette fell to her knees, unable to restrain her sobbing. Tovas knelt with her and wrapped his arms around her shoulders. The warmth of his embrace provided minuscule, yet distinct, comfort against the icy shroud of choking anguish.

Her family was gone.

Chapter 50

Queen of Minds

Desperation. Unrest. Outrage.

The Deia's consciousness left her subjects and returned to the dim, rusty pilot's cabin of the exploration craft as it descended toward the surface of Rwenmar. Jeanette's tragic relapse and the attack on Evamune Palace had delayed her arrival and weakened her forces, but the conditions here were indeed prime. The Sovereign's failure to protect Naleren from destruction had sent ripples throughout the known universe. Many of her subjects had already been protesting at the capitol on Rwenmar before the Sovereign called a secret, emergency, *in-person* meeting of all top officials. Grohs of the Deia's subjects were already well positioned, and more were gathering.

It was perfect.

She looked over at Tess's unconscious face in the seat next to hers, her disheveled black hair splayed out around her pale features. Sorrow dampened her excitement. Tess should be by her side during this remarkable moment. And Jeanette. That fool, Tovas, had somehow broken her hold on the incredible young woman. Belze hadn't been aware such expulsion was even possible. A tragic loss. Hopefully, Jeanette would come to her senses and return to her in time. Perhaps grief over her sister's demise would urge her to return to the unity.

The image of the suit flying at her with remarkable speed played through Belze's mind, and she smiled, pleased with her ingenuity. The execution and timing of the projection portal while anchoring herself had gone off flawlessly. She would have liked to have seen the look of surprise on the girl's face as she suddenly fell helplessly toward the system's star. The feat had required a great deal of energy, however. The obnoxious girl had become quite the nuisance, using Sorcery to enhance that marvelously powerful armor.

If only Delveton had survived his work against Tercast, she might have had an entire squad of suited Sorcerers by now. His death had significantly delayed their progress. Minister Golin was originally supposed to take the fall for Tercast, but if he was reinstated, he might continue that line of work. Even if that happened, however, it would take too long. So much had been riding on Delveton's abilities and unique connections in the Armed Forces.

The memory of the man's perfectly aged, bearded face and muscular body brought a sudden spike of longing and sorrow. She had many other beautiful men to play with, of course, but Delveton had been special. Unique. He had been the first to call her Deia.

And now his death had been avenged.

The view screen displayed clouds dispersing to reveal the magnificent capital city of Anu'avan. Lush deep green trees and groves of well-kept flowering gardens sat between scores of shiny skyscrapers. Some buildings had manicured plant life across their exterior, making the city a breathtaking display of shimmering, vibrant color.

"Stop," she instructed, and the vehicle's velocity slowed smoothly, pushing her body toward the aged console.

This was as close as she dared to approach. The capitol would surely have advanced detection measures on high alert because of the emergency gathering, despite the attempted secrecy. Thankfully, one of the capitol building's staff had found enlightenment through her subjects' proselytizing efforts on Alvior, and had alerted her to the event.

As the vehicle came to a stop, Belze turned and strode into the exploration craft's main bay, which was a depressing mess of bloody and unconscious bodies. The eyes of the few left standing turned to her, and the remnants of chatter died immediately. All bowed their heads in reverent adoration—an appropriate response. She connected to them, evaluating their health and readiness. Most were in awful shape, or near exhaustion. Their defeat was a shameful reflection of their abilities. If only she'd had more devotees with her at the level of Tess or Quade, they may have been able to take back Jeanette before their escape. Those fools from Tercast—with the powerful relics *she* should have claimed from Delveton's efforts—had proven quite formidable in their own right. She felt it unwise to spend any more energy healing her forces, and they had all but exhausted their supply of health potions.

"Taln, Kasem, you will accompany me to the surface. The rest of you will continue to treat the others. Be prepared in case we need a hasty extraction."

"Yes, Deia," rang a chorus of voices.

"Open the bay."

The rear door squeaked and grinded, letting in an icy breeze. Hair flapping in the wind, she stepped over the tangle of bodies, and the two she had called joined her at the rear. Taln, wearing a broken chest brace and black trousers, approached on her left, bearing a longbow. Kasem approached on her right, her blue figure wearing tattered leather trousers and a loose tunic. She gripped a halberd in her left hand.

"Leave the weapons."

They obeyed her command, dropping the weapons to the ground. Belze ripped off a dangling section of Kasem's jumpsuit, then tied her hair into a tight ponytail. It had been ages since she had last constrained her hair with manual effort, but she needed to conserve as much Sorcery as possible.

She took the hands of her companions and enchanted their bodies such that light would bend around them, effectively making them invisible.

The sight of white clouds faded to darkness, and she leapt from the vehicle, which was likewise invisible to electromagnetic radiation. Freezing, wet air rushed past their fall. Belze reached out with Sorcery, observing their descent. They were heading for the top of a skyscraper, so she steered them toward an alley between buildings. Bodies moving inside cast blobs of fuzzy darkness to her perception. When the ground approached, she slowed their descent, and they landed gracefully onto the pavement.

Observing that no one was around, she removed the enchantment enshrouding them, blinding her eyes briefly with bright daylight. An ascender passed by the narrow opening ahead. Belze strode out in silence, her two subjects following closely behind. The alleyway opened to a wide street lined with manicured trees, shrubs, and colorful, bulbous plants. The building they had landed near did, in fact, turn out to be a multi-story ascender platform. Wonderful.

Dohs of people strode in and out of the building, and the trio followed a young family inside. A vehicle landed, letting out a group of giggling women. A few of them gave Belze and her companions curious looks but said nothing as they passed by and took the transport, which contained a lingering odor of flowery perfumes and sugary treats.

"Capitol hall," Belze commanded.

The transport took them out and over the area once more, past a breathtaking garden of blue and pink flowering trees and a high-rise with a manicured tangle of vines cascading down the side. The capital city truly reflected Sovereignty values. Technology uplifting and protecting biological life, working as one. A noble endeavor, but their desperate attempt to maintain such incongruous individualism was a foolish tradition that only brought endless strife, discord, and destruction.

The Molkinar Empire had recognized the futility of such rampant unrestricted liberty, though they sought a gestalt consciousness through inferior artificial machinery, which the human mind understandably and naturally resisted. Biological life was far older, far more experienced, and far more adaptable. It only needed proper control. Unification was the only true path to a lasting, harmonious existence. A people of one mind.

Her mind.

They approached the central capitol building, a structure of remarkable curved architecture, with a contrasting sharp tower in the center that reached toward the sky. A pair of enormous Umeka trees framed the structure, their cascading white racemes reflecting subtle rainbows in the afternoon light. Two massive crowds of people carrying signs gathered outside a temporary barrier, where a few enforcers in bulky Wenkuth armor stood guard.

Two suits strode between the opposing groups of protesters, which were shouting chants against each other. Those on the right bore signs calling for the failed Sovereignty to let deism take control. Those on the left bore signs calling for organized religion to be outlawed. The sight electrified her with excitement.

The ascender turned and landed gracefully onto a spacious nearby pad, and the door opened with a clean whish. Belze and her companions strode toward the chanting crowds. A few others moved off the landing pad with them. They made their way behind the religious side, progressing as close as they could to the capitol building, where the crowd thickened.

She reached out, touching all of those connected to her, and was delighted to find a link to one enforcer standing behind the barrier. He emitted a sense of confidence and quiet anxiety, and seemed to radiate a slight personal favor toward the anti-religious side of the conflict.

Her mind then entered the man in the building. Relaying his auditory signals should allow her to stay in tune with the

Sovereign's response to her actions, so she connected to the tympanic membrane of the man's right ear and enchanted the membrane of her own right ear to mimic its vibrations, closing out the sounds of the nearby crowd.

"—never seen such power displayed by Oblivion before," a male voice said. "This changes everything!"

"We have never been certain of Oblivion's limitations," the Sovereign's echoing voice responded. "I will not impose martial law unless the council unanimously agrees that such action is necessary."

"The instability will only grow with the spreading news of Naleren!"

"Perhaps," a new male voice said. "But Sovereign Aiyla is right. We should not restrict the people's right to organize except in the most extreme circumstances."

"How much more extreme can it get? Oblivion annihilated an entire world under his own intrinsic power!" the first voice contended. "First the destruction of Enck, and now Naleren? We must protect the lives of our citizens. This is undeniably the best way to ensure their safety."

"I suggest—"

"Deia!" a familiar voice said, bringing Belze back to herself.

Fitale bowed deeply before her, his gorgeous blonde hair shimmering in the afternoon sunlight.

"Shh." She prompted him to raise his head. "We must not draw attention."

He bowed again briefly, and subdued his voice. "Forgive me. What caused the delay?"

She let the enchantment on her ear drop in power, keeping it active, but less potent to allow her to focus on her own surroundings.

"Your old friends attacked."

"Kara?"

"Yes. She has been dealt with."

"Where is Urok?"

She sighed, sorrow piercing her at the memory of Urok. "A

young woman destroyed him with a powerful maul—I assume a relic you all took from Tercast—then made a poor attempt against my life."

His eyes widened. "Rose perhaps?"

"I had nearly destroyed her before Kara attacked. She escaped with the others."

"I will go after them!" He moved to rush past her.

She put an arm out, stopping him. "No. We will worry about them later. I want you by my side."

He bowed once more. "Yes, Deia."

Her attention returned to the guard's ear, where the conversation with the Sovereign continued.

"—Oblivion task force to be expanded. We must develop more effective countermeasures."

It was a familiar voice, belonging to a recently elected member of the Legislature of Technical Experts. Realization hit, electrifying Belze's nervous system. This was no small pre-meeting of the Sovereign's close advisors. It was a meeting of all top leadership in the Sovereignty. It was already in progress.

Now was the time.

The Deia re-established her connection to the enforcer nearby, in addition to all her surrounding subjects. She gripped the minds of those in the crowd, minus the Sorcerers embedded within. At her command, they stilled. Scornful shouts and insults died on lips at the sound of crashing signs as the people dropped them.

Uncanny silence settled over the crowd.

Pure confusion emanated from the enforcers. As one, most of the crowd turned toward the building. The enforcers' confusion turned to dread as the throng quickly advanced. All three guards raised their arms, shouting threats. Anti-riot projectiles shot forth, spewing a smog that her Sorcerers swept away with a powerful gust of wind. The immense group rapidly marched forward, throwing their bodies against the superior suits. Touches of Sorcery by those she had planted in the crowd easily thwarted the rounds of gas pellets, stun blasts, and other countermeasures that followed. The remaining mob rushed toward the building and surrounded its exterior.

No one in the swarm uttered a word. Most of the protesters who weren't under Belze's control fled the scene in sudden panic. A few tried, unsuccessfully, to stop her subjects from joining in.

"—keep those who are—"

"Sovereign!" a fresh voice said inside, cutting off the voice of a legislator. "The protesters. The people are surrounding the building!"

"Do not harm them," the Sovereign commanded.

"Reinforcements are approaching, but there are grohs of people. We need to get everyone to safety."

Through Belze's prompting, the people threw themselves against the exterior windows and doors, breaking through them. Bodies—many trampling over each other—flooded into the building. She fought a wave of fatigue, striding with purpose up the stone front steps with her entourage of Sorcerers. At her subtle command, the enforcer under her influence joined her side.

Inside, she navigated her way down the marvelously decorated halls, full of people swarming the guards, to the immense circular meeting hall, where more chaos ensued. A pleasant flowery aroma filled the air while bodies clamored around her, assaulting the leadership and overwhelming the enforcers.

The Sovereign retreated with her guard into a back room.

"All members of the Armed Forces," the Sovereign said, her determined voice ringing through the helmet of the Deia's unwitting subject among her staff. "The capital is under assault. I'm enacting code seven doh nine. Protect the people. Enga—"

Belze pushed her subject to subdue the Sovereign, and metal clashes rang from the closed area they had retreated to, followed by gunfire she could hear with her own ears. She continued across the enormous space with its stunning, weaving ornamentations. Two slim-suited guards in black armor advanced on Belze. The enforcer following her clashed with one, while Fitale spun a white-hot sword at the other. The bodies of her other subjects flew by all around, among the frantic cries of government personnel.

She entered the back room, the Sovereign's personal office, where one of the elite guards had restrained her subject. The Sovereign herself had somehow received her own suit of armor. Belze lifted herself off the floor and hovered, reaching toward the woman.

A portal unexpectedly appeared behind the Sovereign's suit, cast from the air itself, opening into a dark, metallic interior. She flew backward into it, after which the portal closed abruptly. Belze could only gape at the back wall of the office, where the symbol of the Sovereignty protruded.

She let her feet settle onto the floor as her weight returned.

Taln and Kasem engaged the remaining member of the Sovereign's guard, who soon fled into the hall.

So close. She had been *so close* to having the Sovereign herself under control. Still, the rest of the government would be hers in a matter of minutes. Their enemies were already retreating with the threats against hostages, leaving government officials to the control of her subjects.

Belze sat in the Sovereign's padded chair behind a handsome, intricately carved desk. She crossed her legs, looking out into the grand hall at the few remaining flying bodies and listening to the screams of terror.

"The Intergalactic Sovereignty of Rwenmar," she said with a smirk of self-satisfaction,

"you are mine."

Ryan Sivek has been developing aspects of the Source's Edge story since he was in his early teenage years. He loves spending time with his wife and kids and enjoys his day job as a software engineer. He currently resides in the eastern United States.

www.ryansivek.com

www.ingramcontent.com/pod-product-compliance
Lightning Source LLC
Chambersburg PA
CBHW020328010826
48973CB00005B/1179